Fallen Stars, Bitter Waters

Also by
Gilbert, Lynn, and Alan Morris

The Beginning of Sorrows (Book 1 in the Omega Trilogy)

Fallen Stars, Bitter Waters

America Has Fallen, the Antichrist Reigns . . .
and God's Remnant Is Sealed

Gilbert Morris, Lynn Morris, Alan Morris

THOMAS NELSON PUBLISHERS®
Nashville

Published in Nashville, Tennessee, by Thomas Nelson, Inc.

Scripture quotations are from the KING JAMES VERSION of the Bible.

Library of Congress Cataloging-in-Publication Data

Morris, Gilbert.
Fallen stars, bitter waters : America has fallen, the Antichrist reigns ... and God's remnant is sealed / Gilbert Morris, Lynn Morris, and Alan Morris.
p. cm. — (The omega trilogy)
ISBN 0-7852-7001-9
1. Antichrist—Fiction. I. Morris, Lynn. II. Morris, Alan, 1959– III. Title.
PS3563.O8742 F35 2000
813'. 54—dc21

00-028070
CIP

Printed in the United States of America
1 2 3 4 5 6 7 8 9 QPV 05 04 03 02 01 00

To Brother and Sister Mitchell

In loving memory
of how you enriched our lives
and our walk with Him.

Angels are bright still, though the brightest fell.
Though all things foul would wear the brows of grace,
Yet grace must still look so.

—MALCOLM, FROM MACBETH BY WILLIAM SHAKESPEARE

Prologue

EXACTLY AT MIDNIGHT, the eighteenth-century beechwood longcase clock in one of the fortified towers of Halle Eisenhalt began to sound its long notes of doom as it had done without fail each hour for the past three hundred years. Count Tor von Eisenhalt stood at an arched casement, the leaded window swung aside, looking out into a frozen, impenetrable night. To any other man, it would be like staring at a blank wall, for no earthly feature of sky or mountain or star was visible. There was only a simple, cold blackness.

But Count Tor von Eisenhalt was not any man. Indeed, he wondered fleetingly if he was still a man at all. Instantly he dismissed the speculation as one evidence of his unwelcome humanity: the thought itself was wishful thinking. He was, regrettably, still a man.

He was a very special man, however, the only one of his kind who had ever lived. He would never die. It gave him satisfaction to know that, and he gathered his senses to concentrate and to focus his inner eye.

Tor was Nordic in feature, with the bone structure and sweeping jawline of his Viking fathers. His deep-set eyes, piercing and direct, had the intensity of a fierce bird of prey. People under his authority swore that those eyes could penetrate right into the heart—and most solemn secrets—of a man. Inexplicably the wings of pure silver at the temples of his raven-black hair gave him a more youthful appearance. Though his complexion was fair, a touch of ruddy color in his high cheekbones accented his intense vigor. His 180 pounds were perfectly distributed over a six-foot frame, and his strength and agility were proverbial.

He gazed westward, and shapes began to take form, much as a photograph comes to life in developing solution. He glimpsed Brussels; Paris; turned aside to glance at Greenwich, the longitudinal center of the world; faster and over the ocean, ignoring the ruins of the eastern seaboard of America, the empty heartland, over the white-topped sheer falls of the Rockies, the cat . . .

"Cat?" Tor said, visibly startled. The grimace that crossed the handsome planes of his face was forbidding. Tor disliked cats; and even more, he disliked these sudden jags, these jarring interruptions of the reaching out of his mind. And cats . . . ? A cat? Like—spotted . . . wildcat? Or was it two—small—half-grown kittens? Kittens! Why in the world was his mind touching on such vermin as kittens? He struggled to know, to see, what had crossed his line of sight, but it was gone, dissipated like a tendril of mist rising into cold air. It was unsettling. Or even worse, Tor felt his all-too-human heart beat a little faster with fear; he wasn't supposed to be subject to such weakness of will.

Finally, with rigid determination and an incomprehensible oath under his breath, Tor again turned his eyes to the West.

Cheyenne Mountain was unremarkable, a bleak granite rise of only seven thousand feet, much overpowered by the sensational Garden of the Gods and Pikes Peak to its north. But inside Cheyenne Mountain was a quite remarkable hollowed-out warren where the rats were hiding. NORAD—the North American Air Defense Command—was still the brain of America's military defense. Though Tor had all but annihilated the physical body, he had left the brain alone. But he had been watching the soldiers ceaselessly.

"They'll be coming out soon," Tor said expressionlessly.

In his vigilance, with his newfound knowledge and understanding, he knew they wouldn't just open the twenty-five-foot-thick blast doors to the central tunnel and come staggering out into the sunlight. Oh, no. Tor knew—could already see—that soon three groups of Marine Raiders would crawl out of the air ducts, the secret lifelines that ranged from thirty to fifty miles away from the heart of the mountain. With his supernatural perception, he'd already found the openings, and now he watched them, stared at them, his eyes never blinking, his pupils dilated to cover the irises completely, dead black unblinking eyes that never closed . . .

And he waited.

Zoan started, jerked, his eyes wild, his face contorted with fear. Though he hadn't felt a human touch that startled him, he had sensed something that was much, much worse.

"It's that man—that Wolf-Man," he whispered to Cat, the North American jaguar that was his sometime companion. "He's looking, he's trying to find me, I think . . ."

Chaco Canyon was about four hundred miles from NORAD, but Zoan, being the kind of man he was, felt cold dread, for Tor von Eisenhalt's malevolent gaze was almost a physical sensation to him. Zoan didn't know it exactly, as a person knows facts or has perceptions of emotions or reactions. It was pure instinct or unearthly insight that warned him when the Wolf-Man's eyes turned his way. It made Zoan feel cold, his flesh rising in prickly goose bumps, and he always had slight vertigo, a feeling as if he were about to fall down.

"He can see in the dark, like me," he whispered forlornly.

Cat growled deep in her throat, a rumble of distress with an edge of fear. The hackles rose slightly along her back, and she lithely jumped up and paced restlessly in Zoan's stone room. She had a wondrous beauty, while Zoan was so unremarkable as to be almost invisible. He was small of stature, his hair an indifferent brown, his features plain—except for his deep eyes, all pupil, with no colored iris to be seen at night.

Zoan was suddenly worried about his friends. What if the Wolf-Man could see them? What if he was looking for them, too? Zoan knew that his friends had even less protection from the Devourer than he did. For Zoan knew God, and God knew Zoan. To Zoan, God was exactly like a veil over his face and all-seeing eyes when he was afraid—God hid him and kept the Bad Things hidden from him. This man, this ravening Wolf-Man, could see his friends clearly if he looked, for they had no veil; and if they saw the Wolf-Man and what he was, they would be so frightened, they might go mad.

Zoan ran, with Cat striding along silently at his side.

As he had known they would be, the members of Fire Team Eclipse (Zoan simply thought of them as his soldier friends) were all together in the central community room of the small enclosed village where they'd chosen to live. Sergeant Rio Valdosta was, as always, polishing a gun. Captain Con Slaughter was feeding small mesquite sticks into the fire on the clay-lined center hearth and kicking the larger logs with satisfaction, making them spark and roar. He was smiling and shaking his head as he listened to Ric Darmstedt, Deacon Fong, and David Mitchell talking about Custer's Last Stand (Zoan thought his name was Custard, and with his somewhat limited intellectual powers decided they were talking about the last roadside stand where he sold his custard) and arguing about the military strategies, both Custer's and the Indians'.

Zoan stopped and did a quick assessment of the others in the room. Hs best friend, Cody Bent Knife, was sitting cross-legged on the floor by the fire, talking quietly to Rio Valdosta. Little Bird and Benewah Two Color, Zoan's two second-best Indian friends, were sitting behind Cody, watching and listening with barely contained amusement to the heated discussion of the soldiers. Ric Darmstedt was insisting loudly that the "Injuns had 'em dead to rights because Custer's tactics were as dumb as dirt . . ."

Gildan Ives was not exactly Zoan's friend, but Zoan worried about her just the same. She simpered and tried to stay in Ric's line of vision, but he appeared not to be able to see her at all. At least, he never looked at her, though she flitted close around him, as annoying as a gnat.

No one saw him except David Mitchell, Zoan's very special friend. David was the only other Christian in Chaco Canyon. David had his back to the door, but he turned and saw Zoan, smiled, and started to call out to him. But Zoan, who had no social understanding or skills, returned his gaze for a moment and then hurried back outside.

He saw the two special ones, the New Zionists they called themselves. Darkon Ben-ammi and Vashti Nicanor were sitting on a high promontory of rock just ahead of him. Black outlines against the blood-red of the rock, they had their backs to the setting sun, looking longingly to the east, to their homeland. For a moment Zoan was anxious, for they were looking right in the Wolf's direction. But then again, that made no sense, and he knew it. It didn't matter whether you were looking in the Wolf's direction or not; he could see you if he wanted to, and hiding your eyes made no difference. Somehow, Zoan felt easier in his mind as he recalled that these two, the special ones, were God's chosen people. From the beginning of the world until the end, He would keep a special watch on them, the Israelites, the apple of His eye.

Though there were twenty-nine other Indians in the canyon, Zoan wasn't worried about them—not because he didn't care about them, even love them, but because he knew that Cody Bent Knife was the key to his people, and whatever state Cody was in, so were his followers. At the moment, Cody and the soldiers seemed to be unaware of the danger and immune to the fear. Zoan thought that must be a good sign. Sometimes—as he knew all too well—ignorance was bliss.

But there was one last friend that Zoan had to see, to know that he was all right, that he wasn't afraid—or even worse, maybe looking back at the Wolf-Man, wondering about him, thinking about him, considering him and his power.

Dr. Niklas Kesteven was sitting alone by an open window in his solitary cabin. A single candle burned on the crude table in front of him. He looked up without surprise as Zoan soundlessly materialized at the door. "Hello, Zoan," he said in a helpless and weary tone. It was an odd contrast to his powerful frame, strong features, and thick, virile beard.

"Hello," Zoan said uncertainly. He wasn't a very good communicator, so he simply stared at Dr. Kesteven, his unusual eyes, liquid, full of light in spite of the pupils that grew to twice their diameter in nighttime, raking over him scrupulously.

"What's the matter?" Dr. Kesteven asked.

"Nothing," Zoan said helplessly. He was incapable of telling anyone how he felt, what he knew.

Impatiently Niklas demanded, "Zoan, what do you want?"

Zoan frowned a little. "What are you thinking about, Dr. Kesteven?"

Niklas sighed. Such a conversation with a normal person would be ludicrous, but it was typical with Zoan. His thick shoulders sagged a little, and Niklas turned to look out into the gathering darkness. "I was just thinking . . . wondering . . . about Alia. You remember, Zoan? My friend, my lady friend, Alia Silverthorne . . ."

Alia Silverthorne, chief commissar of the Sixth Directorate of the Man and Biosphere Project Executive Council, and personal bodyguard to the president of the United States of America, stared at her friend in dismay. Minden Lauer, the lovely Lady of Light, was slowly descending into madness before Alia's eyes, and there was nothing that anyone could do about it.

Of course, the entire world's gone barking mad, Alia mused. She wondered if maybe she were the last sane person on earth. In her extreme weariness and the beginnings of delusions and even visual hallucinations from what must be akin to combat fatigue, Alia grew vaguely amused that she thought *she* was the only sane person left on earth. She was the classic crazy person who didn't know she was insane.

". . . Tor is watching over us. I can feel him. I know when he's near," Minden was saying. Her calm demeanor and lovely, ethereal appearance created an unnerving contrast to the demented words. "Our destiny is with him, and he will not leave us to die here."

The president of the United States, Luca Therion, listened with what seemed to Alia to be besotted rapture. "But, Minden, my love," he said in a low, troubled voice, "there are such forces arrayed against us, and we—"

"No!" Minden almost shrieked. "No! We are the forces, the elemental forces, the powers, Luca! You must understand this! Tor will triumph, now and forever!" She swallowed, then reduced her voice to its hypnotic thrum. "He is more powerful than that inconsequential rabble," she said with delicate disdain, pointing toward the window. Though it was thick bulletproof glass, they could hear the indistinct growl of the angry mob outside. "He is more powerful than you can imagine. This world, this whole earth, is his . . ."

Sky Rock, a flat promontory that overhung a hill in the pastoral woods of Arkansas, didn't belong to Tor von Eisenhalt and never would, for Jesse Mitchell, a strong man of God and a prophet, stood upon it by night.

Jesse didn't look much like a holy man. He was eighty-eight years old, slight of frame, with shoulders bent from years but not with weariness, and ever-twinkling blue eyes. His white hair and mustache gleamed cleanly in the gathering darkness.

Tenderly his wife of sixty years, Noemi, thought that he could still be considered a handsome man. At least, he was to her. Frowning a little as he coughed, she asked, "Jess, you're not thinking of building up the signal fire again? You've only been out of your sickbed these two days."

"No," he said with a touch of sadness. "The fire was a promise, God's promise to them." He pointed down the mountain, to the south. "But a wicked and perverse generation seeketh after a sign. The Lord's told me that they must come on in faith now, Noe."

She nodded uncertainly. Sometimes she didn't quite comprehend Jesse's intimate conversations with God, but that didn't worry her. It wasn't her business; it was her husband's business. Jesse's total dedication to the business of the Lord had been, all their long lives, both their greatest joy and their greatest hardship. And somehow Noe knew that the worst trial Jesse had ever experienced faced him, and she knew that she must be extravigilant to take care of him, for that was her calling. She sighed heavily. She wasn't as strong as Jess, and she dreaded the coming darkness. It would be a heavy burden on him and also on her.

She stole a glance at him as he stood still at her side. His face was oddly unlined for a man of his age, and right now no fear or trouble marked it. Jesse Mitchell was a man at peace, and with satisfaction Noemi knew that she was a pillar upholding Jesse's peace.

For his part, Jesse was deep into the consideration of the nature of prophecy inspired by God as opposed to the mockery of it that the old devil had made: *It's not telling the future, or those awful personal psychic people that prey on the lost and the ignorant, telling them of their dirty little secrets . . . A true prophet exhorts the church, inspires people with the Word of God . . . It always must be true and agree with Scripture in every jot and tittle . . . has nothing to do with telling the future . . .*

"That little lady's looking up here at us right now," he said suddenly, pointing toward Hot Springs, unaware of the strangeness of his words. "Say a prayer for her, Noe. That little girl's got some hard and dangerous tasks facing her . . ." His voice trailed off. Jesse couldn't pronounce Xanthe St. Dymion's name, but Noemi understood that he was talking about her. She obediently bowed her head and closed her eyes, her lips moving a little.

Jesse continued his musings. *Fortune-telling, divination, soothsaying . . . all perversions of a great gift that God bestows upon His children. And that old Wolf, that old red-eyed demon, he's using all those deceptions and more. The magicians of Egypt were powerful, Lord, and I'm no Moses . . . What on this blessed earth do You expect me to do?*

And He answered, *Be still, and know that I am God.*

"Amen, Lord," Jesse murmured. Still staring down into the darkening land spread out below, he whispered, "Let them know You, God. Let them be still and know that You are God . . ."

"Amen," said Merrill Stanton to his wife's blessing on their food. He began to apportion the still-sizzling deer steaks and fried bread to his family. His wife, Genevieve, was flushed from bending over the heat of the fire and looked uncommonly pretty. She smiled mischievously at him and nudged her plate toward him, signaling "more." His daughter, Allegra Saylor, was willow slim but ate like a plowhand; his grandson, Kyle, was only four but could easily put away two good-sized deer steaks. Their friend—almost an adopted son—Perry Hammett, generally ate more than all of them did, but now he took only a modest portion, strongly refusing Merrill's kind offer of double helpings. Perry was losing some of his chubbiness because he had become determined to eat no more than they did.

Two other fires burned in the valley, and the groups huddled around them might have been in distant cities. At the largest fire, in the most welcoming camping spot, Pastor Tybalt Colfax and his wife, Galatia, and their four friends ate deer steaks and sopped up the delicious gravy with slightly stale soda crackers.

Galatia Colfax was irritated that the Stantons had fried bread but offered them none; never mind that the Colfax faction had never offered the Stantons so much as a crumb of either food or consolation, and Galatia couldn't boil water. Galatia made a spiteful comment, which ruined their dinner—for about fifteen seconds. They were too hungry, and the fresh meat was too delicious, to worry about the nobodies at the other fires for long.

The Stantons were certainly not nobodies, but as Merrill worriedly tended the third fire and the food for the other group, he despairingly thought that these people were, as a group, almost without human identity. They were the lost ones, the frightened ones, the weakest ones, the ones who lagged far behind and who could never keep up the fire and who had no hope. Merrill had to do and be everything for them. Poor Olivia Wheatley was almost catatonic; her ten-year-old daughter, Dana, was so pale and listless and thin that she looked like a small lost child; the Hartleys, both in their sixties, were fading like aged photographs.

With a sudden lurch in his heart, Merrill had a queasy sensation that someone was going to die. That was all. Just an odd thought in his head that seemed to be put there deliberately, fully formed and certain. With despair he stared at the lost ones and wondered which of them it would be.

About half a mile away from where Merrill stood staring at his forlorn little flock, Riley Case threw his Marlin .30-30 rifle to his shoulder, squinted one dark eye, and aimed. He surveyed the dark woods painstakingly through his notched sight. He didn't breathe, so he could keep his hand and eye steady.

Nothing. Only shadows and glimmers among the thick evergreens.

But I did see it, Riley thought. He wasn't a man given to having nervous tics or seeing goblins in the dark. He'd seen the eyes; they reflected the red of the dying sun's last rays, and they'd been the eyes of a wolf.

Victorine Flynn Thayer put both arms around her daughter and kissed her cheek. Dancy was small, her frame delicate, her bones thin, her skin white and translucent. Victorine hugged her just a little tighter.

Together they turned to watch the sun set. It was two sunsets since Tessa Kai Flynn, Victorine's mother and Dancy's grandmother, had died. Both evenings Victorine and Dancy had gone out onto the balcony of their beach condo to watch the sun's last moments. It was late fall, and though they faced due south, across the Gulf of Mexico, the earth had tilted enough so that they could see the sunsets at the corner of the high-rise condominiums.

It was breathtaking, stunning, as it always was, but for both Victorine and Dancy, it was a desolate beauty. The sky was empty and growing a forbidding shade of purple; the sea was bleak and dark; the beach stretched for miles in both directions, abandoned and sad.

Victorine, in a moment of weakness and despair, wondered if they were the only two people left alive on earth.

Dancy was smiling.

PART I

THE VALLEY OF DECISION

Multitudes, multitudes in the valley of decision:
for the day of the Lord is near in the valley of decision.

—JOEL 3:14

Whither should I fly?
I have done no harm. But I remember now
I am in this earthly world, where to do harm
Is often laudable, to do good sometime
Accounted dangerous folly.

—LADY MACDUFF, FROM MACBETH BY WILLIAM SHAKESPEARE

The Rainbow comes and goes,
And lovely is the Rose;
The Moon doth with delight
Look round her when the heavens are bare,
Waters on a starry night
Are beautiful and fair;
The sunshine is a glorious birth;
But yet I know, where'er I go,
That there hath passed away a glory from the earth.

—WILLIAM WORDSWORTH, ODE

ONE

RILEY CASE COULDN'T decide whether to tell them about the dead man.

He had never intended to tell the wanderers in the mountains about the body he'd found the day before he'd joined the group (the "dunkhead dunces" he'd originally named them).

The man, whoever he was, had been young, healthy, and strong, and he'd been following the Christians' path faithfully, but he'd always been two marches behind them. Riley never knew whether he'd been friend or foe, but he did know that the man had died badly—apparently from a wild animal attack. Riley hadn't thought it would do any good to tell the poor wanderers about it.

But now Riley was seeing the wolves.

With further consideration, he decided that the only person who might need to be told about the wolves was Merrill Stanton. Riley sure wasn't going to tell that movie-star preacher, who was supposed to be leading the group, or his shrewish wife; they might collapse with hysterics. None of the others, except maybe Allegra Saylor, could cope mentally or emotionally with the thought of a constant and very present threat. But quickly, with some discomfort, Riley decided not to tell Allegra. It wouldn't help her, and certainly Riley wasn't going to let any wolves or anything else touch her or her boy, Kyle. Not that he would ever tell her that. Riley wasn't much of a man for confidences, either giving or receiving.

Riley was a strong, sturdy man, with coal-black hair, a pugnacious jaw, a beard that shadowed by two o'clock in the afternoon, and dark eyes that gave nothing away. He had quaint, old-world manners but kept a long distance from everyone, man or woman.

He proved to be as invaluable to the wanderers as he was an enigma. He was a skilled hunter, and each day he provided enough meat for the entire group. Though he obviously had woodcraft skills that no one else had, Riley insisted that Merrill Stanton continue to scout ahead, which meant in effect that Merrill was leading the way.

Merrill Stanton hardly looked the part of a wilderness guide. He was a lanky six-footer, almost skinny. His features were homely, his expression kind, his mannerisms like an accountant's. Ty Colfax's "group," which had been ready to run at top speed in the opposite direction from that which Merrill led them in after the signal fire disappeared, somehow became more amenable to going on after Riley Case came along. Perhaps that was why Riley insisted that Merrill continue to lead. No one knew exactly, for Riley kept very much to himself. He provided food for them, he helped them in their hard travel in daytime, and he guarded them at night. He was not a comfortable man to be around, and so he gave them no solace; but neither did he ask for any in return.

The only person that Riley made any effort to talk to was Perry Hammett. Riley didn't spend very much time with the gawky child-man, but he sometimes spoke to Perry as they walked or after they finished supper. The boy's eyes shone when Riley paid the least bit of attention to him. Aside from the fact that the entire group regarded Riley as some sort of superman, Riley was probably the only person in the world who had actually *chosen* Perry. It seemed that, even in the few days since Riley had joined them, Perry stood taller, didn't blush so much, and had lost at least some of his shyness. He seemed to fall down less, too.

Wonder if Riley was an outcast like Perry? Allegra thought, observing Riley as he pointed out a landmark to Perry. *I wonder if that's why he takes time with him—kinship? It's not pity. He's not a pitying sort of man . . . and evidently that's not what Perry needs.*

Allegra disciplined herself not to watch, think about, or wonder about Riley too much. There was something between them. No, that wasn't right. Allegra was a married woman, happily married for five years, and the fact that she was so cruelly separated from her husband didn't change her outlook or her moral strength. There was nothing between Riley and her, except a glance once or twice, and a knowledge, deeply buried and deliberately kept that way, that there could be something between them. Sometimes that happened. There was no sin in being intelligent enough to know when you were attracted to someone. The sin was in what you did with the knowledge. Allegra ignored it, and to her relief, so did Riley.

Her mirror told her that she was an attractive woman, tall and willowy, but with a figure that made men steal a second glance. She was not beautiful in the garish Hollywood/Los Angeles way, but her warm green eyes, smoothly curved lips, and tawny hair gave her a sensuous appearance. She knew that Riley found her attractive, though he rarely spoke to her, hardly ever looked at her. But he was never unkind to her. In some visceral way, she knew that he was watching out for her and Kyle especially—just as she'd immediately known that she was the reason Riley had been following the group for so long. In this world, where all standards of human interaction were being redefined, it didn't seem odd to Allegra at all.

This terrible autumn in the year of our Lord 2050 was sinking slowly and inexorably into winter, and the days were gloomy and chilly. Night began to overtake more and more of the afternoon. On this day, their twentieth day of wandering, it seemed that the sun had never risen, only that the day had been a little lighter gray color than the night before. The shortened days had slowed them down even more. For most of the members of the group were so weak that they could walk only for a short time in the morning and again after lunch and a long rest. Merrill told Riley worriedly that on this dark day he didn't think they'd have time for two marches, so he was going to go far enough ahead to find a place to camp at about two o'clock in the afternoon and stay for the night. Riley agreed.

Sure enough, by noon it seemed that instead of the day waning, the twilight was beginning to fall. There was no wind, but the air was chilly and filled with unseen droplets of water that made their clothing feel damp and smell dank. All of the group—even the older couple, the Hartleys—seemed to have gained new strength with Riley Case's provisions of fresh food and his protection. Yet the world's oppressiveness overtook them, and they soon began to lose strength again.

"Excuse me, Mr. Case," Allegra said as he passed the straggling column. He'd been weaving in and out among them, sometimes flanking them on either side, out of sight. The set of his shoulders seemed taut to Allegra, and his secretive eyes darted, quick with watchfulness.

He didn't stop, but he turned to her and slowed his pace to match hers. "Yes, ma'am?"

"Is there something wrong?" she asked bluntly.

"Aside from creation and everything in it?" he parried. Already he was looking away from her, toward a thick stand of hardwoods on their left. The shadows underneath them were an impenetrable charcoal gray.

She tried again. "You seem . . . vigilant . . . even more so than usual."

To her amazement, he chuckled, although it was a desolate sound without real amusement. "You're not the first person to call me a vigilante, ma'am. Guess the leopard really can't hide his spots. Anyway, we're going to reach your father just up the trail here, and he's found us a good spot for the night. This march will be over soon. Now, if you'll excuse me." As he always did—a quaint, old-fashioned, rarely seen gesture these days—he yanked on the brim of his cap and said, "Ma'am."

Allegra felt reassured. It wasn't until he disappeared, half-running up the trail far ahead, that she realized he hadn't really told her anything. She reflected somberly, *It's as if he's watching for something . . . or watching something, something we can't see . . . Or is something watching us?*

Merrill found a campsite, though it was not quite as pleasant as some they'd had. They had been going slightly downhill all day, loosely tracing the bottom quarter of a high, brooding mountain with twin jagged peaks, unlike most of the gently rounded time-worn Ozarks. The trail was clear. It was the remains of an age-old dirt road, likely a logging road or a hunter's access built a hundred years ago. But it was treacherous and sometimes disappeared in tangles of briers and thickets, and small landslides had buried parts of it under sharp boulders and pebbles as edged as broken glass. It dipped and turned and then sank down into a foggy and thickly wooded valley.

In this valley Merrill set up their camp. As night fell, he wondered about the wisdom of his choice, for the notch between the two high peaks seemed to be like a wind tunnel. A caustic wind out of the north cut through, rising and falling like the atonal cries of women in mourning. In the valley were mostly old hardwoods, tall and stern, almost impossible to hew down with just an ax. Deadwood was scarce, and the fires were difficult to start and tiresome to keep going. A stream was nearby, but instead of running icy cold and fresh, it was one of the hot mineral springs that bubbled up all over these mountains. The pool, which was formed from a small fissure in a rock, looked sullen and dark, and metallic-smelling mists rose from it. Even though it was warmer by the stream, no one made camp by it. For the first time since they'd left the city, the group huddled closely together instead of dividing up into their three distinct "groups."

Allegra, who was sitting with Kyle and Perry and playing a silly game called Stick-Knock-Stick that Kyle made up, saw her father and Riley standing off to one side, talking quietly. Her father's face was grave, lined with care and worry. That was nothing new. But once again, Allegra saw, or perhaps sensed, something more.

"Perry, will you watch Kyle?" she asked abruptly.

"Sure, Miss Allegra. Only sometimes I think he watches me."

Absentmindedly Allegra smiled, then hurried to her father. Riley had his back to her and was blocking her father's view. She approached soundlessly, though she wasn't actually trying to sneak up on them.

". . . saw them three times today," her father was saying in a low voice. "I couldn't tell if it was the same one or not. I just saw a—movement, really, and gray fur, and once I thought I saw eyes, but I couldn't be sure."

Riley nodded, his heavy features drawn into a dark scowl. "I saw them. I've been seeing them all along because there are a lot of them in these hills. But I've never known them to stalk a big group of humans before. It doesn't make sense. They're sure not hungry. They've got more than enough easy prey, like deer and rabbits."

Allegra's voice shook. "Wh—what? What are you talking about?" She stepped up close to her father.

Merrill sighed and put his arm around her shoulders. "I really wish you hadn't overheard, Allegra," he said reproachfully. "No one ever heard anything she needed to hear from eavesdropping." It was probably the harshest thing Merrill had ever said to his daughter.

"But—but I want to know," she said tremulously.

Merrill and Riley exchanged glances. Merrill was clearly worried, while Riley shrugged. With a resigned sigh, Merrill said, "Wolves. We've been seeing wolves along the trail."

Allegra's indrawn breath was ragged. "W-wolves . . ."

Both men waited silently.

She buried her face in her hands for a moment, pressing her cold fingers to her temples. Then she gave her father a quick hug. "Thank you for telling me. I—I trust you. Both of you. Excuse me."

Allegra said nothing else to anyone, not even her mother.

They wrapped up in all of their blankets or sleeping bags or whatever they had, but no one seemed to be able to settle down and go to sleep. Merrill walked restlessly around the camp, stopping to talk to this one and that one, sometimes standing at the edge of the woods and staring out into the darkness. Riley was nowhere to be seen; in fact, no one could recall ever seeing him asleep, in a bedroll, at night. Allegra, Genevieve, and Perry were sitting around their fire. Kyle was a big mound of blankets and covers, with his head in Allegra's lap. He had on a Ty-wool stocking cap, but some of his thick brown curls had escaped around the nape of his neck, and Allegra was absentmindedly playing with them, thinking of how Kyle's hair was exactly like Neville's, except that Neville, being a marine to the core, kept his hair cut so short it was almost shaved.

She saw yellow eyes peering at her in the murkiness just beyond the wildly wavering firelight. For long moments she stared, unblinking, as the primeval slanted eyes stared back at her, into her eyes, burning into her brain, searing her with terror. Panicked, she jumped up and looked frantically around for her father or for Riley.

Ten-year-old Dana Wheatley, who had hardly said a complete sentence, suddenly started a low moan that went up in a sliding scale to a high shriek. "Maaa-maaa! Eyes!"

Pandemonium was instant.

People scrambled up, screaming, running this way, falling, shoving.

Allegra saw her father, then took one step toward him. "Father! Here! Here!" she screamed, but her cry was lost in the din. Merrill caught sight of her, though, and he was coming, running, pushing panicked people aside. She turned to pick up Kyle—

He wasn't there.

In his fear and confusion, Kyle had tried to run to his grandfather. He was between Allegra and Merrill now, with Perry behind him, clumsily trying to reach down and grab him and stop him.

Easily seen within the circle of firelight now were the smoky gray coats, the red eyes and tongues, and white teeth. There were many wolves, not just one or three or a pack. Dull booms, shots from a big rifle, sounded in the forest ahead. Some people panicked and ran into the darkness of the woods; others screamed at them to come back. Some fell, shrieking, to their knees.

One of the big males, a pack leader, suddenly turned and watched Kyle, the smallest and slowest of the prey. He padded toward him, not running, but slinking, his teeth bared and ears flat. Kyle saw him and stopped, his eyes round and unseeing as if he were hypnotized. The wolf lowered his haunches, and they quivered for the spring.

Perry miraculously moved fast. He grabbed a long branch out of the fire and jumped in front of Kyle, directly in the wolf's path.

The wolf leaped, and he and Perry went down together in a heap of fur and teeth and fire. Perry screamed, a terrible sound, but he was fighting. Merrill stopped and had his gun out, aimed, steady and sure, but there was no way he could hit the wolf and not hit Perry.

Allegra ran by the furious tangle on the ground, and she could already see the black-red of blood and smell the burning. Something brushed her leg as she passed the boy and the wolf, but she couldn't look, couldn't help, and couldn't bear to see. She scooped Kyle up in her arms and kept running.

Riley loomed in front of her, and she ran full speed into him. The force of their collision and the hardness of his body almost knocked her down. He didn't speak. He grabbed her arm, whirled her around, and took her back to the fire.

Riley ran to Perry. Allegra pulled Kyle's face tight against her shoulder. Riley lifted his rifle and brought the stock down on the wolf's back in a crashing blow. The wolf jumped, yelped, and threw itself backward off Perry.

But it didn't run. It snarled, holding its ground, staring up at Riley as if it were sizing up its new opponent. Riley pressed his rifle to his shoulder, and the wolf leaped into the sheltering forest. Riley shot once, but the wolf melted into the depths.

As if by some signal or infernal dark magic, all of the wolves disappeared.

Allegra felt as if she were wading in some deep, sticky substance that slowed her footsteps and made them unsure. She had to go to Perry, though. He lay on the ground, still, his face a chalk-white moon, holding his hand to his chest. There was a lot of blood. In the fury of the fight it had splashed all around.

Riley shoved his rifle into Merrill's hands, then knelt. "Let's have a look at that hand, Perry." He pulled gently, then took a deep breath. "We'll have to do some patching, but it'll be all right."

"It—it will?" He sounded more like a lost, frightened child than a seventeen-year-old boy who'd just valiantly fought a wolf.

Allegra gave Kyle to Genevieve, then knelt down by Perry. He looked up at her, searching her face with desperation. She couldn't smile, but she tried to make her voice as calm and reassuring as possible. "We'll take care of you, Perry. Don't you worry about that."

He nodded and closed his eyes.

They moved him closer to the fire, and Riley brought enough wood to keep it burning high. Allegra was glad for the mineral water, for the hot springs were sterile, and the minerals seemed to have some healing powers. Merrill had a small supply of strong painkillers, so soon Perry's hurt was numbed, though his fear was not. Allegra washed his mangled hand—she could see the bone in one place—and spoke softly to him of trivial and light things. She bandaged it as carefully and meticulously as if she were performing neurosurgery. Then she sat with him, holding his good hand.

In a dreamy voice, he asked, "Am I going to be all right?" His voice was weak, a little thick from the drugs, but the fear lurking in his eyes told Allegra everything.

"You're going to be all right, Perry," she said quietly. "You'll heal. You may have some scars, but they will be your badge of honor. You have great courage, Perry. I can never thank you enough for my son's life."

"Don't thank me," he said, almost pleading. "Just—talk to me, please."

He was deathly afraid.

"I'll read to you. Would you like that?" she asked.

"The Bible, please," he said numbly.

"May I use your Bible? It's so nice to have such a big Bible, with such big print, to read by firelight," she said, pulling it from his pack onto her lap. It was a huge display Bible, with dozens of prints of old paintings and with Gothic curlicues in the margins. It was marked and had notes all over it, and the spine and back were held together by sticky duct tape. Many of the crackling yellowed pages were held together by Scotch tape.

"It was my grandmother's," he said dully. "It's all I have of hers."

Allegra read, mostly Psalms. Perry slept after a while. She stayed by his side, reading to herself, watching him, praying a little, sometimes weeping. He clung to her hand, and through the night, he cried, a small child's whimper. Allegra finally pulled him up to hold him close, and she held him until dawn.

"He's not going to make it," Allegra said bitterly. Her voice was cold and edged with resentment. She looked over with despair in her eyes to where Perry lay—too still—under extra blankets.

Merrill huddled down over the fire, clasping his knees. He was weary to the bone. He and Riley and two of the other men had carried Perry in a stretcher made from saplings and blankets. He was so tired, he could only murmur helplessly, "I didn't think the wound was that bad. It's killing him."

Riley stood up, holding his rifle at the ready, ever the vigilante. But his eyes were clouded with weariness and perhaps sorrow, though it was difficult to tell. His voice and his will seemed strong and invulnerable. "There was something odd about that wolf. There was something odd about the whole thing—the stalk, the attack, the way they left. And that boy doesn't have gangrene. That wound shouldn't be life-threatening. Makes me sick." With that, possibly his longest speech to date, he turned and stalked off into the woods.

They were all sick at heart. Perry Hammett was dying.

Tears stung Allegra's eyes, and she felt hot traces down her cheeks.

"Don't cry, Mama," Kyle pleaded, but tears were in his eyes, too. "Don't cry, Mama. Don't cry."

She held him close, so hard that she knew he could barely breathe. "I'll try, baby bear. Why don't you get all your blankets and Benny and go over there with your grandmother and ask her to tell you a story?"

"I want to stay wif Perry. And you. I promise to go to sleep." His eyes were enormous and pleaded eloquently.

"All right, little bear," she relented. She had, after all, been staying with Perry for the last two nights. Kyle needed her, too. "Get all your blankets and your cap, okay? And go right to sleep."

The night was long, and Allegra was exhausted, so she dozed. Perry never moved or spoke. Occasionally Allegra jerked awake and leaned down to make sure he was still breathing. Already his face was sunken; the outline of his skull, hidden until now by the richness of youth, could be clearly discerned.

Allegra thought she heard someone—she didn't know who—shout her name. She came awake with a start and knew that the imperious call had been in her dreams. Riley Case was there, sitting cross-legged on the other side of Perry's bedroll. She sat up and rubbed at her gritty eyes with her palms.

"Go back to sleep," Riley said quietly. "You can't stay awake forever."

At that moment Perry said in a faint but clear voice, "Allegra—Miss Allegra?"

"Yes, Perry, I'm here." Quickly Allegra bent over and put her hand on Perry's forehead. It was cold and clammy. Trembling, she slipped her hand beneath his ugly green sweater and laid it over his heart. She could feel nothing. The heartbeat was so faint, it was imperceptible.

"Miss Allegra . . . you know . . . that scripture you were reading to me?" His eyes were only half-opened and were dull, as if the light of life had already been put out.

"Which one, Perry?"

He licked his lips and said laboriously, "About the seeds . . . planted. Some of them the ravens ate . . . some of them were choked out by thorns . . ."

"Why, yes," Allegra said quietly. "The parable of the sower."

"I—I was just wondering," he whispered, "if I'm like the seed that fell by the wayside and got trodden down, and the ravens devoured it . . ."

Allegra swallowed hard, for she had a burning in her throat that seared all the way down to her chest. "No, Perry," she said firmly. "You are the good seed that fell on good ground, which has an honest and good heart. Because of you, my son lives. What more precious fruit could be borne?"

He looked dimly surprised, then nodded. If he'd had the strength, perhaps he might have smiled, but he could only close his eyes with exhaustion. "I wanted to go see that light, Miss Allegra . . . and I thought I wouldn't get to . . . but now I think I'll see it . . . before all of you. But you'll make it . . . you'll see it . . . I see it now . . ."

The death was so quiet and simple that it was impossible for Allegra to tell when he slipped from this world into the next.

Riley Case dug his grave, and Pastor Ty Colfax spoke. He was a still-faced man of thirty-five, coldly handsome. His eyes were not the warm blue found in many people in the South, but were sharp and rather calculating. Not a tall man, Colfax kept his trim body as straight as any West Point cadet's—perhaps in an attempt to add an extra inch to his stature. His voice was clear, but there was little warmth in it, though it was obvious that he worked at adding the quality.

Galatia Colfax, eight years younger than her husband, was one of those women who fought the constant battle against aging, and she had already had several corrective surgeries. Her dark brown eyes clashed with her platinum blonde hair, and her expression always revealed a touch of unhappiness that she could not hide with cosmetics or surgery. Without all of her facials and hormones and correctives, she was looking rough from the hardships of the past few weeks. Her expression, too, had grown uglier. Right now she was staring at Allegra Saylor with what Galatia truly believed to be righteous anger but was actually nothing more noble than petty envy. Even in her grief, Allegra looked lovely.

Allegra realized that she was not paying attention to Ty Colfax's words. She knew only that she was cold and Kyle was crying, and she was conscious of the weight of Perry's Bible as she held it close to her breast. Galatia said that it would seem more fitting to bury it with Perry, but Allegra lashed out, "My son will have this Bible, and his son, and his son's son. By this Bible, they will know God, and they will honor Perry's memory."

Galatia flinched as if Allegra had struck her, but she said nothing else.

That night, Ty Colfax called the group together. Allegra was surprised to see Riley leaning against a tree, outside the circle of people as always, but attentive. Usually when the group came together for a discussion, he melted into the woods.

"We have had a death, a tragic and senseless death," Ty said mournfully. "I believe we must face the grim reality that we've made a terrible mistake. The night of the blackout, we were all confused and panicked and filled with fear. We saw—something—and it gave us hope. But we must reason together. By now, I'm certain that the authorities have recovered order in Hot Springs. Perhaps the power is back on. It's time to return."

Low murmurs of assent ran like the sea's undertow throughout the group. A few sidelong glances were cast in Merrill Stanton's direction. He, Genevieve, and Allegra sat close together. The discussion—which generally consisted of how quickly they could leave—grew more lively, and still Merrill said nothing. Ty and Galatia Colfax didn't take their eyes off them, though, and finally Ty cleared his throat. Everyone quieted down. "Mr. Stanton? May I ask your intentions?"

"Certainly," Merrill said calmly. "My family and I are going on."

"But why?" Ty demanded.

"For the same reason we began this journey. We believe that the Lord is leading us to a place, and He has shown us the way. We believe that we are following Him."

"But we've had Perry's death and the constant threat of wild animal attacks. And most important, there is no signal fire!" Ty blustered on. "I'm beginning to have my doubts that there ever was one! It's a proven fact, you know, that people in traumatic situations can have mass delusions, hysterical hallucinations!"

Merrill asked in his kindly way, "And, Pastor Colfax, you honestly believe that is the truth?"

"I—I don't know! I'm—that's what I'm saying! We don't know the truth!"

Sadly Merrill said, "But we do, Pastor. We always have. We are

His sheep, and we know His voice. My family and I are going on with Him."

Ty Colfax's mouth tightened, and he nodded curtly. "I see. You are free to make your own choice, of course. But I must warn you, Mr. Stanton, not to try to convince any of these poor people to follow you. I believe you are terribly wrong and you will pay a high price for your blindness."

Allegra jerked and rose halfway to her feet, her face filled with anger. Genevieve put her hand on her daughter's arm and yanked hard. "Sit down, Allegra. He is still a man of God, and it's not our place to correct him."

"But I can't stand to sit here—"

"Please, Allegra," Merrill said softly.

Allegra sat down, but she crossed her arms and stared mutinously at Ty. Ty didn't meet her eyes, but Galatia shot her a savage grimace.

Ty turned to face Riley Case. "What about you, Mr. Case? You don't seem to be the type of man to go on a blind and hopeless quest."

One of Riley's black eyebrows arched up. "You mean I'm not a man of faith? Like you?"

Galatia cried, "Faith has nothing to do with this! We've all decided—except for them—that this aimless wandering in the wilderness was a dangerous and stupid thing to do! God expects us to use our common sense! And, Mr. Case, we need your help. Much more than they do! If they're determined to be martyrs, no one can help them anyway!"

Riley replied evenly, "Mrs. Colfax, I hate to disabuse you of this fine notion you've got that I'm the world's baby-sitter, but I've got to. I'm not going on so that I can help the Saylors and the Stantons. I'm going to find that signal fire." He added with extra emphasis, his dark eyes sliding to Ty, "The one that was there, that we all saw and knew and know is real. Anybody that happens to be taking that road, well, I'll be pleased to travel with him if he wants. But I'm going on, alone or not."

"But why?" Galatia demanded in a high, strident voice.

With obvious reluctance he answered, "Because it's what I want to do. I've always hated living in the co-op cities."

"But why go to that one spot where that stupid fire was? Why not help us get back to Hot Springs and then melt back into the woods?" she pleaded.

Riley, who'd evidently had more than his fill of conversation, set his jaw and shook his head.

Ty finally spoke up again. "Galatia, Mr. Case is obviously not going to help us, so don't beg. It's unseemly. The only thing that I must insist upon, Mr. Stanton, Mr. Case, is that you leave us one of your weapons. I can't allow you to take the only weapons that the group has."

Riley bristled. "You *insist*? You can't *allow*?"

Merrill said quietly, "No, Mr. Case, he's right. I'll leave you my .357, Brother Colfax."

Ty's face lit up like a spoiled child's at a birthday party. But Riley said brusquely, "No need for that. I've got a .22 pistol stashed and a box of shells. That's it, Mr. Colfax. That's your deal."

"With a group this size you should leave us your rifle," Ty said with a decisive air.

Riley shook his head with exasperation. "Do you know what the killing range of a .30-30 is, Mr. Colfax? No, thought not. It's about a mile. How many people do you think would have been killed if one of you had been firing this rifle during the wolf attack the other night? And besides, you can't use this for small game like rabbits or squirrels. There wouldn't be enough pieces left for a stew."

"But it would kill wolves," Galatia insisted.

"Excuse me, ma'am, but in case you've forgotten, neither of these guns killed any wolf the other night," Riley retorted darkly.

"And I don't know about Mr. Stanton, but I can tell you that I'm a good enough shot that I should have gotten three of them. So just forget shooting wolves. There's not enough ammo in the state to kill all of them. Your best bet's going to be fire. Build up two good ones and stay between them."

Colfax, seeing that this was Riley's final word, shrugged. "All right. We'll take the .22."

Riley nodded and turned away. "At least," he muttered to himself, "they'll have to go to some trouble to kill each other with that."

Two

Chaco Canyon and some of the bluffs and ravines tracing out in jagged lines from the central community of vast Pueblo Bonito had faint signs of new life. It was not teeming with vitality, but it was not a ten-mile mausoleum any longer.

Horses ranged up and down day and night. Four burros could be seen in a low three-sided canyon boxed in by a rough line of tumbleweed, though they occasionally chewed on their makeshift gate and meandered around. They never went far. A jaguar paced up and down, apparently about her own personal business. An old dingo, whose constant companions appeared to be two domestic brindled cats, ran and roughhoused in the warmth of the early afternoons. Eagles circled overhead constantly.

If one looked very, very closely, one could occasionally see human beings.

Native Americans, it would seem from their cultural history, might form a tribal enclave and live communally in one of the larger, finer centers such as Pueblo Bonito or Casa Rinconada. Cody Bent Knife's followers, however, had been solitary wanderers in one way or another all their lives, and they were scattered throughout the canyon in single dwellings in voluntary isolation.

A small group of Chaco Canyon wanderers stayed together in what might once have been a small enclosed village, though it was nowhere near as grand as Pueblo Bonito. Fire Team Eclipse of the 101st Airborne had chosen a structure that ranged along a south-facing crescent backed by a soaring bluff. A single central community room with a massive clay-lined hearth was the main entrance to the complex, with antechambers large and small radiating out both sides. A small but very hot fire snapped merrily on the hearth, and what little smoke there was from the dry mesquite tinder jetted straight up toward a smoke hole in the roof.

Captain Concord Slaughter kicked a log, then looked up speculatively at the convenient hole as the smoke dissipated and disappeared through it. At six feet four inches, he was the tallest man in the room, but then he was generally the tallest man anywhere. With long arms and legs and a rangy build, his shadow from the firelight looked oddly like the stick-man hunter paintings that graced the canyon. He had spiky sandy hair, a no-nonsense mouth and chin, a sun-creased face. Even a stranger viewing the scene would know that he was in command of the group of soldiers.

A noise, alien and forbidding, intruded on the homey sounds of the fire and low conversation: the low growling thumps of Messerschmitt-Daimler *Dolches,* or Daggers, the newest, most deadly attack helicopters ever designed. They flew over constantly. No one knew where they were coming from or going.

"Amazing how those air passages built into the ceiling dissipate the smoke before it filters out into the air," Niklas Kesteven mused. He looked like a great grizzly bear drowsing by the fire, his thick shoulders slumped, his unkempt beard growing almost up to his eyes and falling down his chest. "I'm certain the Anasazi weren't trying to be covert—it's obviously a crude heating and cooling system—but it does work for our purposes."

"Those Daggers are sure to have thermal imaging," Lieutenant Deacon Fong said. His dark eyes were wistful as he looked up to the soaring ceiling of the great room as if to try to see the helicopter through the six feet of stone. He was the fire team's helicopter pilot, and a pilot without an aircraft was a sad thing to see. "They're going to register the heat aura sooner or later."

"If they're looking," Con Slaughter said sturdily. "And I don't think they are."

"Maybe not now, but will they?" his sergeant, Rio Valdosta, asked darkly. Short, with rich walnut skin, he was built like a tank. As the team's gunner, he was performing one of his favorite rituals: cleaning Captain Slaughter's 12-gauge shotgun. It already was so highly polished inside and out that it looked as if it were made of onyx instead of blue steel.

"They might sometime, but for now I guess they're pretty taken up with invading the inhabited parts of America," Ric Darmstedt said. He was subdued, almost unrecognizable from his usual rowdy Texas swagger. He was in his stocking feet, for he was cleaning and polishing his boots. Ric had to be the only soldier in the world who still spit-polished his boots every night. Such meticulous habits were one of the things that gave away his Germanic heritage—that, and his tall, muscular, blond, blue-eyed Nordic good looks. He could have been a poster boy for the Aryan *Wunderkind*.

Only two women were in the room, and both hovered by Ric, Con Slaughter noted with some amusement and some envy. He'd never been very good with women somehow, though he had a rugged appeal. Slaughter felt awkward around them, while Darmstedt seemed to be able to make himself perfectly at home with women or girls, regardless of who they were or what they were like. The scene was a perfect example of how all women seemed to be drawn to Darmstedt, for there were never two women more different from the two who managed to stay close by him. Seated behind him now, excluded from the circle of soldiers, but still determined to stay close, was Gildan Ives; she was a fashionably skinny woman with much-corrected, but still pretty, facial features and outrageous cherry-colored hair. She was a veterinarian, and now she was playing with the two brindled cats that lived in Chaco Canyon.

By Darmstedt's side—very much a part of the team—was the grave and dignified Colonel Vashti Nicanor of the Israeli Air Force, lately inextricably joined to Fire Team Eclipse. She had a quiet, unobtrusive beauty, Con decided, with her shining black hair and liquid dark eyes and olive skin, now darkened attractively by the sun. She never looked directly at Gildan, though that woman shot Vashti looks of intense dislike every time Vashti spoke. Vashti always ignored her.

Her fellow wandering New Zionist, Colonel Darkon Ben-ammi, who was seated on her other side, suddenly sat up straighter, training his sharp eyes on Dr. Niklas Kesteven.

"Dr. Kesteven, it appears that you are well rested," Ben-ammi said in a low, concerned tone. Niklas and Gildan had slept night and day since the fire team had rescued them from the ranch with the death house of a lab underneath it.

Niklas nodded. "Yes, it's amazing how well I've been sleeping and how relaxing this place is, considering how primitive it is."

"So you are feeling recovered, and stronger?" Ben-ammi persisted, albeit politely. He gave Captain Con Slaughter a peculiarly intense glance, but Con couldn't decipher the meaning. He wasn't a very subtle man.

"Oh, yes, I'm feeling very well, thank you," Niklas responded with an air of importance. On their journey none of the soldiers had shown him such concern, though they had taken very good care of him and Gildan in the physical sense. Niklas Kesteven was an acknowledged genius, a very important man in the scientific world. He was accustomed to being treated with more homage.

With the slightest hint of exasperation, Colonel Ben-ammi directed to Con Slaughter: "Then perhaps Dr. Kesteven, as he was obviously an important scientist working in the Man and Biosphere Project, might be able to help us, Captain Slaughter."

Darkon outranked Con, but he tried, as much as possible, to defer to him as the leader of the team Darkon had voluntarily joined. Sometimes it was hard, though. Darkon was a member of Mossad, and his greatest expertise was intelligence gathering, while Con was first and foremost a combat soldier.

"Huh?" Con said. He was still wool-gathering about Ric and his women. "Oh—yes, sir, Colonel Ben-ammi, I—yes. Dr. Kesteven. As you know, we all came from Fort Carson, and our communications went down in this massive blackout. As I understand it, Zoan and the Indians have been here for a couple of months. So no one here has had any contact with the outside world since the autumnal equinox. What about your lab? When did you lose power?"

Niklas suddenly looked wary. He realized that Darkon Ben-ammi had set him up for a debriefing, and he didn't much relish it. While Con questioned him, Niklas was thoroughly uneasy, and his speech showed it. Usually an articulate, even pointed, conversationalist, he stuttered and faltered as he related the three days after the equinox when he and Gildan had been "up top."

That one's hiding something . . . or a lot of somethings, or a really Big Something, Darkon Ben-ammi thought shrewdly. *I'm glad we adopted him and that silly woman and cared for them, but I'm also glad that the team remains suspicious of him. Anyone who works that hard to hide something definitely has something important to hide. He's so very bad at it, too.*

"Look, Dr. Kesteven, I'm not going to stick bamboo shoots under your nails or burn the soles of your feet with hot irons," Con stated. "Valdosta here might, but I won't. So why don't you just spit it out? We need every bit of information we can get, and you don't have anything to lose by letting us know everything we can about this blackout and how it's affected the rest of the country. What's your crisis?"

"I don't have a crisis," Niklas blustered, his face growing red. "I'm just telling you that I hardly paid attention to the Cyclops broadcasts. I thought the alerts were some kind of stupid hopped-up Sixth Directorate drill."

Niklas had long ago decided—on the night that the lab had lost power, in fact, when the deadly effects of the blackout had been so personally illustrated to him—that he must never tell anyone that he'd been the man who'd discovered *Thiobacillus chaco* and brought this terrible scourge to the United States and loosed it. He didn't shirk from that fact or try to shift responsibility onto Alia Silverthorne or anyone else—in his mind. But he saw no reason that anyone else should ever know. Certainly not these grim men whose fellow soldiers had been killed. Even though they had died from German bullets and bombs, their deaths had still been an indirect result of Niklas's criminally careless handling of a dangerous organism. Everything had started with that, and he knew it. But he was determined that no one else should know it.

"So what's the crisis, Captain Slaughter?" Niklas went on arrogantly. "America's blacked out. We're in the Stone Age. We have to learn to deal with it."

Slaughter said in his best professional-soldier-to-ignorant-civvie rasp, "The crisis is, Dr. Kesteven, that we don't know that's true of the entire continent. We're fairly certain that the western half of the U.S. is down, especially since you've given us the information you have, regardless of how scanty and careless that information is. How, exactly, do you know that the entire continent's down?"

Niklas reddened, though whether from discomfort or anger no one could tell—except maybe one person, and Niklas had dismissed Zoan from his calculations. "Because, Captain Slaughter, this blackout must be the result of one of two things," he said in his most superior lecturing voice. "Either it's solar flares or an EMP detonation."

Niklas had thought of these two plausible scenarios long ago. An electromagnetic pulse detonation was an explosion of a device at a very high altitude. With no air to absorb the shock wave, instead of converting to mechanical energy—like the air blast in ground explosions—it reached and then traveled through the atmosphere in its simplest form: electrical energy, or more precisely, an immense electrical surge. At least that was the theory. No one had ever actually used an EMP, though it had been invented nearly a century earlier.

Slaughter merely glanced at Ric. Ric spit heartily onto the toe of his right boot, then polished in slow, deliberate circles. "Dr. Kesteven, either you're delusional, or you're not nearly as smart as you should be. Our compasses still work, and you know that would be impossible if it were solar flares. Aside from the fact that our tech-heads, not to mention your people, would have given us a heads-up long ago.

"As for an electromagnetic pulse detonation—yes, it could have wrecked the power grid and Cyclops network. But, sir, it wouldn't have blasted your car's electrical systems or your flashlight or your battery-operated toothbrush. Perhaps you weren't aware of this. And finally—"

Niklas wasn't a very humble man at best, but this grunt questioning his intelligence—even though he'd set himself up—enraged him. He roared, "And perhaps you aren't aware of who I am and what I do. What do you think we did in that lab? Do you think maybe it might have had something to do with *advancement in weaponry*? Did it ever occur to you that I might know more about EMP detonations than you do? Maybe, Lieutenant Darmstedt, you ought to let someone else use the team brain tonight."

David Mitchell and Zoan were slightly back from the others, talking together in half-whispers. Now David started, his eyes narrowing. Zoan slowly shifted his luminous black eyes to Niklas with an expression of deep sadness. Niklas started visibly; Zoan couldn't possibly comprehend the connection between his long-ago questions about the ohm-bug and Alia Silverthorne and Niklas's cover stories, could he?

Could he?

Con said nothing; his eyes flickered dangerously. Beside him, Rio growled and made a sharp movement, but Con made a curt gesture and Rio remained still. "I think that was uncalled for, Dr. Kesteven," Con said in an ominously soft voice. "I think you'd better apologize to me and my team. We're all hot-wired these days."

Niklas looked angry and seemed to be staring at Zoan, but then his face fell. "I am sorry," he said and was openly sincere. "It was uncalled for and also untrue. All of you please accept my apologies."

"Forgotten, Dr. Kesteven," Con said shortly.

"You can call me Niklas," he said awkwardly.

"You can call me Captain Slaughter," Con retorted. "Go on, Darmstedt."

His eyes an Arctic blue, Ric continued, "So, Dr. Kesteven, if you're such a genius about EMP detonations, can you tell us how the Germans have a defense against them?"

"What—what do you mean?" Niklas asked, startled.

"The spray," Darmstedt elocuted carefully. "The glue-salt spray they protected all their electronics with. You know, the helos that fly overhead all the time, the Tornadoes that blew our base to bits!" His voice grew angry.

Niklas's eyes opened wide; he was astonished. Jumping up, he paced with heavy, shambling steps. "What do you mean? A spray preventive? I thought—I knew all those helos and planes could have auxiliary fuel tanks fitted for Atlantic crossings—I thought they'd flown over from Europe."

Con and Ric glanced at each other uneasily; they realized that they hadn't yet told Niklas about observing the Germans at Holloman spraying all their equipment before the blackout. They'd been disrespectful to Niklas and without just cause. It made straightforward, honest men like Con and Ric uncomfortable.

"I apologize, Dr. Kesteven," Con said in a rough half-whisper. "I didn't realize that you didn't have all the facts. The Goths have a spray that they used on all their electronics. We saw them at Holloman, just before the equinox. We procured a sample of the spray and had it analyzed. It turned out to be a compound of—of—what was it, Darmstedt?"

Darmstedt frowned. "I don't recall the chemical compounds. It was a sticky spray with a high concentration of sea salt."

"What?" Niklas blustered. "You're—saying they sprayed this stuff onto delicate electronic equipment? What—never mind. Let me think." His beard dropped onto his chest again; his eyes grew thoughtful but unfocused.

Con Slaughter then turned to speak to Colonel Ben-ammi hulking on his left.

Though the individuals were sitting close together, the intricacies of human interaction were readily apparent. Slaughter and Ben-ammi talked in low tones that no one could overhear, and no one tried to. Rio Valdosta had never stopped cleaning his and Captain Slaughter's weapons. He and Deacon Fong talked animatedly about weapons and choppers, and sometimes laughed. Ric Darmstedt meticulously polished his boots and occasionally joined in with them. At his side Vashti Nicanor said very little, watching the three men—particularly Ric—very closely. Gildan Ives leaned up to occasionally whisper something to Ric, and he gave an automatically polite nod.

David Mitchell and Zoan, sitting by themselves on the far side of the fire, had returned to their private whispers. The dingo, which adored Zoan as all animals seemed to, had begun by lying at Zoan's feet but had managed to sneak up until his head was in Zoan's lap. Absently Zoan stroked him, and the dog's mismatched eyes were half-closed.

Most peculiar of all were the two Indians, young, whipcord-thin Cody Bent Knife and old Benewah Two Color, the dull gleam of the white streak in his hair gleaming like red gold in the firelight. They were seated cross-legged on single blankets, back in the shadows, isolated from each other and everyone else. They never spoke or moved. Cody and Benewah might have been ghosts of the children of light who'd lived and died here so long ago.

After a long time, Con rose, went to the stack of tinder by the door, and returned with an armload of small, dry sticks. He tossed them onto the fire one by one, and everyone grew silent, expectant.

"We completed our mission, Eclipse. We got the burros and the horses, even though there's no base to take them back to," he said in his short, to-the-point manner. "So what's our next mission?"

Rio spoke up in a hard voice, "I say we go kill Goths, sir."

Con nodded slowly, to the Indians' astonishment. "That's our job, Rio, no doubt about it. To make war on our enemies. But to do that, we have to have a plan—a clear objective and a strategy to accomplish it."

Rio shrugged. "Let's go shoot Germans. They die. Mission accomplished."

Con couldn't stop the corner of his mouth from twitching. "Rio, you have a lot of good qualities, but tactical planning isn't one of your brighter lights. Let somebody else use the team brain, huh?"

"Fine with me, sir. As long as I have the guns," Rio replied carelessly.

"C'mon, Colonel Ben-ammi, we're all friends here," Con said. "Give me a hint, would you? I never expected to be the commanding general of the American army, you know."

Colonel Ben-ammi spread his hands, palms upward. They looked like picnic hams. "Captain Slaughter, you've read the books. How do you think the commanding generals decide on strategies? By the books, of course."

The light dawned. Con said slowly, with growing revelation, "I don't know what I'm doing . . . because I don't have information. And I don't have any information because I don't have any intelligence. And if you say one word, Dr. Kesteven, I'm going to do that orthodontist work I promised you when we first met. Of course, I can't map out a battle plan if I don't have a clue who or what or where I'm fighting."

"Sir, I know I gave up the team brain, but—" Rio began, frowning.

"Can it, Rio. We know the Germans bombed Fort Carson. But we don't know squat about the big picture. What about this power blackout? Can we fight it—and undo it? How long is it going to last? Forever?"

In a very subdued voice, Niklas said, "Captain Slaughter? Some things that I've been considering might address that. One is that no one—at least, no one as intelligent as the Germans, if in fact they are responsible—would have used a complete power blackout as a weapon if it was going to be permanent."

"That is very true," Colonel Ben-ammi agreed heavily. "That would make even less sense than using nuclear devices to devastate a country. Only a madman would do such a thing, for the conquered territory would be useless to him."

The team absorbed these comments.

Niklas went on, "And finally, Lieutenant Fong told me that the Germans didn't harm any of the planes and helicopters when they bombed the base. Obviously they plan to use them—and expect them to be functional again. The spray they employed was a preventive measure, not an antidote. Therefore, your darling helicopter, Lieutenant Fong, probably won't be grounded for too long."

"Hold up, Dr. Kesteven," Deacon Fong said, sitting up alertly. "I missed a step there somewhere."

With admirable patience, Niklas explained, "They could prevent it, but they can't fix it after it's already happened. Preventive measures versus antidotal measures, you see. However, they are anticipating the effects wearing off, or reversing, or disappearing in a big puff of smoke or something because they're planning on using your helicopter, Lieutenant Fong."

Con asked awkwardly, for he had trouble visualizing what

needed to be done, "Dr. Kesteven, do you think you could—figure this thing out somehow? I mean, we're talking big here about defeating it, but all of us—even Rio—know we can't just shoot it. Couldn't you get a line on what's causing the blackout? And then maybe you could figure out how to fix it?"

Under normal circumstances, Dr. Niklas Kesteven would have swaggered for days with his chest stuck out, bragging that he could conquer any scientific mystery. But these were hardly normal circumstances, and then there was Zoan's reproachful gaze burning into his conscience, if not his soul. Niklas ducked his head and mumbled, "Sorry, Captain Slaughter. But unfortunately it's like a computer loop. I can't analyze the problem without equipment. Equipment takes electricity. The problem is that we don't have any electricity."

Con nodded with an air of defeat. "Well, thanks anyway, Dr. Kesteven. If you come up with anything else helpful, like you have been, sir, we'd all appreciate hearing about it."

"Sure." This turned the knife in the wound, and Niklas's voice was almost inaudible.

Sighing a little, Con went on, "So I guess I'll stick to what I've got a slight chance of figuring out. What about the rest of the million or so military men and women in this country? Where's the front for this war with the Goths? All the military bases are so isolated here in the West, it would be easy for them to pick us off. But most of the eastern half is still like a regular country, with unconsolidated towns and unfinished co-op cities and farmers spread out. The bases are much more interconnected with the civilians . . ."

No one could answer any of these questions.

After a long, brooding quiet, when they all stared into the spitting flames, David Mitchell spoke up. He was the youngest and the quietest of the group—a lean six-footer with straight sandy hair and guileless blue eyes. His absurdly long, thick lashes he would have given willingly to any of the young women who envied them. He was their Everyman. "Captain Slaughter, permission to speak?"

"Go ahead."

"Sir, I would like to volunteer for a reconnaissance mission. To the East."

Con's head snapped up. "How far east?"

David swallowed hard, then answered, "I'd like to go at least as far as Arkansas, sir. But I'd do my best to go all the way to Washington and back if that's the mission you need."

Con stared hard at him across the leaping flames. "Mitchell, you just want to go find your grandparents, don't you? Puppy's real cute. Well, I'm sorry about that. We've all got family we'd like to visit, but we're soldiers in the United States Army and we have duties and responsibilities. Personal vacations aren't part of those duties right now, Mitchell. Permission denied."

He was harsh, and his voice echoed sharply in the large room. All of the men on the team averted their eyes and said nothing. Con Slaughter was their commanding officer, and his word, right or wrong, was set in stone.

But Colonel Darkon Ben-ammi and Colonel Vashti Nicanor watched and listened to Con curiously. Niklas seemed uninterested as he busied himself feeding the fire with the small bits of mesquite and piñon. Zoan was watching Con, but as usual, his face was a blank slate.

Then with his most easygoing manner, Colonel Ben-ammi said to Con, "Captain, it's not been my experience that Sergeant Mitchell prefabricates in any way."

Con stared at him accusingly, then laughed shortly. "I think, Colonel, that you mean 'prevaricates,' don't you?" The rest of the team chuckled uneasily. Vashti clearly recognized Darkon's little trick of using the wrong word to amuse Americans, which unfailingly put them at ease. But she smiled with the team anyway.

"Yes, of course," Darkon said good-naturedly. "Anyway, I

wouldn't presume to question your decision, Captain, but I do not think that you should base that decision on a misunderstanding."

Con glowered at David, who still kept his head down. "Okay, man of truth, what do you say? You going to tell me you don't want to go look for your grandparents?"

"No, sir, I'm not going to tell you that," David said, his voice muted because he refused to look up.

"Then what?" Con blustered more gently. "Look up, Mitchell. Quit mumblin'. I'm gettin' old and hard of hearing."

Everyone snorted at that, and David finally raised his head with the slightest ghost of a smile. "Sorry, Captain, I forgot about your advanced age of thirty-five. Anyway, I'm kinda embarrassed, I guess, for all of you to say those things about me and all that, but the truth is, I guess I was 'prefabricating' a little."

He straightened his shoulders, then plunged in. "I've been praying and asking the Lord what to do ever since this happened, Captain Slaughter. Usually I don't have to do that because I know my place, I know my superiors, I know my job, and I know my duty. But this situation—it's different. I have to tell you that I do feel that the Lord is telling me to go find my grandfather. He's—in trouble or danger . . ." He made a helpless gesture with one hand. "I know that sounds stupid, like everyone in America isn't in trouble or in danger. But—that's just what I feel. No, that's what I *know*. And I know I need to go help him."

Con stared at David in open disbelief. "You just said, Mitchell, that you know your superiors and your place and your duty. Suppose I still don't give you permission to go?"

Instantly David responded, "Then, sir, I wouldn't dream of going. You're my commanding officer, and I took an oath. I'd never break my word."

Colonel Ben-ammi poked Con sharply in the side and said airily, "See?"

Con grimaced, and Niklas muttered dourly, "I wouldn't do

that if I were you, Colonel Ben-ammi. He hates being poked at. Believe me, I know."

"I, too, know this," Ben-ammi said amiably.

The tightly knit group started easy conversations again, while Con sat unmoving, his arms crossed, his craggy face set in deep concentration lines. Darkon, who knew that Con needed to think it out for himself, spoke up, "As for me and Vashti, we would try to do the same thing if it were possible, Sergeant Mitchell."

Vashti nodded her head in agreement and added, "And I'm not certain that our motives would be as pure as yours are, either. I would volunteer immediately for a mission that would take me to my father and mother and sisters in Beersheba . . . And I'm not too certain that they wouldn't take precedence over the mission."

"But you would perform your mission, and then you would come back," David said quietly. "And so would I."

She nodded, then turned to Rio. "What about you, Sergeant Valdosta? You've never said anything about your family."

He shrugged carelessly. "I'm an orphan. Left at St. Thomas of Baja when I was just a baby, in the Mexican famine of '27. An old priest ran that orphanage, him and two old nuns. Not much new blood in the Oldest Church, you know, not then and sure not now. Anyway, they were the only family I ever knew, except for the army."

Vashti had noticed that the rough-and-tumble Rio Valdosta had a respect that was almost a reverence for the elderly Benewah Two Color. His history explained that instant attachment.

Moodily Deacon Fong kicked at the floor with one booted heel, chipping the brittle sandstone slightly. "I got a big family in China. Four sisters and a brother. My parents are so stubborn. I've tried to move them over here a hundred times. But they said we couldn't afford it until after my little brother gets his education. They were going to send him over here this summer. He's already been accepted at NYU next fall. He was going to study this summer and take his citizenship test. After graduation, he was going to try to join the Screaming Eagles."

"He was actually going to become a citizen?" Niklas grunted. "I didn't know they still gave those tests or required citizenship for any reason."

Fong shrugged. "They don't. But I did the same thing, even though the INS had a good laugh. 'Til they had to dig up the test because I raised such a stink about it. It's a matter of honor."

"They probably never knew whether you passed it or flunked it," Niklas said.

"Probably not," Fong agreed. "But I knew." He turned to Ric Darmstedt, who had brought out his whetstone and was sharpening his boot dagger. "Hey, Ric, how about you? Your folks are in Texas, aren't they? Your people are probably closer than anyone else's! Haven't you thought about jogging over there to check on 'em?"

Ric mumbled, "They're on an extended vacation right now. My parents and two sisters. All of them are traveling until after the new year."

"Traveling where?" Fong persisted. "Do you know?"

"Yeah," Ric answered shortly.

Everyone waited. Ric's knife went *scritch-scratch* across the rough stone. He looked up, glowering. "All right, all right! They're in Germany! They've been all over Europe, and this month they're in Germany! They're Germans, and we have lots of money! That's probably why they were able to get such extended visas!"

The silence was thick; even Con Slaughter came out of his brown funk to stare at Ric in disbelief.

Suddenly Vashti laughed, a sharp, derisive sound. "Is that what is wrong with you, Lieutenant Darmstedt?"

"What?" he growled.

"You feel guilty because you're of German ancestry?"

"Yeah!"

"Funny," Slaughter rumbled, "all the time I thought you were a soldier in the *American* army, Darmstedt. I didn't know your heart was with the Goths."

Ric jumped to his feet, his aquiline features heavy with anger. "Sir, I'm no traitor! I'm Airborne, Fire Team Eclipse, and I'm as loyal to my country and my comrades as you are!"

"I know," Slaughter said casually. "Why don't you?"

Ric's jaw almost, but not quite, dropped. He sat down quickly and stared into space. After a few moments he picked up his boot and polishing cloth and began all over again. "Huh," he muttered. "That's a real good question, sir. I'll think on that question, I sure will, sir."

"You do that, Darmstedt," Slaughter said dryly. "I'll even let you use the team brain for a while."

Niklas dared to sigh and say, "I think I'm going to heartily regret that crack for the rest of my life."

"Yes, sir, Dr. Kesteven, I'll make sure of that," Slaughter assured him.

Colonel Ben-ammi was staring at Slaughter in a peculiar way. "You know, I just thought of something . . . Captain Slaughter, it appears that out of the seven members of Fire Team Eclipse, only two members have family here in the United States."

Slaughter didn't answer.

Ben-ammi went on quietly, "That would be Sergeant Mitchell—and you, Captain Slaughter. Your parents and grandparents in Elegy, Alabama. On their horse farm."

"You know, and remember, too much," Slaughter commented without heat.

"Maybe," Ben-ammi replied. "But I think Sergeant Mitchell has a good idea. We do need information, Captain Slaughter. But no one should ever go on such a difficult and complex mission alone."

Again, no one spoke for a long time. They all watched Slaughter with ever-changing mixtures of curiosity, sympathy, and for David

Mitchell, sudden hope. Slaughter started pacing, his head down, his eyes unseeing.

When Slaughter spoke, it was with his old quick confidence. "Okay, Mitchell, let's talk about a plan. And Darmstedt?"

"Yes, sir?"

"Get over it. That's an order. You'll be next in command."

Darmstedt gulped. "Uh—yes, sir."

Zoan sighed and hung his head so low that the other members of the team noticed. "What's the matter, Zoan?" Slaughter asked. He liked the odd young man.

He looked up and stared solely at Slaughter, as was his wont even in group conversation. "I don't want David to go," he said sadly. "I'll miss him so much. But if God tells him to, he needs to, I guess. It's just that he's the only Christian, like me, here. All the rest of you are real nice, and you're my friends, but you are heathens."

This sincere and perhaps too precise declaration cracked up the group, but some laughed more heartily than others. Slaughter, for instance, felt a twinge—not of offense, but a fleeting sense of loss. Maybe Mitchell—and even Zoan—knew something more than the rest of them did after all?

In his slow way, Zoan looked from one person to another as they laughed and teased each other smartly about their heathenish ways. When they'd calmed down a bit, Zoan went on, "Captain Slaughter, sir? Can I ask you a question?"

"Sure, Zoan."

"I don't guess you'll be wanting to walk or even ride horses. It sounds like it's a long way to the East. Is that right?"

"Yeah, you sure got that right, my man."

Zoan's face wavered, like an image underwater that ripples pass over, at Slaughter's idiom. But he let it go because he was concentrating so hard on what he had to say. "Then I guess," he said with a sigh, "I can show you where you can get a helicopter."

Deacon Fong jumped up as if he'd been shot out of a cannon. "What? A chopper? You mean a live one?"

Zoan frowned, then nodded. "Yes. Not dead. A live one. One of those big fat ones, not the skinny ones that look like hornets."

Deacon hurried around to grab Zoan's thin shoulders and yank him to his feet. Zoan submitted to this outrage gracefully. "You mean a big German chopper? A Messerschmitt-Kawasaki BK 2000?"

"I don't know its name," Zoan answered obediently. "But I know where some of them are. You could get one."

"You bet I could get one," Deacon almost shouted. "Captain Slaughter! I volunteer for the mission! Please, sir?"

"Permission granted," Slaughter said, grinning. "Glad to have the best helo driver in the army aboard. Not to mention the fact that with a helo, and you driving it, we might get there and back before the next millennium."

"Begging your pardon, but that would be the best helo driver in America, sir," Deacon corrected him with dignity. "Maybe in the world."

Slaughter nodded. "Forgive me, Fong. I lost all sense of reason there for a minute."

"I forgive you, sir," Deacon said magnanimously. "So, Zoan, where is this big helicopter?"

Zoan was staring at Deacon in a peculiar way. The two men were the same height, and they were still facing each other. Zoan took a small sliding step even closer and looked unblinking into Deacon's delicately slanted eyes. It gave Deac an odd feeling, both the close perusal and Zoan's eyes that were almost all pupil, dark and bottomless, all-seeing.

"What—what is it, Zoan?" he asked hesitantly.

Zoan blinked once, twice, slowly. Then he shook his head as if he were coming out of a difficult dream. "I don't know," he answered, childlike. "I thought I was going to tell you not to go. But now I'm not going to."

Deac swallowed hard, though he didn't know exactly why he felt such foreboding at Zoan's opaque, but honest, words.

Much later, everyone in the room would recall Zoan's words. And then everyone would be filled with fear.

The three black lumps on the ground looked much like mounds of dirt in the midnight murkiness—until they started crawling, but even then they were hardly noticeable. A few feet ahead of them was a knife-edged glare of light that extended four square miles or more. The cloak of darkness that covered most of America was lying heavily on the city of Albuquerque. But not even the most obscure corner of Kirtland Air Force Base, where the 77th Luftwaffe Air Wing had been based for three years, was dark. Great kliegs powered by freestanding generators blazed everywhere.

The Germans, methodical and practical people that they were, had put Albuquerque International Airport to good use, and it was lit with their external sources, too.

"Zoan was right," the black lump named Con Slaughter whispered softly. "They're keeping the helos at the airport instead of at the base with the military choppers."

"He was right about something else, too," Deac Fong whispered back. "We can get one, easy. They're not even bothering with military guards."

"Yes, sir," David Mitchell added hesitantly. "But what are we gonna do with it once we get it?"

"Fly away home, boys," Deac said, and they saw the white flash of his teeth in a grin. He was having a famously good time.

Directly in front of the three shapeless humps on the ground loomed the brooding mass of a Messerschmitt-Kawasaki BK 2000, the Rolls-Royce of helicopters. There were three of them on this most isolated runway at the airport. The three men surmised that the head Goths didn't want their fine, expensive choppers quartered at the base with the grunt helos. Of course, this runway was the closest in proximity to the luxurious Villa del Sol Hotel, which could have been named a palace, and it was brimming with high-hat Germans. The high command of Commandant Tor von Eisenhalt's army and air force would never quarter on a military base.

"Well, boys, looks like we might as well go for this closest one. We'd have to stop off and deal with the janitor there anyway." A man in a plain jumpsuit and leather jacket with insignia was fussing with the nearest helo, polishing this and that, coming in and out of the chopper with small tools, humming.

Moments later the three shadows looked larger and much more dangerous than dirt humps. One of them, the largest man dressed in black from head to toe and with a blacked-out face, loomed over the pilot. A funny gurgling noise was heard, and then there was a loud thump. Soon all of the shadows melted into the chopper, and the passenger's side door silently rolled shut.

The German was sitting in one of the six luxurious armchairs in the cabin, with his arms behind him, his wrists neatly bound with a plastic choke-tie. Con Slaughter was sitting next to him with his businesslike boot dagger to the German's throat. The German was about Con's age, thirty-five or so, with flashing blue eyes and thick brown hair cut short. Slaughter never took his eyes from the man's face. "What's it look like, Fong? Can you do it?" he asked in a normal tone. They could speak in normal tones, for the four-billion-dollar helicopter was completely soundproofed. The passenger seats were about two feet behind the cockpit, with a reinforced door that Fong had left open.

"You kidding me, sir? Easy as booting up a Drone." Still, he sat for a few minutes, studying the myriad panels and gauges and displays.

In the copilot's seat beside him, David Mitchell frowned darkly, then said tentatively, "Lieutenant Fong, it's all strange looking to us, of course, but you know there's got to be the same stuff that makes this helo work as makes any other one work. So—so—don't you think that's the HUD input? And, okay, that's probably the navigation array, laser/Doppler—what's this, sonar? Yeah, sonar . . . radar altimeter, hey, yeah, this is good. We got NavStar/LORAN, AHRS . . . that's—I dunno what that is—this must be the main targeting console, don't you think . . ."

"What do you think this is?" Fong asked.

"That's gotta be the Coke machine, sir."

"Puppy's funny," Fong said acidly. Rio Valdosta's little riff on David had sort of stuck with the team. "Okay, Captain, I got this baby down. You think maybe Attila there would give us a hint about how to tell the tower that he needs to go for a little ride?"

Slaughter had learned, and had conscientiously developed, a fast and effective trick. It involved putting pressure on a certain group of muscles and nerves in a man's neck that sent screeching, blinding pain up into his skull and burning pinpricks all down his spine. Men who normally would gladly die before giving up information were supposed to be able to take this pain for only a short period of time because theoretically they would never pass out, and it would never lessen. The pilot lasted about twenty seconds. Gasping, he blurted out something—but it was in German.

David Mitchell said, "Uh, sir?"

"I'm busy, Mitchell!" Slaughter grunted, struggling with the German. He was going to give it another, and better, try.

"But, sir, I'm working on the radio here—I think—yeah! Listen!"

David had managed to pick up some chatter from the tower to a Tornado squadron leader.

They were conversing in English. It had been the international language of all air traffic for close to a century. Even Fong, who was still deciphering controls, had forgotten this.

"We're not very smart," Slaughter growled, relaxing his grip on the man's neck—but replacing the knife at his throat.

"No, sir," David agreed. "Anyway, sir, I think you'd better do the talking. Your voice sounds more like his. Just speak with a German accent."

"You gotta be kiddin' me. I'll sound like—like—"

"An impostor and an imbecile," the German growled with a thick accent.

Slaughter nicked the man's chin, no more than a shaving cut. "I was going to gag you, but maybe killin' you would keep you quieter." The man's eyes flickered, but he didn't flinch or show fear. He did, however, grow very still.

After long moments Slaughter said, "You're being so good, I'm going to let you live. Once we get this bird in the air, I think you might have what you call a vested interest in keeping it up. 'Til then, you better be quiet, or your life's going to be short, brutish, and nasty."

The German remained expressionless, but he gave a short nod.

"Give me the comm, Deac," Slaughter ordered. Deac handed back an earpiece and wire mike.

"What's this bird's designation?" Con asked the German quietly.

The pilot blinked.

"I'm going to start chopping off your fingers," Slaughter said conversationally. "I'm going to take them a knuckle at a time, so we'll have plenty of negotiating room. I'm going to start with your right thumb. If you don't tell me the designation of this helicopter after your right thumb is gone, then I'm going to start on your left thumb."

"Fenrir Nine," he said sulkily.

"Tower, this is Fenrir Nine," Slaughter said immediately, with a guttural Teutonic accent. "One of my auxiliary fuel pod gauges is malfunctioning. Permission to take a test run, due east eighty kilometers at one thousand."

A bored German-accented voice responded, "Permission granted, Fenrir Nine."

Fong started up the chopper, which sounded as smooth and rich as a big cat's purr. They lifted up into the sky and sped due east.

"You're not going to let me live, are you?" the pilot asked. To his credit, he didn't sound afraid, merely curious.

Rage filled Slaughter. When he looked at the man, he thought of his dead comrades whose bones, surely cleaned by wolves and vultures and bleached white by the sun, must still litter Fort Carson. Slaughter taunted him, "Your Luftwaffe hasn't been too merciful to us. I'd say you were in some mortal danger, mister."

Deacon Fong and David Mitchell and anyone else who had been around Con Slaughter for very long knew that when he barked—as he was now—he wasn't biting. When he talked slow and soft, he was most dangerous.

Of course, the German pilot didn't know that.

In flight over Texas, Deac and David—as if Slaughter's careless choice of words had hexed them—had problems deciphering the fuel gauges. The BK 2000s had four auxiliary pods, which enabled them to fly across the Atlantic. The main tank was low on fuel, and Deac and David couldn't decide whether they had actually switched over to an auxiliary.

Listening to their low, tense voices, Slaughter took his eyes off the German only a few seconds. But the German was fast and strong and well trained—and unbound. He'd managed to work his small dagger out of his zippered sleeve pocket.

He jumped up, knocked Slaughter a stunning backhand in the mouth with his bunched fist, and then stabbed Deacon in the carotid artery.

Slaughter, who had reeled but not fallen with the force of the blow, slit the German's throat only a moment later.

David switched control of the helo to the copilot.

They winged on into the night.

Neither Con nor David spoke for a long time. The helicopter, which David had immediately reset to autopilot with the ground-hugging terrain sensor, pretty much flew itself. David risked a look back into the dimly lit cabin. Con, one hand still gripping his bloodstained knife, was slumped into an overstuffed armchair. His head was bent, and his bloody fists pressed his eyes.

"Sir?" David said softly. "You can't go there, you know. It wasn't your fault any more than it was mine or Zoan's . . . or God's."

Dully Con asked without raising his head, "What are you talking about, Mitchell?"

"I saw him coming. I watched him do it," David answered in a pained voice. "I couldn't move."

Eventually Con murmured, "And Zoan?"

"He knew. He must have."

"Then why didn't he go ahead and stop him?" Con ranted, stiffening.

"Because, sir, we don't like it much, and we understand it even less, but sometimes it is the time to die. Tonight was Deac's. And his."

Con said nothing. He stared blankly at the dead German sprawled on the floor of the cabin. His blood had soaked into the thick sky-blue carpet, Con noted, and his eyes were wide open. With a touch that was not ungentle, Con closed them. Whatever else he was, he was a soldier, and he died fighting. No man could ask for a more honorable death than that.

"Sir?" David said in a stronger voice. "We're going to be at the border soon. We'll have to do some navigating. So I'd appreciate some help."

Con looked as if a heavy dark veil had dropped from his eyes. As gently as he could, he maneuvered Deacon Fong's body out of the seat. Deac was the smallest of the team, and Con carried him with ease. After hesitating only a moment, he laid him down beside the dead German pilot. Quickly he arranged their blood-soaked hands to lie in peace across their chests. *Both of them have such fine hands, agile-looking, clever fingers . . . mortal enemies in life, but brothers in death. Good-bye, Deac. I'll miss you, and I'll mourn you.*

At dawn, an enormous black helicopter hovered over a five-mile-square patch of fallow field just north of Elegy, Alabama. A figure dressed all in black, a man with long legs and arms and a grim face, rappelled out, released the line, and waved. As the chopper angled tail-up to turn and soar north, he raised both his arms in a long farewell.

The chopper flew straight and unchallenged over deserted miles of fields and empty little towns and houses and barns. About two-thirty, it landed, a perfect and smooth textbook landing, in a high field of winter goldenrod just south of Hot Springs, Arkansas.

David Mitchell turned off the helicopter, gathered up his pack, stepped outside, and slowly closed the door. The conscientious and complete soldier that he was, he first camouflaged the helicopter so it could not be seen from the air.

It took him all of the remains of the day to dig the two graves, refill them, and fashion two crude wooden crosses from the sweet green branches of a nearby dogwood tree. He stood for a long time at the graves, his head bowed, his lips moving, tears rolling down his face.

After a time of mourning, he turned his face north and began to walk. Within moments he was just another gray shadow in the soft southern night.

THREE

JUST AS TESSA KAI had predicted, the weather turned bad. A low cloud cover sank in, hiding the heavens. The dingy gray sea squalled. It grew cold. The days were bleak and lightless, the nights bitter and lifeless.

Victorine decided, after Tessa Kai's death, that she and Dancy had to leave Perdido Key. The only logical place to go was Pensacola Naval Air Station, about twenty-two miles east. It would be tough. They would have to journey at night, along the beach, which was hard walking and cold traveling. Victorine would have to find Dancy some clothes and shoes, and she would have to find exactly the right supplies that they could carry.

"I'm going with you," Dancy insisted.

"It's too dangerous," Victorine argued. "You know, Dancy, that right here in the condo is the safest place on the island."

Dancy merely looked at her. At sixteen years old, she was a lovely girl, delicate looking with her ash blonde hair and small frame and wide blue eyes. Right now they shone, luminous and vulnerable, and a hint of tears shimmered in them.

Victorine softened a bit and said, "You don't want to stay here alone because of—your grandmother?"

"No," Dancy said vehemently. "I could never be—afraid of Tessa Kai. It's because of you, Mother. Suppose you just walk out that door and never come back?"

Her statement jarred Victorine. Dropping her eyes, she murmured, "All right. I suppose you'd have to come anyway if I'm going to fit you correctly. Especially boots. It's very important, if you're walking, to have boots that fit well."

"Oh, thank you, Mother," Dancy cried with such a torrent of relief that Victorine felt a little ashamed of herself. But Victorine, as soon as she had closed and locked the door on her mother's crypt, had changed. She allowed herself to feel savage anger and a hot desire for revenge for a feasible time; then she consciously shifted her mental state to cold calculation. The only fierceness she felt now was determination that nothing—*nothing*—was going to happen to Dancy. Not one hair of her child's head was going to be touched, not if she was still drawing breath.

After that, everything Victorine did and thought about was how best to protect Dancy.

It took them two days to gather clothing and supplies, even though both were anxious to leave. For one thing, the Pikes, including the man who had killed Tessa Kai, had wandered on to the west—and had never come back east. Victorine thought they might still be on the Key, although they might have gone on over to Gulf Shores or even out to Fort Morgan. She doubted it, though. The cottages and condos were about as scarce in Gulf Shores as they were on the Key. Fort Morgan had been uninhabited for years.

Still, they had to bike seven miles west to the Commissary, the only place Victorine could be sure of getting the foodstuffs they needed. She'd already been there twice and hadn't seen a sign of the couple who ran the big store in the winter. Actually it was more of a supplies warehouse. When Victorine had gone to get supplies, she had been constricted by what she could carry on her bike and then up seven flights of stairs. She'd always gotten fresh fruit and vegetables, and juice and canned goods. Now they needed different kinds of food.

They loaded up on dried fruit, nuts, dried beef, candy, powdered milk packets, coffee and tea, honey and sugar. Victorine scrounged around in the aisles of clothing stacked to the cavernous ceiling in the storeroom, but almost all of it was casual summer wear, which was exactly the kind of clothing that Dancy had. In dusty boxes in a back corner, she found some winter clothing, even though it was unorthodox. It was commissars' uniforms. About 40 percent of the Commissary were women, so Dancy found clothing that almost fit: Ty-wool blouses, canvasette breeches, Syn-tex underwear. The best find, however, was the boots. Dancy found a perfect fit in the black lace-up paratrooper's boots. When Victorine saw her as she tried them on, she bowed and said deadpan, "You look wonderful, My Commissar."

"Troll, you mean," Dancy said, making a face. "At least I'm glad they don't have the insignia. I feel like I'm wearing a Halloween costume as it is."

"They're warm clothes, they're sturdy, and the boots are wonderful. I wish I could find some my size," Victorine said. "But I guess my old hiking boots will do."

Victorine had thought that they could pack and rest the next day, and then leave the next night. But as they were getting everything ready to go, Victorine realized that she'd forgotten two very important items: warm socks and warm headgear. Unbelievably the thermometer at the Commissary had read thirty degrees. Victorine had to go back, which meant that Dancy had to go back, and Victorine could have kicked herself. The fact that there was no reason for her to be sharp about cold-weather hiking didn't matter. She was angry at herself.

They found wool socks with the commissars' clothing and the berets, but Dancy refused to wear one. Finally they found a box—it must have been ancient—of black ski masks. They were wool and itchy, but Victorine insisted that they at least wear them as hats and cover their ears. The wind off the sea, with the temperature at thirty degrees, was probably close to twenty.

By the time they got back late that evening, Dancy was too tired to leave. If Victorine hadn't been quite so absorbed in her calculations, she might have noticed that Dancy was very pale. But she didn't notice, and if she had, she probably would have thought it was because of Tessa Kai. Victorine was feeling the strain of being in the condos where her mother was lying in state down the hallway.

The next day passed with Dancy sleeping quite a bit and Victorine reading and pacing restlessly. It was again dreary and rained a hard-spitting splatter that lasted only a few moments. But the weather didn't clear.

They left as soon as the sun set, though they couldn't see it. The darkness came swiftly.

Victorine's backpack was about twice as heavy as Dancy's, yet after the first hour, Dancy's pace was agonizingly slow. The raw wind caught at their words, and the tide was high and roaring, so they had to shout to make each other heard. After a while, they didn't try to talk. They struggled on in the wet cold and raging salt wind. The lovely powdery sand, which was so fine for beach picnics, sucked at every step they took. Dancy began to stumble. Victorine took her arm.

They had gone only about three miles—it seemed as if they had been walking in the howling nightmare for eons—when Dancy wrenched away from Victorine and stumbled to the surf. Victorine ran after her. Dancy bent over double and vomited. Shaking, almost falling, Dancy turned, wiping her mouth. "I'm sorry, Mama," she said.

If Dancy had shot her in the heart, Victorine couldn't have felt worse. She put her arms around Dancy and said as calmly as she could in her ear, "Is it a migraine, darling?"

Dancy nodded shakily.

Victorine took a deep breath. An ugly flicker of anger rose in her: *Why didn't she tell me!* Victorine had been acting like a drill sergeant so, of course, the child didn't want to tell her that she was coming down with one of the horrible two- or three-day afflictions that all three of the Thayer women had been cursed with. None of that mattered now.

Victorine said, "Give me your backpack. See up there? Can you see? That's Perdido Quay. We can stay there. Can you make it, darling? Because I could carry you and then come back and get the backpacks."

Already the pain must have been seeping into her like acid because Dancy held the left side of her face as she shook her head. "I can make it," she said. Victorine could barely hear her.

The condominium was about a mile ahead. It took Dancy and Victorine two hours to reach it. Dancy vomited twice more and fell down three times. Victorine was almost despairing and thought that surely she'd have to carry her. But Dancy kept going somehow, and they reached the high-rise.

The lobby, which was elegantly and expensively furnished, and enclosed entirely in glass, had been broken into. The offal of the gangs' parties was offensive to the eye and left a stench, even though the sea wind howled through the broken glass. Dancy was as pale as a wraith, but Victorine steeled herself and insisted that they go right up to the twelfth floor. Sure enough, they saw signs of gangs on the first and second floors, but none after that. It took another forty minutes. The penthouse wasn't locked. In the world that had existed long ago, before the autumnal equinox, no one would have dared break into a Man and Biosphere Directorate Diversionary Facility.

But that world was long gone, and this one was much more dangerous, much crueler, and much colder.

The entire penthouse was glass-enclosed from floor to ceiling. It was a little warmer than downstairs, and Victorine was very glad that she'd insisted they come all the way to the top floor. Dancy fell onto an enormous overstuffed sofa, and Victorine took a quick look out the north windows that faced the road.

Now she could see the torches, even though she couldn't hear the gang and never would have. There were perhaps a hundred of them. They came into the condo and stayed on the first and second floors. Some hardier ones staggered up to the third floor, but that was as far as they got. They built an enormous bonfire on the beach and ran up and down in the night, screaming and fighting and coupling.

It never occurred to Victorine how very fortunate it was that Dancy had come down with a migraine just when she did.

The next day, the gang seemed to break up. Some stayed in the condos. Some wandered over to the cottages and town houses across the street. Others left and went back to the east. All day and all night, Victorine saw groups of three or four going here and there, always drinking, always quarreling, always staggering.

Dancy suffered but never cried or complained. The facility, which was likely one of the most expensive in the United States, had a mud room with a full rick of aged wood stored in it. Victorine kept a roaring fire going day and night. If anyone saw the smoke coming out of the chimney and took the time to cipher that it was from the penthouse, so be it. She cleaned her gun and kept it loaded and in a snug holster that fit on her belt in the small of her back.

On the second day Dancy was a little better. She told Victorine that she thought they could probably leave the next night if all of the gangs had cleared out. They hadn't, not all of them; Victorine still saw them, furtive shadows, two or three or four at a time. The thought occurred to her that maybe they had annexed the Key and were settling in instead of wandering up and down the rich beach.

What if the bridges at both ends were held?

She was standing at the window, staring down at the road

below. A sound came to her ears, but it didn't penetrate her brain. Behind her Dancy, lying weakly on the sofa, asked, "Mama, do you hear that?"

"Hmm?"

"It's a plane, Mama. An airplane. L-look!"

And so it was. A fat, full-bodied plane with lights and the loud roar of a low jet's intake floated by, leaving a trail of white smoke.

The sight was so poignant that neither Dancy nor Victorine could speak until a long time after it was gone.

"Now listen to me, Dancy," Victorine said, cradling Dancy's face and tilting it upward. "We hike as fast as we can. No talking, okay? There's nothing between here and White Dunes, so we'll walk about halfway up the beach, by the dune line. That way, if we see anything, we can hide in the dunes. If you see anything, anything at all, or if you—you—hear something, or—or—"

"Know someone's coming?" Dancy finished the odd sentence without a trace of self-consciousness.

"Yes," Victorine said awkwardly. "If you feel that something's about to happen, then don't shout. Just pull on my sleeve and lie down flat in the sand. Okay?"

Dancy nodded, and Victorine released her. Dancy dropped her eyes and asked in a small voice, "What will you do, Mama? If—if—something happens?"

"I'll kill anyone who comes close to us," Victorine said calmly. "And if anything happens to me, Dancy, you take the gun and run. All right? Run and get away if you can, but if you can't—shoot them."

Her head was still bowed, and a mulish look came over Dancy's face. Though Victorine didn't see, she knew it was so. She'd already tried to make Dancy carry a gun and learn how to use it. But Dancy flatly refused. She would give no reason, and no amount of cajoling or reasoning or insistence on Victorine's part moved her.

Victorine sighed; she'd done all she could do. Now it was time to go again.

Like two shadows that were just a little blacker than the darkness, they crept down the stairs and out onto the beach. It was still freezing cold, but the wind and tide had died down somewhat. Victorine took Dancy's hand, and they slipped up to the undulating dunes, walking just on the edge of them. The darkness was oppressive. Clouds covered all the stars and the dying half-moon. Victorine could barely see Dancy's white face, even as she walked close to her.

They reached White Dunes much more quickly than Victorine had thought they would. In fact, they were right in front of the first unit before Victorine saw it in the murky blackness. These condos weren't a columned high-rise like Summer Sea. They were twenty single units connected by only one wall, all of them up on pilings with parking pads underneath the terraced balconies. The pilings were partially screened by decorative wooden lattices, and Victorine hated walking by the dark and impenetrable spaces underneath. Something might jump out . . . or slither out . . . or reach out and grab her and Dancy. With a superhuman effort she shut out the imagined horrors, grasping Dancy's hand like a vise.

Then she remembered Gerald Ainsley's body, swaying and creaking in the wind, and her head shot back to try to see the roof. But they couldn't see the front slope of the roofs from the beach side of the condos. She had never told Dancy about Gerald, but once Dancy said something sad about him that told Victorine that she knew he was dead. With an inward sigh Victorine thought, *She knows too much, sees too much, hears too much . . . She's just a child. It's not right that she should be burdened like this—*

A coarse shout, almost lost in the high wind, sounded behind them.

Victorine jumped so fiercely that she might have been shot. She whirled, shoving Dancy down to the ground.

Behind her, three shadows, down at the far end of the condos, were running. One of them was carrying a weak flashlight. The dirty yellow beam hopped crazily as the man ran with jerky steps through the soft sand.

Victorine was actually moving fast, but she seemed to be fumbling and slow as she reached behind her, pulling up her sweater, unsnapping her holster, grasping the .38. "Run, Dancy," she shouted when she saw how far back the men were. "Get up and run! Hurry! Run!"

Dancy struggled, got up, and disappeared out of Victorine's peripheral vision. Victorine didn't know that she ran a few steps, panicky, then stopped and turned around. Victorine was busy aiming.

After that, Victorine had a hard time recalling the exact sequence of events. It was weeks afterward before she could replay the scene in her mind without the galling darkness of fear and the red haze of fury.

Another man, only a few feet from Victorine, suddenly materialized. He was a tall man with long legs, and he stepped out from the cavernous underside of the condos. A short, thick barrel pointed up by his right shoulder. His back was to Victorine, so she couldn't see anything except his broad shoulders, and then the gun barrel disappeared from her vision as he lowered it.

"Stop, or I'll shoot you down!" he shouted, a hoarse, but powerful voice.

One of the men skidded to a stop, bent his knees in a ready stance, and pointed with both hands. A small explosion and a red flicker of flame came from his hands.

The two men, one with a flashlight, kept coming.

The man standing between Victorine and the three men moved. She heard a metallic *chuk-chock* sound, an enormous explosion sounded, and he was momentarily outlined in a red glare.

Noxious smoke rose. One of the men was lifted up and thrown backward several feet.

Chuk-chock!

"Stop, you idiot!"

The idiot didn't, there was another explosion, and he fell.

The third man had been shooting, but in the explosions of the 12-gauge, his little .32 caliber spits were lost. Now his gun was empty.

Shotgun's 12-gauge was empty, too.

The gang member, evidently filled with rage and probably on one of the more violent recreational drugs, drew a knife and ran, yelling like a madman. Victorine stepped aside, then aimed.

"No, Mama!" Dancy screamed, knocking her arm down.

Shotgun had stepped right in front of Victorine's line of fire to meet the madman running at him.

Victorine grabbed Dancy's arm, then yanked her around and started running. She had to drag Dancy because Dancy kept looking back and crying out, "No, no, Mom, we can't leave him. We have to help him!"

"No!" Victorine shouted. "He's probably one of them, Dancy! You know they kill each other off for—no, Dancy! Come on!"

Dancy dug in her heels, then torqued her arm out of her mother's grip and skidded to a stop. Tears were running down her pale face, and her eyes were stark, staring. Still, her voice was reasonable and calm. "Mama, he's not a Pike. He's a soldier. He was helping us, Mama. And we have to help him."

Gritting her teeth, Victorine turned to look back.

They had run far enough that they could barely see anything. They couldn't see either of the two men who had been left alive only moments before.

Dancy started back, but Victorine again grabbed her roughly. "You stay behind me, and I mean it, Dancy," she warned. Holding the gun at the ready, she took slow, careful steps.

They saw a big, untidy lump on the ground.

It was the two men. The Pike, a small and wiry man with tangled and filthy black hair and a beard, was dead, his head lolling at an odd angle, his eyes staring blankly up at the empty sky.

The soldier was still alive. But he was bleeding a lot. They couldn't see the extent of his injuries, but they could see black smudges all over his clothes and hands and face.

Victorine's jaw worked, and her eyes narrowed. "We have to leave him."

Dancy's voice was soft. "I'm sorry, Mama, but I can't do that. And I don't think you can, either."

"Sure I could," Victorine said in a hard voice. But then, after a few silent moments, she said, "We'll never get him up the stairs. He's huge. He must weigh two tons."

"Not quite, ma'am," a weak voice sounded. Victorine started, but Dancy laid her hand on his chest and bent down close to him. "Shh, don't try to talk."

He coughed, then said, "Why not? Looks like I gotta try to walk. I think—if you two ladies would get this scumbucket off me—I could get up."

But he couldn't, not by himself. Dancy and Victorine had to help him and then support him. Dancy didn't even reach up to his shoulder, so she wasn't much help at all. Grunting, Victorine gasped, "Okay, Dancy, you happy? Now what are we going to do with him?"

"Help him," Dancy said. She sounded embarrassed.

"I'd—appreciate—it, ma'am," the soldier breathed weakly, "if you'd at least get me inside one of these condos. Then if y'all need to move on, well, I understand."

There were only ten steps up to the first floor of the units. When they got him inside, the soldier, like a fallen redwood, crashed to the floor. Dancy and Victorine, trying to support him, fell with him.

Breathless, Victorine muttered, "Dancy, this man is not a sick puppy you can nurse. He—he might be badly hurt. And I don't know the first thing about taking care of wounds."

"I do," Dancy said evenly. "I know how to take care of him. His name is Captain Slaughter, and he's hurt, but he won't die."

"Wha—how do you know?" Victorine demanded.

Dancy shrugged. "It's on his name patch."

"But how do you know he won't die? And—you can't see his name patch! You can't see the end of your nose in this darkness!"

"I must have seen it," Dancy said reasonably. "Anyway, Mom, he's here, and we're here. The Lord sent him to save us. Now we have to save him."

Something in Victorine rebelled against this logic, but she merely sighed. "All right, Dancy, we'll see what we can do. But I can't save him. I can't save anyone or anything—but you. That's all I care about. So if I decide that we need to leave him to keep you safe, then we'll leave him. Do you understand?"

"Yes, Mother," Dancy said docilely. "I understand."

But in the darkness, unseen, she smiled.

He thought that he was swimming in icy cold water, far under the surface, the heavy burden of hundreds of feet of water above him fighting him, smothering him. He was drowning.

Jerking, he came awake.

"It's all right," a woman said. "You just had a bad dream." She had a nice voice, not soft or babying, just soothing in some way.

He squinted, for even the dim flickering glow of the single candle hurt his eyes. Everything, in fact, hurt him. The heavy blankets burned his wounds; the cold on his face and hands stung him; the pillowcase beneath him seemed to rub his throbbing head raw.

Licking dry lips, he rasped, "I'm thirsty."

The dim form of the slender woman dressed in solid black drew near to him. With difficulty he focused, and then only for a few moments, but long enough to see that she was probably about thirty, with pleasing but not pretty features, sharp hazel eyes, and lovely long dark hair.

He could smell her; she smelled like the tang of salt air and the slightly musty smell of damp wool. Then she leaned over him, holding a glass of water, and he smelled the scent of her thick, luxuriant hair, a freshly washed, clean scent. He inhaled deeply as he sipped. He didn't know which refreshed him more, the cool water or the scent of her hair.

"Your hair smells so good . . . ," he murmured, falling back against the pillow again. She looked at him, astonished, but his eyes were closed. Settling back down in the armchair by his bed, she picked up her book and began reading again.

He spoke again. "My name is Captain Con Slaughter, ma'am, of the 101st Airborne, Fire Team Eclipse." His voice was weak but clear.

She looked up. "I'm Victorine Flynn Thayer, Captain Slaughter. It's a pleasure to meet you."

"My pleasure, ma'am." The mindless niceties were reassuring to both of them.

"Thank you for helping me," he said, finally opening his eyes.

She studied him. "I think you know that I would not have done it if not for my daughter's insistence."

He nodded wearily. His craggy face seemed too sharp and sunken for the strong, muscular body and the thick, youthful brown hair. "Doesn't matter. I owe you both, and I hope to have the honor of repaying you someday."

Victorine leaned back and spoke in a gentler tone. "No, Captain Slaughter, I must be honest. You saved us both, probably our lives. Let's call it even."

They were quiet awhile. Slaughter shifted restlessly, and Victorine asked, "Are you in pain?"

"Yeah, feels like I got stung by hornets after the cattle stampede ran me down. Am I stabbed?"

"No, just cut up pretty badly," she answered, a little taken aback by the tinge of fear in his voice. She hadn't realized how frightened he was, but then he couldn't possibly judge how severely he was injured, could he? "You're not—mortally wounded, Captain Slaughter. You have a long cut across your chest, a small nick on your cheekbone, but your left arm and hand are the worst. I think your arm needs stitches, but I'm afraid I don't know how to do that. We bandaged it up as securely as we could. It did stop the bleeding," she said calmly. "But I don't know about your hand."

He looked down at the thick white bandages that completely covered his hand and fingers up to the fingertips. "I had to grab the blade . . . ," he muttered. "Funny how scary that was, and hard to do. Seemed kinda worse, in a way, than being stabbed."

Victorine shuddered a little. "I know what you mean."

He looked at her curiously. "You do? You mean I'm not just talking crazy because of delirium?"

She didn't smile, but he could see the merest flicker of amusement in her eyes. "No, you're not talking crazy, and you're not delirious. You went into light shock because of blood loss, I think. But you're lucid . . ." She looked around the room and finished in an almost inaudible tone, ". . . unfortunately."

"Yeah. Does seem like a nightmare you can't wake up from, doesn't it?"

"Worse. You do wake up. It's still there."

He felt very sorry for her. In a gentle tone he asked, "May I ask where you and—I don't know your daughter's name—my guardian angel." She almost smiled at that, he saw. At that moment, Con Slaughter thought—hoped—he might be spending some time making this sorrowful woman smile.

"Her name is Dancy Flynn Thayer. We're going to Pensacola Naval Air Station. We've been here, on the Key, since the blackout.

But—my mother—she—we—" She stopped, cleared her throat, and continued, "She was killed by one of the gangs. So I thought it would be best if I could get Dancy onto a military base."

Con frowned so fiercely that for a moment Victorine thought he was in terrible pain. Which, she realized after a moment, he was. "Yeah, you'd think that would be best. But I'm here to tell you, Ms. Thayer, that it might not be. Have you seen any Germans around here since the blackout?"

"No," she said, growing very still.

"Any German planes? Fighters—like black wasps, kinda? Low, fast, swept-back wings?"

"No, none. We saw a plane yesterday for the first time since the blackout, but it looked like one of the great big passenger liners."

He nodded. "I saw it. It was an American plane, a C-6 Ajax Starlifter."

She looked at him curiously. "Where were you? Where did you come from?"

He dropped his eyes. "My family lived—lives—in Elegy. You know where that is? Well, I went there to try to find them. They're gone. My parents and grandparents. No sign of them. All of our horses are gone, and the houses have been broken into. But I thought they might have tried to get to Pensacola NAS, so that's where I was headed, too."

"But—I mean, where did you come from—out of nowhere, just when we needed you—" Victorine stammered.

"I saw you," he said quietly. "You and Dancy. When you went to the Commissary last week. I didn't want to—try—and talk to you because I knew about the gangs, and I figured you'd—do exactly what you did. Think I was just another one of them."

Victorine shifted restlessly. "You've been following us?"

It was a long time before he answered. "Yes, ma'am."

"But—you mean, you waited—while Dancy—we stayed in the Quay for three nights and two days—"

"Yes, ma'am. I—I—was holed up down on the eleventh floor."

She stared at him with narrowed eyes as if she were trying to see inside his head, into his brain, and discern him. He met her gaze squarely.

Victorine dropped her eyes first. "I think, sir," she said in a muffled, hesitant tone, "that I owe you a very great debt. Perhaps we aren't so even after all."

"I think so," Con answered as casually as he could. "I was guarding you. But Miss Dancy, I think, was guarding me. Enough about debts already. One thing about anarchy. All your bills are canceled." His voice was growing weaker, with the bone-weary tone that only the very ill and the gravely injured have.

"I'm going to give you something for the pain," she said decisively. "It'll make you sleep. I was afraid to give it to you before, but now I think it'll be all right." She gave him a tiny white pill and more water, and he drank more thirstily this time.

He settled back, and Victorine sat back down in the chair. She began reading again, and he seemed to have drifted off to sleep.

But after a while Con asked in a dreamy tone, "You have a place to sleep?" He'd seen Dancy, a shapeless lump under a mound of covers on the nearby sofa. Con, to his bemusement, realized he was on a fold-up Murphy bed and vaguely wondered who Mr. Murphy was.

"Yes, upstairs," Victorine was saying. "But I usually prefer to stay up late and read and then sleep late. No sense in getting up early if you travel at night."

"Hmm," he said pleasantly. Either the drug was already taking effect, or the final stages of exhaustion—a nice numbness—were setting in. "What are you reading, ma'am?"

"Call me Victorine," she said as if it embarrassed her.

"Whatcha readin', Victorine?"

She leaned closely to look at him and suddenly was conscious that he turned a little and was inhaling deeply of her hair as it fell over her shoulder and swung against his face. Acutely embarrassed, she sat back with a jerk. "Richard Lovelace," she replied a little curtly. "You've probably never heard of him."

"Sure have," he said lazily. "Seventeenth century, huh? 'Stone walls do not a prison make, nor iron bars a cage . . .'"

Victorine was astounded. "Why, yes—that's from 'To Althea, From Prison.' How—"

"Tell you everything 'bout my life later," he whispered. "Read me one, Victorine. Please?"

Slowly Victorine turned a few pages, settled back, and said, "I will read you 'To Lucasta, Going to the Wars.'"

"To Lucasta . . . ," he echoed sleepily. "To Victorine . . ."

Tell me not, Sweet, I am unkind,
That from the nunnery
Of thy chaste breast and quiet mind,
To war and arms I fly.

True, a new mistress now I chase,
The first foe in the field;
And with a stronger faith embrace
A sword, a horse, a shield.

Yet this inconstancy is such
As you too shall adore;
I could not love thee, Dear, so much,
Lov'd I not honour more.

The White House
Washington, D.C.

Beneath the West Wing of the White House was a labyrinth of decrepit glass cubicle offices, dank storage rooms, dusty closets, forgotten maintenance passages, odd angles and corners. Only very junior staffers and bug-eyed interns were relegated to the Stygian maze where they got lost with tiresome regularity.

In the last weeks, First Commissar Alia Silverthorne had wandered the much-painted concrete floors countless times. Though she was ghostlike because her only light was a weak flashlight, she didn't look like a wraith. She was still sturdily built, strong looking, since they had plenty of food in the White House. They'd been short of water, so she wasn't groomed to a knifelike perfection as she usually was. Yet she was a militarily neat woman, her figure, though short, of perfect symmetry with no fat, her short hair still combed neatly with the commissar's queue bound with silver, her hazel eyes clear. Somehow her skin was still healthy looking, with a light tan.

But her mind was not perhaps as sharp as her looks. Her mission in wandering the maze was to figure out the best strategic place for a last stand. Miraculously, considering the irrational layout of the enormous basement, and Alia's battle fatigue, she had formulated a plan.

Exhausted, she reflected, It might not even be a last stand. We might just make it . . . if I can stay sane and conscious long enough . . . Now all I need is some bread crumbs to mark the path . . .

It was a certain indication of Alia's state of mind that she found this uproariously funny.

Four

THE SHARP AROMATIC smell of evergreens came to David Mitchell, then other odors that brought memories swept in and trooped through his mind. Mostly it was the smell of loam, and as he came out of a deep sleep, he felt the soft pressure of the earth beneath him, cushioned by the boughs out of which he had constructed a bed. Emerging quickly from his dreamy state, he remembered that he was in the foothills of the Ozark Mountains, the Ouachitas. Not far from where he'd camped, a German helicopter, with its two dead pilots buried near it, was hidden, perhaps for him to return and fly back west.

The thought of his friend Deacon Fong, and the memory of his gut-wrenching flight and landing in the strange helicopter, made David feel bone chilled. *I'm no flier like Deac . . . was. It was just by the grace of God that I got that bird down in one piece . . . and me in one piece.*

He tried to recall the landing in the high field with the tall, slender grasses and yellow flowers. He couldn't recall any part of it, only watching the ground come closer and the helo shifting, wavering, then settling like a live animal making its bed for the night. With an effort he dismissed the unsettling vision.

Cold never bothered him a great deal, and now he felt pleasure as it stung his face. For a while he lay totally still in his sleeping bag, warm and content. Finally he opened his eyes into mere slits and saw that dawn had come. By turning his head slightly, he could see the apple red color over in the east. It was that time of day he had always called the cobwebby hours, and he luxuriated in the warmth and the looseness of his body and the faint sound of the woodpecker far away. *Rat tat tat tat tat!* It was a comforting sound, one that brought back old remembrances. Suddenly, as if in a vision, he saw himself walking through the woods beside a small man with a sweeping cavalry mustache, carrying a single-barrel shotgun under his arm.

With little effort he focused on the face of the boy and knew that it was he when he was only eight or nine and the man was Jesse Mitchell, his grandfather. David was born in Albuquerque, but because his parents lived the kind of life they did, David spent most of the summers of his youth with his grandparents. Several summers they had returned here to visit with Uncle Jonathan, Jesse's brother. He and Jesse had been the last of a family of twelve children. Jonathan had died when David was—eleven? Twelve, maybe? Attending his funeral in these old hills had been the last time David had been here.

The memories reminded him of Deac again. It was hard for him to leave the warm cocoon of his sleeping bag. He knew that as soon as he got up, he would have to face whatever lay before him, whether it was enemy aircraft overhead, snipers, or looters. The only thing he was relatively sure of was that life would be difficult.

But David, being the kind of man he was, pushed away all depressing memories and got up. He didn't stop to make coffee. He made a quick powdered juice drink with fresh springwater he'd found the day before and halfheartedly ate some crackers. He was anxious to get into Hot Springs, for he suspected he might have some trouble finding his grandparents. Their letter to him was short and peculiar. They were leaving and going back to the hills in Arkansas, close to Jesse's old home. With an exasperated shake of his head, David thought that as eloquent as his grandfather was, his letters always left much to be desired.

As he walked along steadily, his eyes swept the trail, except for those times when he automatically—continually—raised them to search the sky for aircraft. He saw nothing overhead, and it was startling to realize how much the threat of the deadly Tornadoes and Daggers had ruled his life lately. Also, David was shocked at how many wolf prints he saw. *Always a few wolves around the hills here—but I never realized there were this many . . .*

Impatience was in him now, for he felt that he was at the end of his journey. He had not formalized it, but somehow he thought, *If I can get back to Hot Springs, I can put things together.* He hurried on, making good time, even though he'd decided to walk in a straight line through the national forest instead of following the rather winding southern highway. He climbed the south side of the Ouachitas, which curved around the city, holding it as if in a tight embrace. Walking through these fragrant woods and gentle hills seemed like a vacation to David after scrabbling through the merciless desert.

Redoubling his pace, he reached the last hill. His feet scrambled over the slate that girdled the mountain, and then with one surge he pulled himself up and stared down, anxious for his first glimpse of the city that had played such a prominent part in his youth. It had always been a special place to him, a place of sweet, clean memories of him and his grandfather and simpler days. David had always thought about coming back to these hills when he was out of the army.

Now his sensitive nostrils were assailed by a terrible stench. Nearing the crest, he slowed considerably. At the very top, an overlook of the old heart of the city, he stopped dead still, and his face seemed to freeze.

It was to David much the same as if he had been a lover who had come to the bed of his sweetheart—as he had approached the bed where she lay under a filmy curtain with his heart filled with expectation and bursting with love. Then, as if he had drawn back the curtain and she had turned to him, he saw that instead of a beauty, she had become a leper with flesh eaten away, with holes for eyes, and with skin rotting and falling from the bone.

"Oh, dear God!" David gasped, a prayer, not an oath.

A pall of sickly yellow smoke hung over the city, an ugly exhalation, fed by what seemed to be thousands of small spirals of stinking fires, burning something loathsome. Buildings that had been alabaster white or creamy beige were now a leprous gray. The Arlington Hotel, for decades a symbol of the city's pride and old-world elegance, was a shell. He stood staring with disbelief at the windows, thinking that they looked like burned-out eyes. It was a ghost of a building, and he thought, as his eyes went over the rest of the city, of the black-and-white photographs of the Last Great War. He thought particularly of Dresden, Germany, which had been firebombed beyond all beauty until it was nothing but an obscenity.

Taking a deep, choking breath, he tightly gripped his grandfather's 20-gauge Remington shotgun. As he made his way down the mountain, the stench grew more pronounced until it seemed to be tangible, a thick slime in the back of David's throat. He kept hawking and spitting, trying to cleanse himself, but without success. When he entered the city, he could pick out its ingredients, garbage and raw sewage mixed with a rank smell of old fires and thick smoke—and the sickening odor of the dead. David knew that smell now, all too well, but somehow this was worse. The men and women and even the children at Fort Carson had died fairly quickly and cleanly. The dead here had not found such mercy; the smell was of disease and rot. David had to stop for a moment and command his body to stay under control, for he thought he would vomit. He conquered it—barely—and moved toward the center of town.

Gangs roved throughout the city, apparently without fear or conscience. They traveled like schools of predator fish, shouting, cursing, pushing, or harassing anyone who was foolish enough to be within arm's reach. Most of them, he saw, were drunk and wild-eyed from drugs. As he went down Magnolia Street and turned the corner, he saw a group of them. They'd gotten some fire axes and were smashing the wire-netted windows of an old dusty and dim pawnshop. David paused, considering the scene and his vague impulse to try to restore some order, when they caught sight of him. One man, with an ugly, oozing cut on his jaw, shouted, "Hey, look, he's got a shotgun! Whaddya think, boys and girls?"

They were all sky-high, for their eyes were bright with a false incandescence. David lifted his weapon barrel-up, pulled the trigger, and watched the aftermath of the explosion. They all stopped. Slinking, muttering obscenities, they turned back to their work. The man with the cut face watched David out of the corners of his wild eyes to see if he would stop them. Grimly holding the shotgun at a ready position, David backed across the street, then kept walking. There were too many of them, too many axes, and too many windows to break. He didn't have a chance of stopping all the madmen in this nightmare.

Confusion was everywhere. The cold gripped the city, and people were bundled up in all the clothes they could gather. Most of them, seeing David's gun, kept far away from him. One woman was sitting on the curb, her legs sprawled, and she was holding a baby to her breast. Her eyes were closed, and she was rocking back and forth, singing a little tuneless song.

David hesitated, thinking he should at least try to help the poor woman. Finally he drew close and said, "Ma'am, could I help you find a safe place for you and the baby?"

The woman did not hear him until he spoke to her again. When she turned to him, her eyes had the blankest despair he had ever seen in a human being. "She's dead! My angel's dead!" she whispered.

David's flesh crawled, for the woman hugged the dead child

back to her breast and sang again. He tried desperately to think of some way to help, but he only had to look around to see that he was far outnumbered by the tragedies. Small children, dressed in every pitiful rag they could find, some barefoot, were roaming in and out of the wrecks of buildings. Everywhere could be heard the wails and screams of women, though most of them were unseen. Men were thin, hollow-eyed, stumbling and wandering, helpless and hungry and lost. It was hopeless.

A man with a thin, pale face and staring eyes appeared. He was dressed in filthy jeans and a ratty-looking blue sweater. He came warily, like an animal afraid of meeting with a whip, but he approached David with desperate determination.

"You—you got any whiskey, soldier?"

David shook his head. "You need food worse, mister."

"Food!" The mouth opened in a soundless laugh. "Food! What food? I got some bacon from an old storehouse three days ago. Everybody was taking what he wanted, and I had to fight for it, but I got it, the last bit. But that meat was bad. It killed some, and I nearly died. Now even the bad meat's gone, soldier. You—you sure you don't have any whiskey?"

"No. No whiskey."

David watched as the man staggered off on rubbery legs, and he thought, *The fountain! There'll be fresh water in it at least.* He made his way warily down the rotting shell of Central Avenue.

"At least there is water," he murmured to himself, "and even some kind of order . . ."

Two lines had been formed, and the people standing in them held containers. Most of them had white Ty-plastic five-gallon jugs that Proto-Syn milk came in. Moving closer, David studied the people who seemed to be in charge—two men and a woman—commissars, he observed with mixed emotions. None of them had rifles, but all had pistols on their hips. They carried their batons, slapping their open palms, and walked slowly up and down the lines, their faces stern. At least they were keeping the crowd under control.

As David watched, he discerned that the woman seemed to be the authority. Observing this scene—the only shred of sanity that seemed to remain in this place—he decided to talk to the woman commissar. Perhaps there was some central authority left in the Commissary.

He moved closer, cautiously putting the safety back on his gun and cradling it barrel-down in the crook of his elbow as Jesse had taught him. She had her back to him, walking slowly down the line. But someone said something to her, and she turned to stare suspiciously at him, her hand going down to unsnap the leather holster flap at her side.

David, at first, as fighters will, eyed the holster. But then his eyes rose, returning to look closer at her beret. Instead of the holographic image of a jaguar that all commissars wore, it was something else, something familiar . . .

He took two long steps, and he was right on her. Her eyes widened and she half-lifted the baton, but she wasn't as quick as David. He grabbed her by the arm and shook her like a small terrier. "Where did you get that?"

"You're hurting my arm! Where did I get what?"

"That brooch on your beret. Where did you get it? Did you steal it?"

"No, I did not steal it! Let go of me!"

David was suffering one of those uncontrollable rages that had taken him only twice in his entire life. Reason seemed to have flown, and he knew his hand was biting into the woman's flesh. Pain was reflected in her eyes, but she refused to back down. She stared up at him defiantly.

"This is my grandmother's. What did you do to her?" He reached out and jerked the beret from her head, staring down at it in anguish.

The eyes widened—even in David's anger he noticed that they were an unusual shade of blue-gray—and she cast a cautious glance over her shoulder at the people waiting in line and especially at the other two commissars who were watching curiously. She hissed, "Keep your voice down. Are you David?"

Stunned, David could only nod.

Her square features hardened, then she whispered furiously, "Kiss me."

"Wha—wh—"

She mumbled something again under her breath, then threw her arms around David and planted her lips on his, hard, but only for a brief moment. Then she hugged him and whispered in his ear, "Play along, David. You have to. I can take you to your grandparents, but we'll have to slip away."

David, who was not much of a covert ops expert, stood still and wooden as a bowling pin. She drew back, then turned to wave at the two male commissars, who were grinning. "Can you cover for a little while, Bryce? I've got some unfinished business here."

"Sure, Xanthe. Looks like you've got some order to impose over there."

She made a quick, ironic sketch of the fist-pound-heart salute, then grabbed David's arm in a viselike grip and turned him around almost bodily. "Walk, David. You can walk, can't you? Listen to me. I can take you to your grandfather and your grandmother, but we have to sneak out of the city. There's no way that I could allow anyone to know where they are."

"Yeah? And what was all that production back there?" he blustered.

She gazed up at him, her eyes steady now. "They don't need to know that I'm helping your grandparents. It wouldn't be—healthy—for me."

David was instantly suspicious. His jaw hardened, and he said, "All right. I'm walking. You talk. What's your name?"

"Xanthe St. Dymion."

David followed her until they had gone down a side street and moved into an alley. There she stopped, ostentatiously let go of his arm, and turned to face him. "I would appreciate it if you would give me back my beret. Your grandmother Noemi gave me that brooch, and so it now belongs to me. Do you believe me?"

David was studying her. She was, he guessed, around twenty-five and was of average height. She wasn't chunkily built, but she looked strong, her body firm. Her man-cut hair was an indifferent brown, and she was not pretty, except for her eyes. They were almond shaped, that mysterious smoke-and-mirrors color, and framed by perfectly arched dark brows. He sized her up as he did most people, in one phrase. *Capable, very quick, not very feminine.*

"I don't trust you," he said.

"That's good. You're showing sense. Don't trust anyone. But give me back my beret and my brooch. Then I'll take you to your grandparents."

By the time David had pedaled the bike to the top of the steep hill, he was panting. They had been riding for four hours, and he discovered that the woman was better on a bicycle than he was. She had explained almost nothing, except that she had made friends with Jesse and Noe at church, and she knew exactly where they had gone. He demanded no more. Suddenly he saw that she was looking back at him with a slightly amused expression.

Xanthe observed that David was awkward on a bicycle. "Time to take a break," she said, not thinking that she sounded as if she were ordering him. But he allowed it with only a slight grimace. David must have really wanted to get off that bicycle.

They parked their bicycles beside an empty field filled with dead grass. David and Xanthe walked aimlessly, stretching their legs and arms. Xanthe saw him rubbing his rear gingerly. "What's the story with that bicycle seat anyway?" he muttered darkly. "New torture device, especially designed for the Commissary?"

"No, I think they're supposed to be ergonomically correct," Xanthe told him.

"Yeah, well, my ergonomic hurts," he said, his face softening but not quite breaking into a grin.

It was the first break she had seen in David Mitchell's stern face. He was built as a man should be, six feet tall, muscular but not bulky. She studied his spiky sandy hair and expressive blue eyes, envying the long, thick lashes. Now that he had lost some of the tension, she saw that he was probably a relaxed, easygoing man when anger did not overcome him.

Xanthe had never had much luck with men, and David Mitchell was exactly the kind of man—attractive, competent, easy with his masculinity—that she could never seem to attract. She had had sad experiences with unworthy men, and as a result, she had adopted rather curt, mannish ways to cover up her insecurity. "You want to rest more?"

"No, I want to get to my grandparents ASAP."

She shrugged carelessly.

They rode all day, stopping only to drink water and once to eat one of David's MRE's. Xanthe ate gritty, bland creamed corn and a slab of alarmingly pink mystery meat with eagerness. David, who could hardly swallow the tasteless food, watched her, feeling a stab of guilt. Food must have been scarce in Hot Springs for the past few weeks. In contrast, it seemed that he and Fire Team Eclipse hadn't had it so bad, after all. "I could have probably gotten us a deer," he said lamely. "But I'm in such a hurry . . ."

Her wide-spaced eyes lit on him with alarm. "You—you mean, kill a deer?"

He nodded, one corner of his mouth twitching. "Yeah, My Commissar, that's exactly what I mean. You gonna arrest me for it?"

She stared at him, bewilderment plain on her stolid features. Then she replied evenly, "Only if you don't share it with me."

"I'll share," he said. "Don't you worry about that."

They rode until the shadows were growing long and the wind whistling down from the brooding heights of the mountains above them started turning icily cold. Gray clouds like tufts of dirty wool were moving in from the north, plodding slowly but inexorably along to cover the entire sky.

Watching the troublesome signs, David moved up beside her bike. "I think it's going to snow. We'd better stop and find a good spot with lots of firewood."

She nodded, casting an anxious glance upward. "I'm pretty sure I remember a place up on that little ridge just in front of us. It's got a rock overhang and a flat shelf facing south. The woods behind it have lots of pines and some hardwoods, too, I think."

They reached the spot, and it was a good place, sheltered from the north wind, with enough of an overhang to sleep under. "I think we'd both better haul wood," he said worriedly. "It's going to get full dark pretty quick with that cloud cover, and we don't need to fall and break a leg."

They gathered a good pile of wood, though Xanthe, who evidently didn't understand the finer points of fire-making, hauled in a lot of pine that was still green. David started to explain to her that it wouldn't burn very well, but she had worked so hard, so steadily, and without a word of complaint that he didn't have the heart. He redoubled his efforts and picked up all the dry pieces of oak and elm he could find, even the smallest sticks. She obviously didn't have a clue how to make a fire, but he quickly built it, pretending not to notice. By the time they had a good blaze going just under the rock overhang, it was already the dead of night.

"Sorry I didn't have time to get us some supper," he said as she made coffee with David's small tin coffeepot.

"That's—all right. It doesn't matter," she said brusquely.

This time, he gave her an MRE of her own. He'd brought along about a dozen of them, hoping devoutly that he wouldn't have to eat them. But they were very nutritious, about three thousand calories each. He suggested they share one at lunch only because he could barely stand to choke down half of the prepackaged, dried, processed, tasteless meals. She ate all of it, just as hungrily as she had at noon. When she finished, she delighted in the small soap, the package of gum, and the two cinnamon-flavored toothpicks as if they were her birthday gifts.

"These things are great little kits to have," she commented.

"Uh—yeah. They're great. More coffee? Here, let me . . . so, My Commissar, why did you decide to stay in Hot Springs instead of going to stay with my grandparents?"

She sipped the scalding brew with appreciation, her eyes somber over the rim of the tin cup. "I'm not a high commissar. You know that, of course. You may call me Xanthe if you want." She almost smiled. "Your grandfather couldn't say my name. He just called me 'miss,' and then he started calling me 'daughter' . . . it was . . . nice." As if she regretted revealing even this small piece of herself, she went on rather stiffly, "As to your question, it would seem that you, of all people, would understand."

"Understand what?"

"Understand the concept of duty," she replied a little self-consciously. "It's my duty to stay at my post and take responsibility for protecting this biome and the people in it. You're a soldier. I'm sure you didn't desert your post to come out here."

"No, I didn't do that," David said hastily. For some reason, it was important to him that she didn't think that of him. "My commanding officer gave me permission to come here. And I've—" He started to say, *I've got to try and gather some useful information,* but he stopped himself. After all, Xanthe St. Dymion had told him not to trust anyone. "I've got to go back," he finished lamely.

She seemed to discern his discomfort—David wasn't really very good at hiding anything—but she merely nodded. "Then you understand why I stayed in Hot Springs."

David said quietly, "Well, I've got another explanation."

She stared at him curiously. "What's that?"

"You'll probably think I'm crazy, but I think you stayed there because the Lord gave you a mission."

"What do you mean?" she asked, leaning forward intently. "Tell me."

"I believe—I know—the Lord wants me to find my grandparents. So you were there. If I hadn't found you, the chances of my finding my grandparents would have been practically nonexistent."

"Maybe," she said hesitantly. "I'm—I don't—know or understand much about dunk—I mean, Christian things. Your grandfather and grandmother led me to the Lord and prayed with me, and I asked Jesus to come into my heart. But I still—don't know much."

David grinned, and he looked years younger. "You're doing all right, Xanthe. Those of us who think we know everything are in a lot worse trouble. You kind of remind me of someone, a friend I made, a friend God sent me to, out in the desert. He doesn't think he knows much, either. But he's one of the wisest Christians I've ever met, I think. He's—special. And so are you. Maybe it sounds—uh—plebeian, but I think the Lord uses special tools for special jobs. I think He used you to help me."

A warmth came to Xanthe then as she finally felt assurance that she had done the right thing. "I think you may be right, except maybe you didn't go far enough."

"What does that mean?"

"I mean, I think I have more work to do in Hot Springs. I believe that the Lord is telling me, or making me, or directing me, however it works, to go back and stay in the Commissary."

David said uneasily, "That could be very dangerous, Xanthe. I don't think what happened in the autumnal equinox is the worst that's coming, not by far. I don't even think that the nightmare that the city's in now is the worst . . ."

A chill crept over Xanthe, and she shivered slightly. "Neither do I." She remembered Jesse Mitchell's words about the coming darkness.

As if their bleak words were a signal, the snow began to fall. It was not fat, cheery flakes swirling; hard businesslike snow, wet and heavy, was instantly like a thick curtain. David tossed a sizable oak log on the fire, and the two shrank back into the shelter of the rocks.

Both had the realization at the same time—their startled, then guilty glances met—and then Xanthe dropped her head awkwardly.

"Well, My Commissar," David said with false heartiness, "looks like it's going to be cramped quarters in here." The shelter was just big enough for two to lie down if they stayed very close together.

"No. This—won't work," Xanthe said desperately.

"Sure, it will. After all, we've already had our first kiss, shared our food, shared our fire. Relax, Xanthe. We've both got on about forty layers, and these sleeping bags are thick. Please, My Commissar, don't make me crawl out and sleep in the snow. I promise to be good," David teased her.

"Oh, for goodness' sake," she declared in her curt manner. "I'm certain you can manage to control yourself, even from my considerable charms. Let's get situated. I'm getting cold."

They shifted and jabbed each other and squirmed and zipped and pushed, and finally Xanthe got settled on her side, facing the fire, her sleeping bag zipped up to her chin. David was lying on his side behind her. She was watching the flames, hypnotized, and was drifting a little and perhaps dreaming a little when she heard him faintly.

"Xanthe?"

"Hmm?"

"You do have charms. Considerable ones."

Her eyes flew open, and she was grateful he couldn't see.

Behind her, again in that lazy, gentle voice, he said, "I don't suppose we could try that kiss again? I didn't do too good the first time around. I think I need to work on it."

Swallowing hard, Xanthe said, "I thought soldiers were supposed to go off to sleep just like that."

"Yeah, okay, I can take a hint. But if you reconsider, you know, about that kiss—"

"David," she said, a clear warning.

"G'night, Xanthe."

She said nothing more. But for the first time that long, hard day, her lips were turned upward in a very small smile.

She woke up, frightened, her heart racing, and sat bolt upright. David was already struggling out of his sleeping bag.

"What is that?" she asked, her voice shaking.

"Wolves. Lots of them," he answered.

He stood up, and the snow was still falling steadily. "Oh, man, look over there. Is that—could that be a wildfire?"

Xanthe stood up, hastily pulling on her beret and wrapping a blanket about her shoulders. "That's where they—the wolves' howling—is coming from, isn't it? David, a wildfire? In this snow? It's got to be—"

"People. In big, big trouble."

They said nothing more.

They left their gear, throwing on their heavy jackets with hoods, and David reminded Xanthe as they ran to the bicycles to put on her goggles. They rode along the road, but then the road swung right, while the fire was burning at the base of a mountain in a direct line to their left.

"That—that's the mountain where your grandfather is," Xanthe said shakily. "No, no—not right there. He's in a cabin, up at the top, on the east side."

David and Xanthe let the bicycles drop and started toward it on foot. They ran when they could, though it was extremely dangerous to run over unknown terrain at night, and their visibility was reduced even more by the thick snow. But they hurried, never hesitating, and Xanthe easily kept up with David.

Their view as they drew closer was obscured by thick woods and snarling undergrowth. They fought their way through it, and finally together they stood on the edge of a small rise that overlooked a clearing at the mountain's foot.

Two women and a small boy clung to one another, and they were almost standing in an enormous bonfire. Two men were brandishing sticks and logs. They were surrounded by wolves, at least thirty of them.

"What are they doing?" Xanthe whispered, taking her 9 mm pistol off safety and chambering the first shell. "The wolves . . . they're stalking . . . circling them . . ."

Grimly David shook his head. "I don't know, but the fun's over. Shoot the pack leaders."

David leveled the shotgun and aimed at the most aggressive male. He pulled the trigger, and the wolf was knocked ten feet by the impact of the heavy slug. About half the pack left, but David, who advanced, saw that there were two pack leaders left and three distinct groups. One of them, a group of four, headed straight for him. Xanthe began shooting, but she was frightened half out of her wits, for she'd never shot anything or anyone before. She missed them all.

David got off one more shot before the four were on him. He missed the leader, quickly turned the gun and bashed the wolf who leaped for him right in the head. The wolf landed on his side, shaking his head.

Instantly one of the men who had been standing by the fire was there, savagely clubbing with the butt of his rifle, shouting. Finally the three wolves disengaged themselves, snarling and growling fiercely, and ran off.

Riley Case was breathing hard. "Screamin' Eagles to the rescue."

"Huu-ahh," David said weakly, scrambling to his feet.

The other man, who had been standing protectively over the women, came forward. David saw that his hand was out, and he almost was running toward him. Instinctively David stepped forward, his arms opened wide, and the older man practically fell into them. "A soldier! It's a miracle, a miracle! Thank God! Thank God!"

Gravely David said, "Air Assault, sir, and amen."

FIVE

I'M FINE. I can make it."

Victorine thought that Con did not look at all fine. He still looked like death, though he had, in the last two days, grown much stronger than she'd thought he would. She wavered, but then decided to remain totally neutral. After all, if you went around advising people and they took your advice, it sort of made you responsible for them. Victorine, of all things, did not want to be responsible for another human being as long as she lived, except Dancy, of course. So she said nothing.

Dancy said eagerly, "You look much better, really you do, Captain Slaughter."

"Your good nursin', ma'am," he drawled with a small mocking bow.

"No, I've prayed all the time for you," she said earnestly. "That must be it."

He ruffled her hair as if she were an endearing small puppy. "You'd know a lot more about that than I would, Miss Dancy Doodle."

Dancy's eyes widened. "My—my grandmother Tessa Kai used to call me that."

"Yeah?" he said gravely. "Your mom told me about her. I sure am sorry, Dancy. I won't call you that again."

She thought about it, and Victorine watched her curiously.

Dancy hadn't mentioned Tessa Kai to her, not once, since her death. Then Dancy said slowly, "No, it's okay. I—I don't mind." She made a little face. "Guess I just look like a doodle, huh?"

With great gravity he replied, "Yes, I'm afraid you do."

She poked his arm, and he grimaced horribly. "Well, you look like a corpse," she said with relish. "A zombie . . . that died of tuberculosis."

"That's because I'm wearing this silly dress." He sighed. "If I had on my uniform, I would look like a mighty warrior again. So—could I have my clothes, please? Slow as I'm moving, it's gonna take me 'til tonight to get dressed anyway."

"You don't have any clothes, Captain," Victorine said crisply. "And that is not a dress. It's a gentleman's lounging robe. I went and got it for you, and it wasn't fun, so I'd appreciate it if you wouldn't complain."

"Wait a minute," he said slowly. "What do you mean, I don't have any clothes? Where's my uniform?" He looked wildly around the tiny one-room apartment. "Hey—where's my shotgun? And my gear?"

Victorine sighed. "Captain Slaughter, the clothes you were wearing, as you've obviously forgotten, were sliced to ribbons and dripping with blood. As for your gun . . ." She frowned and gave a quick, cautious glance at Dancy. But that was merely one of the old habits left over from the old life. In this life, she couldn't—and shouldn't—try to shield her from the harsh realities. "I went outside yesterday as soon as it was light to get your shotgun. But it was gone. And so were the gun and the knife the dead man had. All three bodies had been—rifled. And I figured you had a pack, so I looked around a little for it, but I didn't see it."

He stared at her. "You mean—since I've been out of it, the gangs have been back?" He cast a look of concern at Dancy. "They didn't—"

"No, I haven't seen a soul in the last two days," Victorine said.

"I think I know what happened, though. I haven't seen any of these stinking male gang members yet wandering around without a woman or two. I think there must have been a woman with those three the other night, hidden, watching. When you killed her buddies, she probably stole everything and took off."

"Blast!" he grated. "I've worn a uniform for the last seventeen years. Especially now I don't like the idea of slinking around in civvies like a coward." Neither Dancy nor Victorine had an answer, so he grumbled, "Ma'am, please tell me that at least I'm not going to have to wear this dress."

"No, I got you some clothes from—another one of the condos here," Victorine said dully. "The hospitality manager here was—is—about your size. Your height, anyway."

Dancy said quietly, "Mom, I know Gerald's dead. You don't have to keep trying to hide it from me."

Victorine nodded dumbly. Dancy may have known Gerald was dead in her little weird way, but she had no idea how badly he died. Victorine hadn't really realized it until she'd gone into Gerald's condo. The gangs had evidently broken in and probably beat him before hanging him. The wooden door was splintered as if with an ax, the condo was wrecked, and there was blood smeared in a long, terrible path out the door.

Con was watching Victorine curiously. Then his face hardened, though his voice was light. "So, ladies, I've got a new wardrobe for the first time in seventeen years. I'll be a real dude if this dress is any indication."

"It's not a dress," Victorine repeated with exasperation. But Dancy's woebegone face lightened, and that was enough for Con.

Victorine set about heating some water and lighting a candle in the single bathroom, since Con insisted he was going to wash and dress. Dancy, meanwhile, removed the dressings from his chest and arm. Unfortunately Con was left-handed, so he had trouble doing much of anything with his right hand. And though it had been hard for Victorine to admit to herself—or allow—Dancy seemed to have a soothing touch. On the now-rare occasions that Victorine had a migraine, Dancy was the only person she could stand to touch her, put a cool cloth on her forehead, smooth back her hair, or stroke her hand. Victorine, she knew, had an ungentle touch. That was just the way it was for both of them.

The White Dunes condos were very small, one-room units with a tiny open loft above that barely held a double bed. The bathroom was downstairs, and while Victorine was puttering around in there, arranging Gerald's—now Con Slaughter's—clothes and some men's toilet articles, she listened to the two talking as Dancy took care of him. They were—to Victorine's disgust—practicing belching. It had at first dismayed her that the two seemed to be growing so close. Victorine had not yet met a man that she trusted with Dancy. But it didn't take a genius to see that it had never entered Con's mind to think of Dancy as anything but a child. He'd never, by look or gesture or word, acted otherwise.

And of course, there is the fact that he's—that I—that we—

"Stop it," she hissed to herself. *There is no "we." That first night, after such a trauma, it's only natural for two people to feel closeness and intimacy. It's not real. It's artificial. I don't even like him.*

But Victorine Flynn Thayer, though she did at times have tunnel vision, was not a dishonest person. *That's not true. I do like him . . . even better, I respect him. And evidently I must trust him. I just wish . . . I just don't want to have to take care of anyone else! So there it is, God! If that's being selfish, so be it!*

Such was Victorine's prayer for the day.

Con washed up and shaved, and Dancy reapplied clean dressings while Victorine cooked lunch, such as it was. Because the condos had no fireplaces, she kept a small fire going in the stainless steel sink. Gerald had had a good supply of Proto-Syn lava rocks, so the smoke was kept to a minimum. She fixed a beef stew from bouillon cubes and dried beef strips and canned vegetables. There were rye crackers and raisins and four old satsumas in Gerald's pantry. The skin on them was leathery, but the fruit was still surprisingly sweet and juicy.

Con, meanwhile, was trying on his new wardrobe, and he kept calling out to Dancy from the bathroom. "Wait'll you see me, Miss Dancy Doodlebug. You're going to have the laugh of the day," he grumbled. "Man! These breeches are—oh, forget it. I'm Airborne, Screaming Eagles, I can hold my breath for a day or two. But I'm afraid I'm gonna walk like a duck. Uh—you're sure these aren't girl's clothes?"

"Stop griping, big man," Dancy said, her eyes bright. "C'mon out, I want to see."

"I'm comin'. I'm comin'."

He came out slowly and breathing a little heavily. Victorine sighed; he really was still weak. No doubt about it, they were going to have to move slowly and probably help him if they left tonight.

"I look," he announced sadly, "like an idiot."

"What are you talking about?" Victorine snapped. "It's a black turtleneck sweater—and a really nice one, of real silk and wool that I wish I had—and black Ty-jeans! What's so idiotic about that?"

"I dunno," he muttered. "I just think I look like that Ultimate Reality star, the one that's s'posed to be so bad. You know, the Invincible Vampire Hunter and the One-Man S.W.A.T. Team."

"Marcus Iago," Dancy supplied with delight. "But he's the quirk, a real slay, Captain Slaughter. You don't look at all like him."

"Gosh, thanks," he grumbled, looking down at himself. He studied Dancy—who was wearing her would-be commissar outfit—and then Victorine, who was wearing black Ty-twill pants and a shapeless charcoal gray sweater. "Well, at least we're all color coordinated," he said with a lisp. "We can have our own gang. The Deadly Nightshades or something like that."

"That's not funny," Victorine said sharply.

"Aw, Mom, we're just fooling around," Dancy said.

"Just fools is more like it," Victorine muttered, stirring the thin stew savagely.

Dancy came up behind her and slid her thin arms around Victorine's waist, laying her head against her back. "I love you, Mom. So much."

Victorine dissolved; who wouldn't? "I'm gripy, aren't I?"

"Yes," Dancy whispered. "But I know why. It's okay, Mom. It's going to be okay."

"I hope so, darling," Victorine sighed.

Neither of them saw the look on Con Slaughter's face. In fact, no one had ever seen the like of it on the tough soldier's craggy, desert-hardened features. It was gentle, with much sad longing, and it did not soon pass away.

"They're commissars," Victorine whispered in Con's ear.

He was angry that Victorine had had to belly-crawl up to the little tussock by the side of the road so she could see who was on the bridge. He was a soldier, blast it! And he was good at things like covert night surveillance! And here he sat like a great lump, letting this poor overtaxed woman do all the dangerous work!

The fact that Con couldn't belly-crawl anywhere unless he wanted to reopen the long gash on his chest and probably bleed to death made no difference to him.

"Am I bothering you, Captain Slaughter?" Victorine hissed viciously. "Did you hear me?"

"Yes, I heard you," he grunted. "Sorry. Commissars? Are you sure?"

"I'm sure. I know one of them." Dancy, who was huddled close to Con, perked up. "It's Mitch Day, Dancy," Victorine told her. "You remember him? Greek food and sandalwood incense in his room."

"Oh, yeah. And long-legged blondes," Dancy said.

"You're not supposed to notice things like that," Victorine intoned.

"Can't help it," Dancy said, shrugging.

Con was thinking hard. *So the bridge is held by commissars? I don't trust them, either . . . If I'm going to just sashay up to somebody and turn myself in, I want it to be our military. I could get court-martialed for desertion, I guess . . . if there is a military here . . . but I'd rather take my chances with them.*

So what are our options here? Double back, go through the scrub and down to the waterway? Can we cross it? Bloody well can't swim it, not in this weather. Boat? Maybe, maybe not . . .

"I think we ought to ask them to help us," Victorine said firmly. "At least they have some semblance of maintaining order. Presumably they're here to aid refugees and maybe contain the gangs on the Key."

"You didn't see any Germans? None? And no civilians who might be Germans?" Con asked.

"How the heck do I know what Germans look like?" Victorine asked crossly. "I mean, they don't all look like Aryan supermen, do they? Anyway, there are no civilians. Just commissars."

"Are they armed?"

"They have side arms but no rifles that I saw. And, Con, there's the truck."

"Truck? You mean, it's running?" Con demanded.

"Yes, it's idling."

"That's not good," he intoned. "Far as I know, the Germans are the only ones who still have toys that work. What did it look like?"

"It's just a truck. No markings," Victorine said impatiently. "And have you forgotten about the American planes?" They'd seen two more of the big transport planes in the last two days.

"Yeah, there is that . . ." Still, Con was hesitant. He didn't like it. He didn't like the smell of it or feel of it or something. "I think we ought to try to go to Pensacola on our own."

Victorine was quiet for a long time, frowning. Finally she took a deep breath and said evenly, "Dancy and I are going to go to the commissars, Captain Slaughter. You, of course, can do whatever you like."

It was too dark to see the niceties of expression, but Dancy must have sensed his intent. "Captain Slaughter," she whispered softly, "I would really like for you to stay with us. Please?"

After a moment's silence he muttered to Victorine, "How do you ever say no to this girl?"

"Rarely," Victorine sighed, "and with great difficulty. So how do we—um—turn ourselves in?"

"If we're gonna do it, then let's just do it," Con growled in a normal tone and stood stiffly. "I'm trekkin'."

He walked up to the bridge, followed by Victorine and Dancy. The four commissars who were carelessly guarding that end of the bridge came to attention, then fumbled for their pistols. "Halt!" one of them—a young woman—cried out.

"Stay frosty," Con grunted, holding up his hands in the universal gesture of surrender. "I'm unarmed. Unfortunately."

Victorine pushed forward and called out, "Commissar Day? Do you remember me? I'm Victorine Flynn Thayer, the hospitality manager of Summer Sea."

Mitchell Day lowered his pistol and squinted in the darkness. Then he took a small flashlight and shone it on Victorine's face, then on Dancy, and finally on Con. "It's okay," he said at last. "I recognize them. They're hospitality managers for the diversionary facilities on the Key. She's who she says she is, and that's her daughter, I forget her name. C'mere, sweetheart, it's okay. And the big guy is Gerald Ainsley; he's at White Dunes."

And that was how no one ever knew that Con Slaughter was a captain in the 101st Airborne (Air Assault), Fire Team Eclipse. He didn't have to cower, and Victorine and Dancy didn't have to lie.

They hustled them across the bridge, Mitch Day escorting them, talking all the time. Victorine had never exactly been friends with the gregarious young commissar, but she had found him less offensive and demanding than most.

"We've done a pretty good sweep from Pensacola. We've already picked up about two thousand refugees and arrested a couple of hundred looters and criminals," he told them confidently. "We've been driving the gangs east. Bet the Key's no place to have fun these days."

"No, it's not been fun," Victorine agreed ironically. "Where are you taking us?"

"We can do some initial processing here, at the temporary camp down at the other end of the bridge," he replied. "Then we'll take you to Pensacola NAS. It's where we're processing all refugees."

"Processing?" Victorine said cautiously. "What does that mean? And what do you do with us after we're processed?"

"Just keeping track of everyone, Vic," he said, swaggering a little. "And protecting innocent civilians. We'll take care of you people. Don't worry."

"Gee, I feel so much better," Con growled under his breath. Dancy grabbed his hand—his injured one—and squeezed it, glowering up at him. "Ow," he mumbled, but said nothing else.

Mitchell Day, who seemed to be trying to impress Victorine, took them personally to a mobile trailer and told a gum-chewing woman commissar inside with a Cyclops drone who they were. She typed fast, then without looking up or saying a word, printed out three small cards and laminated them. They had their names, their Social Security numbers, and another long code number printed on them. Day presented them to Victorine with a flourish. "Keep this with you at all times," he said with importance. "You can go over to the mess shack and have some coffee and something to eat. Some cots, too, if you want to catch some z's." He squinted up at Con Slaughter's gray-tinged face. "You don't look so good, big guy. Some gangster jump you?"

"Three of 'em did," Con answered darkly. "They're gull feed."

Dancy, behind Day's back, gave Con a look that might have withered fresh flowers.

Day was twenty-two years old, had never been to college, and never expected to be anything better than a commissar; but then again, he wasn't a blind fool. He stepped closer to Con and searched his face carefully under the mercury vapor lights in the trailer. Con stared back at him defiantly.

He's busted, Victorine thought, and she was a little taken aback at how frightened she was. Day must not have ever really had a conversation with Gerald Ainsley, or he wouldn't have taken Captain Concord Slaughter for the slightly effeminate and much more slender man.

Someone had to do something. And it sure didn't need to be Dancy.

Victorine stepped forward and laid her hand on Day's arm. Softly and prettily she murmured, "My Commissar, I must thank you so much for taking such good care of me and my daughter. We've been so very frightened."

Day was a low commissar, and had no right to the courtesy title. Victorine, of course, knew this, and Day probably suspected that she knew it. Still, he was flattered, and he responded to Victorine the way most men did when she took the trouble to seek their attention. "Victorine, it's been my pleasure," he said, covering her hand with his and pressing it fervently. "I must report back to my post, but could I escort you to the mess tent first?"

"Oh, yes, I'd appreciate it," she replied, taking his arm snugly. They left the trailer, Day having forgotten all about Gerald Ainsley and Dancy, too. But Victorine hadn't. She cast a look of pure disgust behind her at the captain, and he grinned and winked at her. Almost flouncing, she turned back around and smiled oh-so-warmly at the smitten Day.

The mess tent had long metal tables at one end and twenty cots at the other. Con quickly assessed the situation: four commissars cooking and attending and generally lounging around, and twelve other refugees, eight men, two women, two children. Didn't look too threatening, but the hairs on the back of his neck were prickling. Though it galled him, he was somehow glad that they thought he was a scared civvie.

Mitchell Day said what seemed to be an overlong good-bye to Victorine at the entrance to the tent, while Con and Dancy went inside. Dancy's nose wrinkled. "That soup doesn't smell too good," she observed. "Mom's was better."

"You haven't even eaten any yet," Con chided her. "You don't know that."

Gravely she told him, "Your sense of smell is very important, Captain Slaughter. You should always pay attention to what it tells you."

He looked surprised, then said, "You're right, ma'am. You sound like a soldier. You'd make a good one."

"No, I wouldn't," she retorted spiritedly, "and if you don't quit acting like one, I'm going to pinch your hand again."

"Can't help it," Con said defensively. "That's what I am. That's who I am." He stared closely at her, then asked quietly, "Dancy, what difference does it make? I mean, we're assuming that these people don't have anything to do with the military situation in the West, right?"

She looked uncomfortable. "Maybe. I don't know. It's just—better if they don't know about you."

He nodded. "Smells funny, doesn't it?"

"Guess so," she agreed, shrugging. Victorine finally joined

them. Dancy took her hand, looking up at her, and said mischievously, "Wow, Mom. You can sure turn it on when you want to."

"Be quiet, Dancy," Victorine blustered. "And you, *Mr. Ainsley*. I'm not going to do that for you again."

"You're not?" he said with wide-eyed innocence. "Why not? Like Dancy said, you're sure good at distracting men when you want to."

"I'm not having this conversation," Victorine declared. "I'm going to go eat something, and then rest. You are, too, Dancy. You, Mr. Ainsley, can go take a flying leap off this bridge for all I care."

"Mom," Dancy protested.

Con Slaughter watched them go, the light of appreciation plain on his face.

No more refugees arrived that night. Victorine and Dancy slept soundly for the first time since the blackout. Con, who was still weak from his wounds, even rested quietly. Though Dancy had been right about the soup—it was watery and had no meat at all, only Proto-Syn canned vegetables—the breakfast of scrambled eggs and toast was pretty good. Con was a little surprised at just how good he felt. He seemed to be recovering from what were serious, though not life-threatening, wounds very quickly. Dancy prayed for him again at breakfast. The other refugees stared when she bowed her head and took his hand. Two of them, who were sitting down at the other end of the table, got up and moved.

They left at dawn. In the truck, all twelve of the others, even the two children, sat as far away from Victorine and Dancy and Con as possible. One of the men and both of the women kept giving them dark, suspicious looks. Victorine either didn't notice or, in her own self-possessed way, didn't care. Dancy pretended not to notice. Con did take notice, though, and glowered back at them.

Dumb heathens, he thought uncharitably. *I'm no saint, but it always riled me when people treated Mitchell like that . . .*

But it was more than just the widespread disdain people had for Christians in these times. They would find that out at Pensacola Naval Air Station.

They had their first hint that something was wrong when the truck reached the guard shack at the main gate. It was manned by commissars, not naval men. As they drove through the base, they saw commissars and civilians everywhere, but not a single man in a military uniform. They were in the back of the plain gray truck, which was like a military transport truck with a canvasette flap top and benches along the sides. Con raised the end flap and took in the surroundings. One of the men murmured darkly that he ought to sit down and not be so nosy. Con suggested that he mind where his own big nose was pokin' before Con adjusted it for him. Dancy almost, but not quite, stifled a giggle, and Victorine shot her a foreboding look. But the man didn't say anything else.

The truck pulled up in front of one of the big hangars, and Con jumped out before the truck stopped completely. The pain that shot through him from the jarring almost took his breath away, but he wanted to look around as much as he could before some busybody commissar hustled them inside.

Lines of planes—fighters and transports and surveillance—all neatly parked. More commissars driving—

I knew it! Those are Vulcans! German vehicles! Not a single seaman in sight . . . so where are the Goths? Man, I don't believe it! I walked right into it!

Con was seething, but he knew there was no place to run and no place to hide. He'd never get off the base.

And he had to consider Dancy . . . and Victorine.

He squared his shoulders, shook himself loose from the commissar trying to herd him, walked inside the hangar, and finally found the Goths.

About twelve of them were walking around in their arrogant way, shoulders thrown back, eyes cold and narrowed, mouths and jaws hard. They seemed to be merely observing the commissars who were processing two lines of refugees. And they were observing the refugees themselves.

Two of them, who were standing by a table containing a coffee urn and pastries, stopped talking and looked hard at Con Slaughter as he came striding in. Con stopped dead still and stared back at them, his gaze as cold as frozen steel, his stance tense. The two German officers started toward him.

Dancy slipped her hand into Con's. He almost, in his fury, shook her off; but her hand was icy cold, and somehow that made him ashamed of himself. He looked down at her and made himself smile. Her eyes were wide and wary. "Please don't," she said through gritted teeth.

He took a deep breath and made himself not look back up at the Germans. "Okay, baby, I'll try."

She nodded tremulously. Victorine, standing slightly behind them, said in a low tone, "They've stopped. Please, for my daughter's sake—for my daughter's life—don't start any trouble, Cap—Gerald."

"Okay, okay, I'll be good," he said rather ungraciously. It was the best he could do under the circumstances.

"Let's get in line," Victorine said with great relief. "Just—slouch a little, can't you? You look like you're standing at attention all the time."

"Don't push it, Victorine," Con muttered. "I'm not going to walk knock-kneed and lisp, you know."

"I know, but you could try to look less like a captain of the Screaming Eagles."

"How the—oh, forget it. Ladies first."

Con estimated there were about eighty refugees in the building. Some of them had already been processed and milled around, talking and drinking coffee and asking the commissars questions. They made a wide swath around the Germans, though every once in a while some woman would simper at one of them, or a hail-fellow-well-met would try to talk to them. They apparently answered any questions or comments that such fools directed to them in a courteous manner, but no one carried on lengthy conversations with them. And they looked like hawks guarding a nest of field mice.

The lines weren't too long. About fifteen people were in front of Victorine. But they did seem to be taking a long time on each person, even the children. Three or four Germans stood behind the commissars on the drones at all times, watching the screens, watching the people, watching the commissars.

No Cyclops II, Victorine observed. *That means they've downloaded some information to the drones . . . but they must not have physical ident capabilities like thumbprints or retinal scans or vox scan . . . no one's being scanned. That's good, or they'd catch Con for sure . . . Wonder if a captain of the 101st Airborne would be a valuable prisoner? Wonder what they're talking about? Guess they're trying to figure out the best way to place people . . . at least, I hope that's what's going on . . .*

They moved up slowly, and Victorine strained to hear what the commissars were saying to the people in front of her. But they spoke in low tones, so Victorine couldn't hear much of anything until the woman in front of her stepped up to the table. It sounded fairly innocuous: who she was, did she have any family, did she have any preferences as to temporary relocation . . .

Then it was Victorine's turn. Was it her imagination, or did the Germans step closer and become more intent? Were they staring hard at her—or behind her, at Con Slaughter?

"Your ID card, please," the bored commissar said.

Victorine handed it to her. She typed, then shot a keen look up at Victorine. No mistake, the Germans stepped closer. "You are Victorine Flynn Thayer?" the commissar asked. She was a very young woman, maybe twenty, with eyes that were too close together and lips that had been surgically enhanced too much. She looked as if she'd just gotten them unstuck from a frozen pole.

"Yes, I am," Victorine said. Now that she was in the thick of it, she was as cool as winter.

Fat Lips typed some more. "And you came in with your daughter and Gerald Ainsley? You are hospitality managers at diversionary facilities on Perdido Key?"

"That's correct."

The woman craned to look behind Victorine. "And is that Dancy Flynn Thayer and Gerald Ainsley?"

"The short one is Dancy," Victorine said caustically and immediately regretted it.

Fat Lips's beady eyes narrowed. Smugly she turned around to the Germans and tapped the drone's screen.

The German officers stepped up. Both of them were tall men, with frigid blue eyes and imperious expressions. One was blond, about thirty, and the other was a distinguished-looking man of about fifty with jet-black hair. He wore the silver eagles of a colonel on his shoulder. "Ms. Thayer, Miss Thayer, Mr. Ainsley, I'm afraid there is a slight problem."

"Sure is," Con said behind Victorine, but low enough so that no one but she could hear.

The German pointed to the drone. "Your human records indicate that you are a member of the United America Church. Are you, Ms. Thayer, a Christian?"

Hot blood pounded in Victorine's ears and rumbled against her chest, but it did not alter her composure. She merely looked at the German colonel with a slightly amused, apparently unconcerned expression. But her thoughts were in turmoil.

Do I lie? Can I lie? Why does it matter . . . but it does, something's—very wrong . . .

Dancy won't lie.

"I am," she said calmly. "What of it?"

The icy blue eyes flickered. "We have had many problems with fanatical Christians, Ms. Thayer. You see, your countrymen believe that it was right-wing fundamentalist Christians, a militant arm of the United America Church, that caused this power blackout and initiated this terrible national crisis. We Germans, who are here only to assist your country in this crisis, have had great difficulties in protecting you and your people."

Close behind her, Con Slaughter jerked, a tension reaction, and Victorine could literally feel the heat of his anger at her back. She tried, in some ephemeral way, to become even cooler, to counteract him, to calm him on some subliminal level that it seemed the three of them had established.

He relaxed just a little, but Victorine could feel it.

"My people," Victorine repeated in a respectful tone. "You mean Christians? Protecting us from what?"

"Why, from your own countrymen, of course," the colonel said icily. "We don't wish to become embroiled in your internal security matters, but it has become necessary for us to intervene on behalf of professed Christians."

"I see," Victorine said. "So, may I ask exactly what it is you are obliged to do with us Christians?"

He leaned forward, his strong hands flat on the desk. "We've managed to establish two camps to separate you. But I must tell you, Ms. Thayer, that neither of them is a very pleasant place. Unfortunately we had neither the time nor the resources to provide special accommodations for subversive groups." His voice became low and menacing.

Victorine didn't respond. She met his cold gaze, but could think of nothing more to say.

Very slowly the colonel's eyes went to Dancy, who was standing a little behind Victorine, her head down. Victorine clutched her close. In a less-threatening tone he said, "Miss Thayer? Look at me, please."

Dancy raised her eyes. He studied her for a few moments.

They were the longest seconds Victorine had ever lived through. "Your records say you, too, Miss Thayer, are a member of this militant church. Are you, too, a Christian?"

Dancy's face was utterly blank, like a slate just washed. She couldn't look away from the commanding German officer questioning her.

Victorine exclaimed, "What good would it do to deny it? As you say, it's right there in the human records!"

He didn't look away from Dancy's hypnotized gaze. "It would be fine to deny it, Miss Thayer. In fact, that's all you have to do. Just tell me that you're not a Christian, and you don't have any loyalty to their lies and crimes against the nation and the American people. That's all. You will be well cared for, I promise, Dancy."

Victorine was frozen with horror. Con Slaughter stepped close to Dancy—to do what, he never knew—but Dancy finally spoke. "No. I'm a Christian, sir, as is my mother, and as was her mother before her."

He frowned, an ugly grimace of disgust and disdain. "So be it. What about you—Ainsley, is it? Your records don't show any affiliation."

"I'm an American," Con rasped angrily. "And that means I don't think any of my people ought to be treated with disrespect because of their religious beliefs. I'm staying with my friends. I'm going wherever they're going."

The German colonel nodded, suddenly bored. "Fine. Then you'll all be sent to the Isolation Facility in Albuquerque."

The man said it as a threat.

But inwardly Con was laughing. *Albuquerque? Back to New Mexico? Back home to my team? You're too dumb to know it, you sleazy Goth, but I won!*

It wasn't until much, much later that Con realized that perhaps he had had some heavenly help in his unlikely victory over the Germans that day.

SIX

THOSE STARS sure are pretty tonight, Noe."

Jesse Mitchell stood looking out the window at the canopy of darkness that surrounded the earth. A falling star made a brilliant scratch of light across the sky, and Jesse grinned, saying, "When I was just a kid and I'd see a falling star, I always made a wish."

Noe was mixing biscuit dough, adding ingredients to a large brown bowl. "I did that, too," she said and smiled. "What would you wish right now, Jesse?"

For a moment his lined features grew despondent, but then Jesse's eyes twinkled, and he came over and put his arm around Noe. "I'm wishing you could put on a new red dress, and we could go to a camp meeting like we did when we were just married."

Noe sniffed. "That's what you say you wish, but I know you're really wishing for something bigger than that."

Only for a moment did Jesse falter, for she had touched a sore nerve. The catastrophic events that had fallen upon the earth had not shaken his faith in God, but more and more he was wondering what God was up to. To disguise his thoughts, he said, "You're not mixing that biscuit dough right. You need to put a little bit of grease in it."

"I've been making biscuits for you for more than fifty years, Jesse Mitchell! If you're not satisfied, you can get another cook."

"Nope. That would be too much trouble to break in another woman. I'm just gonna have to teach you better ways."

The argument about biscuit making had gone on for years. Jesse considered himself an authority on cooking, while Noe was just as certain that he had not one-tenth of her ability in the culinary arts. It was one of their homey, personal little jokes.

Suddenly Jesse lifted his head. "Did you hear that?"

"Hear what?"

"I hear voices."

Noe put down the bowl, her eyes growing bright. "Are they here?"

Jesse hurried across the room to open the door. Snow had fallen, carpeting the mountain with three inches of fine, glistening dust. The dawn was just beginning to lighten the skyline in the east. By the gray light Jesse saw a group emerging from the first-growth timber that lined the edge of the property. There were seven of them, one of them a small child. Still, these days one never knew what form evil could take. His eyes narrowed, then he murmured, "You wait here, Noe. Might be them, but it might be some other—something."

Stepping off the porch, Jesse noted that Noe paid no attention at all to his warning. He heard the crunch of her footsteps in the snow, but his whole attention was on the people moving toward them.

Suddenly a voice cried out, "Grandpa!"

Jesse blinked, for he knew that voice. "David, is that you, boy?"

David Mitchell shoved his weapon into Xanthe's hands and raced across the snow. They had been leading the others up the side of the mountain since well before dawn, but the sight of the two people he loved most in the world made David's weariness and caution vanish. He reached the couple and threw his arms around Jesse, literally picking him up off the ground. Since he was muscular and tall and his grandfather was a small man, worn thin by time, it was like picking up a child.

"Put me down! Who do you think you are, David Mitchell?"

David laughed, but was obedient. Setting Jesse down carefully, he turned to his grandmother. Folding her in his arms, he whispered, "Grandma, it's me! I'm home!"

The others—Merrill and Genevieve Stanton, Allegra, Xanthe, and Riley—watched with the touch of awkwardness that adults feel when witnessing an intimate scene. Only Kyle was unembarrassed; he plodded forward, a short, fat sausage in red, and threw his stubby arms around David's knees.

Xanthe whispered, "I wish someone would be that glad to see me."

Allegra's eyebrows raised slightly. She had not missed the interest that Xanthe St. Dymion had shown—and tried so hard to hide—in David Mitchell. "Maybe he will be someday."

Xanthe blushed slightly but made no reply, for David called out loudly, "All of you! Come and meet my grandparents!"

The group struggled forward. David scooped Kyle up and said, "These are my friends, Grandpa: Merrill and Genevieve Stanton, Allegra Stanton Saylor, Riley Case. This is our boss, Kyle Saylor. And I think you already know Commissar Xanthe St. Dymion."

Jesse moved at once to stand before Xanthe and took her hands. "Daughter, it's good to see you again. Noe and I have prayed for you every day."

Xanthe felt a sudden warmth at the words. "I wondered if we'd ever meet again."

"I don't believe in accidents. Have you told this grandson of mine how the Lord used you to take care of us?"

David spoke up quickly. "She's been pretty quiet about it. I'll have to hear the whole story from you."

Now Jesse, in silence and without self-consciousness, went to each of them and studied each face. Somehow each member of the group felt as though the faded blue eyes penetrated right to the very center of the mind—or of the spirit. Such face-to-face meetings and perusal were not the norm in this world of cybercommunications, and Allegra felt awkward. But as Jesse studied her, she experienced a warmth, not physical, but in her spirit. *This old man is something,* she thought, and her lips curved upward in a smile. "I'm so glad to see you, Mr. Mitchell. You'll never know how glad I am to see you."

"Almost everyone calls me Dad Mitchell. I guess that would do for all of you," Jesse said. "Now then. Come in out of the weather!"

David herded them all into the cabin, which crowded the small room. "Kyle, you get over there and warm yourself at the fire," David said, plunking him down solidly. The boy had formed a real attachment for him and for Riley Case. David noticed that Riley immediately, upon entering the cabin, stood with his back against the wall and was studying the older couple carefully.

"Let me stir up this fire, and we'll have a little tea. I've been cutting some sassafras. Always use the root, not the branch. It has more bite that way. Wish we had some coffee but we're out," Jesse apologized.

"Anything hot would be fine, and we're all pretty hungry," David said.

"Noe, let's cook these folks up some breakfast."

"We have lots of that venison that you killed last Thursday, Jesse, and we can make up a bigger batch of biscuits."

"That would be great, Grandma," David declared, rubbing his hands together in anticipation. "My grandmother's biscuits! Are you all in for a treat!"

"Could we help with the cooking?" Genevieve asked.

"Guess you might at that," Noe said warmly. "I'm so used to being the only cook around, it's really nice to have some women here to help out. You men just stay out of the kitchen, and especially, Mrs. Stanton, don't let Jesse there tell you how to make biscuits. His bread isn't fit to eat!"

With Xanthe, Allegra, and Genevieve helping (at least, Genevieve was some help), soon the cabin was filled with the delicious aroma of venison steaks and fresh baked biscuits. Jesse did not ask any questions directly about how the group had arrived, but his sharp eyes went from face to face. He brushed his sweeping mustache in a habitual gesture, listening as Merrill told the story of their journey from Hot Springs.

Finally the meal was ready, and there were just barely enough plates, including saucers and cooking pans, to give everyone a steak. Noe had fixed white gravy, and the spicy fragrance of sassafras tea overlaid the other delicious smells.

There were only the three rocking chairs, but David found the boxes that the Mitchells and Xanthe had brought their belongings in—the Mitchells never threw anything away—and soon everyone had a seat and a plate. Jesse said, "We'll thank the Lord for this." He bowed his head and prayed simply, "Lord God in heaven, I thank You for bringing our brothers and our sisters safely to this place that You have prepared. Bless the food and give us strength and let us use that strength for Your glory. In Jesus' name. Amen."

"Amen," David echoed. He had no fork, so he picked up his steak and bit off a huge chunk. "Ow, that's hot!"

"It's good, though," Genevieve said with a sigh.

"Hunger makes a good sauce," Noe replied. She moved around the room, seeing that everyone was fed, eating very little herself.

When the meal was finished, Noe asked, "Now, David, I want you to tell me how you got here. East, I mean. Xanthe told me about that old brooch—I'm glad it did somebody some good. But how did you get to Hot Springs? I just know you jumped out of a plane or something like that."

"Mm, not quite like that," he said, smiling, but then he grew grave. He told them sketchily of the sudden German attack on Fort Carson and how the team had finally ended up in Chaco Canyon. Then he related briefly how he and Captain Slaughter and Deacon Fong had stolen the German helicopter. He hesitated momentarily, grief etching lines into his boyish face and tingeing his voice as he spoke of Deacon Fong's death. Finally he looked at his grandfather and said, "I think Deac died so I could get to you."

The others listened to his story with some shock. David had not told them, not even Xanthe, of the German attacks on the military or of the death of his friend.

Jesse said quietly, "I know that some of you were searching for a hiding place in the wilderness. That's why I built up that fire. The Lord God told me to give a signal for those who needed a refuge."

At these words, Riley blinked and stroked his scratchy two-day growth of beard thoughtfully. Allegra studied him out of the corner of her eye; Riley had admitted that he'd been drawn to the beacon built by Jesse Mitchell, but that was about all of a personal nature that he'd ever said. He was an intensely private man—even secretive.

Jesse went on, "I know that many turned back. And I know that two of you died. These are evil days, but God will bring us through."

Merrill frowned. "When you say two of us died, I assume you mean the young pilot that David just told us about."

"No. There were two besides him."

Riley asked sharply, "How do you know that, Mr. Mitchell?"

Jesse did not answer for a moment. He looked down at his folded hands. They were thin now and had liver spots, the hands of an old man. He looked up and said directly to Riley, "There was one more."

Riley had not told anyone of the body that he had found, and for some reason he did not want to bring it up now. *The old man must really mean Perry Hammett and Deac, the pilot. That's all it could be. He couldn't know about my finding the other body.*

Jesse watched Riley closely, but simply said, "The Lord has brought you all here."

"It was hard for me to come, Grandpa," David said, dropping his eyes. "I hated to leave my team. But I knew I was supposed to be with you."

Except for Riley, all of the others were feeling a sudden, soul-deep relief. They had seen so much horror. It had seemed that all the rules were being broken, that everything was out of sync, that nothing made sense anymore. It had been hard for all of them to know the right thing to do.

But in the warmth of the old cabin, peace came over them. There was reason. There was a plan—each of them had been selected and had followed God's leadership. This assurance, this certainty, also had to do, Xanthe knew for a certainty, with the old man who sat at the table calmly examining them. He was not impressive, for he was small and his face was lined with age. The sweeping mustache and the hair were the pure white of long years. In Jesse Mitchell there did not seem to be the strength that one sensed in his grandson or in Riley Case. Still, something emanated from Jesse Mitchell, a power she sensed, yet could not quite define.

Jesse stood up and with a mischievous grin aimed at his wife said, "These womenfolk aren't the only ones who have chores, no matter what they say. Why don't you men come out with me and we'll cut some firewood and shoot us a pig."

"You have some pigs, Grandpa?" David asked with surprise.

Jesse answered, "Well, some pigs have been coming to visit. I've been putting some scraps out for them, about a half mile from here, so they'll make it part of their run. Must have been domestic pigs a long time ago, but some of the old hogs are growing their razorbacks. You know that, Kyle? Old pigs grow razors along their backs up in these hills if they run wild. And mean and vicious beasts they are, too. But whichever of you is the best shot can probably bring one down. They usually come early in the morning like this."

"Can me and Benny go, Mama?" Kyle asked, holding Benny the Blue Bear (who was one-eyed and definitely not blue) up for inspection.

"*May* Benny and I go?" Allegra corrected him automatically.

"Me, too!" Kyle pleaded. It did make sense to him.

David looked at Allegra. "Will it be all right, Allegra?"

"But—you just said those hogs are dangerous, didn't you, Dad Mitchell?"

Jesse smiled. "Yes. But I guess David and Mr. Case here look pretty dangerous to the hogs, too."

Allegra considered, then asked Riley, "You'll watch out for him, won't you?"

"Yes, ma'am," he said. "Always do."

"You watch him, too, David. All right, Kyle. You may go."

"Can I shoot the pig?" he asked earnestly.

"*May* I shoot the pig?" Allegra said stubbornly. "And these days, it wouldn't surprise me a bit."

"Uh, don't think so this time, hoss," David answered Kyle, pointing to Riley. "Right there's probably the best pig killer."

Riley nodded and quickly moved out of the cabin, followed by the others. As soon as they were outside, Jesse said, "I have one ax and a splitting maul. I used up most of the wood that was already down, and I burned it for the beacon. But thank the good Lord there's plenty of hands here now."

"Sure, Grandpa," David said. "Just leave it to us."

"Why don't you take that white oak over there? It isn't too big, and white oaks split easy as anything and burn real good," Jesse said.

"Merrill and I will chop firewood," David decided. "Riley can take down a pig without my help."

"I'll help," Kyle solemnly promised.

"Thanks, kid," Riley said, almost smiling.

"I'll just go along with you, Mr. Case," Jesse said, "and show you where the pigs are. Might even shoot two if you have a fancy repeating rifle."

"I have that," Riley said. "Just show me those razorbacks."

The day was soon gone. Merrill and David cut, split, and hauled enough firewood to last a week. Riley brought down two fat pigs, and he and David dressed them out. The women decided on the sleeping arrangements, with the Mitchells taking the single bedroom, the two women and Kyle upstairs in the tiny attic, and the men downstairs. All of them had sleeping bags, and Allegra and Xanthe collected soft, fragrant fir boughs to cover the hardwood floor. Though the sojourners had been sleeping in their sleeping bags among the pines and firs and oaks for weeks, somehow the same rough beds in the cabin seemed luxurious.

Reaching the relative safety of the cabin lightened their hearts. Riley Case even talked a little more. Their supper that night was fresh pork ribs that Riley cooked on an open fire outside, while the women fixed more biscuits and a huge blackberry cobbler. A festive air filled the room. Xanthe said nothing about Hot Springs, but David watched her eat ravenously and thought that some people would consider them as having hardships; yet the shelter of the cabin, the fresh food, and the company were soft living compared to conditions in the rest of the world.

"I've been picking loads of these wild blackberries for a long time," Noe said with satisfaction, watching the cobbler that bubbled on the woodstove. "We've got plenty of sugar, and they'll keep for a long time, cooked up in simple syrup. Thank the Lord for His abundance."

They all sat down, and Jesse turned to his grandson. "Then, David, you do just that."

David bowed his head and said a quick prayer, simple, very

much like that his grandfather had spoken earlier. When he glanced up, he saw that Riley had a strange expression on his face, somewhat puzzled and a little strained. *First time he's ever bumped into God,* David reflected.

They all ate heartily, speaking mostly of small, comforting things, like the lovely snow and how good a real fire smelled.

After the meal, David said, "Grandpa, I want us to have a Bible study."

"Why, that would be good," Jesse said at once. "Anybody that wants to stay, just sit right where you are. After we clear the table, we'll look into the Word of God."

The women cleared the table and washed the dishes while the men talked quietly of everyday things. When the women came back, they all sat down and discovered that there were only four Bibles, the two possessed by Jesse and Noe, the one that Merrill had carried faithfully, and the large, oversized one that Perry had treasured.

Allegra pulled her box up to the table, holding Kyle on her lap. He put his hand out on the Bible and said, "I like this book. It was Perry's." Looking over at Jesse, he stated solemnly, "Perry died."

Jesse did not answer, but studied the boy. His eyes lifted to Allegra, who added, "He died saving Kyle's life, Mr.—Dad Mitchell." Somehow it gave her a good feeling to call Jesse Mitchell "dad." She related briefly how the bite of the wolf caused the death of their young friend.

"I've thought about Perry a lot. It wasn't a natural thing," Merrill said, shaking his head. "That boy shouldn't have died."

"There are many unnatural things in this world right now," Jesse said quietly. He looked around the table and asked, "Anyone got something particular to study in the Word?"

It was a question that David Mitchell had heard often. One of the most treasured memories of his youth had been his grandfather's Bible studies. Great numbers of people had come, for Jesse

Mitchell's teaching drew people from everywhere. The studies always began with the same question: "What do you want to study?" Someone would say, "Justification." And Jesse would turn to the person on his left and say, "You turn to Romans, chapter 7, verse 15." To the next person, he would assign another scripture, perhaps from the Old Testament. He would go all the way around, assigning everyone a scripture, and then would begin by saying to the person on his left, "All right, read." After the scripture was read, he would speak. It had always been miraculous to David how his grandfather seemed to know every scripture and could tie them all together. Now David said, "I'd like to pick a subject."

"All right, grandson. What is it?"

"The end times."

A sudden silence fell over the group, and Jesse's eyes gleamed. "The end times! Well, I think that would be a fine study. Wish everyone had a Bible, but we'll do the best we can." He turned to Allegra. "Sister, why don't you turn to First John, chapter 2, verse 18." Xanthe huddled close, looking down at the big Bible with curiosity. She'd never seen such a book.

Allegra found the verse and put her finger on it, with Kyle doing the same. "I've got it, Dad Mitchell."

"All right, sister, read!"

Allegra read in a clear voice: "'Little children, it is the last time—'"

Jesse interrupted, "Now stop, sister, right there. That's the foundation of everything we need to know about what's happening. You'll hear preachers talk about *one of these days* the last times will come, but the apostle John was living in the last time. That's what he said. *It is the last time.* Now, read the rest of that verse, sister."

Allegra continued, "'It is the last time: and as ye have heard that antichrist shall come, even now are there many antichrists; whereby we know that it is the last time.'"

"There it is again," Jesse stated. "All of us are living in the last time *right now.* The church lived in the last time in the days of Martin Luther. It was the last time in the days of John the apostle . . ."

Riley sat apart, close to the fireplace, idly whittling small kindling splinters. But his eyes were watchful as Jesse moved from scripture to scripture. He was amazed at the ability of the old man, who apparently had memorized the entire Bible.

Finally Jesse asked if there were any questions.

Merrill looked uncertain, and then reluctant, but he finally spoke. "Brother Mitchell—there are many other teachings about the end times. It's—it's a little confusing."

Jesse smiled and brushed his mustache down. "You know, brother, people used to do charts and graphs and drawings and timetables and calendars and such. They all used to try to pick out the Antichrist from living men. They picked out Stalin, but he died. They picked out Hitler, but he died, too. The fact is, their antichrists kept dying off!" His sharp blue eyes glowed with merriment, but then he grew grave. "And that's the story of all of the antichrists, you see. They're all going to die."

He paused a moment, and the silence in the room grew thick. From far off came the thin howl of a wolf. Kyle visibly shivered, then drew closer to his mother.

"I don't think the book of Revelation is primarily prophetic," Jesse said slowly. "I think it's a pastoral book. There's prophecy, of course, no doubt about that. It comes and goes, but the pastoral remains." He leaned far up in his chair, like an eager teacher, and his hands were expressive. "You see, when you think you're at the end of everything, brothers and sisters, the book of Revelation is the place to go. When you come to the end of yourself, the end of all your dreams, when everything is tumbled about you, you make a beeline for Revelation!"

"But what about all the teachings we've heard over the years, Brother Mitchell?" Merrill persisted. "I mean, I've always heard that the book of Revelation told us what was going to happen in the future."

"That's right." Genevieve nodded. "Pastor Colfax once brought in a lecturer on Revelation. He had all kinds of charts and pictures of beasts and timetables. If I remember right, he said that all these things had to happen in order."

"Well, you have to be careful with teaching like that. For example," Jesse said kindly, "in the book of Revelation one section discusses herds of horses and locusts that are like scorpions. But the book of Revelation is a book of symbols. Anybody who makes those horses literal or those scorpions literal is pathetic, for a symbol is not the reality. The book speaks of Jesus as a lamb, but He doesn't run around on four feet and eat grass!"

Merrill said, "That Revelation man—what was his name, Genevieve? Lawson? Lawless? Something like that. Anyway, he said those scorpions in the book of Revelation were Scorpion helicopter gunships."

"Big, big error there," David said with an air of superiority. "The Scorpions have been out of service for three decades now. Your Mr. Lawson or whatever his name is needs to update himself on our technological advances."

"Wouldn't do him much good," Jesse said, sighing a little. "Us trying to make out the Bible to mean what we want it to mean is always a mistake. You must let God teach you Himself. Always. Study. Test the spirits. Find it in the Word of God."

David said in a troubled voice, "Still, Grandpa, these are hard times with harder times comin'. America—" He swallowed hard. "America may be gone. We—we don't even know about the rest of the world. But it sure seems that everything's going wrong. Bad wrong. In a hurry."

"Son, I guess you put your finger on what I think is the heart of the scripture about the end times. As I've said, it's always been the end times ever since John was preaching." Jesse held the Bible up high. "You go through the book of Revelation, and you find over and over and over again the same thing. God's people are coming under persecution, and then the Lord Jesus comes and rescues them. That doesn't happen just once at the end of time, folks. It happens in *every* generation. That's the comfort of this book . . . When God's people are persecuted, the Lord Jesus Christ will pull them out of it. Not after a thousand years or two thousand, but when they're in it. Why, what difference does it make to people whether they're being persecuted by the Jewish Sanhedrin or the Roman Empire or Fascists? Whatever it is, it's tribulation—and only Jesus can pull us out of it."

The Bible session went on for an hour more. Finally weariness caught up with the visitors, and the women went upstairs with Kyle. Noe went back to the single bedroom, but Jesse sat at the table for a long time reading the Scriptures.

Jesse was startled when Riley spoke up. The man hadn't said a single word during the Bible study, and though the room was small, Jesse had become so absorbed in his reading that he'd forgotten Riley was there.

"I guess I'll be in your crosshairs, won't I, Preacher?"

Jesse smiled and motioned to the empty rocker across from him. "Brother, it's not me who's aiming for you."

"Well, who is it then?" Riley asked, warily seating himself at the table.

"It's the Lord God almighty. So you don't have to worry about my beating you over the head."

Shifting in his seat uncomfortably, Riley clasped his large hands together and stared at them for a long time. Eventually he said, "I'm not here to join God's little army, Preacher. I came here because I want to be free. Free from the sorry government and the commissars and the stupid laws that keep men from being men."

"What brought you here? I mean right here to this exact place?"

"I decided to help these people, that's all, and I'll keep on helping them, and you, too, if you want. With food and shelter and things like that. It's—sort of a promise I made, and I'm going to stick by it."

Jesse nodded. "So you stand by your promises, do you?"

"A man should."

Jesse studied Riley, and the husky man looked back at him with something like bluster. Riley took a deep breath, held it, then expelled it. "There *were* two who died—besides that pilot. No one knows that but me. So how did you know, Preacher?"

"The Lord told me," Jesse said quietly. "I don't know why He told me unless it's to be a witness to you, son. Make no mistakes, I'm not a magician. I don't have any interest in doing magic tricks. Neither does the almighty God. If He does something that goes against natural laws, there's a reason for it—and usually that reason is to touch someone's heart and to bring him to Jesus Christ."

Riley drew his lips together in a thin line. "I don't see it quite like that, Preacher. All I see is that people died—and died horribly—and it looks like they died for your God." He ran his hands through his thick black hair. "That's not much of an attraction to me at this moment."

Jesse did not answer for a time, and when he did, his voice was soft as a summer breeze. "They made their decisions, young man, both of them. You see, that young man who died in the camp . . . what was his name?"

"His name was Perry. Perry Hammett. He was only seventeen."

"Yes, Perry. Well, he made a decision. A promise, you might say, and he stuck by it. He died, but he's with Jesus and the saints in heaven. Some might not view that as a tragedy. For sure he doesn't."

Riley thought on that a moment. "Maybe. But what about that other one? The one who was alone outside the camp."

Jesse stared into space and then answered slowly. "That poor young man thought he had made a decision. When he left the town, he started for the group, but somehow he never could quite commit himself to joining them. He could have caught up with them quite easily, couldn't he?"

"Yes, I suppose he could."

"*You* did when you made up your mind. I think, brother, he just got caught up in the shadowlands. Indecision and confusion got him. And then the old Devourer got him."

Riley sat very still. A log burned through and fell, showering sparks and startling him. He almost growled, "So Perry did the right thing, and he died. And that guy in the woods, he did nothing, and he died. But if you do the wrong thing—if you're on that other side—the bad guys—they're dying in Hot Springs right now."

Jesse leaned over and put his hands on Riley's clasped fists. His hands looked frail against the strong hands of the younger man. Surprise washed across Riley's face at the unexpected touch and the uncommon warmth of Jesse's hands.

"We're all going to die, son," Jesse said intently. "No choice about that. In this life we've got lots of choices every day all day, but all of us have only one life-or-death decision, just one—and that's how we spend our eternity."

Riley could see the love in the old man's eyes. He had not seen much love in his life. It drew him, but he was still unsure and a bit rebellious. Riley Case was a cautious man. He drew his hands back and shook his head, saying nothing.

"That's a decision you haven't made yet, son," Jesse said firmly. He got up, picked up his Bible, and started for the bedroom. Just before he entered, he turned his head and looked at Case. "But you soon will, Mr. Case. Soon *everyone* will!"

SEVEN

A TOUGH WIND tore down from the distant sere mountains, and the desert wanderer shivered and pulled the motley blanket closer around him. The loneliest of figures, a single man on the vastness of the treeless and barren plain, he lifted his head and sniffed as if with appreciation. The Milky Way was like a filmy veil studded with diamonds draped gracefully across the heavens. Such a spectacular view of the galaxies was one of the few beneficial side effects of the world going dark.

Captain Concord Slaughter found the inhospitable desert night bracing, even like a cleansing after the squalor and despondency of the Albuquerque refugee camp. He felt so invigorated, so light of body and mind, that immediately he felt guilty.

Stupid. Self-defeating reasoning. They can't be free until I figure out how to get them out. I can't figure out how to get them out unless I come out here and see for myself.

He walked in a straight line toward the nearest line of hills. His gait was odd; he walked fast, but he was taking small steps. After a while he unconsciously sped up into a long-limbed half-jog in his desperate straining to get away from the camp, looming like a ghastly rotten corpse behind him. The backlighting from Kirtland Air Force Base, a cheery glow directly to the east, somehow made the decrepit slum look even worse. As Slaughter walked, he never looked back at the sight.

He was jogging again. Cursing under his breath, he made himself slow down and start the peculiar quick mincing again, checking his watch, carefully shielding the green glow in the crystalline night.

Right on time. Big surprise for Germans to keep to a strict schedule . . .

The two helicopters came from behind him, making a wide loop around the refugee camp that was the southwest quadrant of Albuquerque. One was in front, one behind and slightly to the west. They flew low and slow. Great searchlights swept the ground in concentrated arcs.

Slaughter threw himself to the ground and pulled his poncho, which was actually a blanket, over him, completely covering his body from head to toe. This, he had found on his night surveillances the last four nights, was the hardest part. The searchlights always threw their harsh light all over him. He could see the glaring light plainly under the thin blanket, and it made him feel hot and cold at the same time. His muscles always tightened up to breaking point, expecting the .60 caliber shells from the machine guns mounted on the choppers to explode into his body at any moment.

But they never did. The lights always passed, the low roar of the helos always faded, leaving him freezing and exhausted.

Captain Slaughter, when the silence and darkness were well closed in around him again, got up and began his strange trek, staring at his watch and cursing under his breath like a rather crude White Rabbit.

He was checking his watch and watching his gait when the black figures rose up from the hard bare earth right in front of him. One grabbed his right arm, twisted, and swept his legs out from under him in a deadly swift motion. The other fell on him, pinning his other arm and clapping a hand across his mouth.

Slaughter, though much mended in the days since he'd been hurt, was still not in top form. If he had been, the two of them would never have been able to either sneak up on him or down him. Even at less than peak, however, he easily threw off the one attacker, who was much lighter and smaller than he, but couldn't get a good grip on the other, who was much heavier and stockier, and felt like a concrete piling. Neatly he flipped Slaughter and got him in a complicated arm-breaking, neck-stretching hold. "Just stay frosty, man," he said. "I'm trying not to hurt you."

"Try harder," Slaughter gasped.

The attacker jerked, then heaved off Slaughter's back as if he'd been burned. "Cap'n? Captain Slaughter? Aw, man, is it you?"

"Yeah," Slaughter said, rolling over and rubbing his neck. "Rio, you really need to work on your nonlethal submission techniques. You almost killed—"

The stocky sergeant almost smothered Slaughter in a bear hug. "It's Captain Slaughter, that's for sure. Cool as death."

Slaughter hated male hugs, but there was nothing he could do about it, short of breaking Rio's neck. "Man, oh man, Cap'n, am I glad to see you!" Rio was saying.

The smaller mugger came close and extended a black-gloved hand. "Hello, Captain Slaughter," Vashti Nicanor said coolly. "Later I would like to discuss that maneuver you just did. I've never been thrown six feet before."

"Sorry about that, ma'am. Colonel. But you two shouldn't have jumped me like that. Uh—why did you?"

A faint gray shadow, barely visible as he always was, spoke for the first time. "We've been watching you, Captain Slaughter," Zoan said. "But we didn't know it was you. We still don't."

"Huh? What'd you say?" Immediately Slaughter tried to adjust to Zoan's surreal conversational technique.

"That mask you're wearing," Zoan said patiently.

Slaughter was still wearing the black ski mask he'd borrowed from Victorine. "Oh, yeah . . . no camo makeup in the camp," Slaughter growled, pulling off the mask.

Rio and Vashti started talking, but from long years of habit, Slaughter took charge. He held up his hand for quiet, then checked his watch and looked around, squinting. "Might as well sit down here and jaw, I guess," he said. He sounded tired. "No sense in me trying to go farther tonight. Everyone belly-down and under your camo blankets."

Like teenagers at a sleepover, they all lay down in a loose circle, heads close together. Even though no one was around for miles, by much training they rarely spoke above a whisper.

"Permission, Captain," Rio said eagerly. "How about Lieutenant Fong? And Mitchell?"

"Fong's dead," Slaughter said bluntly. "We picked up a German pilot when we stole the Messerschmitt. He got the jump on me and nailed Fong." The raw bitterness in his tone was plain. No one said anything. Rio dropped his head and rubbed his eyes.

"What about Sergeant Mitchell, Captain Slaughter?" Zoan asked.

"Far as I know, he's okay. Last time I saw him he was winging toward Hot Springs."

"I hope he's not dead," Zoan said in his childlike way. "I liked him. I miss him."

"Yeah," Slaughter rasped. "I liked him, and I miss him too, Zoan. And Deacon Fong."

A long silence ensued. Slaughter couldn't see the faces of his soldiers, for Vashti applied camouflage makeup so expertly, they were almost invisible. Interestingly Zoan wore none, but somehow he blended into the earth, the sky, the very air. Slaughter wondered exactly what kind of man he was, but then he brought himself back to the problems at hand. "What are you people doing out here anyway?"

"Surveillance of the refugee camp," Vashti answered, her voice tight. "We started it last month. We had to do something. We had to have a mission. This is it. The beginning, at least."

"Darmstedt? And Colonel Ben-ammi? They're all right, are they?"

"They're okay, Captain Slaughter," Vashti assured him. "They're on the same mission to Santa Fe."

Slaughter's slow gaze slid to Zoan. "They have anybody with them?"

"He's our guide and our front man, Captain," Rio said defensively. "He's like some kind of—of—spirit. But a smart one. No, that's not it. He's kind of like Cat. He can sneak up on and see and smell anything. Course, Zoan's not a killer like Cat. I guess he's—"

"Never mind, Rio," Slaughter said with exasperated affection. "I think I understand what Zoan's here for. The other team have a guide?"

"My friend Cody Bent Knife takes care of them," Zoan offered.

Slaughter thought this was mildly amusing—Zoan and a nineteen-year-old renegade Apache were "taking care" of Fire Team Eclipse. Neither Vashti nor Rio objected, however, so Slaughter went on, "Okay, so what's your situation here? You ride from Chaco? And then what?"

"Camp in those hills," Vashti answered, jutting her chin toward them. "We stay two or three nights. This is our third tour. We've been watching you for two nights, Captain. I decided that if you came out of the camp tonight, we'd try to make contact."

"Yeah, you did make contact, Colonel," Slaughter muttered. "So what's your plan? What's your mission objective?"

"Neither team has formulated one yet," Vashti answered in a professional tone. "We're just observing right now. We really wanted to talk to someone who could tell us about what's going on, but so far no one's left either Albuquerque or Santa Fe."

"They putting refugees in Santa Fe, too?"

"Yes, sir, thousands of them. Just like they have here. It must be making for very crowded conditions."

"You don't know the half of it," Slaughter said quietly. "And I don't have time to talk about it right now. So what you're saying is that you've just got your own supplies for two days?"

Vashti sounded mystified. "Yes, Captain. And you know Chaco's a two-day ride from here."

"Yeah . . . that doesn't help me . . . and I haven't got much time." He checked his watch again.

Rio couldn't stand it. "Sir, what's up? Why don't we just trek, Captain? We can go light on the food and water, and take turns on foot. Get you back to Chaco in three days, tops!"

Slaughter shook his head. "No. I've got to go back to the camp."

"But why, sir?"

"Because I'm not leaving until I can figure out how to get some people out. Some friends of mine."

"Just bring 'em on, man!" Rio grunted. "You've already figured the patrols, and you can make it to the hills in one night."

"I could," Slaughter said slowly, "and maybe other *men* could."

There was a stunned silence. Then Rio whistled softly. "Oh, I get it. It's a woman . . . you gotta figure out how to get a woman outta there. That's tough."

"Actually," Slaughter said dryly, "the woman's not the problem. As tough as she is, she'd probably beat me to the hills. And she probably would've beat you two down, not like some ninety-pound weaklings."

"Then what's the problem?" Vashti asked.

"The problem is her daughter," Slaughter replied. "She's—little and—kinda—delicate, I guess you'd say. No way she could cover the ground in one night." He sighed, a sound of exaggerated exasperation. "And then there's all her orphans she's adopted. She won't leave without them. An old woman, a little boy, and a teenage boy who's kinda gotten lost in never-never land."

"Where's that?" Zoan asked, mystified.

"Uh—I mean he's mentally unable to cope right now," Slaughter said. "He's—not really all there."

"Oh, I see. He's like me," Zoan said thoughtfully.

Surprisingly a low, throaty chuckle sounded from Vashti. "Zoan, there is no one like you, my friend."

"Thank you," he said politely. Vashti had been teaching him the finer points of polite conversation. It didn't exactly apply here, but that hardly mattered.

"Lemme get this straight, with your permission, Captain," Rio said in his careful way. "You want us to arrange an escape for you, a woman, two kids, an old lady, and a crazy teenager?"

"Uh—yeah."

Rio snorted. "I think we should just get the team together, get those crazy Indians, and attack the base. Kill all the Goths. I say that'll solve everyone's problems."

"Yeah? Whatcha gonna do, Rio, throw rocks at 'em?"

"Don't suggest it, Captain," Vashti intoned. "He'd do it. He's been wanting to attack the base ever since our first recon. Just me, him, and Zoan."

"Vintage Rio," Slaughter agreed. "No, Sergeant Valdosta. Just no. We've got to get my people out of there. And I mean ASAP. That place is going from bad to really bad fast."

"I assume you're saying there's no way to walk them out, just like you've been doing every night," Vashti said thoughtfully. "No, you're right. It can't be done by children or an older woman. It's about thirty klicks to those hills, Captain Slaughter. It'd be tough for even you to make it in one night, with having to allow downtime for the patrols."

"I know, I know. You've been watching me out here mincin' around on tiny feet, trying to see if a girl could make it. If I couldn't do it tonight, I was going to give up on Plan A. And obviously I didn't make it far enough," Slaughter said impatiently. "But we've got to think of something, people. And I mean now, tonight."

"Captain, are they hurting people?" Zoan asked in his oddly colorless voice.

Slaughter hesitated before answering in a rough voice. "They weren't until today. I mean, that place is a pit. There's rotten food and no water, and the sanitation is just a hole in the ground. It's cold and we don't have firewood. But at least they were feeding us, and they gave us pretty good clothes and blankets. But today . . . they trotted out a couple who they said had tried to escape the Isolation Facility and infiltrate the regular refugee camp in the city."

"What's the Isolation Facility?" Vashti demanded.

"It's the place where our beloved commissars are guarding the bad guys—the ones responsible for all our problems. The Christians. You know, the right-wing fundamentalists, the extremists, the militant dunkheads."

"That's not true," Zoan said in a wounded tone.

"We know, Zoan," Slaughter said patiently. "I was being sarcastic."

"Oh."

"And they're being persecuted?" Vashti asked.

"You betcha," Slaughter growled. "That couple . . . they branded them."

"What?" Vashti cried, then lowered her voice. "Branded them? You—you—mean—"

"Yeah, with a red-hot branding iron, Colonel. A cross on the left cheek. Rumor was that they had three kids . . . and the kids turned them in."

"Oh, no," Vashti moaned softly. "Oh, no, this is—this is—"

"Bad. It's real bad," Slaughter supplied. "So what are we gonna do about it?"

They were silent for a long time.

Then Zoan's quiet voice sounded in the darkness. "I've got an idea . . ."

The slight bend in the trickle of the Rio Grande had come to be called Laundress's Leg, for the women who came to wash their clothes, beating them against a wide, time-smoothed rock overhanging the muddy water. A woman, tired and drab looking, was just finishing up her wash. She'd been there all afternoon, pounding and rinsing and going through it all again on the pitifully few worn clothes she had. Behind her, a young girl—probably her daughter—waited listlessly. Both of them were gaunt and seemed to be unable to summon the energy to talk.

One of the two commissar perimeter guards who had passed them several times on their rather sketchy patrols remarked, "She won't be taking the trouble much longer."

"They never do," the other sneered. "About two weeks in the camp, and washing clothes kinda goes down to the bottom of the list."

It was true. The people who had been in the camp for more than a couple of weeks were usually sick or malnourished or too weary for hygiene. Most of them were all of those things.

The guards, two men, hesitated on their round, staring at the woman. She seemed not to know they were there. One of them, a dark, surly-looking man who hadn't shaved in two days, squinted at the riotous indigo-and-coral horizon, the last moments of a glorious sunset. "Be dark soon. Think we ought to hustle 'em along?"

"Nah," the other, a sharp-looking young man, replied. "They aren't going anywhere except to crawl back to whatever shanty or shack they're holed up in." They walked on.

Neither the woman nor the girl appeared to notice their passing. The woman kept up her monotonous washing rhythm, even though, as always in the desert, the darkness was closing swiftly.

Only a few moments after the commissars disappeared, an odd and beautiful thing happened. An entire herd of wild mustangs—an old gray stallion leading three dozen or so yearlings, mares, and foals—galloped up to the river and began to drink.

The woman, suddenly filled with life and standing tall, her voice strong and urgent, hissed to the girl. Slender and elflike, the girl jumped up and ran to the nearest house, which was really a shell of an adobe cottage that had died of old age and neglect. It had no roof and only three standing walls. But out of the darkness inside she came running, holding a small child's hand. Behind them, an old woman dressed in black from head to toe hobbled, and a blank-faced boy followed her.

Suddenly on the other side of the river, soldiers in desert fatigues materialized as mere dappled shadows, blending in perfectly with the earth-tone variegations of the evening and the horses' coats. If one looked very, very hard—or if one could see in the dark, as some could—he might see another fainter, even less substantial figure who moved so quietly and easily that he seemed to be woven of the very air.

The tall woman was joined by a big sandy-haired man. As soon as the four reached the couple, they all crossed, wading so as not to splash too much. The big man carried the thin young girl.

Somehow, by a trick of the eye or wizardry of the mind, within a few moments an onlooker might have seen only the herd of horses, calmly watering in the old river.

The stallion, his coat the color of thin wood smoke, raised his head and made a knickering sound. As if they were bound together, all of the horses raised their heads alertly, then turned as one.

By the time they'd traveled a few feet, only a small dusting of the fine desert sand could be seen in the desert twilight.

EIGHT

"ALIA, WE ARE going to freeze to death in here."

President Luca Therion's voice sounded hollow and weak; the clanging echoes of his words sounded more alive. He seemed half-dead in appearance, too. His fine, sensitive features were cavernous; his black hair was dull, his eyes sunken. In startling contrast, his mistress, Minden Lauer, looked as lovely and serene as ever. She floated; she smiled; her skin was translucent and white, her hands soft, the nails polished, her body a study in perfection. In some ways, her apparent well-being was more jarring to observe than the wretched condition of her companions.

Alia's response to the president was slow and stuporous. Her mouth was numb from the cold, and her brain seemed to be slowly numbing, too. "I'm sorry, sir. But this is our best hope of getting out of here alive."

Minden, a ghostly pale shimmer huddled in the corner, said softly, "We're going to live, Luca. I know it. He has told me."

Luca made no reply, and of course, Alia didn't. She was certain now that Minden was irretrievably insane, with this obsession about Tor von Eisenhalt and her powerful companion-spirits. But Minden had remained calm, so at least she wasn't dangerous to herself or anyone else. At times Alia had thought that she had seen a look of terrible strain mar her perfect features for scant seconds. Once, when Minden was staring blankly into the fire, chanting softly under her breath, Alia had observed her face blanch into a ghastly expression of fright, and her graceful hands had clenched into gnarled knots. But almost immediately she was Minden, the serene Lady of Light, again, and Alia had scorned her perceptions again as mild delusions induced by lack of sleep and intense stress.

They were huddled in a maintenance access tunnel, facing double four-inch-thick steel doors, the gray paint peeling in ragged strips. To their backs was a small electrical access room, long abandoned. A passage stretched out to their left, with copper conduit overlaid with a mucous-green patina and with pitted concrete water pipes tangled and snaky overhead. A continuous echo of water dripping slowly somewhere down the tunnel grated on their ears. It was dank and smelled of sour metal and mildew.

Minden had brought a white pillar candle and had lit it as soon as they'd hidden there, but roguish icy drafts kept putting it out. Without speaking Alia had turned on her flashlight—the last 1.5 volt batteries were already dying in it—and had upended it on the damp floor. The light was weak and jaundiced, but it was still much, much better than the dark. Vaguely Alia wondered how she would ever find the way out without even a flashlight, but she couldn't face the total darkness yet. Not yet.

"What are we doing here?" Luca burst out. It was quiet. No sounds of angry mobs above filtered down to them. "Why did we come down here now?"

Alia sighed heavily. She had already explained this carefully to Luca and Minden, but then neither of them seemed to be processing correctly. "You know, sir, that I, my two commissars, and three of your Secret Service detail are the only security people left. We can't keep four snipers on the roof and a guard on you anymore. None of us have slept more than two hours at a time for weeks now. So I decided to put Kev and Bennie as snipers on the roof tonight, and I have placed the three agents at the entrances to this basement."

"But why do you think the mob's going to break through tonight?" Luca hissed. "Why now?"

"Because, sir," Alia went on through gritted teeth, "they're going to see that there are only two snipers. That leaves two gates uncovered. And it won't take them long to figure out that Kev and Bennie are no sharpshooters. They'll break through, sir, and it's going to be tonight."

"But—but surely you could have found a better hiding place?"

With the last tattered remains of her patience, Alia explained, "This is not just a hiding place, sir. That tunnel is an exit. It's a long and torturous route, but I can take us out when the time comes."

"Then let's get out of here right now!" Luca blustered. He raised his voice, and the echoes were so mocking that he flinched.

Alia replied, "No, sir. Mr. President, you're going to need all of us to guard you and Minden, you know. I have orders for all to make the best defense they can, but to fall back in good order and join us here. Then I'll lead us out of here. There's a manhole access out past the fence, and we should be able to slip out."

Though the noise was actually very faint, it sounded obscenely loud to the three desperate people in their dismal hole. They heard thumps, shouts, and the faint thunder of people running. Alia's mouth was suddenly so dry, she almost choked. Though it was ludicrous, all three of them stared upward with wide, frightened eyes.

The distant babble became more distinct. They could distinguish between men's gruff shouts and women's high calls, and the reverberation of running grew more intense. Simultaneously they heard the distinctive chop of two M-60's, one distant, one close.

"Those are the agents," Alia whispered. She took out her .38 service pistol and went down on one knee, pointing it at the door. To her surprise, her hands and arms were steady, though her ears were thrumming and the blood in her chest was pumping crazily.

"C'mon, c'mon," she grated.

A woman screamed, loud and long and close. It was cut off

eerily. More staccato thumps of machine-gun fire. A man's voice raised hysterically, calling the same name or word over and over. The din of a furious mob raged all around them, echoing horribly, multiplying geometrically up and down the tunnel, until Alia thought she would go raving mad.

In an instant, in an eye-blink, the tumult stopped.

Dead silence.

The flashlight went out.

Dead dark.

Minden, without a sound, fell to the floor, unconscious. She looked like a corpse that had been drained of all blood. Luca bent over her, picked her limp body up in his arms, and buried his face in her hair, shutting his eyes tightly. He, too, made not a single sound.

Alia couldn't swallow, and, as if she were observing someone else, she realized that she wasn't breathing. Her hands were clutched around the pistol so tightly that the muscles in her fingers were going into knifelike spasms. But she couldn't loosen her grip. She couldn't move at all.

Like a listless leaf floating down, down into a deep abyss, Alia had only a single forlorn thought: *Am I dead?*

By some of the same infernal magic, both heavy doors swung open silently, smoothly. Count Tor von Eisenhalt walked in.

Still Alia did not move. Still she thought she was dead. Frozen perhaps in some hell where she stayed cold and frozen and muscles screaming and Tor smiling . . .

As always, he cut a stunning figure. His black uniform was perfect, his presence commanding, his careless masculine grace accentuated by a long black wool overcoat draped over his wide shoulders. One raven's-wing eyebrow rose sardonically as he removed his black leather gloves, finger by finger. "It's been a difficult time for you, I see," he remarked casually. "But is that any reason to snub your old friend?"

Behind her, Alia heard the most horrible sounds of low moaning, a mindless keening. Then something hit her with such force and quickness that she was knocked over sideways. Minden was crawling by her like a pale rodent, scrabbling and clawing. Luca had risen, his legs visibly trembling, pressed against the wall. Somehow Alia rose, too, dropping her pistol from lifeless fingers.

"Tor, Tor, my lord, my lord, help me, save me," Minden was gibbering, curled up on her knees and pressing her face against his dully gleaming boot.

He glanced down at her, pleased. "I have. Now control yourself, Minden."

With a quickly cut-off choking noise, Minden stopped ranting and grew still, though she didn't move from her fetal position.

Like a wooden marionette, Luca danced shakily over to Tor. For a moment he looked as if he were extending his hand for a bizarre handshake, then he dropped his arm. His eyes were locked with Tor's, and he shuffled and jiggled forward until he was even with him. Then he toppled over, a terrible stiff-legged, unguarded fall onto his face.

Alia's eyes felt as if they were starting out of the sockets as she looked at Luca. He was still breathing, but a dull ribbon of blood seeped slowly from his face.

"Alia . . ."

The sound was as cold as the winter wind in the most desolate barren plain and as haunting as far-off music in a minor key.

"Alia, come here." He smiled; he seemed happy. Somehow, one corner of Alia's mind gnawed that this was worse than deadly threats.

Yet she walked to him. Her steps were steady, though her heartbeat and breath were not.

He held out his hand.

Eventually . . . inevitably . . . she kissed it.

NINE

SERGEANT RIO VALDOSTA verbally expressed exactly what Con Slaughter was thinking at the moment: "Man, it's great to have the team back together again." He said it with a certain awed reverence that wasn't lost on Con. Suddenly Valdosta looked at the fire team gathered around the huge bonfire. "Except for Mitchell, of course." His gaze went deep into the blaze in front of him, and he whispered, "And Deac."

Con's gut wrenched at the sadness in Valdosta's tone. He was moodily trying to figure out how to dispel the gloom when Ric Darmstedt changed the subject for him.

"I sure hope Mitchell's all right, Cap'n."

"I'm sure Mitchell's fine. He's Fire Team Eclipse; he can take care of himself."

Darmstedt grinned, his white teeth gleaming. "Knowing Mitchell, he's probably taking care of half of Arkansas by now."

"*All* of Arkansas," Vashti Nicanor added. She was seated on a large rock beside Darmstedt. She usually kept a careful physical distance from the man. The evening was turning bitterly cold, but somehow she could sense his body heat distinctly separate from the fire's heat. Inexplicably she shivered.

Her trembling wasn't lost on Darmstedt. "You all right, Colonel? Warm enough?"

"I'm fine," she returned curtly.

"All right, people," Slaughter announced, "down to the business at hand. Colonel Ben-ammi, we know the story at the Isolation Facility in Albuquerque. It's too bad you and Darmstedt couldn't make any contact in Santa Fe, but I'd bet my nine the same thing's going on there."

Ben-ammi nodded somberly. "Sadly I agree." Suddenly his tough features hardened, and with force he threw the prairie chicken thighbone he'd been gnawing on into the fire. "This is unthinkable! Unbearable! What can we do?"

"What *should* we do?" Slaughter countered. "I look around; I see people here who need help. I see kids, I see old people, and they're all going to be hungry and cold this winter. I see hundreds, maybe even thousands more like 'em to the east. Do we stay here and tend to these we know and care about? Do we rescue more? And do what with them?" A frustrated growl escaped his throat as he rose to his feet and began to pace around the fire.

Needlessly Darmstedt commented, "That's a lot of questions, sir."

"That no one has answers to, Lieutenant! And on top of everything else, we're *soldiers,* for crying out loud! We're supposed to be fighting this—this invasion of our country. We're not baby-sitters. We're the first line of defense!" He stopped pacing, leaned toward Valdosta and Darmstedt, and nearly shouted, "Do you people understand that?"

"Yes, sir," both men chimed in, and both straightened their posture considerably.

"Captain—" Ben-ammi tried to speak, but to no avail, for Slaughter was on a true rant.

"And do you know what else I see when I look east, every night in my nightmares? I see Fort Carson, and I see Cheyenne Mountain right by it. I see comrades-in-arms who aren't with us anymore." Slaughter's lips tightened into a line, and he took a deep breath in an attempt to calm himself.

In all the months that Vashti had spent with Fire Team Eclipse, she'd never seen the captain lose control as she'd just witnessed. Not even the horror of the Fort Carson bombing had provoked such an outburst. *But that had been war, something he could deal with. This "baby-sitting," as he calls it, is much different.*

Silence ruled the little group for a few moments, then Colonel Ben-ammi said quietly, "The sad truth is, Captain, that you're in command. Such is the burden of command."

Slaughter fixed Ben-ammi with an intense stare, then said tightly, "Yeah. Yeah, I'm in command." His burly arm swept around the group. "I'm in command of my fire team. I can handle deciding the fate of each and every one of you. That's my job. It's deciding the fate of these other people, the civvies, that gives me grief." His large frame seemed to slump a little bit. "They didn't sign on for this . . . any of this."

"But they are here," Vashti stated evenly. "And it's a soldier's job to protect innocent civilians, is it not? You say you are the first line of defense, no?" She reached down and scooped up a handful of sand. "Defend this? I think not, Captain. This does not make a country." She dropped the sand and wiped her hand on her thigh, nodding toward the cliff where the helpless people were huddled in their caves. "*They* make a country what it is."

Slaughter watched her thoughtfully, not commenting.

Rio spoke up: "Yeah, Cap'n, I gotta admit I've always wanted to just go find the nearest Goths and start shootin', you know? Die in a blaze of glory and all that. But now . . . these people . . . like old Benewah Two Color, ain't he a kick in the pants? Not to mention Zoan. And your friends, Mrs. Thayer and that pretty little girl, Dancy—oh, and that old woman Lystra Palermo, now she's a cutter! Bosses those wild Indians around like they're little kids! Sure can tell she was a tough schoolteacher back in the Stone Age. She's gotta be a hundred years old."

"She's sixty-eight," Slaughter told them. "Her husband died

forty years ago. Can you imagine being alone for forty years? Longer than I've been alive."

"What about that teenage boy, Captain Slaughter?" Darmstedt asked. "What's Dancy call him—Pip? Now there's a sad case if I ever saw one. Kid can hardly even feed himself, and he looks terrified all the time. And what about that little Torridon Carlisle? Only eight years old and orphaned. He handles it pretty well, though. He's got some guts for a little kid."

"This is truth," Ben-ammi agreed. "Eight years old and so grave and dignified. He is much like a midge."

The team, including Vashti Nicanor, looked at him blankly. Then Darmstedt burst out laughing. "A midget! That's right, Colonel, he's just like a thirty-year-old man, only little!"

This broke up the worried tension a little, just as Ben-ammi knew it would. Even Slaughter had to smile. Ben-ammi said to himself, "Midget, midget . . . I must remember this word."

"Yeah, you're sure to use that one a lot, sir," Rio snorted.

The sun was dropping behind the western tip of their world, and they all watched the majestic sight. A curtain of bone-white clouds ribbed along the horizon became tinged pale yellow, then the ultimate vermilion, and finally the tattletale gray of dusk.

As he watched, Con Slaughter knew he should be enjoying the daily spectacle, but his thoughts were turned to more pragmatic, disturbing things. Every evening he saw the sun setting, and he couldn't help wondering endlessly about the West.

What must it be like in those congested co-ops of the Los Angeles and Bay areas? Violent crime had been reduced since the barbaric 1900s and with the coming of the commissars to usher in the Man and Biosphere Project. But that was before *this.* What kind of disorder and rioting would there be among those dark dwellings jammed with people without electricity? Would the commissars be able to keep order? Or was there only the raging chaos of finding that next meal or next sip of purified water?

And what about the military? There were ten thousand servicemen and -women at Twenty-Nine Palms alone. Was that enormous base still standing, or was it a pile of rubble and bones like Fort Carson?

The *not knowing* was like a splinter in Slaughter's brain.

With the coming of darkness came the biting cold of the desert and its unique nocturnal sounds. Slaughter shook off the helpless feelings of dread and turned to his people. "Okay, Fire Team Eclipse, are we ready for dawn? Everybody know where and what and up to specs?"

All of the small population of Chaco Canyon knew what Fire Team Eclipse was going to do, even though they hadn't said anything to anyone. It was a ceremony private to them, but that, by its nature, must be presented to the world. They didn't want anyone to help them, and they didn't want anyone to join them. They made their plans in private for the warrior who had left them.

Rio sighed. "It's a sobbin' shame we don't have the proper weapons for the honor guard." He was mourning the loss of Captain Slaughter's 12-gauge shotgun as much as Deac had mourned his helicopter. David Mitchell had the only other shotgun, his grandfather's 20-gauge single-barrel Remington, and he had it with him in Arkansas. The only weapons the team had left were their 9 mm personal side arms.

"Yeah, I'm gonna get that gun back before I die," Slaughter growled. "Don't know how. No telling where it is now . . . I wonder where they're stashing everyone's private arms . . ." He suddenly looked into space, startled. "Hey, I just thought of something—can't believe I haven't thought of it before! Los Alamos! Rio—Ric—you think the Goths would take that out?"

"Why, heck no!" Ric said eagerly. "With all that research stuff and no tellin' what kind of biowarfare gadgets and—"

"Yeah . . . yeah!" Rio jumped up, very excited. "That place had security almost as good as NORAD! Lotsa firearms and stuff for us there, Captain!"

Slaughter sighed. "Another possible mission. We've only got about a million or so that we can try."

Ben-ammi said kindly, "We're all tired, Captain Slaughter, and you especially. You were injured, yes? In Florida?"

"Aw, just a couple of scratches."

"That is not what Mrs. Thayer tells me," Ben-ammi returned sagely. "And the food in the isolation camp was probably not too nutritious, eh? I think you need to rest down."

"Rest up," Slaughter corrected him wearily. "And I think you're right. I know everyone makes better decisions when he's well rested. Anyway, we all set for dawn?"

They began double-checking their plans with military precision.

Zoan appeared out of nowhere, as he seemed to have done from his birth. He materialized soundlessly out of the darkness by the fire.

"Captain Slaughter?"

"Yes, Zoan, what is it?"

"Can I come with you?"

"But, Zoan, this is . . ." Slaughter stopped. This was a team thing, a very private Fire Eclipse ceremony, and everyone else had understood this as the team prepared. But Zoan was not everyone else; he was in a class by himself. He had no perception of nuance—at least, not the usual human kind—so Slaughter lost his impatience with him immediately. Now that he considered the quiet young man, he reflected that in some weird way, Zoan was a very comforting and peaceful person to be with. "Well, Zoan, we have a certain ceremony we do at times like this. It's for soldiers, for us to . . . perform. But—if you would—maybe you'd like to—um—say a prayer?"

Zoan considered this. "You mean, out loud?"

"That's what I had in mind. You're not shy about it, are you?"

"No. I've just never done it before. Out loud. But, okay, I can do that. I'd like to do that. But what I really wanted to do was sing a song."

"Sing—" Slaughter once again found himself at a loss for words while talking to this strange young man. Visions of Zoan singing "Here We Go Round the Mulberry Bush" or maybe some UR rock song came to him. But Zoan looked so hopeful, Slaughter couldn't bear to disappoint him. "Sure, Zoan. You can sing if you want to."

Zoan nodded. "Good. 'Cause that's one reason why I'm here, you know. To sing."

"You are?" As always, Slaughter was confused about whether Zoan's conversation was very deep and meaningful or whether it was nonsense from Zoan's odd mind. Zoan was opaque at times, but he was rarely nonsensical. You just had to listen to him. Slaughter moved closer to him so that only he could hear Slaughter's words. "Zoan? Can I ask you a question?"

"Sure."

Slaughter searched his face, his incredible eyes. "You say one reason you're here is to sing. Well, I don't really understand that, but I believe it. The thing is, do you—can you—see, uh, I'm wondering if somehow you can see—you know, kind of like you knew about Deac—about the rest of us . . . that is, what I'm trying to get at is—"

"Are you asking me if I know why you're all here?"

"Uh, yeah. I guess so. I think so."

Zoan frowned. "That's a hard question."

"Yeah, I suppose it is."

Zoan thought for a long time, his dark eyes unfocused. "I see some—things. It's hard for me to say it, Captain Slaughter. I can see it, but I can't hardly say it right."

Slaughter swallowed hard with tension. "I know, Zoan, but . . . could you try, please? Take your time."

"All right." Another long silence.

Slaughter was so breathless with anticipation that a popping twig in the fire made him start.

Finally, with difficulty, Zoan said, "I know why we're *all* here. We were brought here by God, for His purpose."

"That's . . . not quite accurate, Zoan," Slaughter said gently. "I brought my team here on orders from my commanding officer, on a mission that he set for us. God didn't have anything to do with it."

"Yes, He did. But I know you can't see that right now. And, Captain Slaughter, that's why it's so hard for me to tell you. You can't see right now. You're blind. Almost everyone here is. But that's exactly why God brought us here, you know? So we'll see, see real good, like I do."

Slaughter mulled this over, then gave up. "Well, thanks, Zoan, but that's not quite what I was trying to figure out. I need to know what to do, what to tell my team to do, what is—the right thing to do. I just thought maybe you'd—advise me, I guess."

Zoan's pupils grew noticeably, even in the face of the roaring fire. Desperately he said, "But, Captain Slaughter, that's exactly what I was trying to tell you. I can't tell you what to do. I don't know whether you're supposed to go kill Goths, like Mr. Rio says, or hunt for food, or stay here and protect us, or go back to Albuquerque and get some more people—that's not for me to see. That's for *you* to see. That's the thing that God has set for you to do. And until you can see, and know Him, you won't *ever* know. So that's why you're here, in this place, in this time. To decide your path. And the only advice I can give you is that you choose God's path . . . because there's only one other one . . . and that's—that's—" Zoan's gaze focused somewhere over Slaughter's shoulder, and his face slowly filled with pain. "If you take the other one, Captain Slaughter, you'll never see. You'll always be blind. Forever."

In the early morning steel-blue light just before dawn, all the occupants of Chaco Canyon emerged from their caves.

Despite the murky light, as they made their way to the base of the two-hundred-foot pinnacle, they could clearly see the top. Rio Valdosta, Ric Darmstedt, Darkon Ben-ammi, and Vashti Nicanor stood in a ruler-straight line at attention. Directly centered in front of them was Concord Slaughter. As they gathered, Slaughter stabbed a pole into the ground. Flying from it was an American flag and the pennant of the 101st Airborne, the rampant Screaming Eagle.

Victorine's thoughts and sympathy went out to Captain Con Slaughter. She thought she knew the pain he was going through as he said good-bye to one of his own—not only a fellow Airborne comrade, but one of his *own.* A life for which he'd taken personal responsibility—undoubtedly, in his eyes, a *huge* responsibility. If she knew one thing about Con Slaughter, it was that he was a proud man. What could be going through his mind right now? That he was a failure? Victorine suspected this was so, for that was exactly how she'd felt after her mother had been killed. Con had never spoken of the details of Fong's death, but Victorine suddenly sensed that even if Con had been a hundred miles away when it happened, he would still blame himself. She certainly had and still did.

"It's cold," muttered Lystra Palermo, an older woman dressed in black from head to toe, much like a Muslim woman. She and the mute, almost catatonic teenage boy that Dancy called Pip filed behind Dancy much like the soldiers behind Con Slaughter.

"You should have stayed by the fire, Mrs. Palermo," Victorine said gently.

A sharp gaze fixed Victorine. "They're honoring a fallen hero, Ms. Thayer. A little cold won't stop me from being here at this place of honor. I was just commenting on the weather, that's all."

"Yes, ma'am." Victorine had yet to figure out Mrs. Palermo. A former schoolteacher, she seemed to be from the old school: full of sharp retorts that left one cringing, yet sometimes revealing incredible kindness.

Ten yards to their left, Niklas Kesteven stood stonily in the predawn, his large head raised toward the soldiers. With surprise he felt the hand of Gildan Ives slip into his. After a glance at her and a moment's hesitation, he let it stay. Her head was bowed, so she didn't meet his eyes, but she moved closer to him, obviously grateful. Gildan was a lonely woman.

The gathering could see the team bow their heads, and the slim, small figure of Zoan, standing a little away from the soldiers, led them in a prayer. His voice, though seemingly insipid, carried down to the crowd below. They couldn't hear the words, but they could hear his tone, a mere whisper on the cold breeze.

As the first crescent of scarlet sun showed on the flat eastern horizon, Con Slaughter called out, "Present arms!"

The four soldiers behind him drew their 9 mm pistols, for they had no proper rifles to present the honor, and aimed at the rising sun.

Slaughter shouted, "Fire!"

It sounded like one single shot, then was repeated over and over as it echoed throughout the canyon. As one, the soldiers pulled the deadly arms close to the chest, pointing skyward.

"Fire!"

Another loud *crack!*

"Fire!"

Their fallen comrade, Deacon Fong, had had a hero's salute, with honor guard.

Zoan began to sing, and it was miraculous, for his voice was a pure, strong tenor. The crowd below could hear him clearly as he sang this most difficult of songs perfectly. The soldiers stood at knifelike attention, saluting. Victorine and Dancy placed their hands over their hearts; Niklas and Gildan were slower, but they did the same. Cody Bent Knife, standing beside Benewah Two Color, saw the older man follow suit. Cody set his strong jaw, but then he, too, placed his hand over his heart and bowed his head with sorrow. After all was said and done, it had been his America, too.

Oh! say, can you see,
By the dawn's early light,
What so proudly we hailed at the twilight's last gleaming?

Whose broad stripes and bright stars, thro' the perilous fight,
O'er the ramparts we watched,
Were so gallantly streaming?

And the rockets' red glare,
The bombs bursting in air,
Gave proof thro' the night
That our flag was still there!

Oh! say does that star-spangled banner yet wave—
O'er the land of the free
And the home of the brave?

Part II

COCKATRICE'S EGGS AND SPIDER'S WEB

They hatch cockatrice' eggs, and weave the spider's web: he that eateth of their eggs dieth, and that which is crushed breaketh out into a viper. Their webs shall not become garments, neither shall they cover themselves with their works: their works are works of iniquity, and the act of violence is in their hands. Their feet run to evil, and they make haste to shed innocent blood: their thoughts are thoughts of iniquity; wasting and destruction are in their paths. The way of peace they know not; and there is no judgment in their goings: they have made them crooked paths: whosoever goeth therein shall not know peace.

—Isaiah 59:5–8

Foul whisperings are abroad: unnatural deeds
Do breed unnatural troubles.

—Doctor of Physic, from Macbeth by William Shakespeare

TEN

IT WAS THE TUNNEL AGAIN, the tunnel that never ended, that smelled of mold and black water, and the flashlight was dead, and it was dark, and Alia was the only one who knew the way out. She struggled, silent, her eyes aching with the strain of trying to penetrate the cold darkness and stay close to Tor. Tor was leading them, but Alia kept trying to say, "You're not going the right way . . . this isn't the way out . . . we're lost . . . we're lost . . ."

In the dream she couldn't talk, or at least, the words she said made no sound. As she fought her way up through the layers of sleep pushing her down and smothering her, she managed to make a grunting panic noise. Instantly a cool, dry hand was lightly touching her forehead.

Her eyes flew open, though she still couldn't move. She thought it was another nightmare, the doctor nightmare, but no, Doctor was real. Wasn't he?

From the shadows beyond the heavy red velvet curtains surrounding her bed, a colorless, tuneless voice said as if by rote, "You've had the nightmare again, Commissar Silverthorne. Wake up, Commissar. Wake up."

"I'm awake," she said testily. "Stop that, Doctor. I'm awake, and I'm fine." The doctor was a corpse-faced man with cavernous cheeks, sunken dark eyes, emaciated body, and sparse hair growing in thin strands across his bald head. He never spoke. The only thing human about him was his hands; they were always white and clean and cool and dry. For decades now no doctor had actually touched a patient without latex gloves. It wasn't sanitary. Not only did Alia find it peculiar that the doctor used his fingers to feel her face, her pulse, her forehead, sometimes her lips, but she was positively repulsed by it.

Doctor's long head swiveled and his fingers moved slightly. The nurse, a blank-faced, square woman with short iron-gray hair, stepped forward into the low lamplight by Alia's bed. "Doctor will medicate you tonight so that you may sleep. But now you must get up and bathe and dress. You are having dinner with Count von Eisenhalt."

As if she functioned on robotics, Nurse squared around and marched out of the room, followed by the spidery, silent doctor. He was unable to hear or speak, and he could not read lips. Nurse was the only person he communicated with in sign language. Alia had never heard of a person who could not hear or speak in these days of genetic engineering and in utero embryo testing. The medical technology had long existed to correct deafness and certainly muteness. It was extremely odd.

But Alia, with a curious lassitude that had been weighing her down in the last ten days since Tor had brought them to Halle Eisenhalt, reflected that it was likely she was mentally incapable of discerning exactly what was oddity and what was normalcy. She couldn't seem to figure out such complexities anymore. Just as she was never quite certain whether she was awake, dreaming, or in a purgatorial trance somewhere in between.

She hadn't seen anyone except the nurse and doctor in the last ten days, and she had barely spoken a dozen words. Perhaps tonight at dinner she would see Minden and Luca. That would help her. That would make the world real again. Deliberately she avoided thinking about Tor von Eisenhalt. Alia Silverthorne was a determined woman, a willful woman, a stubborn woman, and no matter if she was barking mad, she could not and would not admit to herself that she was afraid.

Her bedroom was medieval. The walls were rough blocks of yellowish rock, the floor paved with smoother stones, with a faded but deep rug centered on it. The windows were thick and opaque, with bubbles in the small diamond-shaped panes bordered by ropy black iron. The fireplace was enormous, six feet high and nine feet wide, and Alia had been aware that an enormous fire had been kept going continually. But the room was always cold.

There were wall-mounted lamps, all of black wrought iron. The bulbs seemed dim, but at least they were electric. Alia turned all of them on. Connecting to her bedroom was a thoroughly modern bathroom with all the amenities, and connected to that was a tiny cubicle mirrored from floor to ceiling. It was a dressing room, Alia supposed, for her clothes were hung neatly in it. They were her own clothes, from her apartment in Albuquerque. She refused to speculate on how they'd gotten here, somewhere in the dark mountains of eastern Germany, in this ancient castle. Her commissar's uniform was laid out neatly, including her beret and her 9 mm pistol. Bathing and dressing quickly, she refused to study her drawn reflection in the mirror.

For the first time, Alia opened her bedchamber door and stepped out, steeling herself. She was at the end of a long hallway of the same golden stone. It stretched to her left, and she could not see the end. She saw no other doors along it. The only lights were dim flickering torches in sconces every ten feet or so. Alia felt small, like a lost little girl. But this unpleasant sensation made her straighten her shoulders and set her jaw and stride confidently down the hallway . . . or tunnel, it seemed . . . like the tunnel they'd run down forever and ever to get out of the White House . . . they were lost . . . she was lost . . .

"Stop it!" She didn't shout the words; rather, she growled them. Still the echoes mocked her, an unending "Stop it, stop it, stop it . . ." until she wanted to scream.

Alia almost did scream when the man appeared down the hall, just a black cutout, coming toward her. Then he passed directly under one of the torches, and she could see that he was a man in a black tuxedo, a man with dark hair and eyes and a terribly pock-marked face. "Commissar Silverthorne? I am Fetzen. If you will allow me, I will show you to the dining room." The German accent made the words staccato, and his tone had a hint of arrogance. Alia supposed it had something to do with the commanding cadence of the German language, for it seemed that all German men—even butlers, as she supposed Fetzen was—sounded as if they were giving orders.

"Thank you," she said stiffly.

It wasn't that bad, really. Alia had no recollection of the exterior of Halle Eisenhalt; however, she sensed that it must be enormous. If it was, her bedchamber was close to the dining room and what seemed to be a more inhabited part of the castle. Fetzen led her down the hall, took a sharp left down another hall that had a Gothic wooden door that led into a huge, high-ceilinged room that had no furniture, only rugs and tapestries and some paintings. Across that cavernous, echoing room were two twelve-foot-high double wooden doors. As they neared, the doors swung open, and Tor walked through them.

Though Alia had tried hard to steady herself for this moment, she stopped in her tracks, and her heart pounded.

Count von Eisenhalt smiled warmly and walked confidently forward to stand in front of her and bow slightly. "Alia, I'm so glad to see you are well enough to join us tonight. Please . . ." He turned and motioned to the door.

She walked forward, aware only of the pounding of her heart and the primitive sense of the hairs on the back of her neck prickling as Tor followed her. In the dining room she was enveloped by clouds of white silk and incense scent and Minden's luxuriant voice murmuring to her as she kissed both cheeks. "Alia, Alia, how glad I am to see you well. How wonderful you look, like a stern Valkyrie."

"Thank you," Alia said uncertainly. She didn't know what a Valkyrie was.

Luca Therion stepped forward, and Alia was shocked by his appearance. He didn't look ill or ravaged. He just looked different. Luca had always had the rather dreamy look of philosophers and artists, and his sensitive features enhanced the impression. But now his hair was shorter and sternly fashioned, with none of the studied artlessness of the escaped lock over his brow; his soft doe eyes looked matte black; his features looked sharply carved rather than clear-cut. He looked stern. "Hello, Mr. President," Alia said tentatively.

"Alia, my dear," he said, though with none of his customary warmth. "I'm glad you've recovered and are joining us tonight."

"Yes, well, it seems that I am the last one to rejoin the living," she said rather lamely. "I gather that you and Minden have been—well?"

"Oh, yes, Doctor has been taking marvelous care of us," Minden said, taking Alia's hand to lead her to the fireplace. "Luca and I have dined together the last two nights. Tonight, however, is wonderful because Count von Eisenhalt is joining us."

Alia studied the room as she allowed Minden to lead her. It was high-ceilinged, enormous, ancient, as all of Halle Eisenhalt must be. The table was immense, seating thirty at least, of a wood so old it looked black. Hundreds of candles centered along the expanse gave the wood a dark gleam, and white dinnerware and gleaming goldware were set in four places at one end. No windows showed, for all of the walls were hung with tapestries and great rich burgundy velvet draperies with golden tassels. The fireplace was at the far end of the room, with what Alia assumed were servants' entrances on each side. Even as she was doing her customary military assessment of the entrances and exits of the room, Fetzen came in through one of the rear doors carrying a silver tray with goblets on it. He served the four of them as they stood in a loose circle in front of a roaring, popping fire.

"To our host and our savior, Count Tor von Eisenhalt," Luca said gravely.

"Count Tor von Eisenhalt," Minden and Alia repeated. Then Minden added dreamily, "May you live forever."

Tor smiled at her, then drank.

Alia took her place at Tor's right hand, while Minden and Luca were seated on his left. Fetzen brought two silver platters and one silver flask. He served each of them, and the entire meal was a very rare prime rib and black bread. From the silver flask he poured them more mead, that syrupy but bitter and heady drink made from honey and fermented grains. After that he stood back by the door and did not move or speak or even look at the diners.

During the meal, Tor talked quietly of the history of the castle, of his father, of trivial things. Minden watched him obsessively, unmoving, barely blinking, the look of almost feral love plain on her face. Once Tor told her to eat, and she obediently took a bite, unseeing and unknowing. Luca ate sparingly and was also riveted on Tor, though he didn't seem quite as distracted as was Minden.

Alia could not quiet the deep apprehension that filled her throughout the meal. It was a pervasive sense of unreality, an uncomfortable feeling that something, somewhere, somehow, was very wrong, that none of this was exactly as it looked or smelled or sounded . . . that if she just paid attention and was sharp enough, she could comprehend exactly what was off, what was jarring her. It gave the food, the conversation, even the way Minden and Luca and Tor looked, a nightmarish quality to Alia.

She wondered if she was ill, fevered maybe, or if she had gone insane and they weren't letting on, they were just being nice to her because she was sick in her mind.

Typically of earthy Alia, she reflected sardonically, *Well, if that's the case, they certainly shouldn't have given me a loaded gun.*

The thought made her smile, though it was a small and sour smile, and she looked down quickly.

"Alia . . ."

His hypnotic voice again, and Alia's head snapped up. He was smiling at her, and an idiotic, squeaky little voice in Alia's head gibbered, *What big teeth you have, Grandma . . .*

A frown, vicious and full of malice, darkened Tor's face.

Alia was more frightened than she had ever been in her life. She stopped breathing and started choking. She could get no air into her lungs, into her nose, down into her chest, and she was going to die right here, right now.

"Stop," Tor said quietly, calmly.

Alia swallowed and gasped for air.

He watched her impassively. Luca and Minden still watched Tor.

Alia was nauseated with fear. "I—I'm not well. I'm—please forgive me, Count von Eisenhalt," she said hoarsely. "Will you excuse me?"

"Nonsense," he said. His voice had returned to its usual commanding tone, and he looked handsome, elegant, coolly concerned again. "Fetzen, bring a bottle of my father's special stock. I'm certain it will make Commissar Silverthorne feel better." He didn't turn around to address the servant. His dark hawk's eyes were steady on Alia's face.

Now she felt desperate. She didn't want any more to drink; she felt ill, sick to her stomach already, for Alia rarely drank any alcohol. The food, though plain, had been heavy. But she sat, mute and unmoving, until Fetzen brought in a misshapen bottle with no label and four wine glasses.

"This is burgundy of a very old vintage," Tor said, pouring a generous amount into a glass. Then he rose and handed it to Alia. "Drink it, My Commissar," he said softly, with a caressing quality to his voice that Alia had never heard before. Alia was looking down into the wine glass, and it was a very good thing that she was, for if she had seen the murderous envy on Minden Lauer's face, she might have left Halle Eisenhalt on foot at a dead run.

Alia was sure that it was just the candlelight that made the wine look so black. *Burgundy is darkly colored,* she told herself. But it wasn't the quality of the light that made it so thick. As she swirled it lightly, it clung to the sides of the graceful glass in dark arcs that barely moved as they dribbled back down. Putting the glass to her lips, she smelled the wine; it smelled sour, as wine does, but with a peculiar scent underneath, an acerbic hint of something familiar.

She drank, her eyes closed.

The first taste of the wine was rich, mellow, as a good burgundy should be, but the undertaste and the hidden scent were of salt.

Immediately after she swallowed the thick brew, Alia felt relaxed, at peace, and at the same time fully in control of herself. It was not a physical sensation, as a heady drink of wine can give, but instead a mental and emotional change from turmoil to tranquillity. She opened her eyes and smiled at Minden, who was watching her with narrowed eyes.

Tor took his seat at the head of the table and sipped his own glass of wine. The others did the same. The four sat in silence for a while. Minden, Luca, and Alia were staring blankly, with a kind of inward vision, as if they were seeing things painted on the surface of their eyes. Tor watched them.

Finally he said in a low voice, "I chose you."

He seemed to be speaking to them generally, but each of the three was certain he was speaking only to him or her.

"I chose you," he repeated deliberately. "Never forget it."

"I could never," Minden whispered.

Tor didn't acknowledge her; he was staring down into his wine glass, swirling the thick black liquid around and around. The four concentric circles of the ring on his forefinger glittered silvery bright, twinkling, alive. "Let us talk, then, of loyalty," he murmured thoughtfully. "Many of my men of war have sworn oaths of fealty to the House of Eisenhalt—and to me personally. But before they did, I asked them—each of them personally—one very important question." He looked up, mildly expectant, clinically curious.

Alia felt the barest fringes of the remembrance of dread—what terrible price would this man, this mysterious, compelling, truly dreadful man, ask of them?

Tor almost, but not quite, smiled at her. His eyes seemed to soften a little, as if to reassure her.

He turned to Minden. Before he could say a word, she whispered breathlessly, "Anything . . ."

He seemed pleased. "All I want to know, Minden, is—what do you want?"

Her blue eyes flared as if they had been set aflame. "You, my lord. Just to please you. I'll do anything, be anything, you ask."

He stared at her hard, then nodded. "I believe you, Minden. You have spoken well and truly." His eyes, like a great searching spotlight, slowly swiveled to Luca Therion, who seemed to be in a trance.

Luca guiltily, shamefully, let his gaze slip toward Minden. Before he could recover, Tor muttered in a low growl, "Luca, never lie to me—and never lie to yourself. You want more than that. You *are* more than that. You can have everything, anything you want—if you will join me. I chose you, Luca. But you must now choose."

As if Tor had struck him, Luca drew back, flinching. Then he sat up ramrod-straight, his face stricken and pale. He stared into Tor's searing gaze for a long, long time. Then he murmured, "You, sir, have saved my life, my mind, even my soul. I will die for you."

Tor nodded, then said curtly, "No need for such dramatics, Luca, Minden. And we are all friends here. Let us speak frankly. You, Minden, I know what you long for, what you burn with desire for, what you dream of . . . You want to be loved, to be admired, to be the most beautiful and desired woman on this earth. I tell you now that this will be so. Your dreams will all come true, my dear Minden . . .

"And you, Luca, I know you have visions. You see days of glory, of honor—of power. You know that the breadth of your intellect and the depth of your passion far outstrip those of other puny men who surround you. You, Luca, will have power you never dreamed of. Power that you cannot conceive. I promise you this, in return for the loyalty that you've sworn to me."

Alia was spellbound. No longer did she experience fear, dread, or the discordant feeling that the universe was out of joint and time was out of sync. This man, Tor von Eisenhalt, literally radiated power. The air was thick with it. They were drunk with it.

All three of them slowly turned to look at Alia. She felt exhilarated, poised to run, to shout, as adrenaline pumped through her body. Licking her lips, she stared at Tor, her eyes burning as if she were looking into the naked sun.

"And you, Alia . . . my fierce little shieldmaiden. What say you, soldier?"

"I—I don't know what—good I am—could be to you—sir," she said raggedly. "But I—want to swear my oath of fealty to you, Count Tor von Eisenhalt, my oath as a soldier."

"Do you?" he commented with casual interest, though his eyes on her felt like needles pricking her skin. "It is a grave thing, a serious matter of honor—*unto the death*—for a soldier to swear an oath of loyalty, Alia."

She tried to swallow, then tried again, but the burning in her throat would not go away. Her hands shaking, she took another drink of the thick wine. "I—wasn't—certain before," she said, and her voice trembled shamefully. "But—but I am now. You—you chose me."

He nodded, understanding. Turning to address Minden and Luca, he said, "You see, Alia has never wanted physical beauty, and she's never wanted the love of men . . . All she's ever wanted is to be the best. All the desire she's ever had, all the strength she's ever had, has been directed to achieving that one goal, that one shining, bright, unreachable goal . . ."

Luca murmured, his brow furrowed, "But, sir . . . the best? The best at what?"

Tor's attention was back on Alia, who was gazing at him as if he were holding open the gate to the Garden of Eden, with a dawning, unsure but growing hope. Tor finished in the same low, caressing tone he'd used before as he spoke to her. "Alia wants to be unconquerable. She wants to fight and to win—which means that she wants to defeat everyone else. Isn't that right, Alia?"

"Yes . . . yes . . . how do you . . ."

He suddenly leaned over close to her, his face almost touching hers. She was utterly still, not even breathing. "Alia, I cannot die."

"I know . . ."

"But I do have enemies . . . and Minden and Luca must be protected. For my sake."

"For your sake," she said as if in prayer.

"You will win it all, Alia," he whispered, so low that Minden and Luca couldn't hear. "You will utterly defeat them all. This I promise you, for your loyalty to me."

"I will die for you," she said as if in a dream.

She thought someone was laughing.

But that couldn't be so.

Tor reached up with his forefinger, and she was blinded . . . by the bright silver of his ring, she thought . . . He touched her lips, ever so lightly.

She fainted dead away.

Fort Knox
Near Louisville, Kentucky

It was the most heavily guarded building in the world.

In the first place, it had been built in the Great Depression paranoia of the 1930s on an army base that was now the headquarters of the most deadly heavy infantry in the world: the United States Armored Cavalry. Those ten thousand soldiers, two thousand tanks, and four hundred Bell AH-20 Cobra helicopter gunships weren't there only as a hopped-up security police force. They were the muscle-bulk of America's land force. But they ran full-scale mobilization games twice a year, deploying as guardians of the modest white granite building that stood in the middle of their base.

The Armored Cav wasn't the first line of defense. First and foremost were the nonhuman defenses: the harsh floodlights, the perimeter fortified with solid concrete barriers, the barbed wire, the Cy-II surveillance system with electronic gate sentries.

Next up were the specially trained Justice Department police, half of whom were ace sharpshooters, deployed on the roof of the second story. They patrolled the facility inside the gates.

Outside the barricades an entire squad of army MPs kept a solid twenty-four-hour-a-day, 365-day-a-year vigilance.

All that had changed in the last two months.

Naturally the first and most noticeable change was the lack of lights. The building had been bathed in the harsh glare of fifty-six 800-watt lights every single night since 1936. On September 23, the night of the autumnal equinox, it went as dark as the deepest Congo.

The two thousand M1A5 Abrams tanks squatted on the dark plain like prehistoric beasts. They were dead. They couldn't move; their thermal imaging eyes were closed; their lethal 90 mm electromagnetic rail guns were paralyzed. The tank crews, most of whom regarded their tanks as majestic, roaring live predators, mourned as if they'd lost their families.

The Cobra gunships were dead, too, their pilots and crews distraught, just as Deacon Fong had been devastated when his beloved Apache died.

Like the rest of the army, they all had their MK-20 Techstar rifles. And just like all the rest of the army, they were lost and confused when they didn't work. All they had left were their decorative Beretta 9 mm personal side arms (PSAs). Most of them did know enough to chamber a round and pull the trigger, but since they'd been trained only with high-tech targeting and guidance systems, they didn't have a clue how to aim. Their minds, accustomed to vast amounts of information being spoon-fed to them, couldn't adjust to the instinctive handling of a small pistol. It made no sense to their eyes or their brains.

The sharpshooters of the Treasury police were the worst. They'd been trained on the REM/3000 assault rifle; it had a delicate LOSAP guidance system with a helmet-mounted image display, both of which were utterly useless without the electricity in the power packs. Skilled snipers with only their sharp eyes and quick brain-hand-eye coordination were a curiosity of the last century.

The Mint Police of the Justice Department were the first to go. Unlike the army personnel who were only temporarily stationed on the base, the Mint Police lived in the nearby towns and had families there. As the weeks wore on, fewer and fewer of them reported for duty. Almost all of them had families to take care of. Protection of inanimate objects, no matter how valuable, began to seem an absurd distortion of loyalties.

The Military Police kept up their vigil, however, because they were under orders. They required no emotional reinforcement to follow orders, so they patrolled day and night with their clubs and their 9 mm pistols.

For two months, the loyal guardians had nothing to do except look out over the surrounding empty acres. No one tried to approach the high barbed-wire fences. No tourists came to the gate, taking pictures and asking tiresome questions. No journalists appeared to try to weasel information out of the stern MPs. Not a single person tried to breach the facility's defenses. Of course, that was not unusual. In the last 114 years, no one had tried to attack, infiltrate, or in any way assault the facility.

The first and only assault ever made on the United States Bullion Depository was supremely successful.

First the snipers came, hiding in the shelter of the grove of old oak and elm trees on the west side of the grounds, about four hundred yards away from the main gate. With their old Steyr Aug automatic assault rifles and their six-month-long training, just completed, on a noncomputerized weapon, they picked off the fourteen MPs with ease.

Then the Peterbilt Titan twenty-four-wheelers rumbled down Bullion Boulevard in the white night. A light blanket of snow covered the land, gleaming and sparkling. To the fifty-seven massive Peterbilt trucks, the snow was no problem. Their line stretched all the way back toward, and almost reached, Godman Army Air Field. About forty soldiers wandering around the base saw the trucks. Twenty of them were shot before they could run. The others made it to HQ, but by the time the officers had rounded up a hundred men, gotten them dressed and armed, and run on foot all the way to the west side of the base, the snipers had already turned toward them. Not one of them lived; most of them were killed with single shots to the forehead within the first fifteen minutes.

When the first truck reached Gold Vault Road, it smoothly took a wide right turn and growled its way right up to the Depository's front gate. The MPs guarding it were dead. The titanium-reinforced truck smashed through the steel gate.

The trucks lumbered on to an unnamed road that encircled the Depository, took a right, and went around to the loading platforms in the back. They didn't know, and wouldn't have cared if they had, that the circular road was made out of steel plates on hinges that, in a crisis, could be raised hydraulically to create a second internal stockade of steel. The road would not be raised this night.

In the rear of the building klieg lights, generated manually by fittings on the Titans, were set up. Specially made titanium dollies rolled out the back of the Depository, and the loading began.

The Bullion Depository in the year 2050 held 180,449,666 ounces of gold, or roughly 11 million pounds. The Peterbilt Titan was capable of transporting 200,000 pounds, though driving American highways with that weight was illegal. The drivers were not afraid of being arrested, however.

All together, the fifty-seven Titans removed 439,054 gold bars from the Depository. The bullion was worth about $62 billion, almost half the world's gold supply. America had always owned most of the gold and all of the prestige and power that come with the perception of such unbelievable wealth.

But now it was all gone.

Eleven

THE EARTH ALWAYS looked the same in the photographs taken from the NASA space shuttles that ran their regularly scheduled routes to maintain the myriad satellites spinning in orbit. The pictures made by the shuttle crews, as stunning as they were, were indistinguishable from the pictures taken by the legendary *Apollo 11* astronauts almost a century earlier.

Although the shape of the continents and the borders of the oceans and the ridges of the mountains had not changed, the world had altered dramatically in the last century. If cause and effect could be graphically imposed on the photographs, they would look much like the maps that the commercial airlines published to show their flights, with networks of lines radiating from each hub. On earth, America would be the single central hub, with lines radiating out all over the globe.

The United States of America, the last superpower, changed the makeup of the entire world economically, militarily, and culturally, and these three things combined always result in political change. When analyzed to irreducible simplicity, it was all because of two distinct causations.

The first critical event was the attempted nuclear attack on America's homeland by the Socialist People's Libyan Arab Jamahira in 2006. Only a few months ago, Minden Lauer and then Vice President Luca Therion had discussed this incident and had found inspiration for Project Final Unity, but that had only been the last poisonous fruit from the tree. This episode had had complex, far-reaching, lasting effects.

The fear—and rage—that the American people felt at this narrowly escaped national disaster could not be ignored by anyone. They were well and truly roused. The government listened and complied with the people's (loudly) expressed wishes.

A top-of-the-line military force was developed, and then was kept at home. Thus America's military isolationism evolved, and by 2015, there were only token American forces stationed outside the U.S.

But, as Minden and Luca had observed, this event was also an impetus to perfect a defensive system, and so Galaxy Guardian, a space-based laser weapons platform and antimissile defense, was born. American scientists, in unheard-of unity, worked diligently for two years to perfect the technology and upgraded the accuracy of intercontinental ballistic missile kill capability from 72.3 percent to 99.9 percent. This, in effect, became the ultimate countermeasure for any airborne missiles. Galaxy Guardian made it impossible for any kind of hostile weapon to be transported by air into the Western Hemisphere—or Israel.

Out of this critical event came the final bond of alliance between Israel and America. Following the attempted bombing by the Libyan submarine, every country in the world condemned Libya—except the major Arabic nations. In their oil-saturated arrogance, they spoke meaningless platitudes at the United Nations and praised the dead mujahideen in their Arabic newspapers and Cyclops broadcasts. The only country in the Mideast that took a stand for America—and armed its borders to fight, if necessary—was Israel. America repaid her by enclosing her in the protective umbrella of the Galaxy Guardian system.

America repaid the Arab nations, too. A consortium of businessmen—American, German, Chinese, and Indian—delicately contacted key men in the International Man and Biosphere Project, and in the American government. Over the span of ten years, new electric cars were phased in. In the developing co-op cities, where traffic flows were carefully controlled, electric cars were mandated, and the ubiquitous mass transit buses were switched to electrics. Gradually these businessmen and the American government had leveraged out Arab financial interests. When the fall of the Arabic Confederation occurred, they were well cushioned, as were the markets of their countries.

America started using domestic and South American oil, and the Arabic Confederation countries were, once again, poor desert countries, albeit with fabulously wealthy and propertied kings or sheikhs or abdullahs. The only predominantly Muslim country that managed to prosper was Jordan, which finally aligned itself with Israel (and the United States) in exchange for expelling the Palestinians, who, by 2010, comprised 80 percent of the population of Jordan. The Joint Task Forces of the Germanic Union of Nation-States had accomplished that, with an efficient "police assistance action" alongside Jordan's national security organization.

This U.S. military isolationism caused some wars and lesser conflicts all over the world for a period of about ten years. The European Union stepped in and talked a lot about keeping world peace, but the Germanic Union, with its mighty Joint Task Forces, became the world's policeman.

By then America had become indisputably the ultimate economic powerhouse. As Americans developed the satellite technology for the Galaxy Guardian systems, and the space shuttle technology for maintenance, they developed the Cyclops system along with all the industry giants of communications technologies. Soon the entire world was obliged to use the Cyclops system, for the simple reason that only America had the highly skilled technicians, the outrageously expensive space shuttles, and the billions of investment dollars needed to develop, launch, and maintain space satellites. Just as every civilized person in the world had once owned a television, a telephone, a facsimile machine, and a personal computer, so now every civilized person in the world was on the Cyclops net—and paid dues to the United States of America for it.

And so it was seen that the effects of that ill-fated submarine attack were not limited to the pollution of the Gulf of Labrador. Eventually this one pathetic attempt to injure America affected global military stances, delicate balances of power, and world finance, and reconfigured the global marketplace. Because of it, America developed Cyclops, which greatly influenced the eddies and currents of social and cultural life. For decades American culture had been its major export in every conceivable form, from clothing styles to religious influences. With Cyclops and its centralized heart in America, all American attitudes and beliefs and opinions and desires became the world's, in a fateful marriage, for better and for worse.

The second world-altering event was at America's instigation, too. A major upheaval in the relative power of the world's economies occurred when America legalized recreational drugs. No country in the world, no culture, and no social institutions were ever the same after the use of drugs became legal and therefore socially acceptable—and that made drug use moral.

America had always been the leader in cutting-edge medical technology. American scientists developed cures for several types of cancers; life-remission programs for diabetes; a cure for Alzheimer's disease; a cure for Parkinson's disease; permanent and full remission programs for high cholesterol, heart disease, liver ailments, and kidney ailments. They honed neural electrode implants for many types of brain dysfunctions. They cloned organs, though no one ever cloned a functioning human being. They perfected robotics for surgical devices. They refined genetic engineering, with its accompanying in vitro human embryo analysis. They made a fail-safe abortion pill with no side effects. They made enormous strides in corrective surgeries, including a 97.6 percent preventive of male pattern baldness, a skin renewal program that was 52.9 percent effective, and muscular, tissue, vascular, and bone renewal. All organs, except the brain and skin, were successfully transplanted, some from human donors, some from animal donors, some from cloned materials. Any surgery to make one more beautiful, from fatty cell laser removal to dimple implantation, was readily available.

But one field of medicine that Americans (to the health care field's chagrin) did not pioneer was that of Serum Courses or, as they came to be commonly termed, SCs. This completely new area of medicine was developed by a team of German scientists in Bolivia. SCs were, to put it simply, antidotes to the negative effects of narcotics on the human body.

Until 2005, Americans were still struggling with the war on drugs, but much of the rhetoric had changed. With the realization that some illegal drugs, such as marijuana, were effective painkillers, that drug was declared a controlled narcotic. People began to question the very nature of controlled narcotics; after all, morphine was a much-used painkiller, and it was a derivative of opium. Hashish was a variation of the marijuana plant. It was the second substance to be declared a legal, albeit controlled, narcotic. These were natural substances, after all, gifts from the earth, the mother of us all; they were medicines, much as foxglove had given us digitalis and cinchona bark had given us quinine.

After the German scientists made their findings public, within a year America had declared all narcotics legal and stipulated that with recreational use they were to be combined with the Serum Courses. This legislation proved later to be ineffectual. Drug addicts will faithfully find a way to get and use narcotics, but they are not as conscientious in following protocols of antidotes that do not make them feel good. So, in America, Structured Dependence Zones were created in the co-op cities where the citizens made twice-weekly pilgrimages to the Alterative/SC Clinics to get their poisons and their antidotes.

The countries of South America and Mexico, with their endless fields of marijuana and coca plants, grew fabulously wealthy; India and China, with their millions of little farmers who grew only poppies, prospered; Japan, with its robotlike efficiency, took a huge bite of the processing and packaging business; the European Union took the bulk of shipping; while American and German pharmaceutical companies had great feasts of Serum Course production.

Slowly, over a period of many years, responding to varied forces, the world changed. America was the richest and the most influential country. The European Union, dominated by Germany—which had grown to be the second-richest nation in the world—had the largest standing army and the most influential military force in the balances of power. The Far East prospered; China grew fat and lazy, though it continued to have the menace of a snake asleep in the sun. India had grown in military might, in prosperity, and in sheer population, and it counterbalanced China effectively. The Arabic Confederation was a cipher but, because of the massive populations and the sheer geographical area the members controlled, was still considered one of the Eight Spheres of Influence.

Africa, the largest and richest continent on the face of the earth, practically disappeared—not the land mass, of course, but the concept of African nationalism. Devoted missionaries of Islamic radicalization had taken Northern Africa. Only the collapse of OPEC had kept them from taking the entire continent.

The countries of Southern Africa, so hopeful and fiercely independent in the previous century, had succumbed not to another imperialist expansion, but to a much deadlier enemy. At the beginning of the century, AIDS had infected one-third of the people of Zambia, with comparable infection rates in the other less-developed countries such as Botswana and Malawi. The infection rate of the economically strongest countries—South Africa, Zimbabwe, Kenya, Uganda—was between 10 and 25 percent. The drugs to combat the disease were much too expensive for even the wealthiest South Africans. By 2010, most of them had died, and their children, 98 percent of whom were infected, were already dead or had an even shorter life expectancy than their parents. The numbers increased geometrically, and the strains of the disease increased in complexity. By 2015, Count Gerade von Eisenhalt and the Germanic Union of Nation-States had mercifully come to the aid of South Africa in all ways—loans, medical supplies, teams of physicians and hundreds of clinics, food, water purification plants—and the Joint Forces of the Germanic Union as benevolent peacekeepers.

Germany owned Southern Africa by 2017.

The story was much the same in Tropical Africa. The land area of more than twenty countries had well and truly earned the name the Dark Continent. The Muslims had crept down the eastern side. Vast countries such as Kenya, Uganda, and Somalia still existed, but they had continuous civil wars with the Muslims and the tribal natives who were mostly animists. The state of Eritrea had long disappeared, swallowed by Arabic Confederation member Ethiopia. Djibouti was gone; either African Somalia or Arabic Ethiopia had it, depending upon the status of the border wars at any given point in time. The populations of Tropical Africa, too—especially the central countries of Zaire, Congo, Angola, and Tanzania—had been cruelly reduced by the AIDS scourge. Complete figures and statistics for remotest interior Africa were scanty; it had returned to a pre-nineteenth-century closed continent. News rarely came out of those impenetrable jungles. Germany had some forces stationed along the coasts, but they hugged the coastline, keeping well in sight of their naval fleet. Even the valiant Goths didn't like to venture into the darkness of central Africa.

However, other countries of the world needed armies, too. Since the beginning of time, some countries have needed help to cope with larger, more aggressive neighbors. Though Americans had chosen to ignore it, strength was not measured in terms of economics only. In some parts of the world, it was still measured by a more primitive form: military might. And that was how most of the other great nations melded their spheres of influence.

Germany used a combination of the two to dominate all of Europe; Western Europe had been allied to it, the second-richest country in the world, through the European Union. Eastern Europe had been won over by military force (though not by wars); Russia, after reannexing Chechnya, had started making noises at the other breakaway republics. But the Joint Forces of the Germanic Union of Nation-States had formed a mutual defense alliance, thumbing its nose at NATO, which was powerless without America. Accordingly all of the Eastern European countries that could see the giant rumbling to their east ran straight into Germany's arms.

For Russia, it was a feint. Russians were not like Americans, speaking only a different language, as had been thought in those heady years after the Union of Soviet Socialist Republics, and their wall in Berlin, fell.

The Russians were a downtrodden and splintered people who had no notion of self-governance or self-reliance. Russia had quickly degenerated into a nation of petty criminals run by a few very powerful criminals, and it had stayed hungry and cold and dark. It had no strength at all, except its behemoth size and the world's perception that it could put four million men into a war. The big thieves were stripping the country of the big things—the weapons, the imported moneys from natural resources such as oil and industrial diamonds and titanium—while the millions of little thieves were practicing graft and corruption on a smaller scale, cheating on the weights of bread and watering down the soup and using substandard wool to knit the gloves and rotten leather to sole the shoes.

The only way that Russia commanded attention from the world was a sort of sly blackmail—it needed grain for the starving poor, it needed IMF loans for the broken banks, it needed technological aid for the antiquated industrial complex, and it needed medical supplies and pharmaceuticals for the sick millions. If Russia could not keep the population well and fed and happy, how could it possibly maintain the military-industrial complex, which safeguarded the nuclear arms and materials?

With this sly blackmail, the rest of the world gave Russia an arm's-length respect, while the World Bank gave it loans and America gave it grain (bought from Australia) and medicines (bought from Japan). On paper Russia had 2.8 million in the active forces, and 2 million in the reserves. Even if the figures were accurate, the quality of the soldiers would be highly suspect. Yet millions of men—from Attila's to Napoleon's to Hitler's—were buried in the snowy steppes, and the world could not afford to let the Great Bear roar, no matter how old or decrepit he was.

The only countries that were considered by some to be the last frontiers (and seen by others as backward renegades) were the countries of the Pacific that had, from creation, been set apart from the rest of the world. Australia and New Zealand had stubbornly stayed stuck in the twentieth century, with their strict criminal laws, their disdain for the Man and Biosphere Project, their antiquated social mores. In Australia they still called partners a husband and a wife. Australia and New Zealand had the lowest abortion rates in the world and the largest number of intact families.

They also had robust and noisy democracies, and in 2015, Indonesia signed a mutual trade pact with them that effectively made Oceania a large, influential, and unruly member of the Eight Spheres of Influence. Together they ruled the Pacific shipping lanes. The countries of Europe—particularly England—hated the odd confederation, for they considered it a betrayal of Australia's and New Zealand's historic cultural ties. China and the Far Eastern Sphere hated it because they considered Indonesia a traitor to what they still called the barbaric West. Oceania didn't care. Its countries were prosperous, they had millions of miles of land, they had control of the largest (and most beautiful) ocean, and they minded their own affairs. While they were at it, they formed an Oceanic Task Force to keep everyone else minding his own business, too, and that military was third (in standing army) only to the Germanic Union's Joint Task Forces and China's military.

The pie of the world was split up into eight great juicy pieces: (1) America (with her spheres, Canada and Israel); (2) Europe (dominated by Germany); (3) the Far Eastern Sphere (mostly China, which had not literally conquered anyone but overshadowed Japan, North and South Korea, Southeast Asia, Mongolia, and the Philippines); (4) Russia, the wounded Great Bear, all alone but mighty in sheer size; (5) the Arabic Confederation, as splintered and downtrodden as the conquered and overrun Ottoman Empire had been; (6) India, which warred with, and easily overran, Pakistan, Bangladesh, Nepal, Bhutan, and Sri Lanka; (7) Latin America, which included Mexico; and (8) happy Oceania.

So it was with the representatives from these Eight Spheres of Influence that Tor met personally and showed them that he would own the world.

In 1942 it had been the Reichsbank; in 2000 it had been the German Foreign Ministry; in 2010 it was the German Offices of the Eurobank; in 2022 it became the Germanic Union Headquarters of the World Bank. It was the same building, however, that Hitler had approved, and his banker, Hjalmar Schacht, had

had the same office that, until recently, Count Gerade von Eisenhalt had occupied as chief finance officer of the World Bank. Now Count Tor von Eisenhalt had that same office and that same title.

But the new count did not meet with the twenty-three representatives from the Eight Spheres of Influence in that office or in any of the great meeting rooms with their soaring ceilings and friezes and classical statuettes. He met with them in a cold anteroom in the basement, in a spartan room with only chairs and a long plain table and harsh lighting and no windows. Behind a plain lectern hung dull red velvet drapes from floor to ceiling. Tor's speech was short and to the point. He disdained the podium; he used no electrical sound equipment; he wore his military uniform with no apology. No sound was made by anyone or anything as he spoke.

"America is in chaos. But as you see, here at my right hand, the president of the United States is safe; and so also, by my hand, will America be held safe." He paused a moment to let this statement settle in, and some of the esteemed high persons glanced meaningfully at one another and at Luca Therion. It had been two months since the blackout of the United States, and no one in the world had been able to learn exactly what had happened or why. No one had been sure that Luca Therion was still alive.

Tor waited until everyone was perfectly still and everyone's gaze was fixed solely on him again. "I know that the economies of many of your countries have suffered in the past two months. I know that some of you face severe panics, depressions, inflations, or other market convulsions."

His voice grew deeper, louder, and the assembled men and women, powerful and influential though they were, felt small and inadequate. "But I say to you that this is merely imagination, false visions, nameless fears, ladies and gentlemen. You think, and therefore the people of your nations think, that because America has fallen, you will fall. You think that because the New York Stock Exchange hasn't been open, you will not have food to eat. You think that because you can't get the latest quote on the NASDAQ Exchange, your roof will not shield you from the heat of the sun or keep the rain from falling on you. You think that because the ineffectual eunuchs of the UN General Assembly are lost in the darkness of New York, your country will disappear."

He waited, eyeing each of the twenty-three men and women with something like disdain. The four women, and many of the men, flushed with shame. Some others grew pale with dread, for Tor von Eisenhalt's derision could be intimidating, indeed.

Tor continued in a mocking tone, "I say again, these are just a child's fears. You think your life's blood is in stocks, bonds, derivatives, market shares, trade levels . . . but I am a soldier, and I know that your life's blood has nothing to do with these bits of paper and these electronic impulses that travel over electrical lines that can fail.

"What do you want? What does each of you really want? Corporate records that say you own shares? Pieces of paper that are supposed to represent a piece of wealth? Meaningless numbers attributed to you in Cyclops ether space? I think not. I think what you want, what you need, and what your nations need is real wealth. True wealth. Measurable, tangible, physical wealth. That, ladies and gentlemen, is the worth of the world. And so, my friends . . . I give you the world."

He stood, nodded to Luca, bowed and clicked his heels, and left.

The assembly was so taken aback that everyone sat motionless, in silence, for a long time.

Then Luca Therion rose and pulled back the heavy red velvet drapes behind him.

It was gold. It was tons of gold, mountains of gold, worlds of gold, stacked to the ceiling, extending as far back as the eye could see. Hundreds of thousands of bars of gleaming gold, so bright that it made the eye squint, so pure looking and clean looking that it made one almost cry. There was even a distinctive, heavy metallic scent in the air. The harsh lights looked dim and dreary; the gold shone as bright as the sun.

Luca stood at the podium; no one had spoken a word. The people were so amazed and bemused at the sight of this unfathomable wealth that many of them had stopped breathing.

In a calm voice Luca said, "Count von Eisenhalt has named me second minister of the World Trade Organization and second minister of the World Bank. I'm sure you will confirm these appointments. At present, by his authority I am to assure each of you that your country will be more than insulated against any real losses incurred by the temporary cessation of the American stock exchange. This . . ."—he gestured lightly to the unbelievable wealth behind him—"is Count Tor von Eisenhalt and the Germanic Union of Nation-States' insurance policy for you."

The Chinese prime minister recovered more quickly than anyone. "But—but—none of us have been on the gold standard for many decades! Our reserves are in U.S. Treasury bonds!"

Luca shrugged. If he had not been so cold looking, his expression might have been akin to a smile. "Germany now has the largest gold reserve the world has ever known. Here, in this building, is enough gold to back all the currencies of all the nations in this room one and one-half times. Germany will buy your U.S. bonds either with gold or with German Treasury bonds."

England's prime minister said slowly, "But—but you mean, switch the benchmark currency from dollars to euromarks?"

"Deutsche marks," Luca corrected him mildly, using the common term for the Germanic-based currency that had slowly dominated the ill-fated eurodollar.

The finance minister from Japan blinked rapidly. "But—but—this is—Mr. President, we cannot just pretend that the largest consumer on earth has disappeared, and it makes no difference!"

Luca, whose chiseled face had darkened to malevolence at the beginning of the young man's outburst, suddenly laughed. "Mr. Finance Minister, I assure you that America is still there. And within four months, Count von Eisenhalt will bring her to life again. Within the next year, America will rejoin the world. But Count von Eisenhalt realizes—as do we all—that interim emergency measures must be taken. And be aware, Mr. Finance Minister, that Tor von Eisenhalt is not a simpleton, and to suggest—to even think such a thing—may be a very serious mistake for you to make. Now, we are all intelligent people here. Surely you see that solid gold backing your currency will stabilize your economies admirably.

"Now, for the second phase of Count von Eisenhalt's emergency market measures. The World Finance team of the Global Union of Nation-States has devised a model flow of actual, physical goods that we can use to feed us and clothe us and give us all the luxuries—and the model shows that we can actually prosper."

Another astounded silence met this declaration.

At length the prime minister of Australia, a plump, robust young man, could contain his incredulity no longer. "Do you mean to say, Mr. President, that those German money wonks have actually figured flows of goods for the whole kit? Grains, foods, ice, shoes, Tyvek, pickles, oil, apples, sapphires, natural gas, kumquats, glass beads . . . They counted all of everything that exists and apportioned it to us?"

Luca did not look amused. "Yes," he answered curtly. "That's exactly what I mean. And it will work. It is the only plan that will save you."

Another of the long, uncomfortable silences ensued. No one looked directly at anyone else; there was a lot of staring blankly into space and looking down at twisting hands.

Finally India's prime minister, a shrewd older woman, asked quietly, with a show of subservience, "And this gold, Mr. President? It is America's, is it not?"

"Most of it was America's," Luca said quietly, "but it now belongs to the Global Union of Nation-States—formerly the Germanic Union. America has allied herself with this union, and consequently the name has been changed to reflect its global membership. As a member of the Global Union of Nation-States, America has pledged her gold as currency reserves for distribution to the member-states as the first minister dictates."

They digested this information, and being the intelligent people that they were, they knew exactly what Luca meant: if they were to stabilize their economies, they would have to join the Global Union of Nation-States, with Count Tor von Eisenhalt as the first minister of the Global Union, the commanding general of the Joint Task Forces, the first minister of the World Bank, and the secretary-general of the World Trade Organization.

Tor would own them all. He would, in fact, own the world.

TWELVE

"SO BY TOMORROW I will have a one-page summary of the military postures of the Eight Spheres as I see it. From there we will go on to devise our overall strategy in the Mideast." Tor von Eisenhalt sipped appreciatively from a finely made crystal goblet containing his favorite liquor, mead. His cold blue eyes raked the two men sitting in front of his desk in the spacious study at Waldleiningen.

Oberstleutnant Rand von Drachstedt and *Oberleutnant* Jager Dorn exchanged uneasy glances. Both men were already uncomfortable enough in the imposing study of the Waldleiningen *jagdschloss*—and not only because Tor's father, Gerade von Eisenhalt, had died in mysterious circumstances in this room.

The twenty-foot ceiling seemed nonexistent, it was so high. The room's combination of German Gothic and neoclassic English was heavily masculine. A massive fireplace of neo-Gothic design loomed to their left. For some reason it reminded Jager Dorn of a childhood fairy tale about ogres pitching children through a huge portal into a dark, scary nightmare place where they were lost forever. The fireplace never failed to raise goose bumps along the back of his neck when he managed to look at it.

Tor was watching the two men with something akin to amusement. Jager Dorn, the young first lieutenant, was obviously uncomfortable. His handsome face was unnaturally pale, and he kept running his fingers through his thick black hair and fidgeting with his silver pen. Colonel Rand von Drachstedt seemed a little more at ease, though his craggy, stern face showed some tension.

"Is there something . . . wrong, gentlemen?" Tor finally asked lightly.

"Um, sir . . . ," Dorn began, tugging at the tight uniform collar at his neck, "it was my understanding—that is, I was unaware—"

Tor didn't help him; he merely watched Dorn coldly until the young lieutenant ran down. When he did, Tor said evenly, "*Oberleutnant* Dorn, I expect two things from the chief aide of my General Staff. One is your undivided and unquestioned loyalty. The other is that you speak plainly and truthfully to me always."

"*Ja wohl, Mein Commandant,*" Dorn returned quickly. "Of course, you have, and will always possess, my complete loyalty. I was not questioning your judgment. I simply do not understand. I was not aware that further military intervention in the Middle East was required."

"It is not evident now," Tor said confidently, "but it will be required in the near future."

Rand von Drachstedt cleared his throat. "Sir, it is difficult for me, too, to comprehend why we should get embroiled in the garbage pit of the Mideast. With the downfall of the United States, the Germanic Union practically controls the economies of the entire world. You have brought the vast military resources of America, including the priceless Galaxy Guardian system, into the Joint Task Forces. Your military forces are invincible. It would seem that you already own the world."

Tor said, "No, Rand. I will not own the world until I own Israel."

"Israel?" von Drachstedt blurted in surprise. "But, sir . . . it is of some strategic importance regionally, of course, with its access to the Red Sea and maintaining the Jordan Neutral Zone. The Israelis have a certain military genius and determination, and I must admit that their intelligence operatives are some of the finest in the world.

But still, I cannot see their global importance. Um . . . sir." He suddenly realized that he may have spoken too much against Tor's international policy. Questioning Tor von Eisenhalt on anything was not a very healthy thing to do.

But Tor was unusually tolerant of Colonel von Drachstedt. With the exception of Alia Silverthorne, Minden Lauer, and Luca Therion, von Drachstedt was his most loyal follower. Almost with warmth he replied, "Relax, *Herr Oberstleutnant.* I will not explain Israel's importance to me, for my reasoning is of a personal nature. However, I will tell you about the Arabic Confederation.

"In the coming months, some evidence will come to light that the terrorist group in America that caused the blackout has definite links to some fundamentalist Muslim subversive groups in Saudi Arabia, Libya, Ethiopia, and Persia. This will inflame the Americans—and it will give me an opportunity to increase the forces in the Middle East by at least two divisions—of Americans."

Dorn was confused, though he dared not ask the question: *Why in the world do we want the Americans in the Middle East?*

But von Drachstedt nodded slowly. "Yes. That would provide both motive and opportunity for the Americans to take an active part in any large-scale war that should break out."

"And it *will* break out, Rand," Tor said with quiet satisfaction. "Even without inflammatory propaganda, the Arabic Confederation is desperate. This economic downturn of the Americans hurts them the worst." He took one more sip of wine, then placed the goblet on the desk. "And I am not as weak-minded as the Americans. I have no intention of giving the Arabic Confederation charity, as the Americans have for so long. All of their economies are going to suffer even more."

"Yes," von Drachstedt said thoughtfully. "And then, of course, there is Syria. The Syrians have been making loud noises about that little campaign against them."

Tor shrugged carelessly. "For these reasons, and more that are known to me but that are not pertinent here, I want our team to retask some of the Galaxy Guardian satellites, both photo-recon and ICBM platforms."

"It will be done, sir," von Drachstedt assured him.

"Let's watch them, Rand. You'll see that they have likely already begun their mobilization against us."

"If they fight us, they will die," von Drachstedt said with some heat.

A small smile played at Tor's lips. "There is that distinct possibility." His light joviality was short-lived as he turned his searing gaze on Dorn. "Now, *Oberleutnant* Dorn, I have some thoughts about America. I will dictate more detailed instructions to one of the secretaries later, and I will expect to receive detailed reports. But for now, I want to instruct you to see that all German military personnel in the United States have access to Cyclops. I also want it made available to all Commissaries. I know that we do not have enough treated units, so I want you to form a *Projekt Schlußenheit* field team for America, take them over there, and requisition all the Cyclops units you can find. Instruct the team to kill the microorganism, reseal the units, and reset the electronics. We should be able to retrofit enough for all of our people to have their own personal Cyclops and at least one for each Commissary post."

Jager Dorn started squirming uncomfortably as soon as Tor said "*Projekt Schlußenheit*." Tor noticed this but deliberately kept on with his instructions—possibly to note, and maybe relish, the young soldier's fear. Now Dorn swallowed and began, "Sir, I—" He cleared his throat again and said in a stronger voice (though he averted his gaze), "Sir, our *Projekt Schlußenheit* Team One has just alerted me this morning that some anomalies have appeared in the long-term laboratory models—"

Tor's rising fury was so evident that Dorn, no matter how hard he tried, could not force himself to continue. The two men watched as Tor leaped out of his chair and began pacing like a tiger, his steps harsh and unbelievably loud on the thick carpet. His handsome features were coarsened with anger. He clenched and unclenched his hands, knuckles cracking like firecrackers in the large room. Then he muttered an unspeakable oath through gritted teeth.

The two men exchanged nervous looks. It seemed that the room temperature was dropping. The two men, who had been chilly since they'd walked into the room, now felt very cold. Unable to help himself, von Drachstedt stared at the big fire in the fireplace, wondering how it had grown so cold, almost freezing, so quickly, in the room. Perhaps a freezing draft, winding its way in insidiously from outside? Dorn touched his lips and found that they were numb. He suddenly wanted more than anything to be anywhere but in this place, at this time.

With a movement so rapid that it defied the eye, Tor drew his small dress dagger out of the scabbard at his waist and threw it at the wall behind Dorn and von Drachstedt. Both men flinched, then whirled. The dagger was buried to the hilt in the polished wood of the wall.

Dorn actually began to fear for his life at that moment. He twisted back around, horrified, and saw Tor throw himself down into his chair, his face still flushed with rage. Restlessly Tor shifted, his lips set in a razor-thin line, and the only sounds in the room were the creak of leather and the screech of the chair's wooden support.

Von Drachstedt, as if from a distance, noted two things. One was that the room temperature was suddenly back to normal, and the other was that the two-hundred-year-old grandfather clock behind Tor had stopped. He sincerely wanted to think it was pure coincidence. But he was a practical man, and self-deception was not in him. There was no doubt—Tor's rage had been so electric and complete that it had thrown the very air, the very essence, of the room out of balance for a few moments.

Rand had been under Tor von Eisenhalt's command for twelve years. He had seen these flashes of Tor's murderous temper before, though none had been quite so full of fury as this. Von Drachstedt knew he wasn't as terrified as Dorn was. *I've faced death too many times,* he reflected with a sudden bone-crushing weariness. The thought jarred him; now, here, in this very room, he was facing . . . Death. He shuddered, not bothering to hide it.

No one spoke. Dorn didn't think he could. A long time passed, or it might have been only moments. Neither Dorn nor von Drachstedt looked at the commandant. Finally, in a voice that sounded strained with holding back his anger, Tor said, "I want to see the *Projekt Schlußenheit* Team One leader. Today."

In a half-whisper Dorn said, "Yes, sir."

Tor gave Dorn a withering look. "I'm very disappointed that I'm only just now receiving this bad news, Dorn. Very disappointed."

This time Dorn really *couldn't* speak. He opened his mouth, but the only sound that came out was a pitiful squeak.

"Anything else?" Tor asked. With each word his voice settled down into its normal timbre.

Rand judged the moment and decided, once again, to defy Death. "Sir, there is one thing that has just occurred to me. Regarding the Arabic Confederation."

"Go on."

"I have had some reports from a member of the *Wolfsrudel,* an economics adviser working in Moscow. He says that the Russians sold some components to Egypt about six months ago. They were parts that could be used in manufacturing some high-tech weapons managers, such as the Javelin Field Array. But the adviser also heard rumors that the Egyptians were having secret talks with some Chinese weapons manufacturers . . ."

"Get to the *point,* Rand!"

"To put it simply, sir, there is some indication that the Saudis are trying to develop the LINC-4 system." Rand tensed himself for another onslaught of anger.

As if none of the rage that had consumed him only moments before had ever existed, Tor's eyes lit up with interest. Rand was ashamed at how relieved he felt. Tor murmured, "So . . . they're gearing up that cowardly thing, hmm? Get confirmation, Rand, but I'm certain you're right. You do know what this means, don't you?"

"The tactical implications, sir? No, I haven't thought that far ahead yet."

Tor smiled, and there was a dark fearful glee in it. "It means, *Mein Oberstleutnant,* that we send in the Americans first."

Thirteen

"SHE LOOKS . . . different," Commissar Xanthe St. Dymion murmured.

No one replied, except with outraged hisses of "Shh!"

The giant Cyclops screens, four of them, each six feet wide and four feet tall, had been set up in Fountain Square at the intersection of Grand and Central. Xanthe estimated that about four thousand people were gathered to watch Minden Lauer's first live-comm broadcast since the blackout. The entire platoon of thirty-two commissars surrounded the civilian population in a thin picket, but Xanthe reflected dryly that the dirty, hungry people needed no riot police. After more than two months of being without heat and light and fresh food, the population had been weakened—and decimated—by hunger, exposure, and disease. Violent assaults such as murders and beatings had gone sharply down with the arrival of supplies and a high commissar to organize the Commissary's police duties. Also, the people had grown too weak and listless to fight much anymore.

But on this cold night, they stood silent, transfixed, as the "Children of Light Overture" blared out on Cyclops's great speakers. On the screen Minden Lauer stood, unmoving, her head thrown back, her hands raised high. She did look different; if possible, she looked even more perfect. But Xanthe thought that somehow, the Lady of Light didn't look quite so ethereal, so angelic. Now she looked more earthy or something. More fiery perhaps.

For one thing, Minden had always worn white dresses for her live-comms and left her arms and neck bare, though she did not indulge in low-cut necklines. She didn't have to. But tonight she wore a midnight blue dress of a flowing translucent material; it covered her from her chin to her toes, but it was very thin. Her stunning figure was clearly outlined by subtle backlighting, and the material was shot through with silver gems that flashed coldly. Minden's lips seemed fuller and were a dark crimson color, and her long oval nails were painted red. Usually Minden wore airy pastel colors for accessories and makeup.

And then there's the background, Xanthe brooded. *Usually it's pastoral scenes, like watercolor paintings. Where in the world is she? It looks so . . . Gothic . . . that ancient sharp-toothed battlement looming like a monolith behind her . . .*

Oberstleutnant Reinhart Angriff stared around at his comrades-in-arms with narrowed eyes. In an instant, they had changed.

In one of the luxurious meeting rooms of the Villa del Sol Hotel, all of the officers of the 77th Luftwaffe had come together to see Minden Lauer's first live-comm broadcast, and then United States President Luca Therion was going to make a world address. After that, Commandant Tor von Eisenhalt was going to address the Joint Task Forces of the Global Union of Nation-States on a closed circuit Cy-II channel.

Reinhart cared little for Minden Lauer's speech (or service, as the followers of the Children of Light called it), since he was not a member of Earth's Light. Many of his comrades were, however, for they seemed to believe that the organization's teachings of vast resources of individual inner strength gave them power. For all

Reinhart knew, they might be right; they were certainly powerful men. He had sometimes felt that he needed something, that he had a lack, or a weakness, within himself that he was at a loss to overcome. But Reinhart had never had any faith in Minden Lauer or Earth's Light. He had faith only in his beloved Germany and in his commandant, Tor von Eisenhalt, the greatest leader of men that the world had ever seen.

Reinhart had seen Minden's live communications broadcasts before, but other than thinking that she was a lovely woman, they'd made little impression on him. He thought it curious that she seemed to have such an impact on so many people, from small children to hardened warriors. He also thought it odd that she was to address the world—before the president of the United States, even before Commandant von Eisenhalt. He'd decided to watch, and listen, to her more closely, to see if he could discern exactly what this woman had to do with the catastrophic global events that had taken place in the last few months.

"Is that her?" he muttered. She didn't look like the same woman. In his recollection, Minden Lauer was soft, pretty, ephemeral. This woman looked like a vampire.

"Seid ruhig, Oberstleutnant Angriff!"

"Entschuldigen Sie bitte, Mein Oberleutnant," Reinhart murmured quietly. Though First Lieutenant Jager Dorn did not outrank him, it was wiser to defer to Commandant Tor von Eisenhalt's chief of staff.

Minden Lauer was about to speak.

My beloved Children of Light . . .

We have walked, and breathed, and lived, and loved in the light for so long . . . that we stopped looking into the darkness. We did not see the evil forces hiding there, waiting for their time and chance . . .

And so the evil hour has come. Even now, my beloved country is still under a shadow. But because we are strong, and we have powerful allies throughout the world, we will grow strong again. Soon! In just a matter of a few days, all of our beloved children in America will be walking in the light once again. We have powerful protectors, men and women all over the world, who are unceasingly, untiringly watching over you, and even now are rooting out and banishing your enemies.

Make no mistake, we have been attacked by enemies, people who hate us, who cannot tolerate our beliefs. They teach that we are blind, that we are doomed, that only they are righteous and good. Yet they have brutally and wantonly attacked America with this scourge . . . because they believe that they do God's will.

But you and I, children, know that we walk in God's will. We understand that this earth and all the forces and powers of it belong to us, for our dedication to it and our inner strength! And now, you must call upon those powers, those strengths, that are our greatest defense—and weapons! All of the powers of our beloved Father Earth are yours, from the beginning of time . . . the might of the four forces . . . air, water, earth, and fire . . . Seek them! Use them to fight and conquer!

"I thought it was our *Mother* Earth," Xanthe commented dryly to her fellow commissar, Bryce Atherton. The expression on his face was as confused as Xanthe's. He started to answer, but a young woman behind them snarled, "Be quiet, can't you?"

But what do you have, you alone of all the creatures and forces on earth? It is not of the earth . . . This power is beyond, above the very power of fire, of the air . . .

"What's she doing?" Reinhart Angriff whispered. No one answered. It seemed that all of the men in the room were enthralled.

Drawing a glittering, slender knife from an unseen sheath at her waist, Minden drew the blade across her middle finger. Then she held up her hand, the blood crimson and thin, flowing freely down her hand and dripping off her wrist. When she spoke again, her voice was soft, erotic. But Angriff felt disquieted; this woman was bizarre.

Why do we shudder, feel primitive dread, at the sight of blood?

Because we rarely think of, or see, blood . . . only bloodshed. *We see pain. We see suffering. We see death.*

But I tell you now that blood is life.

Blood is power!

With it you will have the world!

Minden held her hand over a golden goblet, and the blood flowed freely into it. With a seductive smile, she picked up the goblet and drank.

The silent thousands of people in the square in Hot Springs, Arkansas, started clamoring; it could not be called cheering or shouting. It was a primitive roar, a howl of thirst and hunger.

Xanthe St. Dymion shuddered, trembled. For the first time since the blackout, she was truly frightened.

FOURTEEN

NORTH AMERICAN AEROSPACE DEFENSE COMMAND
CHEYENNE MOUNTAIN, COLORADO
***********Z PRIORITY EYES ONLY***********
DIRECTIVE 09096633ZSEP
***********Z PRIORITY EYES ONLY***********
Z REF PROTOCOL X

» APPLICATION

1) THREAT OF UNKNOWN ORIGIN
2) INDETERMINATE EFFECTS ON POPULATION
3) INDEFINITE DURATION

» DIRECTIVES

1) ALL MARINE AND ACTIVE NAVY ON DEFCON-3 ALERT. FULLY MAN ALL SHIPS IN BOTH CARRIER GROUPS USING ANY TRANSPORT (MILITARY OR CIVILIAN) AVAILABLE. CARRIER GROUPS BOTH ATLANTIC AND PACIFIC TO PROCEED TO LASER ARRAY INSTALLATIONS AT DIEGO GARCIA AND MIDWAY IMMEDIATELY TO AWAIT FURTHER ORDERS.

2) ALL PERSONNEL AT LOWRY AFB, PETERSON AFB, AND FORT CARSON ARMY BASE TO GO TO DEFCON-2 ALERT. SELECTED UNITS TO PHYSICALLY SURROUND NORAD AS A LAST LINE OF DEFENSE AND SET UP SUPPLY AND COMMUNICATIONS LINES.

3) COMPLETE LOCKDOWN OF NORAD FACILITY, I.E., ALL TUNNEL ENTRANCE/EXIT BLAST DOORS CLOSED AND SEALED, AIR FLOW REVERSED, WITH AIR PURIFIERS ON TWENTY-FOUR HOURS/DAY.

4) IF SITUATION IS NOT CLARIFIED (WITH SUBSEQUENT RESORT TO ANOTHER PROTOCOL) WITHIN TWENTY-FOUR HOURS, NO PERSON SHALL BE ALLOWED INTO NORAD (IN CASE OF COMPROMISE OF OUTSIDE PERSONNEL).

NORTH AMERICAN AEROSPACE DEFENSE COMMAND
CHEYENNE MOUNTAIN, COLORADO
**********Z PRIORITY EYES ONLY**********
DIRECTIVE 09096633ZSEP
**********Z PRIORITY EYES ONLY**********
Z REF PROTOCOL X

****

NAADC HAD ALL SORTS of Protocols, for every national emergency that the collective brains could devise: Protocol Touchdown (for *T*hermonuclear *D*evice); Protocol CAB (for *C*hemical and *B*iological *A*gents); and the favorite of many of the younger staffers and soldiers in the high-tension underground complex, Protocol ICUS, which they called I-CUSS (for *I*nvasion of *C*ontinental *U.S.*).

Protocol X was a catchall, a miscellany for the unheard of, the junk drawer of the emergency directives. No one ever actually expected to invoke Protocol X, for no one ever expected that the most advanced society in the history of the world could not determine the exact nature of a catastrophic event that threatened the United States. But for the equinox of the autumn of 2050, Protocol X was all NAADC had.

On any given day there were about eleven hundred people scurrying around the granite guts of Cheyenne Mountain. More than half of them were civilians: chemical engineers, electrical engineers, computer programmers, mechanics, maintenance staff, cooks, bottle washers.

Of the five hundred–plus military personnel, only about two hundred of them were NORAD Security, or heavily armed soldiers there for the purpose of defense of the facility. The rest were highly trained and qualified air force personnel who performed the actual job that NORAD was built for: to staff the operational center that kept watch over aircraft, missiles, and space systems that might pose a threat to the United States and Canada. Since the Galaxy Guardian systems umbrella had been expanded, they also kept watch over South America and Israel.

In NORAD, at the top of the food chain was chief duty officer. The duty officer rotated among the Joint Chiefs of Staff, the director and deputy director of the National Security Agency, and the four assistant secretaries of defense. On the fateful day of the ohm-bug, this unfortunate responsibility fell directly on the shoulders of Dewey Driscoll Wallace, commandant of the Marine Corps.

General Wallace, a hard-edged man with a jutting jaw and flashing dark eyes, had knife-sharp manners that could freeze an underling's guts. But as was true with most soldiers of the soul, his truest and best qualities shone through under adverse circumstances. And these days in the vast caves of Cheyenne Mountain were certainly of the adverse kind.

"Let's just all relax, shall we, gentlemen?" He searched the anxious faces of the men sitting at the plain wooden table. It was a junior officers' wardroom and had shining vending machines and a laser-light jukebox. All of them were dark now, the vending machines' wares long since removed and stored. Wallace had chosen the wardroom to meet with the engineers as a sort of neutral—and he hoped more congenial—meeting place than the tense, semidarkened situation rooms and offices around NORAD's heart, the Central Control Room. "Port and cigars, anyone?"

The weak joke brought a smile to the men's faces. Chief Engineer Kronsky, a burly man who looked a little like Father Christmas, chuckled. No liquor was ever on the premises of NORAD, for any reason. And the idea of anyone smoking in this stale, heavy, odor-ridden air was ludicrous.

"All right, now for the bad news," Wallace went on, a shadow passing over his rough features. "My Raiders are gone. No word from any of the teams." Three air duct tunnels existed, for even the most secure installation must have a fresh air supply. For all the high technologies of the century, no one had been able to make oxygen. One tunnel came out on the east side of Fort Carson, in the rocky plains; one was just to the west of Pueblo, at the base of an unnamed and unnoticeable mountain; and one came out in the Royal Gorge. The three six-man teams of Marine Raiders had left the central complex seven days before. Their handheld walkie-talkies with the 9-volt batteries had reached only about a mile; after that NORAD had heard nothing from them. NORAD's all-seeing eyes had noted, of course, the three Messerschmitt Dagger helicopters searching the areas where the tunnels came out two nights previously, but they couldn't afford to retask any of the satellites to monitor any more detail than the flight paths. They hadn't seen the eighteen men die, though Commandant Wallace knew they were dead.

The four men nodded, and Wallace went on, "Guess everyone

knows that already, but this is my official notification to you. Now, Chief Engineer Kronsky, you go ahead and give me your bad news."

Kronsky frowned, and the chubby cheeks above his neatly trimmed silver beard reddened with frustration. "Sir, we're starting to get dangerously high carbon dioxide levels."

"Yeah, I've noticed that it's sorta like trying to breathe in quicksand," Wallace said dryly. "So let's go over my options again, Kronsky."

The older man nodded and said in a neutral voice, "We can divert more power to the air purification systems, sir. I think even with these CO_2 levels we could still knock it back."

Wallace's jaw jutted forward ominously. "But that means that we'd risk the Crays, right?" The fragile Cray-5 computers that were the hardware heart of the Galaxy Guardian systems required a constant seventy-degree temperature and microsensing dehumidifiers. Any change in ambient temperature or the tiniest droplet of moisture in either the hardware room or the monitoring Control Center was likely to damage the delicate components of the powerful computers.

Kronsky shrugged. "Yes, sir, any diversion is likely to result in surges and maybe temporary outages."

"No," Wallace said decisively. "The GG system has to stay up and running. After all, that's why we're here, not to do any silly superfluous things like breathing."

In his kind manner, Kronsky said, "At most it would give us only two more days, anyway. We never foresaw, sir, that this facility would, in reality, have to run off the auxiliary systems for such a prolonged period." NORAD had two backup power sources, diesel and battery, and either was supposed to power the complex for thirty days. The installation also had food and water to last for sixty days. It was now the sixty-second day since the autumnal equinox. NORAD was out of food and almost out of air, and the diesel was getting ominously low.

Kronsky cleared his throat and said uncomfortably, "And, sir, I must remind you that if we let the power go completely down, it'll probably be months before we can get the system hardware checked and cleared to boot up again. I know you probably have Cray techs advising you about this already."

Wallace smiled, a dour stretch of his thin lips tight over his teeth. "Yeah, they've been 'advising' me about that at the top of their lungs for about three days now. I think those drone-heads would actually give those computers artificial respiration if they thought it would keep them going." His dark eyes, bleak and unseeing, focused far in the distance. "Well, gentlemen, if we're out of air and out of power, I guess it's time to hit the road."

The relief on the faces of the four men was almost ludicrous to see. Kronsky, who was the only civilian to dare take conversational liberties with the commandant, asked, "So, we aren't going down with the ship, sir?"

Wallace laughed, a harsh, braying sound. "Not hardly, and those navy pukes wouldn't, either. I just need to know one really important thing, though, Kronsky. If we leave a skeleton crew in here—say, a hundred men, good and true—can they live for a couple of days? I mean, can they breathe?"

"Sure, Commandant," Kronsky replied. "Twelve men won't take up nearly the oxygen that eleven hundred do. There'll be plenty. And, sir—if you open the tunnel doors, naturally there'll be fresh air coming in."

"Well, then, that's it, gentlemen," Wallace said, rising to his lean six feet. "Let's go open those doors."

In the end, it was that simple.

The tunnel blast doors were three-foot-thick slabs of concrete and steel, each weighing thirty tons. Commandant Wallace, in the lead with the 336 men and women of the 721st NORAD Support Group, felt immense relief when they slid smoothly open without a sound. His most secret fear was of being buried alive, and that was exactly how he had felt for the last two months in the underground complex. Though the doors were set about a quarter of a mile down the tunnel, he could still see the faint glow of sunlight—real sunlight!—in the immense cavern. By sheer willpower he made himself march calmly toward the light instead of running like a madman.

Outside, at the tunnel entrance, President Luca Therion and Tor von Eisenhalt waited in an open Vulcan. Because the president was with him, the 721st didn't fire on Eisenhalt or any of the armed men arrayed behind them.

With cold dread, Commandant Wallace stopped in his tracks, blinking in the unaccustomed brightness of the morning sun.

"General Wallace," Luca said calmly, "step forward, please."

Confused, Wallace walked slowly toward the Vulcan.

Tor von Eisenhalt, with calmness and deliberation that paralyzed the American soldiers, took out his side arm and shot General Wallace in the head.

Tor's elite German 571st Mountain Battalion instantly moved up. Out of the 336 American soldiers, only forty-two shots were fired, and only 2 Germans were killed and 1 injured.

Of the 1,062 men and women in NORAD, not a single person survived.

PART III

REDEEMING THE TIME

Wherefore he saith, Awake thou that sleepest, and arise from the dead, and Christ shall give thee light. See then that ye walk circumspectly, not as fools, but as wise, redeeming the time, because the days are evil.

—EPHESIANS 5:14–16

And oftentimes, to win us to our harm,
The instruments of darkness tell us truths,
Win us with honest trifles, to betray 's
In deepest consequence.

—BANQUO, FROM *MACBETH* BY WILLIAM SHAKESPEARE

Fifteen

As Riley Case emerged from the dense woods, he carried his rifle in his left hand while the other grasped a sack that was slung over his shoulders. When he approached the Mitchells' cabin, Kyle Saylor came running up, his short legs pumping. "Hi, Wiley!" he called, his doe-brown eyes bright. With his lisp, he couldn't pronounce Riley's name correctly, and Allegra had laughed and sometimes called Case "Wile E. Coyote." Riley pretended not to recall the silly character from the ancient Roadrunner cartoons.

"Hi, boss," Riley answered. "What have you been up to?"

"I've been helping Mama clean."

"Good for you. I like to see a man who stands by his mom. I got some cleaning to do, too." He nodded toward the canvas sack over his shoulder. "Got some squirrels to clean."

"Clean them? Are they dirty?"

"Uh—sorta. Got to clean them so we can have them for supper."

Kyle nodded sagely, which amused Riley. The four-year-old had seen the kills Riley made for their food—deer, squirrels, rabbits, and wild pigs—but he still didn't exactly connect them to the food on the table. *Gets it from his mama,* Riley thought with some affection. *She's kinda squeamish about the process . . . but she sure likes the end result.*

Merrill Stanton staggered around the corner of the cabin, his arms filled with firewood. He wasn't a very good outdoorsman, though he worked as long and hard as Riley Case and David Mitchell did in this frontier world.

"Grandpa, Wiley's got some dirty squirrels in that sack," Kyle told him solemnly.

"That right?" The older man winked at Riley. "I'll give you a hand as soon as I stack this wood inside, Riley."

"No need, Mr. Stanton," Riley assured him. "It's only about a dozen. I can clean them myself."

Merrill was secretly relieved, for he wasn't certain he'd know the upside of a squirrel from the downside. "Okay, c'mon, Kyle. Let me put up this wood, and we'll go out and get some kindling."

"Can I bring my wagon?" Kyle asked eagerly.

Merrill smiled. Riley had made Kyle a wooden wagon, with wooden wheels painstakingly whittled by hand. Riley had even carved Kyle's name on it and made a little seat for Benny the Bear. Riley might be a rather distant and forbidding man, but he was certainly good to Kyle. "Sure, that's a good idea. We can load it up."

Kyle and Merrill disappeared inside the Mitchells' cabin, while Riley went off to the spot he and David had chosen below the cabin in the thick woods to clean and butcher the kills. It had to be a safe distance away from the cabin. The blood and entrails drew predators—particularly wolves. They heard them howling every night.

Soon Riley brought the meat back into the kitchen, where Allegra, Genevieve, and Noemi Mitchell were discussing cooking wild game. Genevieve Stanton was a pretty good cook, but all her life she'd cooked only meals that were so preprocessed and preconcocted and pretreated and preconstructed that they rarely resembled the original food. Allegra was a competent cook, but she lacked flair or whatever the instinctive quality was that made a really good cook. But Noemi had it, and she'd taught both of them much.

Riley handed Allegra a plain wooden platter piled high with meat cut into small pieces. Allegra made a face. "Thank you, I guess, Mr. Case."

"My pleasure, ma'am," he replied, his dark eyes sparkling. "You still haven't gotten used to fresh meat, have you, Mrs. Saylor?"

Allegra stared down at the bloody meat and sighed. "It's not that exactly. I'm just having a little culture shock. Sometimes my brain lags behind for a few minutes . . . I can't believe I'm holding a platter filled with pieces of dead squirrels, and I'm going to cook them with a wood fire on a cast-iron stove . . ."

Genevieve nodded. "Do you know that sometimes when I walk into a room, I still say 'Lights' to Cyclops? Sometimes it all seems so unreal, like a dream or a hallucination."

Riley Case's penetrating gaze was still on Allegra Saylor. "Is it like a bad dream to you, too, Mrs. Saylor?"

"Hmm? Oh. Um . . . I don't know. It's not really—a bad dream, no. Not since we got here and found Brother and Sister Mitchell. It's just that sometimes your mind rebels at the enormity of what's happened." She looked up at Riley curiously. "Don't you feel that way, too, Mr. Case?"

He shrugged, and Allegra could almost feel the barrier he instantly, always, erected. "It is different. If you ladies will excuse me . . ." In his usual, quaint old-world manner, he nodded to each of them, murmuring, "Ma'am," and slipped out.

Noemi looked shrewdly at Allegra, who watched him go with a thoughtful look on her face. "He's a good hunter, is Mr. Case. Did you know squirrels are about the hardest game to kill? Small target and fast."

"No, I didn't know that," Allegra said. "And I certainly don't have the faintest clue how to cook them. Do you, Mother?"

Genevieve sighed. "No, I can't say I have any experience cooking squirrels."

Noemi smiled. "It's real easy, especially since Mr. Case has butchered the meat into small pieces. We can have some fried squirrel, and then I'll show you how to make squirrel dumplings. Now first you get a bunch of flour, and salt and pepper it and mix it up . . ."

"But—how much flour? How much salt and pepper?" Allegra asked, bewildered.

Noemi shrugged. "Just a pile of flour, and salt and pepper it."

Allegra said with exasperation, "Why do good cooks always say that? 'Just some of this, and a little of that, and no, a lot of the other . . .' Why can't they tell us food morons how to measure it? Like in teaspoons or gallons or whatever?"

Noemi and Genevieve laughed. "All right, Allegra," Noemi said, her eyes twinkling. "Take a gallon of flour, a minim of salt, and a peck of pepper . . ."

As the women cooked, the men sat around the fireplace, talking of the situation with the living quarters. Everyone had been sleeping in the Mitchells' cabin, but David and Riley had found several other cabins nearby. They were renovating three of them—one for Merrill and Genevieve, one for Allegra and Kyle, and one for David and Riley. Allegra had been working hard on all three cabins, too, cleaning and doing some repair work. Soon everyone would have a house.

Riley suddenly lifted his head. He seemed to sniff the air, then said, "Somebody's coming."

Instantly he and David got up, grabbed their guns, and went out on the front porch. David squinted in the falling darkness. "It's a diesel," he muttered and released the safety on his shotgun. "Maybe a Hummer."

"Maybe," Riley agreed in a low voice. He moved over and planted himself beside the cabin as he chambered a shell into the rifle.

As soon as the outline of the vehicle was visible to his sharp eyes, David jumped down beside Riley and threw his weapon to his shoulder. "That's a Vulcan. German military utility vehicle," he said grimly.

"What do you want to do, Mitchell?" Riley asked.

David thought for a moment, then answered, "Don't kill him. Or them. Need to talk first."

They waited tensely.

Riley squinted through the old magnification sight on his .30-.30. "Mitchell, I think it's that commissar, St. Dymion."

Indeed it was Xanthe St. Dymion. She pulled up and jumped out, waving at David and Riley. "It's okay. It's just me," she called anxiously.

"Pass, friend," David said, coming forward and smiling.

Xanthe was bundled up in a heavy coat, and a thick fur cap was pulled down over her ears. "Hello, David," she said, somewhat shyly.

"Xanthe, it's good to see you." David put out his hand. She took it, and her grip was as hard and firm as a man's.

"I brought some supplies. You want to help me? I've got something else, a present for Brother and Sister Mitchell."

The men began to bring in the boxes and bags that Xanthe had brought. They made quite a pile on the floor of the kitchen, and the women were rummaging through with cries of pleasure.

"A whole case of coffee! We've been out for weeks," Allegra cried, holding up a Proto-Syn red-labeled can.

"And look at this—sweaters," Genevieve exclaimed. "I've been freezing to death."

Xanthe had gone outside, and when she reentered the cabin, she held a cat in her arms.

"Well, what in the world have you got there, daughter?" Jesse Mitchell exclaimed.

Xanthe put the cat down, stroking its back. "What do you think it is, Mr. Mitchell?"

Jesse examined the animal thoughtfully. "Well, it looks sort of like a cat—but somehow the plan went wrong. Never saw a cat like that."

Xanthe laughed. "He's a Manx."

"A Manx, you say! He sure is a strange-looking creature."

The Manx was a mottled brown and white. His irregular markings had given him a most comic expression, for one-half of his mouth was dark and one-half was white. He seemed to have a lopsided smile. The most startling features of his breed were the lack of a tail and extraordinary long hind legs.

"That poor cat's got his tail cut off! He backed into something," Jesse observed.

"No. All Manxes are that way. None of them have tails."

"Look how long his hind legs are," Noe said. "He sure is a peculiar-looking cat."

"I like cats," David said, affectionately stroking the Manx. The cat nuzzled his hand and pushed against his fist when he doubled it up. "I always wished I could have one. Never thought I'd see a Manx."

Early in the century, all exotic pets such as parrots, ferrets, and snakes had been outlawed. A strict national program to sterilize stray cats and dogs had been enacted, with the result that within twenty years all of them had died out. Only registered companion animals had then been available, and the licenses for them had become so difficult to obtain, and so expensive, that very few people had dogs or cats. The Man and Biosphere Project Protocols disapproved of domesticated animals. The philosophy dictated that cats and dogs were merely wild animals that humans had perverted and should be eliminated from the earth altogether.

"Manx cats are very rare," Xanthe was saying. "I believe there are fewer than one hundred of them left in the world, and they've all been sterilized. So I guess you could say that makes Mannie here priceless."

Jesse shook his head. "A cat—and a clown-looking one at that. Who would believe what this old world's come to?"

"Where did you get him, Xanthe?" David asked. Mannie had,

in the way of cats, decided that David was worthy of his attention and had promptly climbed up in his lap to demand adoration.

"Two years ago someone found him wandering around out in the biome," Xanthe answered, shaking her head. "He'd been sterilized and well cared for. Why someone would abandon a valuable companion animal like that, we'll never know, I guess. Anyway, the Commissary took him, and he's been held in the biome animal care facility ever since. When the blackout came, nobody cared about the animals there but me. I let the rest of them go—they were just squirrels and raccoons and rabbits. Mannie was the only domesticated animal there." She grimaced. "I got into trouble with our new chief commissar for letting the other biome sample animals go. I figured that First Commissar Wickham would probably want to lock Mannie up again, and I didn't want that to happen—so I catnapped him, you might say."

Kyle's eyes were as round as silver dollars. "A cat!" he said reverently. "Can we keep him, Miss Xanthe? Please, please?"

Xanthe smiled. "I hope you will, Kyle, but you'll have to ask your mother and the Mitchells."

Kyle made a heartrending appeal to the entire room. "Please, can we, please?" Kyle had never seen a live cat in his life.

"Why, of course, we can, Kyle," Noe said warmly. "When Brother Mitchell and I were young, we always had a cat around, before it got to be such a terrible crime. We're getting some mice, and Mannie ought to take care of them."

Kyle was overjoyed, and he immediately grabbed up Mannie, whirling him in a circle, whooping. The cat stayed limp, his lopsided smile intact. "Good-natured cat," David observed. "I thought they were supposed to be arrogant and all that."

"Mannie's not," Xanthe said affectionately. "He's sweet." She sniffed the air and hinted, "Something certainly smells good . . ."

"Goodness, where are my manners?" Noemi said briskly. "Here, sit down, child. The Lord's provided us with plenty of squirrel and dumplings tonight. Guess He knew we'd be having company."

Xanthe sat down and ate hungrily. Between bites, she was peppered with questions. Everyone was avid to know what was happening in the outside world. Riley, as always, withdrew from the group at the table. He stayed by the fire, cleaning his rifle and watching Kyle play with Mannie.

"Well, I've been promoted," Xanthe said slowly. "I've been made a high commissar, second in command of the Hot Springs Emergency Service Commissary."

"Hmm," David said noncommittally. "Is that the good news or the bad news?"

Xanthe sighed. "Not too long ago, that would have been the best news I could ever have. More than I could hope for. You know, of course, that the Commissary doesn't actually have a military hierarchical ranking? I mean, you are either a low commissar or a high commissar, and there are only a few high commissars, the top leadership in each biome. Now, though, under the emergency directives, we're getting rankings."

"So who's in charge? Who's issuing these emergency directives? And what are they exactly?" David demanded.

Xanthe dropped her eyes. "Well, as near as I can tell, the Commissary is being reconstituted as the lead organization in a sort of superagency that includes the FBI, FEMA, and all state and local law enforcement agencies. Chief Commissar Alia Silverthorne is the director. Hot Springs has a new first commissar, as I said. Commissar Wickham. He's a real hard case. Used to be first commissar of the Three Rivers Biome."

Riley, unnoticed by the others, stopped cleaning his gun and stared hard at Xanthe. He rarely spoke to her; he seemed to avoid her, though he was never rude to her. After a moment, he dropped his eyes to his rifle again, though his motions seemed rather automatic.

"So how are you getting your information?" David asked. He thought he already knew the answer.

Xanthe shifted uneasily. "It's the Germans, David. Guess you already knew that from the Vulcan. I know what you told me about Fort Carson . . . but they really do just seem to be trying to help here. I mean, they've flown in food and medical supplies, they've helped reorganize the hospitals and clinics, and they've set up Cyclops for the Commissary." With a cautious look at Kyle, so close in the small one-room cabin, she went on in a low tone, "They even flew in two companies to help with body disposal. That's been a real problem since the crematorium's been out."

Noe murmured, "How many?"

Heavily Xanthe replied, "We aren't sure of the total yet. We're still—finding them. So far we've cataloged more than two thousand."

A stunned silence greeted this news.

"Okay, so what's their story, Xanthe?" David asked darkly. "Are the Germans in charge? Have they actually conquered the United States?"

Xanthe replied, "It's—it's kind of hard to tell exactly. See, evidently Commandant Tor von Eisenhalt rescued the president—and I mean he personally found him and Minden Lauer and Commissar Silverthorne, besieged in the White House. So President Therion is back, and he's announced that we're now allied with the Germanic Union of Nation-States, only the name's been changed. Now it's the Global Union of Nation-States."

"Aw, man," David muttered blackly. "That's just great."

Xanthe slid David a sidelong look. "So you see, now our military is joined with the GUNS Joint Task Force. President Therion has mobilized—everyone, I guess. There's—something going on in the Mideast."

"What!" David exclaimed. "You mean, we've all been ordered to active duty?"

"I think so. At least, the president has ordered all military personnel to report back to their posts. He's given his personal assurance that no questions will be asked of anyone who had left his post."

"Yeah?" David snarled. "Think he's thought to ask the Goths why some of our military *left their posts* . . . as in they got shot to pieces?"

"I don't know, David," Xanthe answered unhappily. "I don't know if the president is a traitor—or just foolish."

"I wish I knew what Captain Slaughter was doing," David muttered. Even as he said it David had an idea, but he knew that he would have to speak with Xanthe privately.

Finally Xanthe finished eating—it took her a long time because she kept having to answer questions—and Noe served all of them some delicious-smelling freshly brewed coffee.

"Count Tor von Eisenhalt," Xanthe pronounced with some wonder. "He's managed to salvage the global economic crisis that exploded after we went down. I'm not certain of the details, but I do know that we're not on dollars anymore."

"Not on dollars!" Merrill exclaimed. "What currency are we on?"

"Deutsche marks. But it doesn't seem to make that much difference to me," Xanthe said with the carelessness of one who had never used pieces of paper for money. "We just get Cyclops personal account credits in deutsche marks instead of dollars."

"But what about the people, daughter?" Jesse asked quietly. "What's happening to them?"

Xanthe was obviously troubled. "It's—odd, Brother Mitchell. All we have is Cyclops broadcasts, you see. It's our only connection, our only communication, our only—touch with the outside world. So we have to rely on whatever they tell us." She shifted in her seat, and her eyes quickly swept over David, who was staring blankly into space, obviously lost in thought. She continued, "The president says that militant religious fanatics caused the blackout as a terrorist attack against the people of the United States."

Merrill, Genevieve, and Allegra all exclaimed in outrage. David started and stared at Xanthe. Even Riley made a low exclamation. Only Jesse and his wife seemed unsurprised. "Uh-huh," Jesse said laconically. "So that's how he's getting to it. Old devil's got him another excuse to persecute Christians. Just like when they accused the Christians of trying to burn down Rome." Noe nodded in agreement.

"Well, that's just great!" David snorted. "Goths crawlin' all over us, shooting down innocent civilians at will, and my commander in chief thinks people like my grandfather are the criminals!"

"Guess we are at that," Jesse said, his blue eyes twinkling. "I know we're not supposed to be living here in one of his little green spaces on the map. That means we're breaking the law, doesn't it, daughter?"

Xanthe smiled dismally. "Yes, you and Mrs. Mitchell are some real desperadoes, you are. So are you, Mr. and Mrs. Stanton. And you, Allegra. And Kyle, too. He's a real danger to society."

Her summary broke the tension a little. Jesse stared at Xanthe, his blue eyes as bright as lasers. Unable to meet his gaze, she dropped her eyes. "Daughter," he said kindly, "we're joking about it, but now that you're a big uppity-up in that Commissary, you're in a bad position, aren't you?"

Softly, without looking up, she answered, "Our orders are to detain all registered members of the United America Church and the Catholic Church for questioning. The public is instructed to report any known Christians who are not members of these churches to the Commissary."

With a tinge of fear Genevieve asked, "What do you do with them, Xanthe?"

"They're being transferred to Little Rock for debriefing, and then they're all being deported to Isolation Facilities. For their own protection, they say. And I guess it's true . . . the public . . . people are very angry and scared, and they want to take it out on someone."

She looked up squarely at Brother Mitchell. "They've been forming lynch mobs and dragging people through the streets to the Commissary. Not everyone has made it there alive, either. And—and—our orders are not to detain anyone who is reporting a Christian, Brother Mitchell. They can pretty much do whatever they want without being questioned, much less arrested."

Jesse nodded calmly. "And so they've turned completely away from God. What kind of poison is that old Destroyer feeding them now?"

At first Xanthe didn't quite understand the question, but then she realized that the people were being indoctrinated with something that sounded like religion but that surely had nothing to do with Jesus Christ. Slowly she answered, "Minden Lauer is doing two live-comm broadcasts a day. Everybody watches them on a huge Cyclops that the Germans have put up in Fountain Square. It doesn't matter whether it's raining or snowing, daylight or dark. They all stand there, thousands of them, even the children, without moving or speaking. It's like they're hypnotized or something. They can't seem to get enough of that woman."

Jesse was silent for a moment, then he leaned forward, his blue eyes piercing as he stared at Xanthe. "What is it they can't get enough of? What's that woman telling them?"

Xanthe hesitated, uncertain. "I have to admit, Brother Mitchell, that I just don't understand it. I've listened to her, but I can't follow. She's—she's *different*. I'd heard her before the blackout. She used to talk about love and beauty and nature and the love and the care of the earth . . ."

"Let me guess," Jesse's voice rasped, "now she talks about how everyone is powerful, everyone is good, everyone can be a god!"

Xanthe shot a startled glance at the old man. "Yes! How did you know?"

"Same old thing, daughter. Same tired old lies the devil's always told."

Xanthe nodded. "But that's not all." She dropped her voice to a rough half-whisper. "Minden talks a lot about our enemies, about how evil has always tried to overcome good and how we've all been attacked. I—guess that part—she means us, doesn't she? The Christians? And there's a lot of talk about—about blood. That's the part I can't seem to grasp. Sometimes I feel she's talking nonsense, but then I see how everyone hangs on her every word. I think there's some kind of key or code that everyone else has—but I don't."

Jesse's Bible was open before him, and he turned a few pages and said, "That's exactly right! In John's gospel, chapter 3, verse 19, the Word says, '*And this is the condemnation, that light is come into the world, and men loved darkness rather than light, because their deeds were evil.*'" He ruffled the pages and said, "Back in chapter 1 the scripture says, '*In him was life; and the life was the light of men. And the light shineth in darkness; and the darkness comprehended it not.*'"

He closed the big threadbare Bible and caressed the old leather cover. "It's a good thing you don't understand that woman. You don't because you aren't on the old devil's wavelength. Don't ever listen to her, daughter. When she's on, you just pray to God and set your mind on Jesus."

The group at the table grew quiet, each one sorting out his thoughts. The only sounds in the cabin came from Riley as he sewed a button on one of his shirts. His movements made the slightest rustle in the silence of the cabin. He had spread out his sleeping bag for Kyle, who was nestled in it, sound asleep. Mannie was sprawled out contentedly next to him.

After a while Merrill asked with difficulty, "Xanthe? If you're rounding up the Christians—have you heard anything from Pastor Colfax or any of the others who were with us?"

Xanthe shook her head. "I've been kind of trying to keep watch for them. I was hoping I might find them first, maybe get them out of town before they get picked up." Xanthe had attended Tybalt Colfax's church, and whatever his shortcomings, Xanthe had first heard the Word of God while attending his church.

"Yeah?" David said, eyeing Xanthe sternly. "And wouldn't that be dangerous for you, My Commissar?"

"Yes," she answered evenly. "I think it probably would. But that's why I'm there, I think, David. That's why I'm where I am and what I am. You all know that you're here for a reason, for some plan or task that God has set for you. And that's why I'm a high commissar in the Ozark Plateau Biome right now, in these times. It must be to help the people of God." She took a deep breath and smiled sweetly at Jesse and Noe Mitchell. "And that's what I'm going to do. Help the people of God in every way I can think of, as long as I can."

"You mean until you get caught," David said quietly. "And you will get caught, you know. Then what will happen to you?"

"A very wise man told me once," Xanthe answered with a nod at Jesse, "'*Though He slay me, yet will I trust in Him.*'"

For more than two hours Xanthe stayed and felt herself safe and at home. Then she said reluctantly, "I've got to go back. I can't keep the Vulcan out overnight, or someone will question me."

"How did you get away?" David asked.

"I told them I was going to patrol the outlying areas—just to be sure no unauthorized persons were wandering around in the biome."

"So, are you going to report us, My Commissar?" David said, smiling.

The corners of Xanthe's rather thin lips turned up. "As far as I'm concerned, it seems that the Lord God of heaven and earth has authorized you people to be here. I don't think it's necessary to explain that to an underling."

Xanthe got up to go, but Allegra came over and said, "Can I talk to you a moment before you leave, Xanthe?"

"Why, of course."

The two women moved over to the far corner of the room, and Allegra said, "Xanthe, can you check military personnel records on Cyclops?"

"Yes, I can do that."

Allegra was troubled; she chewed her lip for a moment and studied her friend's face. "Would—could you get in trouble?"

"Of course not, Allegra," Xanthe said confidently. "I'm a high muckety-muck, and I have access to the Great Red Eye. We have four Cyclops drones at the Commissary, and we're allowed to use them for personal messages. All of us have been Cy-mailing. No one would think twice if I inquired about a friend in the marines. Colonel Neville Saylor, right? At Twenty-Nine Palms?"

"Yes," Allegra whispered. "I—I just didn't want to—my parents are so worried about me and Kyle, I just didn't want to talk about it in front of them."

"I understand." Xanthe nodded. "I'll check, and I'm going to try to get back out here once a week, Allegra. Maybe next week I'll have some news. So would he be trying to send you a message, do you think? Would he use a call sign or a code name?"

"We never set up any code names. It'd just be on the Cy-net from Neville at Twenty-Nine Palms to Allegra."

Xanthe said her good-byes, and David told her, "I'll walk you out."

With some confusion Xanthe murmured, "Okay," and then hurried out, with David following.

Xanthe studied David's profile by the starlight. He had the particular kind of masculine attractiveness, rugged and clean-cut, that she had always admired. In fact, David was everything that Xanthe had ever wanted: he was attractive, resourceful, smart, with a good sense of humor. And he seemed, to Xanthe, to be so out of her league.

"Whatcha starin' at, Xanthe?" he teased. "I got something between my teeth or some crumbs on my chin?"

Xanthe hadn't realized that they'd reached the Vulcan, and she had been standing there like a mooning goon, staring up at David. Blushing furiously, she answered, "N-no, I—sorry—I didn't mean to be rude."

"Rude?" he asked lightly. "You were thinking rude thoughts about me?"

"No! It's just—I know it's rude to stare. I—I—sorry."

"S'okay. I stare at you sometimes, too. It's just the first time I've caught you staring at me."

"You—you stare at me? But—but why?" Xanthe asked in confusion.

Exasperated, David replied, "'Cause I like to look at you. I think you've got the most beautiful eyes I've ever seen."

Xanthe gulped. "You do?"

"Yeah," he rasped. "Go home and look in the mirror, woman. You shine."

"I—shine?" Xanthe was well and truly bemused now, and David couldn't help grinning. He gave her a few moments to recover because he knew that though Xanthe St. Dymion might be a tough, courageous high commissar, his warm attentions seemed to throw her completely off balance. He knew he had to go slow with her, and he didn't want to crowd her.

Finally she recovered and bristled, as he had thought she would. "Did you bring me out here to talk nonsense, David Mitchell? 'Cause I'm getting cold."

"No, My Commissar, I walked you out here so I could say good-bye in private. And also . . ." He frowned. "I—kinda need a favor . . . but I'm having a hard time making up my mind whether to ask you or not."

Xanthe immediately said, "You want me to try to contact your team, don't you?"

"Uh, yeah, but I—"

"David, I can take care of myself," she said stiffly. "No one's going to question my trying to contact friends. So, who are my friends?"

"Okay," he said with resignation. Hesitating, he said, "Uh, if you could send a message to Mama Noc from—uh—Puppy."

Xanthe's eyebrows shot up. "Oh? And you are—Puppy?"

"It's hard to explain," David said gruffly.

"I'll bet," Xanthe said dryly.

"Anyway, put out a message on the 'net, please. Just say Puppy's home and fine, and would Mama Noc please Cy-mail him and let him know she's okay and—uh—what her plans are. Yeah, say that."

"She?" Xanthe grumbled.

"That's Fire Team Eclipse, my outfit, Xanthe. My commanding officer's name—*his* name—is Con. Con—Noc—see? We set up some code names and some simple coded messages, just in case we could get Cy-access. Might be overly dramatic, I guess."

Troubled, Xanthe replied, "Maybe not, David. I have to tell you that you may be in greater danger than either of us thought."

"Yeah? Why?"

"The Germans are furious about the stolen helicopter, and they want it back. They're offering one million deutsche marks to anyone who can give them any information, especially about who stole it."

"They're not likely to find it way out here," David said carelessly. "And I've got it camouflaged so well even the animals probably think it's a tree."

"They might not find the chopper, David, but one of the other commissars asked me about you. I mean, he asked me about the soldier who came to get me at the fountain . . . and then I disappeared for three days. This commissar isn't the sharpest knife in the block because he didn't connect the dates. And the dates match, David. The dates that the chopper was stolen and when you showed up and then I disappeared."

"I see what you mean," he said thoughtfully. "So—what can I do?"

"Nothing," she said calmly. "Except I don't think you need to come into town, especially in uniform."

"No danger of that. I don't want to leave my grandparents that long."

She studied him soberly. "David, how well do you know Riley Case?"

"Know him? Don't know him at all—at least, I don't know much about him. I like him, and for some reason—maybe because my grandfather does—I trust him."

She thought a few moments, then nodded. "That's good. If your grandfather trusts him, then he must be all right."

David asked, "What do you mean?"

"Riley Case is on the Commissary's ten most wanted list."

"What for?"

"He killed a bear in the Three Rivers Biome."

"Killed a bear," David scoffed. "The ultimate crime to greenheads, I guess."

She stepped close and laid her hands on his arms, throwing her head back to look up at him. "Listen to me, David. It doesn't matter how silly it is, especially under the circumstances, but it is a crime. It was a rare black bear, and Riley ran, so he's a fugitive. And my new chief commissar is from Three Rivers Biome. Believe me, David, he's having lots of fun lording it over everyone these days."

"Great," David grumbled. "One of those 'big fish in a little pond' dudes, huh."

"More like a big shark in a little pond," Xanthe retorted. "He has power, David. Don't you doubt that. If people start seeing Riley Case on Cy-net, they might connect his face to the man who was in Hot Springs up until the blackout." She took a deep breath. "I'm just trying to tell you, David, that you may not be hidden as well as I thought. Be careful."

"I will if you will." He grinned suddenly and leaned forward and kissed her on the lips. It was a light caress that startled Xanthe.

"Why—why did you do that?"

"I wanted to. Do you mind?"

"Yes—no—no—I guess not."

"You tasted good," he remarked.

"I—tasted—?" Suddenly Xanthe laughed out loud, then slapped him on the chest with the flat of her hand. She had a marvelous laugh, full and rich. "You fool!" she said, a happy note in her tone. "I've got to go."

David waited until she had disappeared and the roar of the Vulcan had become muted, then he turned back. One thought was on his mind: *It's not that we're not hidden well, Xanthe . . . It's that they're looking for us . . . Oh, yes, he'll be looking for us . . . He'll surely be looking for Brother Jesse Mitchell . . .*

SIXTEEN

OBERSTLEUTNANT REINHART ANGRIFF, of the 77th Luftwaffe Air Wing stationed at Kirtland Air Force Base, had a day off. At dawn he fired up his personal Desert Patrol Vehicle (DPV), drove north, parked by a chunk of three twisted mesquite trees, and hiked into Chaco Canyon.

Unfortunately Sergeant Rio Valdosta of the 101st Airborne (Air Assault) Division, Fire Team Eclipse, saw him first. Rio, as always, was wearing his 9 mm, and he drew it and aimed at Colonel Angriff as he marched straight toward the team's quarters.

Angriff stopped and threw up his hands. "Wait! Don't shoot!" he shouted.

"Why not, you slinking Goth!" Rio snarled.

"I'm not slinking, you fool! I walked right in here in broad daylight!" Angriff shouted back angrily. He was considering drawing his own weapon, a fine .38 caliber Glock, when two other soldiers in dusty BDUs (Battle Dress Uniform) came running out of the doorway behind Rio. That put the odds up at three to one, and Angriff believed in going with the odds. He kept his hands up and remained still.

Con Slaughter and Ric Darmstedt looked at the German pilot in disbelief, then Con said, "Stay frosty, Rio."

"I'm frosty, Cap'n," Rio muttered. "I'm cool. And I got a perfect bead on him."

Con said, "Okay. Let's approach him. Rio, keep your target, but don't shoot unless I give the order. Got it?"

"Got it," Rio replied, though he added inaudibly, "but I don't like it."

The three approached Reinhart Angriff.

Angriff was not by nature an arrogant man, but he was proud. As the dirty, weather-beaten soldiers drew near, he straightened his shoulders and held his head high. He was a handsome man, with clean-cut features and crisp brown hair, and he was immaculately groomed. His black BDUs were stiffly creased; his paratrooper's boots were glass-shined; his black leather pilot's jacket was clean and polished. He wore a black BDU cap and dark glasses. Next to him, the three American soldiers looked sorry, and they knew it. Especially Ric Darmstedt, who had the same regard for meticulousness in his blood as did this German pilot.

"Okay, start talkin'," Con growled. He stopped a little to the left of the pilot, so Rio could get a clear shot. But Rio marched right up to the pilot and pointed the 9 mm at his nose. "Rio, back up a coupla inches. Give the man talking room," Con said with exasperation. Rio obeyed—very slowly.

"I am Colonel Reinhart Angriff of the 77th Luftwaffe Air Wing," he said stiffly. "I protest this treatment. You are Airborne? Screaming Eagles—101st? Why should you threaten me like this?"

"Yeah, well, you might say we got our reasons, Colonel," Con retorted angrily. "We're not too happy with the Luftwaffe right now. Bet you can guess why."

Angriff frowned. "Is this an American joke? Because I speak English, but I don't always understand your humor."

Con studied him carefully, searching his face with eyes narrowed razor-thin. Angriff stared back at him, his eyes hidden by the dark glasses. But Con thought that, at least, the man was no threat. No immediate threat anyway. "You alone?" he asked cautiously.

"Yes."

"How'd you get here?"

"DPV. It's back at the east entrance to the canyon, by that stand of three mesquite trees on the small hill."

"Go check, Rio," Con said.

"But, Cap'n, I—"

"No, Sergeant Valdosta, you're not going to shoot this man. Not right now anyway. I want to talk to him. I gave you an order, Sergeant!"

"Yes, sir!" Rio ran, holstering his pistol.

Ric Darmstedt and Con Slaughter stared suspiciously at the German.

Reinhart Angriff waited, his eyes hidden, his arms crossed, his shoulders ruler straight.

Then Angriff nodded his head slightly, his mouth twisting. "Behind you, Captain. The man I came to see."

Without turning, Con grumbled, "Zoan, right?"

"Right."

"That man," Ric Darmstedt said, rolling his eyes, "could sneak up on a snake."

"*Ja,*" Reinhart Angriff agreed. "*Zoan ist eine Wunderkind.*"

By the time Rio returned from checking that Angriff had come alone, everyone knew that the German pilot was there. All forty-five occupants of Chaco Canyon crowded into the huge common room of the complex where Fire Team Eclipse was quartered. Angriff cataloged them carefully, surprised that there were so many people. Even though, after his plane had gone down in the autumnal equinox, he'd been in the canyon for three days and nights, he'd seen only Little Bird, Zoan, Cody Bent Knife, and a few of the other Indian men.

Now Angriff observed there were quite a few more Indians

than he'd known about, including a couple of families with children; and there were other women and children and civilians—and the soldiers, of course, including two Israelis, or New Zionists, as they preferred to be called. Angriff was certain that the soldiers hadn't been here the night he'd crashed his Tornado and Zoan had saved his life. Instead of Zoan and Cody Bent Knife, they certainly would have taken a hand in deciding his fate back then. It seemed that the American soldiers were in complete charge now.

"I've already answered that question, Captain Slaughter," Angriff said with the first open trace of impatience. "And Zoan and Cody and the others have confirmed my story. I will tell you, once again, that I came here to bring some things—gifts—to Zoan, and to let him and his friends know what's happening in the outside world."

Everyone was still standing in a ragged circle around the flier. He seemed at ease, unafraid, though the air in the lofty, barren room was tense. Zoan stood close to Angriff, his eyes and attention fixed on Con Slaughter, for Zoan had great trouble shifting his attention back and forth in a group setting. Oddly Con felt ill at ease under Zoan's patient scrutiny. Finally he said, "Okay, Rio, let's can the armor. We're not going to shoot this man down in cold blood."

"But, sir, he's the enemy!" Rio protested. "Don't tell me you're going to let him keep his PSA!"

Con stepped toward Angriff, holding out his hand. "Colonel Angriff, I must ask you to surrender your side arm to me."

Angriff crossed his arms again and said calmly, "No. You have no authority to take my weapon—not to mention rank." Angriff was extremely proud of his recent promotion to colonel even though it was from unit citations given to everyone who participated in *Projekt Schlußenheit.*

Con's tanned face grew taut, and his voice grew dangerously soft. "I might declare you a prisoner of war, Angriff. Then your rank don't mean spit."

"But you would be making a grave mistake, Captain," Angriff replied coolly. "We are not at war. Your country and mine, we are allies. I can see that you are not aware of this, so I won't consider your offense as mutinous."

Rio snarled, stepping forward between his captain and the German, "Cap'n! He's Cat meat!"

Zoan said sadly, "Sergeant Rio, Cat wouldn't eat him. He's my friend."

A stunned silence followed this statement, and then, as so often happened, many people—even the cold and aloof Reinhart Angriff—smiled at Zoan's simplicity. That genuine smile changed Con's attitude toward Angriff.

"Colonel Angriff, I won't apologize for my caution," he said rather stiffly, but his voice was a more natural timbre than the hoarse half-whisper that signaled danger to those who knew him. "I will ask you, however, to let Zoan hold your side arm."

"If you and your team will give yours to him, I will do so," Angriff replied.

After a moment's hesitation, Con nodded. "All right. Eclipse, hand 'em over."

"Aw, Cap'n, man, you gonna let this Goth disarm us?" Rio said in disbelief.

Ric handed Zoan his 9 mm easily. With one eyebrow raised slightly, Angriff watched, then asked, "Darmstedt? *Sie ein Deutscher?*"

"*Nein,*" Ric replied gruffly, turning away. "*Ich bin Amerikaner.*"

"*Sie sprechen Deutsch,*" Angriff observed.

Ric shrugged. "And you speak English. Don't make you American, *Oberstleutnant.*"

"I didn't know you spoke German," Con said quietly as he handed Zoan his pistol.

Ric frowned. "Yeah, well, you know I've been having a little trouble with taking pride in my heritage lately, sir."

"I'm sure you didn't mean that Colonel Nicanor and I are to surrender our weapons for this German's peace of mind, Captain Slaughter," Colonel Darkon Ben-ammi said darkly, staring at Angriff as if the pilot were a lobster he was picking out of a tank to be boiled.

Angriff didn't react; he merely watched Con Slaughter with mild curiosity.

Slaughter answered, "Colonel Ben-ammi, Colonel Nicanor, I can't order you to give up your weapons. But you, sir, of all people, should know that we need to talk to Colonel Angriff and listen to him. Do we really need to be armed to do that?"

"Yes, sir," Rio volunteered.

"No, we don't," Con said. "Give it up, Rio. You won't die of d.t.'s."

Rio reluctantly handed Zoan his weapon, still muttering almost inaudibly under his breath.

Darkon Ben-ammi and Vashti Nicanor held a hurried whispered conference, then Darkon said grumpily, "All right, Captain Slaughter. But we do this out of respect for you—not because we recognize this German's right to dictate terms to us."

The crowd surrounding the soldiers relaxed somewhat, then began milling around and spreading blankets to sit on the floor in a loose semicircle around the central hearth. Zoan dropped a gun with a jarring clatter. Rio swore, then apologized to the women and children. Clumsily Zoan piled the six firearms untidily in a corner, then seated himself by Reinhart Angriff, who was facing the crowd. The implication was unmistakable—though Zoan did not consciously align himself as if in defense of the German pilot—and Con Slaughter felt even more strongly that he must be as fair as he could be to Angriff. Even if Angriff was a hated Goth, he was Zoan's friend.

Eventually the Indians and civilians got settled down behind the fire team, who sat in a semicircle facing Angriff and Zoan.

Victorine, Dancy, Niklas Kesteven, and the elderly Lystra Palermo sat close behind the soldiers.

"Captain Slaughter, I assume that you've been out of communications for some time now," Angriff began, "so you must be unaware of current events." Taking a deep breath, he continued evenly, "Your president has been found and is well. It is my understanding that power will be restored in a couple of months; joint German and U.S. teams are working on the problem right now. In the meantime, we have provided emergency generators, equipment, general supplies, food, medical supplies, and personnel in most of your co-op cities."

"We?" Con repeated. "You mean Germany?"

"Mostly, yes, although other countries have contributed much."

Con's desert-bronzed face took on an angry cast. "Yeah? Have these other countries also joined in the undeclared war against the United States? Along with Germany?"

Angriff looked sincerely confused. "Undeclared war? We are not at war with you!"

"You lying—!" With obvious effort, Con made himself calm down. Taking a long, deep breath, he continued, "Colonel Angriff, I and my team witnessed a massacre of our base—Fort Carson—by your Luftwaffe! We were, for all intents and purposes, unarmed, completely defenseless because of the blackout! And your bloody fighter jocks and chop jocks mowed down everyone and everything! Even the women and children . . . even the hospital!"

For long moments Angriff didn't answer. He was clearly troubled. Then he said in a low voice, "Captain Slaughter, I don't know what you witnessed. I know nothing of this. During the blackout, and in the confusion of the days immediately following it, our forces were deployed to recon and observe. Some of our infantry and planes were fired upon. Yes, there were casualties—on both sides."

"Gee golly, I didn't know those rocks we were throwing at you caused any casualties," Ric said dryly.

Angriff frowned, evidently not understanding the sarcasm. Then he repeated carefully, "There were casualties on both sides. But that has been smoothed over. That has been forgotten and forgiven because of the massive chaos that your country was in."

"Forgotten and forgiven?" Con repeated in a strangled voice. "I'm telling you, Angriff, you massacred my comrades! In an unprovoked attack!"

Angriff straightened his shoulders and tightened his jaw. "Captain, I did no such thing. And I'm telling you that this is what your own president has broadcast again and again since he's been back in communication. Listen to me! President Therion—your own commander in chief—was fired upon by some of your military at NORAD as he was attempting to reestablish communications! My commandant, Count Tor von Eisenhalt, personally saved him—again!"

At this, Con, Ric, and Rio looked horrified and fell silent. Growling like an angry bear, Colonel Ben-ammi said, "Captain Slaughter? Why should you believe this—this—Hun?"

Con swallowed and stared hard at Colonel Angriff. Angriff met his gaze, unflinching, unblinking, then said, "What would be my reason for lying to you? Do you actually think I came here, alone, openly walking into the camp—to take you all prisoner or to kill you? Use your common sense, Captain Slaughter. I have no reason to lie. Aside from that, you can easily find out the truth for yourselves. You could report to any military base anywhere, and you would be welcomed back. The president has directed all military personnel who were separated from their units, no matter the reason, to report back to active duty, and there will be no questions asked."

Now Con and his men were utterly confused. What if this German was telling the truth? What if the U.S. military was getting organized again under the rightful commander in chief? If that was the case, then they had a sworn duty to report back and rejoin the forces, or they would, indeed, be deserters.

Vashti Nicanor watched the American soldiers—in particular, Ric. Over the last months, as Vashti had gotten to know (and had thought much about) Ric, she had begrudgingly accepted the fact that not all Germans should be dismissed as monsters.

But she realized, as she glanced at Darkon Ben-ammi's dark and menacing expression, that he had not yet come to this acceptance of their traditional worst enemy. Sighing, she realized that her mentor, and by far the wisest and most experienced soldier on their team, was unable to competently deal with this situation. He was too blinded by hate.

"Just a moment," she said calmly to Captain Slaughter, who still looked lost in confusion. "Let's just back up, shall we? It seems to me that we're jumping ahead without taking into account the context of the situation. Isn't that what you've always taught me, Darkon? To look at the entire picture, not just the pieces of it?"

Frowning, he slowly swiveled his angry gaze to her. Clearing her throat, she went on, "We are confused. And why? Because, as Colonel Angriff has said, this country has been in chaos for two months now. And why? Because of the loss of electrical power in the entire United States.

"Let us go back, then, and trace our steps: Who or what was responsible for this blackout? And most important, why? It resulted in chaos and death and destruction. It literally threw this country into anarchy. Who could have done this? Who benefited from this?"

Her eyes flashing, she went on in an icy voice, "Colonel Angriff, your people knew about the blackout long before it happened. Your people have barely been inconvenienced by this tragedy—because you had an extremely effective countermeasure, a preventive. And, Colonel Angriff, obviously the Americans did not."

Calmly Angriff answered, "But they did, Colonel Nicanor. They did. Our intelligence—the *Wolfsrudel*—learned of this weapon, or anomaly, or whatever it is, last year. Our government fully briefed the Americans of the danger then. At that time, Bishop Beckwith was president, and he was fully informed. But somehow the Americans discounted the intelligence, or in the confusion resulting from Beckwith's death, it was lost or forgotten in the bureaucracy. We've found only two of the Joint Chiefs of Staff, and they had no foreknowledge of it at all. Also we have found around two hundred congressmen and other various governmental officials. None of them were briefed about the possibility of a blackout."

He shifted uneasily, but his voice remained calm. "Luca Therion was vice president then, and he has said that he personally was notified by our government and then turned the information over to the president. But nothing was ever done, and after taking over the massive responsibilities of the presidency, Therion never found any documentation concerning the intelligence. He assumed that it must have been bad information or a false alarm."

Con Slaughter rasped, "Sounds awfully convenient, Colonel Angriff."

"Just a minute, Con," Victorine said suddenly, laying her hand upon his shoulder. "He—he may be telling the truth."

Angriff said tightly, "There is no maybe. I am telling the truth. The truth that your own President Luca Therion has told the American people, my government, and the world."

Con ignored him; he turned to face Victorine. "What do you mean, Vic? How do you know?"

Quietly she said, "I—I do know that a meeting took place between Luca Therion—he was vice president then—and some high-ranking German military people last year. Months before the blackout." She looked uncertainly at Reinhart Angriff. "Was your operation to treat all your electronics with the preventive named *Projekt Schlußenheit*?"

Angriff looked startled, but quickly smoothed out his expression. "Yes. How did you know this?"

Colonel Ben-ammi said angrily, "Wait a minute. Madame Thayer, I hardly think that you are competent to debrief this man. And you should have given us any information you had about—anything—of a sensitive nature such as this!"

"I didn't realize the importance of the information I had until now," Victorine shot back. "After the blackout, it seemed unimportant. And, Colonel Ben-ammi, I really know nothing of sensitive German–U.S. intelligence matters."

Suddenly her head swiveled and her eyes narrowed as she stared at Niklas Kesteven, sitting a few feet away in uncharacteristic silence and stillness. "But I have just realized that there is one person who must know a lot—maybe all—of the background of this crisis . . . Dr. Niklas Kesteven. One of the foremost scientists working for the government . . . and Chief Commissar Alia Silverthorne's consort."

Niklas shifted uneasily as every eye in the room turned on him. Mostly he was conscious of Zoan's clear, penetrating gaze. "I'm not her consort, haven't been for a long time," he said in a low, tense voice. "And I knew nothing about the blackout and secret meetings and the countermeasures." He dropped his eyes, unwilling to look at Zoan, even though he had spoken the truth—but not exactly the whole truth.

Colonel Angriff sat straighter and stared hard at Niklas. "You are Dr. Niklas Kesteven? Of the MAB Second Directorate, Shortgrass Steppe Biome? Assigned to Lab XJ2197?"

"That's me," Niklas said in an almost inaudible undertone.

"Interesting," Angriff said in a clinical tone. "Chief Commissar Alia Silverthorne is looking for you." A stunned silence greeted this revelation. The only movement in the room was made by Niklas; he jumped as if he'd been burned, looked first at the German in shock and then at Zoan, almost with fear. Angriff narrowed his eyes, watching the odd reaction closely, and then said in a low voice, "But then, Commissar Alia Silverthorne is looking for a lot of people."

Everyone from Chaco Canyon seemed to be reeling with the impact of Angriff's news. But one thing Vashti Nicanor realized with some shock: Reinhart Angriff was not a threat to them, and he was actually trying to help all of them. He had perceived that none of them could—should—trust him, and he was giving them every opportunity to hear what he had to say, without trying to extract any information from them. Clearly he understood that they needed time and consideration to sort everything out, and he had not once pressed them for their views or intentions. It was a courageous stand to take, considering his precarious position.

So Vashti picked up the thread. "Commissar Silverthorne is looking for people? What do you mean, Colonel Angriff?"

For the first time, Angriff dropped his eyes as if he were discomforted. "Martial law has been declared by your president. For enforcement, a sort of superagency has been formed, under the umbrella of the Sixth Directorate of the Man and Biosphere Organization. All the personnel of such security agencies as the FBI, FEMA, state law enforcement agencies, even the NSA, have joined with the Commissary. Chief Commissar Alia Silverthorne heads this organization."

"I see," Vashti said thoughtfully. No one else seemed inclined to reply to him. "And who, exactly, are they looking for?"

This time Angriff looked troubled, and he gave Zoan a long look. "Your government insists that this blackout was caused by fundamentalist religious fanatics. The Commissary has directed that all registered members of the United America Church and the Roman Catholic Church report to the nearest co-op city or refugee camp for questioning."

Victorine spoke up again, in a voice laden with suspicion, "At Pensacola Naval Air Station, we were questioned and detained by German military, Colonel Angriff."

Angriff said quietly, "In the days following the blackout, *Fräulein* Thayer, America was in chaos. We simply tried to help what was left of your government—which was the Commissary, mostly—get organized. Now we are completely disengaged from your internal problems and conflicts. Your government, with your leaders, is controlling this recovery and reorganization."

Con, who suddenly sounded half-dead weary, murmured, "And what about the armed forces? What's the situation of the U.S. military now?"

"Your president has joined the Global Union of Nation-States," Angriff said steadily. "Almost all of the nations in the world have joined now, and all of them have come together to assist your country in this crisis. Your president has enjoined the military with the Joint Task Forces of the union."

Con blinked and shook his head as if he'd been struck a numbing blow. "The Joint Task Forces of the Germanic Union of Nation-States? You're saying that we've joined that army? Under—who is the commanding officer?"

Quietly Angriff replied, "Commandant Tor von Eisenhalt of Germany, Captain Slaughter. And it is now the Global Union, not the Germanic Union. As I said, the union is not just of Germanic peoples anymore . . . Almost all of the nations in the world belong to it and are loyal to it."

Colonel Darkon Ben-ammi said in a guttural growl very unlike his own voice, "I would bet my right thumb that New Zion is one of the few that have not joined your new Aryan world order, Colonel."

The look Reinhart Angriff gave his traditional adversary was one almost of pity. "But it has, Colonel Ben-ammi. As a matter of fact, many of the armed forces from the Global Union are deploying to active duty in the Mideast right now in defense of your country. Many of my comrades have been sent to Lebanon and Syria and Jordan. And also"—he glanced quickly at the still-silent

American soldiers—"all American armed forces have been activated and are now detailed to combat duty in the Mideast."

"Combat duty?" Con repeated in a strangled voice. "You mean—there's going to be a war?"

"The war has already begun," Angriff answered. "We are fighting a consortium of Arab nations threatening the Jordan and Lebanese Neutral Zones. Their intention is clearly to overrun and conquer New Zion. My commandant has ordered the Joint Task Forces to defend Israel."

Zoan, who had not spoken a word, now said in a soft, unhappy voice, "Your commandant . . . he's fighting a war for the children of Israel?"

Angriff looked confused for a moment, but then his face cleared. "Why, yes, Zoan, he is. He's protecting them."

Zoan nodded, then looked straight into Reinhart Angriff's clear blue eyes. "I know you think that's true, Mr. Reinhart. I know that there is no deceit in you. You just don't understand."

Angriff frowned. "Then explain it to me, Zoan."

Zoan merely shook his head and sighed sadly.

Angriff said to the group in general—and his voice was now a little too loud—"One thing I do understand. It is not my commandant who is persecuting the religious people in this country. It is your own people, your own government. We—Germany and America—are allies."

"But we—that is, the president—" Con began in a confused, low tone.

Darkon Ben-ammi had had enough with trying to absorb all this information, right in front of a man he considered his own deathly enemy—and the Americans', too, even if they couldn't quite grasp it. "Enough," he said angrily. "We need some time to talk among ourselves, analyze this information, make some decisions, and we don't need to include this German in any of it. You, *Oberstleutnant Übermensch,* if you are our ally and our protector, as you insist, then why don't you do something for us that will truly help us?"

Warily Angriff asked, "And what would that be, *Herr Oberstleutnant* Ben-ammi?"

"Get us access to Cyclops," Darkon replied, watching him closely.

With a quick look at Zoan's downcast face, Angriff said quietly, "I can do better than that, sir. I can let you have the DPV I brought if someone—perhaps Dr. Kesteven—can disengage the ethernet ID so it can't be tracked. I told the mechanics that it was having some electrical problems, and I intend to tell them when I return that it broke down in the desert. We have plenty of them, so I don't think anyone will try to recover it. It won't have Cy-II capabilities, but it will have Cy-net and a broadcast receiver. Then, *Herr* Ben-ammi, you will have both communications and transport."

Darkon said nothing. He stared at the German with ill-disguised suspicion.

Zoan said softly, "That would be good, Mr. Reinhart. We thank you."

Angriff smiled gently at his friend. "For you, Zoan. I do this for you."

The Holy Land

Not since cruel Shalmaneser's Assyrian hordes had razed Israel had the Holy Land been drenched in such blood and tears.

The Arabic Confederation never intended a war of such immensity. As they had done for decades, the diplomats blustered and the generals shouted battle cries of Allahu akbar! *But the overall strategy was for the appearance of aggression to illustrate grievances—not to incite a full-scale war.*

The Arabic leaders did not count on Tor von Eisenhalt's strategy. He was the Destroyer, the Ravening Wolf. War was his meat.

Aside from the strategic miscalculation, the Arabic Confederation made a mortal tactical error in the choice of weaponry. Because of a single weapon used on a single battlefield in this war, all of the armies in the entire world united against the confederation—and came under the control of Tor von Eisenhalt, commandant of the Joint Task Forces of the Global Union of Nation-States.

The Arabic Confederation did not have the high-tech interlocking space-based system of sensors and weapons that was the Galaxy Guardian system. The only real weapon it had was numbers, and the only advantage it had was geography. The confederation decided to array forces tightly against Israel on the south, Jordan and Lebanon on the west, and engage in close combat. Weapons of mass destruction used against the forces would be self-defeating because none of them were precise enough to kill one man engaged in a close-combat situation with another man. Sheer numbers seemed to make this scenario plausible. The Arabic Confederation forces outnumbered Tor's two divisions in Syria and the Israeli forces by four to one. In a small theater of operations, space-based weaponry would be impossible to implement without unacceptable friendly casualties.

The Arabic Confederation members clearly saw the buildup of

Germanic Union forces in Syria and coolly observed the deployment of American forces in Lebanon, Israel, and Jordan. They saw that Commandant Tor von Eisenhalt intended a three-pronged advance into Egypt, Saudi Arabia, and Iraq. They knew that they were outgunned, but they also knew that the Global Union forces were outnumbered.

The global might of the Western world's armies had long been based around laser systems for targeting and ranging devices; however, their use as offensive weapons was severely limited. The problem was that the higher the magnitude of the laser beam, the greater the power required to produce and project it.

The problem with power generation was the obstacle that kept laser beams from being used as antipersonnel weapons. To produce a laser beam of such power and physical diameter to do mortal injury to a human required a power pack so bulky that it was impossible for one man to manage it. Therefore, conventional artillery was much more efficient. Two men spraying an area with two rifles could kill a lot faster and more efficiently than two men operating a clumsy laser weapon with a pinpoint projectile beam.

If the object was to kill, that is.

Lasers are extremely concentrated light amplifications. Therefore, one part of the body is ultrasensitive to it: the human eye.

Lasers had been used in optical surgery for many decades, for the beams will easily and precisely cut the retina. In the 1980s Italy developed a handheld laser gun, based on the same technology as surgical lasers, that was powered by a four-pound power pack and emitted a pinpoint beam. If the ray raked across your skin, you wouldn't feel the warmth. If the ray fell on a newspaper you were holding, you could read the paper by it. But if it hit your eyes, you would be permanently blinded.

The weapon was considered, by even the most backward countries, to be so horrific that Italy never mass-produced it. Even criminals had no use for it, for it required such precision in targeting that the cheapest .22 Saturday night special was much more efficient as a weapon.

But in the China-Taiwan crisis of 2002, China toyed with an antipersonnel phased laser array (loosely translated into English, the initials were LINC, and the Chinese made four prototypes, hence the LINC-4). This secret weapon experimentation never became widely known. When British intelligence found out about it, officials threatened to expose the Chinese experimentation. Even the insular Chinese knew that the wrath of the world would descend upon them if they ever hinted at using the weapon. The LINC-4 project was abandoned.

But somehow the Egyptians either obtained the technology from the Chinese or developed it on their own. Tor von Eisenhalt doubted that they had developed it themselves. The precise technology required to figure the logistics of mounting three laser units in strategic places to rake every millimeter of a battlefield was almost beyond comprehension. No machine, no computer, no artificial intelligence ever invented could conceive the mathematical computations necessary to create such a weapon. Only human beings could create it, and human error can never be reduced to absolute zero; such a precise weapon required a margin of precisely zero.

But the Arabic Confederation obtained this weapon and used it, and it was to be the final millstone that sunk them to the depths of oblivion as a people.

In the terrible Mideast War of 2050, the Arabic Confederation used an antipersonnel phased laser array on the advancing forces of the Joint Task Forces of the Global Union of Nation-States. The first units to be blasted into darkness were the Americans, the most elite forces in the world, the commando units and the rapid deployment forces: the 101st Airborne (Air Assault), deployed first of all; the 82nd Airborne; Delta Force; Army Rangers; and those men who are always first in, last out, and never leave a companion behind—the U.S. Marine Corps.

Tens of thousands of them were blinded in the first three days of that terrible battle on the Sinai Peninsula. Many thousands of them were killed by enemy soldiers as they fell, helpless and terrified, struck by the blazing blue light. Many Americans died by friendly fire, for men panicked and went mad and died shooting at terrors they could not see in their sudden, pain-filled darkness. In the following days, many of them committed suicide, and many died mysteriously of injuries that were not life-threatening.

But within three days after the Egyptian lasers shot across the desolate sands of the Sinai Peninsula, the entire world was arrayed against the Arabic Confederation with a rage born of horror. Killing your enemy in battle was an ancient code that was generally agreed to be honorable.

Blinding him was not.

All of Tor's warships and transports from South Africa moved up to the Red Sea, and by the time they arrived, the U.S. carrier group based around the carrier Reagan *had already obliterated the Arabic Confederation's navy. India, with her two-million-man standing army, literally overran and burned Iran. Russian armies came down from the north through Georgia, Armenia, and Turkey, and scythed through Iraq. Tor's two divisions in Syria advanced into Saudia Arabia from the north, while his southern forces from Africa razed Yemen, Oman, Egypt, and Libya.*

The Arabic Confederation was no more.

Count Tor von Eisenhalt walked the streets of Jerusalem in triumph.

He had disdained any protection at all. The only people allowed to accompany him were Minden Lauer, President Luca Therion, Commissar Alia Silverthorne, the prime minister of Israel, and a Cy-World news cameraman.

Alia thought that he must be mad; no iota of war had touched the people of Jerusalem, and they were literally dancing and singing in the streets, thousands of them. Alia thought that surely Tor would be attacked, and though her mind shied away from it once again, she thought that he might be hurt. Certainly Luca and Minden could be killed. It seemed to be a foolish thing to do, with the riotous crowds in the streets.

But no one touched Tor or anyone in his retinue. People shouted, cries of triumph and glee, but his tall figure cut a swath through the masses of people as if he were parting them with a strong wind. They fell back from him, and they dropped their eyes, for no one dared to return that burning gaze. Some of them even fell to their knees as he passed.

Alia noticed that the confused shouts of the crowd had become a one-word cry, shouted in cadence by thousands of people. "What are they saying?" she asked, her mouth close to Minden's ear.

Minden turned and smiled at Alia. Her eyes glittered as if they were made of stars; her lips were moist and red; her pale cheeks were delicately flushed. "They are saying Messiah. It means the Great Deliverer of Israel. They are proclaiming him their savior, the one who was promised by God, who was sent to save this land and its people from all oppressors." She smiled with ecstasy. "They are worshiping him."

The old streets were narrow, but no matter how many hundreds or thousands of people packed them, Tor always had a clear path. Many of the sandstone buildings looked as if they'd stood for centuries. Alia had no idea where they were going. She hadn't even known where Jerusalem was before Tor had brought them here and had certainly never studied a map of Israel or Jerusalem. She had never quite comprehended the attraction for this ancient, dusty city. Her best understanding was that it was something of an archaeological curiosity because it was so old, and it had some supposed mystical qualities, like the Egyptian pyramids and the Forbidden City of the Chinese emperors.

They moved at a relatively fast pace, for Tor's stride was long.

The cameraman kept a respectful distance of about two feet from Tor's side, but he kept his camera steadily on him. Minden, Luca, and Prime Minister Landau struggled along behind, with Alia anxiously flitting about the four of them, trying to watch everyone in a 360-degree circle around them.

Finally they came to a halt.

Alia nervously took in their surroundings.

They were standing in a large square that was surprisingly open, considering the geography of this crowded walled city. Tor stood at the bottom of a set of white steps that led up into a beautiful building of generally classic design except for the round golden dome crowning it.

Looking behind and around them, Alia saw literally thousands, perhaps even ten thousands, of people crowded into the square. They were still shouting, "Messiah! Messiah! Messiah!"

With lithe grace Tor turned and held up his hands. A silence, so quick and complete that it was eerie, fell.

"My comrades of New Zion," he said. It did not seem as if he shouted, but everyone could hear his words. "Your enemies are dead and dying. This place, that has been a scar on your holy city for so long, I give to you as reparation for your long, bloody war against your enemies." Suddenly savage, Tor turned and spat against the clean white stone steps. "Do with it as you will."

They came like a flood, though they flowed cleanly around Tor von Eisenhalt and his companions. The mosque of the Dome of the Rock was a pile of rubble, literally torn down, stone by stone and brick by brick, by the children of Israel.

Tor watched, and his mouth twisted as if with strange amusement. Minden watched him, her pretty face drawn with incomprehension. He turned to her. "You wonder why, don't you, my lovely Lady of Light?"

Behind Minden, Alia stepped closer. She told herself that she was merely trying to protect them, but the truth was that Alia tried to hear every word that came from Tor's mouth. She was devoured with curiosity about this compelling man, was fired by a zealous loyalty and devotion that she never knew she was capable of. She literally hung on his every word.

Minden said as quietly as possible in the din of the wreckage, "I do wonder, my lord. I—don't—quite understand your—zeal for this place and these people. And I—desperately want to understand. I want to understand everything." The desire that contorted Minden's face was so wholly, nakedly concentrated that Alia was uncomfortable.

Tor nodded. His blue eyes blazed with dark delight, and his shapely mouth seemed continually on the edge of a smile. He seemed full of some deep well of terrible glee. "This land, this country," he said, gesturing with his left arm. "Do you know what it is called?"

"No, my lord, I am so ignorant," Minden said adoringly.

"It is called the Fertile Crescent," he said, now in a low tone of concentration. "It is a rich land, desirable to all men of the ages, fertile and sweet and green." He turned to look at Minden. He looked so forbidding, his anger was so terrible, that she flinched. "Long ago this land was a paradise, untouched, bursting with all the sweetest of fruits in the world. There was a battle fought here, and I won; but my enemy exiled me and those I had conquered. I swore vengeance. I swore I would return. I swore a blood-and-death oath that I would win this garden again . . . and I would curse it and salt it so that no green thing would ever grow here again, world without end . . ."

He turned again and smiled at Minden. It was an awful thing, the smile that could have been from the joy a madman feels at killing or torturing.

"I have come back in triumph. And I will salt this accursed earth with blood enough to choke it forever!"

And again, with rage, he spat.

Alia, as if in a hypnotic trance, looked down. The spittle was of blood, and it burned with a noxious smell and then turned black.

PART IV

THE DAUGHTER OF ZION

Your country is desolate, your cities are burned with fire: your land, strangers devour it in your presence, and it is desolate, as overthrown by strangers. And the daughter of Zion is left as a cottage in a vineyard, as a lodge in a garden of cucumbers, as a besieged city. Except the LORD *of hosts had left unto us a very small remnant, we should have been as Sodom, and we should have been like unto Gomorrah.*

—ISAIAH 1:7–9

Narrow is the mansion of my soul; enlarge Thou it, that Thou mayest enter in. It is ruinous; repair Thou it.

—THE CONFESSIONS OF SAINT AUGUSTINE, THE FIRST BOOK

SEVENTEEN

CON SLAUGHTER stalked along the perimeter of the sandstone high-rises. The setting had become familiar to him, but sometimes the atmosphere of the ancient dwelling places of the Anasazi weighed heavily on him. Those who had carved the dwelling out of solid rock were all gone and forgotten, buried in nameless graves, long returned to the earth. Yet there was a visceral sense of their presence that troubled Slaughter.

They once thought that the Anasazi cannibalized their own people, and that's why they disappeared without a trace, he reflected morosely. *That used to be unthinkable to me, that people could betray their own . . . but it sure seems like that's what's happening to my people here and now. My own commander in chief, the highest military leader in the land, is either mad or a traitor . . . and a Luftwaffe pilot, our bloodiest enemy, seems to be our only friend out there . . .*

Restlessly he worked his way up to the creek that fed their pool, then followed it along a line of piñon trees, his mind wrestling with innumerable images, large and small. Con's attention was caught by a bird perched in one of the winter-sparse trees. He had seen the birds all over the canyon. Even as he stopped, the bird raised its head, pumped it up and down several times, and made a raucous call that sounded like, *Get out! Get out!* In his mind Con had named it the Get-Out Bird. Idly he decided that he would ask one of the Indians or perhaps Zoan about it.

Wouldn't be surprised if Zoan could talk to the thing. It seems that he can talk to birds and animals better than he talks to people. Funny . . . I have this weird feeling that Zoan could help me if I could just find the right question to ask him, if I could phrase it correctly, if I could find the key to him . . . but I don't think anyone will ever know Zoan completely . . . Even Dr. Kesteven, as smart as he is and as long as he's known Zoan, can't seem to get a good hold on him . . .

Con made a wide, ragged circle and scrambled down into a deep ravine where they'd hidden the vehicle that Reinhart Angriff had brought them. The DPV (Desert Patrol Vehicle) was more or less like a megaheavy dune buggy but heavily armed, with two .50 caliber machine guns mounted on the front and back. Rio was greatly pleased—his sergeant could never have too many guns to play with. Ric Darmstedt had remarked that Angriff, if he was planning on betraying them, had certainly left them with a fine arsenal of weapons and five hundred rounds of ammunition.

The DPV could carry two people, with minimum storage in the back. It could carry three if the front gun was removed, which Rio was doing right now. Con studied the tires and the two extra fuel bladders with a soldier's appreciation, for they were made of Tyvek and steel and were impenetrable up to a .50 caliber round.

Con made his way down to the vehicle, and both Rio and Ric jumped to attention and saluted. The fire team had grown closer, more personal, with their commanding officer in the last few hard months, but they still strictly observed military protocol.

"Ease up," Con said lightly. "I'm just checking on our new toy. How's it going, Darmstedt? You get the ident disabled?"

"You betcha, Captain," Darmstedt replied enthusiastically. "Dr. Kesteven had to help me, but we finally found it and killed it. Now I'm just playin' around with it, trying to see if we could maybe grab some Cy-II apps." He shook his head sorrowfully. "But these drones, they don't have anything like the memory needed. I thought Dr. K was gonna cry. He's bored out of his skull, you know. Big brain like that, with no Cyclops, no lab, no switches and dials."

"Yeah, I know," Slaughter said absently. He was watching Rio, who was like a big kid with a new toy, crawling all over the mounting for the big gun with an enormous wrench and industrial-sized screwdriver.

Darmstedt noted Slaughter's distraction and decided to ask his commanding officer about it. These days, Con talked to Ric Darmstedt sometimes. Though Rio was probably Con Slaughter's closest friend, Ric was much more like Con in many ways; they thought alike, and both were officer types, which Rio definitely was not.

"What's up, Cap'n?" Ric asked nonchalantly. "Aside from the usual misadventure and mishap, I mean?"

Con considered the younger man. Ric acted like an overgrown kid, but he actually was extremely intelligent, shrewd, and level-headed. Six months before, Con would never have considered discussing anything with a man serving under him. In these days, however, Con was glad to have Ric as his second-in-command and trusted him as if he were a fellow officer. "Have you noticed that the world's pretty sorry these days, Darmstedt?" he said sourly.

"Yes, sir," Ric answered briskly. "But that's kind of a sweeping problem to address, sir. D'ya think you could narrow the scope a little?"

Con studied Rio, who, after smartly acknowledging Con's presence, had returned to his absorption with his fine new gun. "We got so many problems, Ric, I don't know whether to alphabetize them or number them." He roused himself a little, then went on in a businesslike tone, "We've sure got problems with supplies, and that's what I'm trying to figure out right now. We're short of everything, with the new people. Soap, toothpaste, buckets, forks, tools—you name it."

Ric nodded. "Yes, sir, not to mention food and medical supplies."

"Winter's here, and some of our people don't even have coats or jackets," Con went on with frustration. "And we don't have nearly enough blankets."

Carefully Ric observed, "Yes, sir, and it does look like they're our people. Even the Indians seem to look to us to help them out. They're the best hunters, that's for sure, and even old Benewah Two Color can haul and split wood like two twenty-year-olds. But they do kind of expect us to take care of a lot of the problems." Ric was saying *us,* but both he and Con knew that everyone in Chaco Canyon—except maybe Zoan—pretty much looked at Con as the leader, with all the responsibilities that job entailed.

Con let his eyes drift over the far horizons of the desert that spread out to the east. It was a barren, ghostly place, and the sense of loneliness communicated itself to him in a thousand intangible ways. In his trademark husky half-whisper he said, "Sometimes, Darmstedt, I feel like one of those hides that Benewah Two Color was talking about the other night, how the Indians used to stretch them. Cut, stripped, scraped, and yanked up tight at every point."

Ric nodded, his clean-cut features wrinkled with sympathy. But he couldn't think of anything to say, for in himself he could find no comfort to give.

The meeting had gone on for more than an hour, and Slaughter, as usual, had not been able to be as firm as he'd like. It disturbed him, for he was accustomed to having men under his command. But the Indians were not soldiers. They had to be led, not ordered. He glanced around, studying them, especially Benewah Two Color. At seventy years old, he was thin and stooped, with only the one startling white streak of color in his otherwise matte black hair. He was the strongest member of the group, although he was probably the weakest physically.

Cody Bent Knife became the object of Slaughter's consideration.

He was nineteen years old, a full-blooded Apache with black hair below his shoulders. He was not large, no more than five ten, but wiry as an antelope and could run all day, it seemed, without a break. He was a strange man, and Slaughter had never quite understood him or why the other Indians—especially the older men—were so blindly devoted to him. It was not the sort of loyalty that comes from a sense of duty; Slaughter understood that emotion very well. The other Indians were drawn to Cody as if he were some sort of lightning rod or ensign. Maybe they sensed in the young man a remnant of their past. Slaughter really didn't know, but he did know that whatever he wanted the Indians to do, he'd have to get Cody's approval.

"We're going to take the DPV to get resupplied," Slaughter was saying. "You all know that we need—everything. Basic foodstuffs, cooking utensils, tools, supplies, blankets, winter clothes. Especially we need medical supplies. But I'm not sure exactly where to go first. You people are more familiar with this territory than I am. Any suggestions?"

No one said anything for a long time, and Slaughter despaired of what to do next. No one seemed to know where to go to get the desperately needed items, and no one seemed willing to volunteer any help, either.

Suddenly Zoan said, "We could get some of those things back at the lab, Captain Slaughter."

Everyone turned to look at Zoan with surprise. He rarely took any part in group discussions or in making decisions.

Thoughtfully Slaughter said, "Yeah . . . yeah. That was a big facility, the ranch, I mean. It had quite a bit of farm equipment, tools, and—what about the biome animal care clinic, Dr. Ives? Was it as well stocked as most of the MAB projects are?"

"There were plenty of medical supplies and pharmaceuticals in the veterinarian clinic," Gildan said in a low voice. "But I'm not going back there, Captain Slaughter. Never."

Heavily Niklas Kesteven said, "You can count me out of this one, Captain. I'm no coward but . . ." His thick shoulders shrugged expressively. His and Gildan's weeks in the ranch house—which was essentially a gravestone marker for the two hundred–plus friends buried underneath it—had taken a heavy toll on both of them. Niklas still had nightmares about it.

Slaughter nodded with rough sympathy. "It's all right, Dr. Kesteven, Dr. Ives. I'll volunteer Darmstedt to go with me. If you'll just give him a list of the pharmaceuticals and things we can use, Dr. Ives, he'll be able to figure it out."

"Can I go, Captain Con?" Zoan asked.

Con studied the nondescript young man. Con wondered if Zoan completely understood what had happened to all the people at the lab, which had been his only home and family his whole life. Con wasn't sure if Zoan needed to return to that place of death, but then again, in some ways, Zoan was the strongest of them all.

"Sure, Zoan," Con finally said. "You can keep me and Darmstedt straight."

Cody Bent Knife had listened carefully as Slaughter outlined the emergency though, indeed, he had little need of being told. Now he spoke up, his voice low and somewhat hesitant. "I know where we can get all the blankets and winter clothes we need. Some of the finest clothes ever made."

Instantly all of the Indians turned to face Cody. Slaughter asked, "Yeah? Where's that?"

"The Navajo reservation," Cody answered with reluctance.

"Oh, no, huh-uh, Cody!" Ritto Yerington grunted. He was twenty-five, six years older than Cody and twice his size. But he followed Cody as faithfully as a bullmastiff—usually. "That's some bad medicine, Cody, and you know it."

Ritto's sister, Layna, put her hand on Ritto's arm. "Maybe it's best, Ritto."

"What's the trouble?" Con asked, careful to keep his voice mild. The Indians didn't like anyone interfering with their ways.

Cody seemed to be framing an answer, but Bluestone Yacolt,

who was half Apache, half Blackfoot, spoke up. He had startling turquoise blue eyes and was easily the most quarrelsome member of the group. "You're going to bring a curse on all of us, Cody. I can't believe you even said it out loud."

"I thought you didn't believe in the old ways, Bluestone," Cody retorted.

"I don't," Bluestone responded, "but that doesn't mean we won't be asking for trouble if we do this."

"Hindo Night Singer's two youngest children don't have any winter clothes, and Ravenna Crow Heart and Ventana Ute have to share one blanket," Cody said with finality. "And everyone who came in from that pit in Albuquerque needs clothes and shoes and blankets." Cody turned his back to Bluestone and Ritto to talk to Con Slaughter. "You see, Captain Slaughter, the Navajos always kept to themselves. Their reservation was huge, hundreds of miles square, and they rarely came off it. And they didn't exactly welcome visitors, either."

"I thought all the reservations put in casinos, luxury hotels, golf courses, things like that, for diversionary facilities for the public," Ric spoke up.

"Not the Navajo. There was only one hotel ever built, but the road to it was so bad that it finally closed in 2002, just three years after its opening. After that not many people even saw a Navajo."

"Did the plague hit them pretty hard?" Gildan Ives asked with interest.

"No one knows how it hit them," Cody said with a shrug. "They stayed so much to themselves that no one was really sure how many of them there were. And they didn't go to white men's hospitals when the plague hit. They stayed right there in the desert. I heard that only fifteen of them left the reservation and joined the world."

"That's true. I know because one of those fifteen was our father," Layna Yerington said sadly. "Our mother died in the plague.

And he lived only a year after we left the reservation. Ritto and I were too young to remember much. But our father told the woman at the Indian Child Care Home, and she told us."

Cody's eyes on Ritto and Layna were full of pity, but his voice was dispassionate. After all, most of his people had much the same tragic history. "The Navajo, I think, were the greatest artisans of us all. They wove the finest blankets, used only the best deerskin for clothing, the softest leather for moccasins, the finest furs for winter cloaks. All of those materials have been illegal for decades, of course, but for some reason the Commissary ignored the Navajo trade. And there was just one storehouse—the Old Red Rock Trading Post."

"Where is that?" Slaughter asked quickly.

"Just over the Arizona line."

Slaughter frowned. "To the east . . . and the lab is west."

"No," Cody said quietly. "If anyone is going to go, I need to."

"My father said our people kept on making clothes and sending them to the trading post until all of them were dead. The few who lived didn't touch anything." Layna's face was sad as she turned to study the ground.

"We can't disturb their burial ground," Ritto said harshly. "Stealing from the dead is worse than stealing from the living."

"It's not stealing," Cody said mildly.

"Yes it is!" Ritto argued. "And stealing the things they made for their spirit gifts—that's even worse!"

Cody did not speak for a time. He did not particularly care for this option, but he saw no other way. "I don't believe that our spirit ancestors will begrudge us their gifts to save our lives."

Ritto shook his head, a gloomy expression on his dark face. "Look, Cody, that German who was here said the Commissary is in charge now. They've been pretty good to Indians. Why don't we just go to Albuquerque or Santa Fe and buy the stuff? I mean, we're not involved in the dumb religious wars that the white people are having. Remember your visions?" His face grew savage, his obsidian eyes glittering. "Let them kill each other off! It doesn't have anything to do with us!"

Cody stubbornly shook his head. "I'm sorry, Ritto, I can't do that. All of you know you are free to go anywhere you please. I don't ask anyone to stay with me, and I won't think any less of you if you leave. But I'm going to get those things at the Navajo reservation."

Ritto bowed his head. The loyalty—even love—he had for Cody Bent Knife was strong. "I will go."

"I'm in," Bluestone Yacolt grumbled. "Been following you around like some dumb Tonto for too long now. Bad habits die hard."

Little Bird said in defeat, "Then I'll go with you, too, Cody."

Cody merely nodded.

Relieved at having some of the burden of logistics taken from him, Slaughter said, "All right. My team will leave as soon as we can get the DPV loaded. I suppose the rest of you will ride."

"Yes. We have plenty of horses," Cody said. He was still troubled, and his face was etched with lines that made him look older.

Zoan stepped up to Cody and laid his hand on the Indian's chest, next to his heart. It was a sign between them. He looked up into Cody's eyes, dark and wary, and said quietly, "Go with God, my friend."

As the DPV sped through the night, both Ric Darmstedt and Con Slaughter were glad that Zoan was there. They were traveling without lights, for they did not want any planes overhead to spot them on simple visual. Though the DPV had a neat camo kit that could be thrown over the vehicle in about thirty seconds, they avoided traveling during the day. The air traffic over the wasteland had lessened somewhat, but the odd Tornado squadron or Dagger flew over sometimes. Zoan, who could not comprehend the GPS, seemed to instinctively know their position all the time, and then, of course, he could see in the dark.

"Turn this way," Zoan said, pointing to his left. "You go across this wide plain to those three hills. See?"

"No," Con muttered. "And take my word for it, Zoan, it ain't no fun to drive blind."

"I could drive," Zoan volunteered.

"No!" Con and Ric both exclaimed. They'd tried that once. Zoan didn't seem to understand that hurtling through total darkness was too nerve-racking for the two soldiers. Zoan tried to drive slowly, but it seemed silly to him, and he kept creeping up to what seemed like outrageous speeds. He liked driving fast. He hadn't exactly told Con and Ric that no one had ever taught him to drive, much less let him try.

At any rate, it was a little less tense for Con to drive. Ric was suffering—he would have liked to feel that he was in control, too—but he was Con's subordinate, so he had to tough it out.

The hills reared up in front of them, and Zoan asked, "Now can you see them?"

"Yeah, Zoan, they're right in front of us," Con blustered.

"I know, but I don't understand what you can't see," Zoan said innocently. "Anyway, you follow this biggest hill around to the right, and there's a road curving between it and the other one."

It was true. They came out onto another plain, but this one had brown remnants of grass.

"How much farther is it?" Con asked impatiently.

"I can never see those klicks you're always talking about," Zoan answered, "but it's about five minutes from here."

Zoan's estimate was right. They followed a winding track through the wide expanse of fields and pasture to the ranch house. Zoan eagerly jumped out of the DPV. He breathed deeply of the biting desert night. He had grown up here. He had known every inch of these fields. He had missed them, though he hadn't missed the lab. "I know where all the medicines and things are, and there's some other things I want to get. I'll meet you back at the house."

Ric said, "Here, Zoan, take a flashlight—"

But he disappeared without a sound.

Con said dryly, "He can see better without it than we can with it."

"Yeah, what was I thinking?" Ric muttered. "The Lizard Man with X-ray vision."

Both of them turned to the empty, dark house. Like all deserted houses, it looked a little spooky. But then, both Con and Ric thought that their childish fears had a lot to do with the fact that they knew two hundred people were in the lab buried underneath. Neither of them said anything, however, as they entered.

Dust had gathered everywhere, and decay had already begun to show its effect. The thin beams of their lights waving around somehow made the dark, unseen corners even worse. Con admitted, "This place is creepy. But come on, let's get it over with and get outta here."

They worked steadily, hauling everything they could find that might be useful to them out onto the wide front porch. They brought out all the cooking pots and pans and utensils, the canned and dried food, the cleaning supplies, even the pillows from the sofas and chairs. Finally they stood together at the entrance to the bedroom where the elevator down to the lab was located. Con was past being embarrassed; neither he nor Ric was a squeamish man. But it was a place of death, of a particularly horrible kind, and the very air seemed heavy with it. They stared at the splintered paneling that Dr. Niklas Kesteven—another man who was not subject to hysteria—had torn so desperately, and the cruel titanium steel door behind.

"Think Zoan understands what happened here, sir?" Ric whispered.

Con considered the question, then answered, "Yeah, I think he knows and understands, maybe better than we do. There's nothing in here we need, Lieutenant. Let's get trekkin'."

They went back out on the porch and stared doubtfully at the pile of supplies they'd gathered. "We're never gonna get all that in the DPV," Con said.

"Betcha they've got some trailers in that barn, sir," Ric said. "I could rig up a flatbed if I had any kind of frame, and this old girl will sure pull it."

"Yeah, okay, let's search these outbuildings, see if we can find Zoan."

"We won't find him unless he wants us to, that's for sure, sir," Ric rasped. "That man's a walking stealth weapon. Can see in the dark, never makes a sound, can hear the bunnies talking over in New Mexico. And there's the fact that he's invisible."

Con snorted agreement. They walked and were suddenly conscious of how quiet the night was—it was unusual, for there was no wind—and how loud their movements and voices were. Then Con asked in a casual tone, "Ric, you ever think about Zoan's—uh—dunkhead thing?"

Ric frowned, then said with exasperation, "Yeah, okay, sir, I'm busted. I have been thinking about the dunkhead thing. A lot. I kinda thought, sir, that if I came along and—you know—Zoan was here, and not—uh—distracted—I might just, you know, ask him about it."

Con grinned, and though Ric couldn't see his face, he could hear the wry amusement in his captain's voice. "You thought that, did you, Lieutenant? Funny. I was kinda thinking the same thing."

The two men looked at each other, and Con shrugged his shoulders. "Why is it so embarrassing? I guess people have always made fun of Christians, but, hey, Mitchell isn't weird. David Mitchell, he's a good guy and he's tough."

"I know," Ric agreed. "Is it because we think of them as being sissies? No, that's not right. People make fun of women Christians, too. I don't know. I guess, sir, that we need to ask Zoan. It does seem that we've brought him out here, under false pretenses, for that."

"Sure does, Lieutenant," Con agreed. "Let's get loaded and get out of here first, though. I don't care if we stop just over those hills. We're not staying here. Tonight in camp we'll surround him and make him talk."

"Seeds," Zoan said. "I've figured out how to make a garden in the canyon, and I knew there were lots of seeds in the agri barn." He grinned. That was unusual, for Zoan rarely smiled, though he didn't look sour or morose. When he smiled, he looked like he was about twelve years old. Con had trouble believing that Zoan was actually twenty.

"You never told me about your parents," Con said to him, settling back against a rock and sipping his hot black coffee.

Zoan stared into the campfire a long time. Then he said, "I don't have any—not like you do, I mean." Then he looked up at Con, and the child's smile played across his still features again. "But I was adopted by God through my Lord Jesus Christ. That's good enough for me. That's good enough for anybody, don't you think, Captain?"

"I don't have a clue what you're talking about, Zoan," Con said, but without the usual hint of impatience. "Do you, Darmstedt?"

"No, sir," Ric said.

"Zoan, explain it," Con ordered.

Ric laughed, but only inwardly. *Well, that's like you, Captain, to give a military order to help your soul.* An old memory came to him, a story from the American Civil War. A Confederate colonel had been informed that twenty men from another regiment had been converted and baptized. *Lieutenant,* the irate colonel had commanded, *detail forty men and have them baptized at once!*

Zoan did not take offense—he never did. He folded his hands in his lap and stared down at them for long moments. It was a way he had, for not once had Con or Ric heard him give a quick answer to a question. Always there was the period of incubation.

"We're not just the products of our mothers and fathers. No one is. We were all made by God," Zoan said simply. It was not an argumentative tone, but it did away in a few words with the theory of evolution. "In the beginning God made the heavens and the earth, and then He made man and man was like God," Zoan went on very slowly. They were thoughts from deep within him; this was the first time he'd ever said them aloud.

"But man ruined himself and fell away. And that tore us in two. All of us, we're two things—we're sinful men, but with a spirit that God made and put into us. We're broken; we're divided against ourselves. But God fixed it when He sent His Son here to die for us." Zoan fell silent.

Finally Con leaned forward and asked urgently, "We're—torn in two? I don't understand that, Zoan."

Zoan returned Con's intense gaze, and Con felt as though Zoan could see his darkest thoughts, his most deeply buried fears and longings, just as he could pierce the darkness. His next words proved it to be true. "Captain, inside yourself you feel pain, you feel confusion, and worry and fears gnaw at you all the time. That's because you walk according to the course of this world, according to the prince of the power of the air, and that spirit works great harm in the children of wrath. It hurts."

As if a light was dawning behind his eyes, Con sat back and stared into the distance. "Yeah . . . it's—funny, Zoan, because your words . . . are strange . . . but I know what you mean. I—I do feel that way. I'm—I can't find any peace at all."

"You're torn in two," Zoan repeated softly. "But Jesus Christ is our peace, for He made both one, and He breaks down the wall that divides us, that makes us our own worst enemy. His blood is our sacrifice to our Father God. You understand shedding of blood in sacrifice for another, I know, Captain. And Jesus did it for us all."

Unheeding now of military protocol, Ric spoke up. "But, Zoan, what does that—how does that help us? I mean, I accept what you're saying. I understand the concept of sacrifice. But—I'm not trying to be cute, I just really want to understand—so—then what?"

Slowly Zoan, struggling with his trouble with group conversation, turned to focus on Ric. "When we tell Jesus that we know He died for our sins and ask Him to forgive us, then we're reconciled to a holy God . . . and He adopts us. And we need that, all of us need that, even strong men like you, Lieutenant Ric. We need our Father, we need Him to love us, we need Him to make us feel secure, and maybe most of all, we need Him to give us peace."

Ric and Con glanced at each other. Slowly, then, the captain nodded. "Okay, Zoan, what's the drill?"

"I don't know what that means," Zoan said.

Con shifted uneasily. "I know you don't, and I'm sorry. I—don't understand why it's so hard, Zoan, for us to admit that we need God. I'm sure not ashamed to say that I love my father and need his love."

Zoan nodded. "I know. Your nature wars against God, always. It's part of the way that sin makes us miserable."

"Yeah," Con agreed quietly, "I'm pretty miserable, Zoan. So how do I come to God? How do I—get adopted?"

Once again, Zoan's smile lit up his face. "Easy. Just pray and ask Him to forgive you for your sins. Tell Him that you want Jesus to be your Savior and Lord. Then you'll become a child of God instead of a child of wrath."

"That's it?" Concord Slaughter was a cautious man.

"Yes, sir."

"Okay, I'm ready," Con said firmly. "What about you, Darmstedt?"

"Sir, I've been ready," Ric answered. "I'm—tired."

Con nodded. "I'll go first." He bowed his head and prayed, "God, I'm lost, I'm tired, I'm confused, and I know that whatever I do, however good I am, it's nothing because I'm just a sinner. I ask You now, Jesus, to come into my heart, to save me from my sin and misery, to give me some peace. Amen." He looked up at Zoan and asked anxiously, "Is that good enough?"

Zoan answered, "You have the heart of a lion, Captain Con, and now you have the heart of the Lion of Judah."

"Okay, I can do this," Ric said eagerly and bowed his head. "Lord, I need help. I need You. Save me, forgive me, and thank You for dying for me. Amen."

Zoan said, "Well, thank God. Now I've got two more brothers. And you'll see. Being adopted by almighty God is even better than having a mother and a father."

"For my part, Zoan," Con said, rising to go to Zoan and shake his hand, "I'm proud to be adopted by God, but I've gotta say that it's an honor to be your brother, too." He swallowed hard. "I—I love you, brother."

Zoan looked up at the tall, rugged soldier, and for the first time in his life, his lustrous dark eyes were filmed with tears.

"I think we've got all we can haul. Let's pull out."

Cody looked over the two buckboards that the four of them had found on the Navajo reservation. They were in good condition, like new. It was rather jarring to Cody that the crude wagons were so valuable to them, while all the expensive toys in the world were piles of useless junk.

The half-wild mustangs, who were as docile as pets with Zoan, had to be fought long and hard, but finally Ritto and Cody managed to get them harnessed. Both buckboards were piled high with deerskin breeches and jackets, fancy beaded dresses and fringed skirts, moccasins for outdoor and for indoor wear, and hundreds of blankets woven of all the intense hues of the desert.

Ritto drove one buckboard and Bluestone the other, while Cody and Little Bird rode ahead. As they left the reservation, Ritto turned and looked back. "This is bad, Bluestone," he said, but instead of his usual hard voice, he merely sounded weary.

Cody heard the remark but paid no heed. He drove the horses hard, for Cody, too, felt forebodings, and he was glad to get away from what was now miles and miles of burial grounds.

The Indians traveled during the day, for they were not concerned with German helicopters or commissars. They had long been forgotten, dismissed from America's mind. As soon as the twilight began to veil the east with a dusky gray, Cody stopped at the first likely place he saw, which was a tumble of boulders at the base of a soaring butte.

"We'll camp here for the night," he told his companions. "We could probably make it back to camp, but the horses are tired."

They pulled the wagons up, freed the horses, and fed them with the feed they had brought with them. Ritto and Bluestone quickly built a fire and fried some salted antelope they'd brought with them from camp. It was tough and stringy, but they were tired and hungry, glad that they didn't have to hunt for their supper.

Little Bird talked about the lovely clothes—she'd already picked out a couple of pairs of breeches and one skirt—and what fine weavers the Navajos were. She and Cody had also taken some of the silver jewelry the Navajos had made with the distinctive coral and turquoise stones. Little Bird had insisted that they could give it to their people for Christmas presents. She didn't seem to feel any discomfort at the idea that they were violating sacred ground.

But Ritto and Bluestone had almost nothing to say. Cody knew they were still upset, and he sympathized, for he was starting to wonder if he'd made a terrible mistake. The gravity of the deserted old trading post, piled high with dusty treasures of the dead, weighed on him. *Little late to be getting squeamish,* he mused. "Ritto, you and Bluestone take the first watch. Wake us up at midnight."

The two men, without speaking, picked up their rifles and walked out into the darkness.

"We'd better get what sleep we can, Little Bird," Cody said, interrupting her midsentence. Wrapping himself in his old blanket, he lay down before the fire and instantly fell into a heavy sleep.

Little Bird did not go to sleep at once. She draped her blanket around her shoulders and sat cross-legged before the fire. Her eyes were dreamy as she stared into it, her thoughts drifting. Finally her eyes fell on Cody's face. The chiseled features were plainly highlighted by the flickering amber light of the fire. She studied him a long time, which was something she couldn't do when he was awake. Cody Bent Knife knew instantly when someone's eyes lit on him.

I'm in love with him. There, I said it. At least, I admitted it to myself. Fine. Now what? Now nothing. He's—unreachable. He's not for me. He's too—spiritual or something. He's kind to me, he's comforted me when I've been afraid and felt weak, he listens to me and talks to me . . . and he loves me about as much as Zoan loves those two silly kittens.

Finally she shook herself as if to rid herself of a memory, wrapped up in her blanket, and went to sleep. It seemed she had only dropped off when she heard a voice and felt a light touch on her shoulder. "Time to get up, Little Bird."

Coming awake, she saw that Cody was already standing with his boots on and rifle in hand. Quickly she pulled her boots on, shivered in the coldness of the desert air, and then pulled the low-crowned hat down over her black hair. "Ready," she said.

They moved out, and Cody called out, "All right. We'll take it from here."

The two saw the shadows of Ritto and Bluestone emerge from the darkness. "Anything?" Cody asked.

"Nothing," Ritto said shortly.

He and Bluestone headed toward the small fireglow.

"They're angry," Cody sighed.

"They're superstitious, so they're afraid. But they act angry to keep us from knowing they're afraid."

Cody eyed her with amusement. "You know a lot about men."

She shrugged. "Most men aren't hard to understand. They're just big babies, really."

"Thanks," Cody said dryly.

"I said most men," Little Bird said evenly and left it at that.

They walked until they were well outside the camp perimeter, along the rough base of the butte. Cody stared up at the flat heights. "So you aren't afraid, Little Bird?" he asked with real interest.

"Afraid of spirit ancestors taking revenge on us? No. I don't believe in those old superstitions, Cody. Do you? I mean, really?"

He was troubled and didn't answer for a long time. Finally he replied, "I don't know. I guess I'm confused sometimes. I do believe in spirits. I do believe that there is something after we die, that we don't just—return to meaningless dust. And so the real question is, Are these spirits good or evil? And shouldn't we fear them if there are evil ones?"

His words chilled her suddenly. "I—I don't know. And I—now I'm sorry I asked. Do you want to split up?"

He shot a shrewd look at her face. The rather flat planes of it were stark in the cold starlight, and her eyes were black pools. The smooth skin of her forehead was drawn; she looked worried. Quickly he answered, "I don't think so. We might as well stay together. I don't expect any trouble."

Why have a guard then? Little Bird wondered, but she kept her sudden strange apprehensions to herself.

The two circled the camp, occasionally glimpsing the flickering firelight on their left. A thin sliver of a moon grinned crookedly down at them as they walked, their eyes always searching the darkness on the outside of the camp. They came to a large rock, and Cody leaned up against it, stretching and rubbing his neck and eyes.

"What was your life like, Little Bird, before I knew you?"

"It wasn't much fun." She pulled off her floppy wide-brimmed hat and looked down at it, fidgeting with it. Even under the faint trace of moonlight he could see the black sheen of her hair and the sturdiness of her form covered by the bulky coat. "I made it worse on myself than it should have been."

"Your parents?"

"I didn't know them too well. But I knew my grandfather. He was a great man." She hesitated, still looking down at her hat. "You knew that he was a good friend of Jesse Mitchell's? David's grandfather?"

Cody nodded, though she wasn't looking at him. "Your grandfather, Cholani, was the last chief of the Apaches, wasn't he?"

"He thought so. I guess I thought so, too."

"And was he a dunkhead?" Cody asked with elaborate casualness.

"Yes. Brother Mitchell—he—saved him, or whatever it is."

"So this Brother Mitchell, David's grandfather, he drew Cholani, our last chief, to God? Do you really think they knew Him? God, I mean?" Cody sounded interested, as he always did.

She took a deep breath. "Yes. They knew Him. And they were both great men, strong in God," she answered awkwardly.

Quietness flowed over the land. Far away a coyote howled, and then another answered him. It made a plaintive sound, but it was one that Little Bird had always liked.

The two were standing side by side. Cody slowly reached out and turned her to him. The moon lent its silver light, and he saw that her eyes were watchful, full of knowledge, alert, but not wary. For a long time he simply looked at her. He noted the full turn of her lips, the wash of faint gray light against her prominent cheekbones, the dark hollows underneath. She was not a pretty woman, but she had the wild beauty of a child of the desert. The moonlight was kind to her, showing the full soft lines of her body, and her hair, blacker than the night itself, was intensely beautiful.

They were so alone. Each of them was enclosed in a great circle of uncertainties, fears, longings. Without planning to, he reached out and brought her to him. He half expected her to resist, but she did not. And when he kissed her, he was aware of a desperate hunger—something that seemed to leap into him, shaking his mind. He knew then that this woman had a power over him that no one woman had ever had, and for one moment in his arms he held a sweetness and a richness that filled all his emptiness. He knew that this would be only a short fragment of time, that it was something he desperately longed for, although he had not known it. He drew back and found her dark eyes, unblinking, staring back at his face.

Little Bird did not speak. She watched him, waiting for a sign from him, a break in his impenetrable reserve, an opening into him.

But the moment didn't come, and the door into Cody Bent Knife's hidden heart closed. He turned away from her, and she thought she would—must—cry out. But then he took her hand, and she knew she must accept another defeat.

For a long time they stood together, holding hands like two children. But they were still alone, except for the mirthful moon.

The remains of the night passed quickly. Little Bird and Cody were intensely aware of each other, but he did not touch her again nor did she attempt to make him do so. About an hour before dawn they were back at the tumble of great boulders where they'd kissed. Both of them were very tired and cold. Cody looked up at the sky; it was turning a dim gray, the stars fading to dull specks. "Why don't you go back and get us some coffee, Little Bird?" he asked. "By the time we finish it, it'll be about time to break camp."

"That sounds good," she said in an oddly thick voice. Her lips were numb with cold, which made it hard to speak. She turned and headed back toward the camp, but a quick, primitive sense of danger flared up in her, and she whirled around to stare back at Cody.

He was standing, his head thrown back, his rifle held limply in one hand. "What . . . what *is* that?"

With an unreasoning fear rising cold within her, Little Bird looked up.

Against the dim grayness of the sky, shapes were outlined on the flat crest of the butte. As if she were a schoolchild, Little Bird counted them: *six . . . six . . . wolves . . .*

Her eyes went back down to the slim form of Cody.

"Cody!" she screamed and began to run. "Cody!"

It was as if the wolf had dropped from the sky. He fell on Cody from the rocks soaring above his head.

Before Cody could get his rifle half raised, the wolf struck him. He saw blazing yellow eyes and white fangs, and all he could hear was the guttural snarl that sounded like no animal he had ever heard. He smelled blood and the rotten-meat odor of the animal's hot breath. Cody was driven backward, stumbling, dropping his rifle. Desperately he threw up his hands, reaching for the wolf's throat. The wolf was tearing at his arms, and he felt the razor-sharp fangs rip through his clothing and rip through flesh. *I am going to die now,* he thought with strange detachment. But he fought savagely, grabbing and tearing at the wolf.

Before Little Bird's first scream had died away, Ritto and Bluestone had rolled out of their blankets, grabbed their weapons, and run to the awful scene. Neither could get a shot, for the wolf and Cody were rolling furiously on the ground. The wolf's snarls were deafening in the frozen air.

Little Bird, seeing that no one could possibly shoot the wolf without hitting Cody, snatched up a large burning branch. She smelled the hot coals burn through, but she felt nothing. Running up as close as she dared, she rammed the blaze right into the wolf's face. For a moment she thought he would turn on her. She held the blaze in front of her, shoving it savagely, almost ramming it down the wolf's red mouth.

And then the beast, giving one screeching, unearthly cry, turned and fled. He disappeared into the predawn shadows.

Little Bird's heart grew cold as she saw Cody's blood, black and thin, spread out over him and run into wide pools on the desert sand.

Desperately she looked up at Ritto and Bluestone, who seemed frozen, as unmoving as statues.

"Help me," she groaned, unaware that tears were flowing down her face. "Help me."

EIGHTEEN

A DREARY DAWN BEGAN with dirty gray tufts of thick clouds that heralded a snowstorm. The sun was glorious for only a moment, low on the eastern horizon. Then it disappeared. It was bitterly cold in the desert.

Ritto drove the cart into the canyon at a crashing run. Little Bird and Bluestone—now riding bareback, having left the other cart at the camp—charged in behind. All of the horses were grunting with exertion, their haunches lathered.

"Go on, Ritto!" Little Bird ordered. It was almost a scream. "Take him to the whites! They'll know what to do!"

In the cart, lying on a pile of colorful Navajo blankets, was Cody Bent Knife. He was covered with blankets, too, up to his chin. One-half of his face was swathed in thick white bandages. His one visible eye was closed, and his features were sharp, bony, like an old man's. The natural burnt umber of his skin had faded to a sallow dark yellow.

They had entered the canyon from the north so that they passed all of the huts where the Indians were living. Like an ill wind, Little Bird screamed, "Cody's hurt! We're taking him to the whites! Cody's hurt . . ." Indians on foot ran after the horses. As they rode through, everyone in the canyon followed them.

The soldiers were already up and were stoking the fire in the great room and boiling water for coffee and tea. Hearing the shouts, they ran outside.

Little Bird, drawn and sobbing, jumped off her horse and ran to Con Slaughter. "Help him! He—it was wolves! A wolf! Cody—he's—"

Con and his team pushed through the crowd that immediately surrounded the cart. With one look at Cody's face, Con grew grim. Quickly he searched the crowd, then ordered, "Dr. Ives! Get a move on. He needs help!"

Gildan Ives's white skin grew even paler. "I'm—I'm just a veterinarian, Captain! You know that!"

Con growled, "Well, that's four more years' medical training than anyone else here has, ma'am."

Gildan looked around helplessly as if she were a lab rat in a maze. Everyone was staring at her accusingly. With a gruff sigh, Niklas Kesteven, who looked like a grizzly bear just awakened from hibernation, stepped up to her side. "C'mon, Gildan. I'll help you."

"All—all right, Niklas," she said timidly.

They climbed up into the cart, one on each side of Cody.

"I—I need to see how badly he's hurt before we try to move him inside," Gildan said shakily.

Niklas nodded and pulled back the blankets covering Cody.

Gildan's hand went to her mouth as she flinched in shock.

His entire body was crimson red with blood.

Grimly Niklas peeled back the makeshift leather strips that Little Bird had bound around Cody's torn body.

The silence was complete.

Gildan made herself look closely at Cody's chest and stomach. Then, standing jerkily upright, she said in a choked voice, "If he were a dog, I'd put him down."

She jumped out of the cart, landing hard, took two unsteady steps, and kept her back turned, her head bowed.

Little Bird wailed, "You—you people! You white people know everything. You've—you've made—everything! Do something!"

With unaccustomed gentleness Niklas was covering Cody back up. "Little Bird, if we had a crack thoracic surgeon, a sterile operating theater, the latest laser surgical instruments, I'd still give him only a fifty-fifty shot. Here . . ." He shrugged helplessly.

"It's because we desecrated the burial grounds," Ritto said in a voice so filled with pain that he sounded more like an injured animal. "We never should have gone there." Bluestone was uncommonly quiet, merely nodding sorrowfully.

Little Bird looked around at the gathered crowd, and her face became twisted with anger. No one would look at her. "Someone has to help him," she said between gritted teeth. "I—I don't know what else to do."

Zoan, who was standing right by the cart, stared down at Cody Bent Knife with his characteristic lack of expression. "I guess I have to," he whispered. "I promised him I would if he ever got hurt."

Suddenly Dancy, who was standing close by Victorine, stepped forward. "I'll—I'll help take care of him, Zoan."

"Oh, that's just great!" Little Bird said savagely. "A half-wit and a little kid!"

"Silence, woman," Benewah Two Color said sternly, stepping forward to stand by Dancy. His dark eyes raked over Little Bird. "You shame us—especially Cody Bent Knife—by your dishonorable words."

"It doesn't matter," Victorine said in a tight voice. Her eyes were like flint, and her voice was hard. "Dancy will do no such thing. She can't possibly help someone who is hurt that badly. She—she can't. She won't."

Benewah turned to her, and his face was kind. "Your daughter looks like the little snow rabbits. She is small and quiet and meek. But she has the heart of a cougar. You must let her do this."

Victorine did not seem as much absorbed in the Indian's words as she seemed stunned. Her eyes widened as she stared at Benewah, unblinking. But after long moments she dropped her eyes and looked away.

Con, Rio, Darkon, and Benewah carried Cody into the great

room. As gently as they could, they laid him by the roaring morning fire on several of the beautiful blankets. Benewah said, "You go. Zoan and the girl and I will see to him."

Like embarrassed children, the three soldiers shuffled out.

Benewah began to tend the fire and see to preparing water to cleanse Cody with. Zoan knelt by Cody, gently removing the sticky red strips from his body and replacing them with big sterile Ty-gauze pads that were brought from the vet supply at the lab. Cody never moved, and his one eye remained closed. His breathing was shallow, ragged.

Dancy stopped and stared around. It was dark, for this led into a great warren of rooms cut back into the heart of a mesa. The only light came from two window openings cut beside the door, and the soldiers had tacked canvas over them for the winter. Strange shadows from the firelight danced on the remote stone walls, and the ceiling was hidden in darkness. It was a bleak, barren room that offered no comfort. With a small shiver she hurried to Cody's side.

"Benewah Two Color," Zoan said, the sound hollow in the big empty room, "we need more of these pads. They're in a storeroom, down the first passage, left, then left again. And I guess you better get some morphine-X, Benewah."

Without a word Benewah hurried through a door at the back.

Dancy sat cross-legged by Cody, and her eyes met Zoan's over his still body. "He's hurt really bad, Zoan," she said. With a feather-light touch, she began to remove the bulky bandage from Cody's face. He had three raw scratches down his cheek, from just beneath his eye diagonally down to his jawbone. But they weren't deep at all, only raw and swollen. They were minor compared to his other injuries, and his eye was untouched. Little Bird had bandaged his face rather clumsily in her distress.

"That's better, hmm?" Dancy whispered.

Cody opened his eyes. They were clouded, unseeing, but then he focused on Dancy's face. "You . . . Dancy? You're . . ."

"Yes, it's me, Dancy. You're home."

"I'm here, too, Cody," Zoan said in his childlike tones. "I'm going to take care of you, just like I promised."

Benewah Two Color hurried back into the room and knelt by Cody with a big stack of rolled bandages and pads. "Cody, my son," he said in a deep voice, "I'm here."

Cody nodded slightly, then licked his lips. "I'm thirsty. Can I have some water?"

Benewah jumped up, but Dancy said sternly, "No, Benewah. Not yet." To Cody, she said, "In just a few minutes, Cody. But no water, not now."

Benewah seemed angry for a moment, but then his shoulders slumped with resignation. "All right, little girl. What do you need?"

Dancy frowned. "I—I don't know . . . let me think . . ." She bowed her head for a moment. Then she looked back up, her eyes a clear light blue. "Heat that water to boiling, please. And—and—" She turned to Zoan as if to appeal to him. "Would you go and get some sage, Zoan? Some fresh sage that's still green?"

Zoan made a move as if to get up, but Benewah laid his hand on his shoulder. "No. I will go."

Cody asked with difficulty, "Dancy? You—how old are you?"

She swallowed. "I'm sixteen. I'll be seventeen in two months."

Cody didn't smile, for his face was riven with pain, but it did seem as if his haunted expression lightened for a moment. "Sixteen . . . when I was sixteen I went on a vision quest . . . I went out into the desert alone, and I didn't eat, and I didn't drink . . . The sun burned me and the nights chilled me . . . I was seeking death, for the Apache believe that when you draw near to death and stare at it, you have visions . . . and I did." His voice trailed off, and he tried to move his body. The pain grew to a savage heat, and he almost cried out, but he bit his lip so that no weak groan would escape him.

Dancy said, "No, don't move, Cody. I'll go ask Dr. Ives how much morphine to give you—"

"No," he panted. "No drugs. I don't . . . want to . . . die . . . not knowing . . . not understanding . . ."

"All right, Cody," Dancy said soothingly. "Here, let me see if I can make you a little more comfortable." She rearranged his blankets, adjusted the rolled blanket under his head, covered his legs and feet with another blanket. All the time Zoan never looked up from searching his friend's face.

Finally Benewah Two Color came back in with a bunch of wild sage in his gnarled hands. He hurried to Cody's pallet. Cody had closed his eyes again. "Is he—" Benewah asked fearfully.

Dancy shook her head. "No, he's just resting. Thank you, Benewah. Will you help me a minute?" She and Benewah went and stoked the fire underneath the cast-iron pot of water. It was almost boiling. Dancy picked out the smallest, most tender shoots of the hardy plant. A delightfully spicy scent, like a cold and clear day in the desert, permeated the room.

Cody's eyes were still closed, but he shifted his head a little. Zoan watched him and saw that he was sniffing. "That smells—refreshing . . . it's a clean smell . . . so clean . . ." He opened his eyes and almost smiled at Zoan. "Sweet smells . . . a hot fire . . . a good friend . . . not a bad way to die, is it, Zoan? This death . . . it's better than my visions . . . they were—they frightened me . . ." He was quiet for a moment, watching Zoan's somber face. "They were lies, weren't they?"

Zoan answered in a strong voice, "I don't know. Maybe it was God trying to talk to you, Cody, in a way that you would understand. He talked to me that way until I could hear Him. He talked to me with music."

A dark light, perhaps of hope, lit Cody's eyes. "Do you—do you think—He still would talk to me, Zoan?"

Zoan almost smiled. "I think He's always talked to you, Cody. I think He's talking to you right now."

Cody was silent a moment. His shadowed, pain-filled eyes met Zoan's fathomless gaze, and neither of the two young men moved.

But something, something felt rather than seen, perceived rather than known, passed between them. They were brothers, and they loved each other as much as two men, so unlike, so alien to each other, possibly could.

"He's your Father, too," Zoan said quietly.

A single tear slid down Cody's carved cheek. "It—seems—cowardly. Self-serving . . . for me to—to—pray to Him now. Now that I'm—dying . . ."

Zoan took Cody's hand. There was blood on it, and it smeared onto Zoan's palm and fingers. "I don't know what that means, Cody. All I know is that He will hear your voice, and He will know the truth of your heart. '*The word is nigh thee, even in thy mouth, and in thy heart: that is, the word of faith . . . that if thou shalt confess with thy mouth the Lord Jesus, and shalt believe in thine heart that God hath raised him from the dead, thou shalt be saved.*'"

A shadow, whether of pain or doubt, twisted Cody's face. "My heart longs to be saved . . . my mouth—I'm—thirsty for God . . . but faith, Zoan? Do I have faith?"

"You've always been a man of great faith, Cody," Zoan said in his childlike sincerity. "It's just never been faith in the right thing. In Jesus Christ."

Cody took a breath; it was long, shuddering, and deep. "Will you pray with me?"

"Sure, Cody."

Cody Bent Knife, the last of the true Apache warriors, closed his eyes and prayed, "God, I believe in You, and I believe that You sent Your Son, Jesus, to this earth as a man. I believe that He died for my sins, and rose from the dead in three days, and now reigns in heaven. Forgive me, Father, for my sins. Thank You for Your Son, Jesus, who died for me. Thank You . . . for . . . my life . . ."

Dancy was bending over the steaming water, slowly dropping the small leaves of the desert sage into it. Her eyes were closed, and her lips moved in prayer. Benewah Two Color watched her, amazed, for her face was lit, though the light was uncertain, and she seemed to glow. As he watched, a single tear slid down her cheek and dropped into the steaming water below.

When Cody fell silent, Benewah hurried over to the pallet. Every time Cody closed his eyes, Benewah was afraid he'd died. "My son, Cody . . . he is at peace now?" he asked. His voice was filled with fear.

Zoan looked up. "He's at peace now, Benewah. But he's not dead. God hasn't taken him home yet."

In a low voice, Dancy said, "It might be—a while yet. I'm going to . . . wash his wounds. It will make him feel better, to be clean . . ."

Though his eyes were still closed, Cody murmured, "Clean, yes. I want to be . . . clean . . . again . . ."

Dancy set the heavy pot down on the floor beside Cody, then knelt down. She dipped a clean rag into the water, wrung it out carefully, then sponged his face and neck. Cody shifted, just a little, and said, "All my life I've had the smells of the desert in my nostrils. I never knew that sage, just a desert weed, could smell so . . . wholesome, so refreshing . . ."

Zoan lifted his sad eyes to Dancy. She nodded slightly, and Zoan pulled down the blankets, then lifted the pads that covered the wounds on Cody's chest and belly. They were already sodden with blood. Dancy's mouth twisted, and for a moment she looked like what she was: a frightened half-grown child. Then she washed the cloth out in the fragrant water again, set her jaw, and began to wash Cody with a touch as light as a butterfly's wing. Benewah, sitting beside her, flinched as she touched Cody's skin.

But Cody seemed comfortable, even happy. "God is good. The pain . . . it's not as bad as it was. I even feel a little warmer . . . Zoan? Would you please . . . sing to me? Something about . . . Jesus?"

Zoan was thoughtful, then he straightened his shoulders and began to sing in his clear, light voice:

Tell me the story of Jesus,
Write on my heart every word;
Tell me the story most precious,
Sweetest that ever was heard.

Cody had a deep, long wound from his right shoulder down across to the left side of his chest. It was wide and bleeding freely. No gauze pads would staunch it. He also had savage bites, and some tearing from sharp fangs, on his side and right arm. Even his legs were bitten, some of the bites leaving long gashes and shredded flesh.

But those wounds alone would not have been life-threatening. It was Cody's stomach, torn open, that would surely kill him. It was impossible, in this time, in this world, to repair that kind of internal damage.

Dancy hesitated for a moment, then decided to cleanse the mortal wound last. She reflected—with a calmness that surprised her greatly—that probably Cody would die when she cleaned it. But she also knew that God was telling her insistently to wash his wounds with the sweet-smelling water. *Is this Your way of—of—taking him home, Lord? He's in so much pain . . . but I know that he could linger on for—hours, maybe even days . . . and if I let him drink water, he'll get rehydrated and the blood will flow . . . But, Lord, wouldn't it be better for him to—to—bleed to death instead of—going into shock when I clean out that wound? I—I don't think I can—it would seem like I'm killing him!*

"He's not dead. He lives."

Dancy jerked, splashing the warm water onto her lap. "What—what did you say?" she asked Zoan accusingly.

He stared at her, his eyes enormous in the half-light. "I was singing. I didn't say it, Dancy."

"Oh," she said uncertainly. Looking down at Cody, now with wonder, she saw him looking back up at her with a sweet expression, so unlike the hard, distant desert wanderer he'd always been.

Dancy swallowed hard. "Cody, do you—would you—um—" Feeling a bit desperate, she looked up at Zoan.

Zoan looked puzzled for a moment, and then his plain features lit up. "Cody? Do you believe that God can heal you?"

Cody answered dreamily, "Of course. He's God, isn't He?"

Zoan nodded to Dancy.

She stopped her hands from shaking. Then she slowly laid the damp cloth on Cody's shoulder—right where the wolf had begun his long, tearing path. Almost imperceptibly she moved the cloth down, tracing the wound, but just above the cloth, where Dancy had started, there was no wound. There was only clean, bronzed skin.

Benewah Two Color started, then muttered, "What—how—"

"It's all right, Benewah," Cody said, watching him. "It's all right."

Dancy, her eyes as wide as the sky, moved the cloth a little more.

The wound, as if it were being cleaned off, was disappearing.

Dancy carefully, unhurriedly, kept moving the cloth down the long, jagged red road across Cody's chest.

Behind the cloth's trace, there was only healthy skin, not even new scar tissue.

In front of it were blood and torn skin and muscle.

Dancy's cloth moved.

Finally she had traced the entire long wound, and it was gone. Dancy lifted the cloth.

Benewah, his age-creased face stunned, snatched it out of her hand and stared at it. It was clean, damp, smelling of the sweet savor of the sage. No blood was on it. Benewah blinked.

"That didn't even sting, Dancy," Cody said dreamily. He wasn't looking down at his torn body; he was watching her face, thinking what a pretty, ethereal girl she was. How odd he'd never noticed the light that shone in her face and eyes and lit her dark golden hair. Idly he thanked God that he could see such innocent loveliness for his last sight of this world. "I'm getting warm . . . I almost feel . . . normal, like I'm just tired or something . . ."

Zoan was staring at Dancy. "Go ahead, Dancy. Keep praying."

Dancy nodded tremulously.

As if he were in a death trance, Benewah Two Color handed the cloth back to her. Dancy dipped it in the water, wrung it out, and began cleaning all of Cody's bite wounds and tears from the wolf's claws. At her touch, they melted, dissolved, became unreal, never real, as if the skin had never been touched.

Finally she looked down at Cody's death wound. She looked back up at Zoan. He smiled. "Go ahead. You think the others were just fine for God, but this one is too big?"

Shakily Dancy smiled back. "N-no, I guess not."

She closed her eyes and whispered, "It's just You, God. Guide my hands. And—and thank You."

"What . . . what . . . ," Cody breathed, stirring.

"Shh," Dancy said softly. "Just—another—minute, Cody."

Steeling herself, she applied the cloth to Cody's side, where the wound began, and began to glide down his stomach.

The wound, the blood, the horror—all was gone.

Cody moved stiffly, but the growing strength in his body was evident. "Dancy? Zoan? I—something's—different. I'm feeling—stronger—and I don't hurt—" He rose up on one elbow, then looked down at his chest. His skin, with all the glow and elasticity of youth, bronzed by the sun, was clean and without mark. Cody's narrowed eyes widened. "Zoan—Zoan?"

Zoan said, grinning, "No. Not me. And not Dancy, either. It was God, Cody. He healed you. Jesus Christ of Nazareth . . . *'His name through faith in his name hath made this man strong . . .'*"

The only sounds in the air outside the room where Cody Bent Knife lay were deep, tearing sobs from Little Bird and the harsh crunch of Niklas Kesteven's footsteps as he paced the cold, hard earth.

All of the Indians were seated cross-legged on blankets and skins, not speaking, only waiting. They were, on the whole, a patient people. For generations they had been waiting for a man such as Cody Bent Knife to lead them out of their darkness. Now, with resignation borne of centuries of defeat, they waited for his death and the death of their visions of the Indian living again as master of his world.

Lystra Palermo, ever the practical schoolteacher, gathered the children around her and settled them in the cart, huddled under the new blankets that Cody and the others had brought from the Navajo reservation. When Lystra told the children to get into the cart and cover themselves with the new blankets, Little Bird screeched, "They've got his blood all over them, you stupid old woman! How dare you!"

Bluestone Yacolt grunted, "The price of those blankets was much too high, and they are cursed. We should burn them along with his body, and maybe that would free his spirit and those of the old ones who died that we have offended."

Lystra was a high-tempered woman, and she had struggled for years to keep her fiery temper under control. Now it flared uncontrollably in her, but she was a lady of the old school, and she never would raise her voice in anger. She said calmly, "Bluestone Yacolt, I am an old woman, I am cold, and these children are freezing. Don't be a sad and superstitious fool. I thank God for these blankets. And so should you."

In a businesslike manner she picked up the top blanket, which was indeed stiff with blood. Little Bird darted forward and snatched it from her, then turned and ran a little way, crying hysterically. Lystra sighed, then helped Pip, the catatonic boy Dancy had practically adopted, and eight-year-old Torridon Carlisle into the cart. Tenderly she covered their shoulders with two of the blankets, casting foreboding glances at Bluestone and Little Bird.

But Bluestone and the rest of the Indians ignored her. All of them had a thousand-mile stare as if they could see past the canyon, past time itself, into the spirit-place they believed they had violated. From the expressions on their faces, it seemed to be a bleak vision, indeed.

Con, Rio, and Ric stood together, talking in low, uneasy tones. They felt as if they should be doing something, for they were men who were accustomed to taking charge and initiating action. But there was nothing they could do, and for some obscure reason, they all felt guilty. Darkon Ben-ammi and Vashti Nicanor sat a little off to one side, by themselves, apparently observing in a clinical manner. Darkon's face was heavy, and Vashti's usually cool, aloof eyes were shadowed with sadness. Both liked Cody Bent Knife, but more important to them, they respected him. Not many people earned the two hardened soldiers' respect.

Gildan was sitting cross-legged on a flat boulder, her back to the complex and the people gathered around. She stared into space, her pretty face haggard and lined. She had been attracted to Cody Bent Knife, but he had ignored her flirting, and then he had even been sharp with her when she tried more aggressive tactics. Gildan had hated him for that. And now she hated him for putting her in this position. One couldn't help feeling guilty for hating someone (and if the truth be known, wishing him harm) if he died, and especially if he died so horribly. Gildan, too, was staring far away in her mind, wishing she could be back where people behaved civilly, according to the rules. Back there—wherever it was—men seemed to find her more attractive and more desirable. Gildan had never been so lonely and miserable in her life as she had been since she'd come to Chaco Canyon.

Victorine leaned against the stand of boulders where Gildan sat in desolate solitude. She was pale and nervous. She fidgeted with a stone she'd picked up, rubbing it, tossing it from one hand to the other, feeling the soft grit that could be so easily rubbed off the rocks in the canyon. Victorine couldn't decide whether to march into the complex and snatch Dancy out of the horrible situation, or whether to go in there to offer help, or whether to hold her peace and stay still and calm and ready to help Dancy if she was upset, or whether to just cry. She didn't see the continual concerned looks Con was furtively giving her. And it never occurred to her to pray.

Suddenly, in the leaden air, loud shouting came from inside the great room. Little Bird stopped her harsh sobs. Niklas Kesteven stopped pacing midstride.

"What the—" Con muttered.

It was, indeed, shouting, and not cries of grief.

Oddly it sounded like—Cody Bent Knife.

He came running out, shirtless and barefoot. His leather breeches were still covered with blood. But there was no mark on his body, except for three scratches on his cheek. "Look at me!" he shouted, throwing up his arms and whirling around. "I'm alive! I'm strong! I'm *healed*!" For sheer joy's sake, he ran. He ran in a circle around the gathered crowd, shouting, "Ay-yi-yi-yi!"

Benewah Two Color had come out with him, and behind them came Zoan and Dancy together. All of them looked exhausted—much more worn out than Cody did—but all of them, especially Benewah, glowed with joy. The grave older Cherokee, whose face normally looked as if it would crack if he smiled, was grinning like a young boy.

Soon the three stopped, and their happy expressions slowly faded away. In the heavy silence, Cody's triumphant cries rang out, but as he ran back to Benewah, Zoan, and Dancy, he suddenly grew quiet and whirled around to face the people gathered.

"What's the matter?" he asked, genuinely astonished. "All of you look—"

He couldn't describe how they looked. All had different reactions, and none of them were what Cody and the others had thought they would be.

The Indians, for the most part, seemed frightened. Some of the women jumped to their feet, grabbed their children, and started backing up, their black eyes wide and stark. Bluestone and Ritto stood up, staring at Cody—and the three behind him—with suspicion.

Con, Ric, and Rio seemed stunned with disbelief. Ric took a tentative step toward Cody, but then stopped, his face riven with confusion. Unconsciously Rio fingered his gun. Con just stared, his tanned, rugged face frozen.

Victorine, too, was still. She was the only person in the gathering who wasn't looking at Cody. She was staring at her daughter with incomprehension, as if she were having trouble recognizing Dancy. Beside her, Gildan had turned around, and her wide blue eyes were strained open with mild revulsion.

Niklas Kesteven was the first to recover. He hurried over to Cody and roughly ran his hands over Cody's chest, arms, stomach, turning him like an errant child to study his back, stepping close to peer at his skin. "It's impossible. This can't be. There must be some explanation."

Cody, who might be a Christian now but who had not had time to learn meekness, pushed Niklas hard, even though it was like pushing on a great heavy punching bag. "Yeah, there's an explanation, Dr. Kesteven," he said with a hint of crossness. "I prayed for God to save my soul, and while He was at it, He saved my life, too. Dancy healed me. Zoan prayed and sang, and Dancy healed me."

Every eye swiveled toward Dancy Flynn Thayer, and she visibly shrank. The light, the joy, was gone from her, and she seemed small, vulnerable, a frightened sixteen-year-old child. Victorine rushed forward, threw her arms around her, then shoved Dancy protectively behind her, like a she-bear protecting her cub. "What are you all looking at?" she hissed. "She's just a child! Stop—staring at her!"

Uneasily Zoan said, "Wait a minute. You don't understand. Dancy didn't heal Cody. He just doesn't realize that he shouldn't—say it that way. God healed Cody. Just God. Cody had faith, he believed, he confessed his belief in Christ Jesus, and by faith he was saved and by faith he was healed."

Niklas nodded in a clinical manner, then asked in a cool voice, "But what were the physical circumstances, Zoan? I mean, how exactly did those wounds go away?"

Benewah Two Color stepped forward because Zoan seemed confused, and Cody seemed lost in amazement at the hostile reactions of the people he loved. Benewah said in a low, reverent voice, "I was a witness, Doctor. I will tell you that I saw, and I know that God our Great Father healed Cody. Zoan was singing a song of life, and the girl was tending him with cleansing waters. And I? I was witnessing, and then I was praying to Jesus, the Son, and our Father God. And so was Cody healed."

Niklas nodded absently. "Water? Cleansing water? What is this?"

"They don't understand, Benewah," Cody said sadly.

"They will," Benewah said calmly. "We must make them understand. We must tell them."

People had been backing away, distancing themselves from Cody, but now they were almost unconsciously creeping forward. They had been staring at Cody, but now they looked only at Dancy. Somehow, she and her mother had become the center of an ever-tightening circle of people. Not every face was merely curious; not every expression was friendly. Some people looked fearful; some looked awed. But some looked resentful, and some had ugly expressions of suspicion.

Victorine stared around at her friends and comrades with a sudden dreadful comprehension. "Oh, no, you don't! She's not going to be your little patron saint, and she's not some whacked-out psychic, either! She's just a little girl, and—oh, get out of my way!"

Victorine Flynn Thayer, a tall, dark woman with flashing eyes, could be commanding, indeed. The crowd parted as she strode forward on long legs, hauling Dancy with her like a small rag doll. They marched off toward the pool and soon disappeared in the ravine leading up to it.

A foul wind, sharp and long, swooped down into the canyon from the east. The snow began.

German Foreign Ministry, Berlin
December 15, 2050

". . . not permanent or inclusive of each member of the generation but seem to be almost an attempt at experimental evolutionary defensive permutations by the organism so that our studies are continually diverted from the intended goals . . ."

Dr. Gudrun Schaecht, a young woman with a lumpish face and thick body, droned on and on about the ohm-bug. Alia Silverthorne's mind wandered; she wondered about many things. Alia wondered why Minden Lauer and President Therion were always present at all of Tor's meetings now, even with his military advisers. She wondered why Count von Eisenhalt was letting this woman speak to him in such a supercilious manner.

Mostly she marveled that Dr. Gudrun Schaecht truly seemed to have no hint of the danger she was putting herself in by attempting to make excuses to Tor. True, the woman was brilliant. But she was somewhat unworldly in that she seemed to think and see only in terms of her little world of microbiology. Surely Dr. Schaecht was aware that her predecessor had been gone for three weeks? That is, he had disappeared; he had been erased from this world. The last anyone had seen of him, he had been on his way to a private meeting with Tor von Eisenhalt. No one, including his wife and three children, had seen him since.

There had been no investigation, of course. No one on this earth would dare to question Tor von Eisenhalt about it. And no one would question Tor even if he killed and ate this woman right here and now . . .

Alia was shocked at her own idle musings. Killed—and ate the woman? What in the world am I thinking? What's happening to me? Am I going totally insane?

But Alia Silverthorne was nothing if not stubborn and determined, and she put the thought—and horrible vision—out of her mind. Lately she'd had to do that often. It seemed that something—her imagination, her innermost thoughts, the most secret and hidden parts of her brain—had been intruding on the conscious workings of her mind. Quickly, hastily, so she wouldn't have to think about it too much, she made a decision to ask Doctor for something to calm her. She was already taking a strict and strong regimen of various body and mind enhancers, and she thought they might be resulting in some odd side effects. Doctor would know—she jumped at the sound of Tor's voice.

Tor demanded, "Dr. Schaecht, are you saying that you cannot kill this organism?"

The woman's muddy brown eyes suddenly grew wary. "Why, why—no, sir. We can kill it. Any physical entity can be killed under controlled *circumstances."*

"You're wrong," Tor said in a deadly quiet voice. "This is a waste of my time. March 23 will be six months after the autumnal equinox. I will be generous. I will give you until April 1."

Dr. Schaecht looked confused, and then the first hint of fear began to show. Tor seemed to be pleased, and when he spoke again, his voice was its usual deep, commanding tone. "So, Dr. Schaecht, I have just one more question for you. What do you need? You can have anything—equipment, personnel, consultants—anything. What do you want?"

Dr. Schaecht's first thought was more time, *but she had finally become aware that she was treading on a dangerous road, full of pitfalls, and she'd better watch her steps very carefully. Taking a long, deep breath, she began, "Sir, I would like to have two more lab technicians, and I have two biochemists in mind if you would be so kind as to add them to the staff—"*

She cut off her words midsentence.

Tor von Eisenhalt abruptly sat upright, and his face clearly showed that he was angry. Enraged, in fact. Every man and woman in the room—except Alia, Minden, and Luca—flinched, and some shuddered with abject fear.

Dr. Schaecht frantically thought, What did I say? What did I do? Am I going to die?

Suddenly, jarringly, Tor jumped out of his chair and hurried from the room.

Gathering all her courage, Alia followed him. Minden and Luca had become his constant companions, and Alia was always with them, for she was their personal—and only—bodyguard. But she felt privately that she must guard Tor, too. He can't be killed, *she thought for the thousandth or maybe the millionth time,* but he can be hurt. *For some reason, this mantra came to her so much that she wholly believed it to be true. It terrified her.*

She followed him almost at a run, for Tor was a tall man with long strides, and Alia was small, though she was strong and sturdy. He marched through the long hallways, his steps making no sound on the thick carpeting. No expense had been spared for the renovation of the old Reichstag; it was a Gothic palace, with stern statues of warriors and bas-relief carvings of great battles everywhere. Tor went out a side door to a small, secluded garden near the west wing. Alia doggedly followed him. Tor had always seemed to be slightly amused at her lapdoglike devotion.

It was noon, but the sun was too weak to give much warmth. In the small square of garden, the grass had long since withered, and a few dead leaves from the great oak tree crackled underfoot. Alia knew that they would be raked up by the afternoon. Germany, all of it, was the cleanest, most well-kept country she'd ever imagined. There was never an iota of litter in public places, the sidewalks were never dirty, and it was amazing to her that every window in every building always sparkled like polished diamonds.

Tor stopped with his back to Alia, so she stopped, too, and studied him. He lifted his head, and Alia could have sworn he was sniffing . . . but no, that was ludicrous . . . It must be another of the peculiar imaginings that had plagued her for so many months now . . .

She didn't know how long they stood there. Tor stood absolutely still, not speaking, not moving. Alia fidgeted a little; she fingered the pistol at her side, and her gaze continually swept around the small garden, noting the two pathways converging on the small enclosed square, the shortest way to the street, the shortest way to the entrance of the building behind them.

Abruptly Tor turned and looked at her with a gaze that froze her bones. "You," he said in a low growl. At least, Alia thought she heard a growl . . . growling . . .

"Do you hear it?" he asked her. He seemed clinically curious.

Alia licked her lips. "Hear—I—I hear the wind, sir. Just the wind."

He nodded, then turned his back to her again. Alia had the strangest feeling that if she walked around to look at his face, it would not be Tor von Eisenhalt's face at all. It would be someone—no— something *else entirely, something not human, something not even animal . . . something . . . Some thing . . .*

With an almost physical effort, Alia controlled her mind. "Sir," she said between gritted teeth, "you should not go anywhere without protection. I know you—feel—confident that—you—that no one—that nothing—"

"Silence," he said, and Alia felt as if someone had hit her on the head hard, and it had stunned her. Naturally she fell silent.

"America . . . that accursed, sprawling—" He went on in a language that Alia didn't understand, but the rebellious little imp in her mind insisted that it did, too, sound like growling . . .

"They're fighting me," he said. He turned to her again, and Alia felt a relief all out of proportion that it was Tor von Eisenhalt, the man, though his expression was forbidding. "It would seem that the sheep are putting on wolf's clothing, Alia. Foolish, weak-minded, stupid little children are trying to fight me. Me!"

"Who, sir? Who is fighting you?"

He studied her. "You must *find them, Alia. You* will *find them."*

Despairing, Alia cried, "But, sir, I don't know who they are! I don't—I can't see!"

He nodded. "I know. I know. It's all right, Alia. I will show you. They will be some of your renegade religious crazies, a small group, hiding . . . not in the camps . . . somewhere . . . in the West, I believe. California maybe?"

"I'll find every last one of them, sir," Alia stated evenly. "I swear to you that I'll find every one of them who would dare to try to fight you."

He smiled, and the smile was as terrible as his wrath. "Don't kill them, Alia. Just bring them to me. Especially the young ones."

The noon sun seemed to grow bigger, hotter, as the two stood there in the square of light.

The sun was hidden in Chaco Canyon, for it was just past the dawn, and the lowering clouds hid the sun from them, and it also hid the canyon from ravening eyes. Zoan and Dancy and Benewah Two Color were praying for Cody Bent Knife, and his body was being healed of a deadly hurt. The light shone bright around them.

For now, Tor von Eisenhalt, the Wolf, could not see.

NINETEEN

A SKIM OF ICE caught the bright afternoon sunlight. Overhead the pale sun seemed almost without heat, and the spectators who had come to line the circumference of the pool wore heavy clothing and their breath made puffs like incense rising up in the frigid air.

Zoan wore only a pair of faded Ty-jeans and a thin blue shirt, but he never seemed to feel the cold. Usually his face was empty, but now he looked happy as he stood hip deep in the water. He was dwarfed by the tall men who stood beside him, Con Slaughter on his left and Ric Darmstedt on his right.

Standing on the very brink of the pool, watching with frowning concentration, were Rio Valdosta and Vashti Nicanor. Colonel Darkon Ben-ammi had flatly refused to attend the baptisms. Niklas and Gildan had disdainfully refused. But all of the Indians were there, and so were the "civvies," as the refugees from the Albuquerque Isolation Facility had come to be called.

Victorine Flynn Thayer stood very close beside Dancy, holding her cold hand. She had found it difficult to accept the fact that these two fighting men had given their lives to Christ, when neither of them had ever said a great deal about God. *Especially Con . . . he always closed up tight as a vise whenever Dancy mentioned the Lord to him . . .* It struck her with a sudden pain when she realized that she had never talked to Con Slaughter about the Lord. She rarely spoke or thought about her Savior much at all these dark days. The focus of all her thoughts was Dancy Flynn Thayer.

The baptism itself was simple, as was everything that Zoan did. He asked, "Are you ready, Captain Con?"

Con nodded, and Zoan put his hand on the back of the taller man's neck. With his left hand he closed Con's mouth and pinched his nostrils together and then said, "I baptize you in the name of the Father, the Son, and the Holy Spirit." The words echoed over the open space as he lowered the big man backward until he was completely immersed. Con was a full half foot taller than Zoan, and the smaller man struggled a bit. Ric stepped forward to help. "Is this—legal, Zoan?" he asked.

"Sure," Zoan said. "We're all brothers in Christ."

When Con came up, he shook his head, wiped the water from his face, and then said calmly, "Thank you, Zoan."

Zoan nodded. "Will you help me with Lieutenant Ric?" he asked, then turned to Ric. He baptized the big man, saying the words again. When he came up, Ric gasped with the shock of the water, but his eyes were bright, and he laughed exultantly. "Thank you, Zoan, and Captain Slaughter, it's a real honor." The two men rather awkwardly embraced.

Zoan turned to motion Cody and Benewah Two Color into the water, only to see Rio Valdosta wading out toward him, his face grim with determination. He was like a great tank lumbering along, the water making small waves from his stocky body as he moved.

When he reached the three men, he looked at Con Slaughter and said, "I've always followed you, Captain. If you're gonna live and die as a Christian, then I'm gonna live and die with you."

"It—it doesn't work like that, Sergeant Rio," Zoan said with some distress. "This is what a man does for himself. He gives himself to God, not for his loyalty to somebody else, no matter how much you admire him."

"I know that, and I understand that this is between me and

Jesus. I'll get all the finer points down later, but I'm telling you right now—" He turned and spoke louder so that those on the bank heard him clearly, "I'm asking Jesus Christ into my heart. I've always been kinda embarrassed about it—who knows why—but I've read the Bible enough to know that it means He takes first place in my life. And Captain Slaughter is the gutsiest man I've ever known. If he's not ashamed, then I'm sure not going to be."

Zoan smiled. "If you will follow Jesus, then it is right you should be baptized."

Rio's sturdy form was steady as he nodded. "I believe in Jesus Christ as the Son of God."

"Then in the name of the Father, the Son, and the Holy Spirit, I baptize you."

Rio came up from the water, and the three men waded ashore where they wrapped themselves in blankets and laughed and talked loudly, as men will.

Zoan said, "Cody, Benewah." When the Indians came to him, he said exultantly, "Now we'll really be brothers."

"Yes," Cody said and smiled up at the pale sun.

Zoan was struck again by the three long red scratches on Cody's face. They were going to leave ugly scars on the handsome young Indian, but Cody had just laughed and said that maybe God knew he was vain about his looks, and that's why He hadn't healed them.

"I live," Cody said quietly, "and that's a miracle. This baptism is the same miracle. Now I die, but I will be alive in Him."

Zoan baptized his two best and closest friends, true friends of the heart. Benewah was smiling, but shivering, so Cody and Zoan hurried to help him ashore. Cody was astounded when he reached the bank and looked up at Ritto Yerington. Easily the largest, heaviest man in the group, Ritto was standing rigid, his fists clenched, bloodless, at his sides. But what amazed Cody was that tears were streaming down Ritto's coppery cheeks.

"Ritto, my brother. Let me pray with you," Cody said kindly, laying his hands on the man's thick shoulders.

Ritto seemed to collapse. Beside him his sister, Layna, her head drooping so that the black satin fall of her hair hid her face, was sobbing. Turning, she threw her arms around her brother and whispered, "Ritto, Ritto, we have to come to God. We have to know Him . . . We're so lost . . . we've been so lost, so alone, all our lives . . ."

"Listen, listen to me," Cody implored them. He loved these two—especially Ritto, who had always loved Cody Bent Knife as fiercely as he had hated his enemies. All of the Indians, who kept a certain stolid distance from white people, drew near and listened eagerly as Cody simply and calmly explained his dedication to Jesus.

Finally Ritto nodded and said, "Yes, Cody. Yes, I must have this Jesus. If you say that He's our Father God, then I must come to Him."

The huge Indian, holding his sister by the hand, waded out into the pool. It was all that both Zoan and Cody could do to handle him. Ritto, with understanding, had taken them out into even deeper water so that they didn't have to lift his massive weight, but even so it was a struggle. Ritto, however, came out of the water so handily, he almost leaped from his own great strength.

The Indians gathered around them, talking and asking questions. Lystra Palermo, with Torridon and Pip in tow, joined them. The Indians had tacitly accepted them, partly because Torridon had made fast friends with Hindo Night Singer's two youngest children, and partly because they had a vestige of an old superstition that Pip with his mental illness was special—touched by the gods, they thought.

Zoan and the soldiers were together in a tight group. Vashti had hurried to put a blanket around Zoan, though he didn't appear to be cold. Ric came up to her, grinning. "Do I look different, Colonel?"

She considered him coolly. "You look wet. That's different."

"I feel different," he said with boyish excitement. "I am different. Think you'll still like me, Colonel, sir?"

She was startled for a moment, her raven's-wing eyebrows raised. She quickly recovered, however, and grumbled, "You were a Gentile before, and I liked you. You're still a Gentile, so I suppose no irreparable harm's been done."

"A Gentile, huh?" He laughed, a genuine, rich laugh. Ric had been laughing a lot in the last few days. "As opposed to a Jew?"

"Of course," she rasped.

"A Jew? A child of Israel? One of the chosen ones—like you?" he teased, his blue eyes sparkling like struck steel.

"You're still an idiot, too," she said dryly.

"Yeah," he agreed, "but the sad part is that you still like me, Vashti."

"That's 'Colonel, sir,' to you, Lieutenant," she said sternly, taking his arm. "C'mon, all of you get out of those wet clothes. That's an order . . ."

Standing apart from them, Victorine and Dancy watched the two knots of people talking and laughing. For once, no one noticed them. Most of the time, people gave Dancy sidelong looks and sidled up to her as if they were frightened of her or in awe of her. Everyone but Zoan, Cody, Benewah, and Con seemed uncomfortable around her. Dancy hated it, but since she was still a child in many ways, she didn't know how to handle it.

But Victorine did—or at least she thought she did. "C'mon, Dancy," she said, her voice filled with anger. "Let's go for a walk."

Hand in hand, they turned and walked alone for a long time by the stream.

Cody heard no sound, for Zoan appeared at the open door with his characteristic ghostlike silence, but Cody sensed his presence. Without turning he said, "Hello, Zoan. Come in."

Cody was standing at the window at the back of his hut, by his bed. He'd pulled aside the Navajo blanket he'd hung over the square opening and was staring out at the frosty night. It was breathtakingly beautiful, with the light dusting of snow and the unending vista of the heavens.

Zoan did not answer as he came to stand by his friend.

The two men stood, silent, motionless, for a long time.

Zoan had been out for hours, walking alone in the frozen wastes. Thoughts had formed in his mind, disturbing thoughts, troubled thoughts. As usual, however, he had not been able to figure out how to express them. He did know that somehow he could make Cody understand.

Cody waited patiently.

Zoan finally said, "I've been walking and thinking."

Cody nodded and waited.

Zoan's smooth, unmarked forehead drew together in worry creases. "You remember I once tried to tell you about that Man-Wolf, Cody?"

Cody nodded, and slowly his fingers went up to brush lightly the three raw welts on his cheek. "Yes, I remember, Zoan. I've been thinking about that a lot since that thing attacked me and almost killed me. Would have, but for the grace of God." He hesitated, then his voice dropped with uncertainty. "Do you think, Zoan, that the wolf that attacked me was . . . real? I mean, was it just—a wolf or—or—something else?"

"I don't know, Cody," Zoan said, and he sounded afraid. "I don't understand much sometimes. But I've been having these dreams . . . bad dreams. About wolves, hunting, always hunting . . ."

Cody frowned. "Dreams . . . I think your dreams probably have a meaning, Zoan. I think maybe what they mean is that he's looking for us. The—the Man-Wolf. Maybe the wolves that attacked us are like his servants or something, but—they don't know everything. They don't understand everything . . ."

Suddenly Zoan's face cleared. "I think that's true, Cody. I think you're right. Just like sometimes I can't understand everything. I know the devil doesn't know everything, can't see everything." With a touch of unhappiness returning he murmured, "But he is looking . . . he would be looking for strong Christians, Cody. Like you. Like Dancy."

"Like you, Zoan," Cody added, almost whispering.

Zoan nodded, then sighed. "Yes, he's been looking for me. I can see him sometimes. I mean, not with my eyes. I just—see him in the dark."

"I know," Cody said. "You're not afraid, are you?"

"Yes," Zoan answered honestly. "I am."

Cody returned his searching gaze out into the night. "I am, too, Zoan. But that's nothing to be ashamed of, you know. In fact, I think we'd be loco if we weren't afraid."

Zoan didn't answer. Both of them stared out, unseeing, into the night for a while longer. "There's more," Zoan finally said. His voice was as soft and light as a snowflake.

Cody swallowed hard. "I thought so."

"We have to—let him find us, Cody," Zoan said, almost as if he were pleading. "I'm—not sure—but I know—that God's telling me that we have to—let him see us. We—we can't hide anymore. I can't hide anymore."

"I know," Cody said, and he sounded weary. "And I know why, too. I've been too afraid to face it, to admit it to myself." He turned to Zoan and laid his hand on the smaller man's heart. He took Zoan's hand and placed it on his own chest. "Our hearts, our blood, between us, Zoan, my brother. We two together are strong." Zoan nodded wordlessly, watching Cody's face with his unfathomable gaze. "It's because of a man, one man, one frail man named Jesse Mitchell," Cody told him quietly. "I felt it when Little Bird spoke to me about him, even before I was listening to God speaking to me. And now I know because God has told me. We can't ever let him—the Man-Wolf—find Brother Mitchell. We can't even let him—look that way."

The two men broke their brothers' embrace, and together, they left the cabin. Cody said heavily, "We have to tell the others. I guess we need to talk to Captain Slaughter and the soldiers first. But everyone has to know. People have to—make their own decisions."

"I know," Zoan said gravely, but he felt tremendous relief. Cody had understood. Better than that, Cody had known.

Zoan wasn't alone anymore.

"Wait a minute!" Con rasped in his trademark throaty half-whisper. "Let me get this straight. You're telling me that we're nothing but cannon fodder?"

"I don't know what that is," Zoan said solemnly.

"Dead is what that is!" Rio said heatedly. "Forty-five dead corpses!"

"Dead corpses?" Zoan asked, a puzzled look on his face. "What other kind is there?"

Ric broke in. "Maybe not, Rio. We're pretty tough. I'm not just talking about the team, but everyone here is tough in his own way."

Rio shook his head stubbornly. "Look, for all my big talk, sirs, you and I both know that the only hope we have is in stealth! You know, black ops? The kind where they don't even know we exist—much less where we are? And now you're telling me we've got to paint a target on our foreheads and say, 'Hey, Mr. Werewolf, over here! No, don't look that way. Come over here and kill me!'"

Incredulously Colonel Darkon Ben-ammi said, "Stop right there. Do I understand that you, Captain Slaughter, and you, Lieutenant Darmstedt, are considering some sort of—foolish—gesture, just as a decoy? For some little old man in Arkansas that you've never even met? Is this some dunkhead madness, or are you all truly insane?"

Con was far from offended; the corners of his eyes crinkled with amusement. "Sir, I'm not insane, and neither is Darmstedt. We're not considering any action at all right now. I just want this information, sir, all of it."

"This is not information," Darkon muttered. "This is contusions."

"Delusions," Vashti corrected him gravely.

"*Ja, ja,* whatever."

Con managed to keep from laughing as he turned back to Zoan and Cody. "I believe you," he said sturdily, "and I even think in some weird way that I knew something like this was coming. Still, I'm a practical man. Do you think we have any other kind of options here? Is there anything else we can do?"

Zoan considered this before answering in a slow, kind voice, his eyes on Darkon Ben-ammi. The older man quickly averted his angry gaze. "Nobody has to stay here, Captain Con. Anyone can leave anytime. Cody says there's no shame in being afraid, especially of something you—you don't know how to fight." He took a deep breath. "But I'm here, and Cody's here, and I'm pretty sure Dancy's going to stay here. I know the—Man-Wolf is going to be trying real hard to find us. Especially Dancy."

"Wait just a bloody minute!" A furious voice sounded from the doorway. Victorine stamped into the room, propped two tense white fists on her hips, and growled, "I've been listening to all this crazy talk! Who do you people think you are? *What* are you? Do you actually think for one instant that I'm going to allow my daughter to be some kind of a—a rallying point for your stupid, hopeless little war? Well, you can think again! You're all crazy, and you're all going to die! But Dancy Flynn Thayer is not!"

Whirling furiously on one booted heel, she marched out. Con leaped to follow her.

"I think she's mad," Zoan said morosely.

"Can't blame her," Rio said in a low voice. "Little girl's kinda—delicate."

Victorine was walking fast, but when she saw Con coming after her, she began to run.

He easily caught her, though, and grabbed her arm.

"Let go of me, you—you troglodyte!" Victorine hissed.

"Vic, listen—please listen just a minute." Con let go of her arm, and she stayed still, even though she was poised for flight. "Look, Vic, this has hit me pretty hard. I always thought becoming a Christian meant putting on a suit and tie and going to church, but I see now that it's more than that. When I gave my loyalty to the service, I thought there couldn't be any higher loyalty, but I know now that there is and it's to Christ. I still don't exactly know what I'm supposed to do. Not yet."

Victorine stared at him. She relented and relaxed a little.

With relief he went on, "One thing I do know is that we can't ignore Cody and Benewah—and especially Zoan. They're—they're like some kind of prophets of old times. You know it, you must. You've been a Christian for a long time."

Victorine's head was bent, and her heavy hair, unbound, swung in front of her face. In a muffled, choking voice, she said, "Yes, but I can't see that God truly intends to make Dancy some sort of a decoy for all of the evil forces in the world. The idea is absurd! Zoan is a half-wit, and Cody Bent Knife's a crazy renegade Apache! How can you think that I'd let them tell me what's best for my daughter?"

Con shifted restlessly. "I'm not trying to tell you that, Vic. I guess I'm saying that all of us have to let God tell us the right thing to do. Do you believe God's telling you to take Dancy away from here?"

She didn't look up. Her voice was very small. "No."

Gently Con took her arm again and then pulled her close. He held her for a moment, and the scent of her fragrant hair came to him. "Can't you trust God and then trust me? How could you think for a minute, after all we've been through, that I'd stand by and let anybody harm Dancy or you?"

He thought she was weeping, for her shoulders trembled slightly. "So you would fight? You would help me try to protect her?" she asked.

"Try? Why, ma'am, don't you know I'm the biggest, baddest troglodyte in the West?"

She didn't pull away from him. She turned slightly to rest her cheek on his chest. "This is no time for jokes, Con."

"You called me a troglodyte."

"I know. But I didn't mean it. Just like I didn't mean what I said about Zoan and Cody." She pulled back slightly to look up at him. "I'm scared, Con."

"We're all scared." Cupping her chin, he lifted her face and bent closer to her. "But, Vic, I want to tell you something. I'm going to say it plain because that's the kind of man I am. I love you. I think I fell in love with you the first time I saw you—when you and Dancy were riding along on those dumb bicycles, laughing and talking. I thought you were the loveliest woman I'd ever seen. I still think so. I've never loved anyone before. I never even thought I was in love before—until I saw you."

Victorine stared up at him, her eyes wide. In the darkness it was difficult to read the niceties of expression. She seemed unable to speak.

He watched her but was unable to decipher her. At least she hadn't tensed up or turned and run from him. He went on, "I had to tell you all this now because I want you to know that I'll protect you and Dancy always. As long as I live, no harm will come to you. I promise."

She held her head still as she looked at him, and as he met her glance, he saw the shadow and shape of fear come and go. He knew that he would always love this rich and headlong quality of a spirit sometimes hidden behind the cool reserve of her face.

Victorine saw the day's growth of whiskers glittering like metal filings on his face, and she noted the breadth of his shoulders and the solid neck muscles. He was a strong man in many ways. With a sigh of relief, she nodded wordlessly, an acceptance of all he'd said, and all the promise it held.

For now, it was enough.

PART V

THE OLD PATHS

Thus saith the LORD, Stand ye in the ways, and see, and ask for the old paths, where is the good way, and walk therein, and ye shall find rest for your souls.

—JEREMIAH 6:16

We are not now that strength which in old days
Moved earth and heaven, that which we are, we are,
One equal temper of heroic hearts,
Made weak by time and fate, but strong in will
To strive, to seek, to find, and not to yield.

—ALFRED, LORD TENNYSON, *ULYSSES*

Ye sow in tears to reap in joy. Why fear ye the power of evil?
Above the earth, above Rome, above the walls of cities is the Lord,
who has taken His dwelling within you.

—APOSTLE PETER, FROM *QUO VADIS* BY HENRYK SIENKIEWICZ

TWENTY

AT FIRST HE COULD see it only as a shape so black that it made a dark ebony blot against the night. He was standing in the middle of a forest, but he did not know where the dark wood was or when the time was. A sharp, cold wind bit at him as he strained his ears for any sound that the creature—or man or whatever it was—made, but he heard nothing.

A quick thought detonated in the recesses of his mind: *This is death. It's come for me . . .*

The wind purled around him, sighing with a hungry sound.

As the shape came closer, it loomed larger, but he couldn't see clearly. The night surrounded him like a wall, caliginous, blacker than the interior of a tomb. The darkness was more than a lack of light; it was a solid thing, and he thought that if he reached out his hand to touch it, his hand would come back shriveled and smudged with it.

In front of him, but far off, he saw the shape, the movements. He stared at the shape, straining to make it out, and then swifter than light his mind suddenly received the images given through his eyes.

A huge wolf emerged from the darkness. The creature was lupine, but larger than any wolf, and the quality of the face was almost human. The eyes gleamed and glowed with a calescent heat until the pupils were yellow like iron on a blacksmith's forge submitted to intense heat.

He tried to turn and run, but he couldn't move—and he knew that he never would. His will and his flesh were disconnected, as if a cord had been cut between the two.

He saw the monster break into a run, moving toward him with a speed beyond anything in nature. The beast left the ground in a leap, and then the mouth seemed to grin. The yellow fangs, sharper than razors, opened—and he felt them as they tore away his throat and the blood incarnadined the face of the beast. His cry came in a bubbling scream as the life poured out of him.

Jesse Mitchell cried out in the darkness, threw his arms out, and sat upright in bed. For a moment he could not think; his mind was blinded with the force of the dream. It did not fade at once, as a normal dream might, but lingered. He had once, as a young man, looked too long at a welder's blazing torch, and for several hours, no matter where he looked he could still see the bright orange dot of fire before his eyes. And so he knew that this dream would not fade as other dreams.

Noe, disturbed by the sound and by the wrenching of the form beside her, sat up and reached out to grab Jesse. "What is it?" she whispered. "What's wrong?"

"Nothing, Noe. Just—just a bad dream."

Noe sat up straighter and brushed the sleep away from her eyes. "The same dream?"

"It's always the same."

"What does it mean?"

"I don't know," Jesse said, but he was not entirely honest. He knew that the nightmare had more reality than most dreams. He believed strongly in dreams: God often gave them to men, and when He did, they had a meaning; they were put into the mind for a reason. It was one way of God's speaking.

Although Jesse believed the nightmare had a meaning, he was certain that the dream did not come from the Lord God. The stench of evil was on it. He drew himself up and crossed his arms across his chest, then shivered lightly.

"Was it that wolf again?" Noe whispered.

"Exactly the same. It's always the same, and I wake up just as he's pulling the life out of me."

Noe sat silently, and the two older people did not move. Outside the light was gathering, and dawn was almost upon the earth. Finally Jesse sighed deeply, then threw the covers back. "I'll build a fire. You stay in bed until it gets warm, Noe."

"Let me get up and fix your breakfast."

"Just wait until it gets warm."

Rising from the bed, Jesse pulled on a pair of itchy wool breeches that Xanthe had scrounged up, a red plaid shirt, and his beloved beat-up moccasins. They were so old and soft, they were like wearing thick comfortable socks. Jesse smiled a little as he remembered the old Apache woman who had made them for him. She'd been a godly woman, and she had died with the plague. But she'd had joy in her heart and praise on her lips.

He padded into the kitchen–living room and lit the lamp. Grumbling a little to himself, he went to the cookstove. Opening the door to the firebox, he took the poker and raked away the white ash. Jesse knew exactly how to leave a fire at night so that the next morning he would not have to go to all the trouble of starting one. Uncovering the glowing cherry-colored coals, he reached into the woodbox and pulled out several pine knots rich with sap. He threw them on the coals, and at once they burst into flame. Quickly he added splinters of pine, nursing it until a fire blazed, crackling and popping. He laid several small sticks of oak, forming a pyramid so that the draft would carry the flames through them, then he shut the door and stood up a little stiffly. He felt the cold more every winter.

Moving over to the table, he pulled the worn black Bible forward. It lay open to Job, and he thought that was as good a place as any to start his studies.

The crackling of the wood in the stove sounded like miniature rifle fire. Outside the morning wind was dragging the limbs of the ancient apple tree across the roof of the house. It sounded almost like fingers scratching, like a beast seeking entrance. With the whisper of the wind, it seemed to urge, *Let me in . . . let me in . . .*

Shaking his thin shoulders, Jesse forced his eyes to follow the print. He whispered the words aloud, but for the first time in many years he found that the words of the Scripture were meaningless. This frightened him more than the wind's song, even more than his nightmare. He closed his eyes, put his hand over the pages of the Bible, and sat still, quieting his mind. He did not pray in words, but his spirit reached upward beyond the fragile roof of the small cabin, beyond the clouds and stars and out into the vast reaches of space. Jesse had no idea of finding God in a particular location, but he had always found Him by simply waiting. Often he had advised others, *Don't work so hard to get God's attention. He's been trying to get yours all your life. Just sit and let your mind reach out for Him. He'll pull those thoughts right back into your heart . . .*

As he sat with his eyes closed, growing calmer, he was startled when a furry form flung itself into his lap. Jesse jumped, then smiled to see Mannie digging his claws into the fabric of his trousers. "Hello, you old tomcat," he murmured affectionately. "Seems like you like these breeches better than I do. They're itchy, aren't they?"

He had grown fond of the animal and had learned that Mannie, like all cats, had a unique personality. Mannie was gentle and good-natured, never fussy, not even when Kyle pulled him in his wagon, smushed in with Benny the Bear, or carried him like a sack of flour. Many people who did not know cats thought that they were all alike, but they were vastly mistaken. Jesse and Noe had always kept cats, and Jesse had been very glad to have this fellow traveler along life's way.

Mannie looked up into the old man's eyes, his purr like a miniature jet engine. It seemed to shake his whole body and was so loud that Jesse could sometimes hear it even when Mannie was sleeping by the fire while he himself was in bed. Its sound always gave Jesse a sense of comfort, of well-being. He murmured, "I wish I didn't have any more problems than you have, Mannie."

Suddenly Mannie reared and stood up on Jesse's lap. The claws dug into his chest, and Mannie arched his head forward until his nose touched Jesse's chin. He moved his head around, the golden eyes glowing as if there were a light behind them. He seemed to be seeking something, and Jesse sat very still.

"If you're looking to see what's inside my head and my heart, Mannie," he said and ran his fingers down the cat's backbone to the funny hollow in his rump where his tail should have been, "then you let me know what you find. I'm not sure myself sometimes."

"That cat certainly makes himself at home." Noe had entered the room, fastening the belt of a faded chenille robe. She came to sit beside Jesse. "You and that cat are partners."

"Can think of worse ones. Fool cat follows me around like he's a dog I'm walking."

"I think he's walking you, Jess." Affectionately Noe scratched Mannie's ears. "Now tell me again about this nightmare."

She listened carefully as Jesse described the dream. Then she said, "It's always the same."

"It's got a meaning. The Lord just hasn't given me the answer to it yet."

"He will, Jesse. He always does."

"I know it, but sometimes I get a little impatient."

"You always did want to run ahead of God."

"I know. It's the only fault I ever had, isn't it?" He took her hand and squeezed it and saw her smile.

"I could think of two or three more if you pressed me a little," she teased. "All right, Brother Mitchell, time for me to fix your breakfast. I know what you're going to do."

"What am I going to do?"

"You're going out and walk in the woods and find a place and wait for God."

"How'd you know that?"

Noe sniffed disdainfully. "I know more than you think, Jesse."

"I guess you do. 'Whoso findeth a wife findeth a good thing, and obtaineth favor of the LORD.' I always loved that verse. Soon as I read it, I knew God favored married men. That's why I came up and proposed to you that morning. I just couldn't stand not to be favored."

"That wasn't what you said to me."

Jesse shook his head. "Guess I've forgotten."

"No, you haven't. You never forget anything."

With economical, efficient motions of one who has practiced half a century and more, Noe fixed a breakfast of pork sausage, grits, and sawmill gravy. She warmed up biscuits, put two of them on a plate, and set them down, saying, "Eat all you can. You haven't been looking well lately."

Jesse ate half of what was on his plate, then pushed it away. "Just not very hungry, wife. Put it in the oven. I'll eat when I come back."

Noe did not answer but got his heavy black Ty-wool coat. It was a commissar's overcoat. She and Jesse were always amused at the paramilitary garb that Xanthe brought them. She helped him into it and handed him his gloves and a bright red toboggan cap that she hated. "This is an awful-looking cap, but it'll keep your ears warm."

He reached out and put his arms around her, kissed her cheek, and then left without another word.

As he stepped outside, he saw that a light snow had covered the ground. But Jesse paid it no heed, for his heart was already beginning to be heavy, and his eyes were looking beyond his surroundings. Leaving the clearing, he entered the woods, following the old path that led deeper and deeper into the pine forest.

The cold seeped into the small cabin that David and Riley had fixed up for themselves. It was only two hundred yards from a larger place where Merrill and Genevieve had settled in. Allegra and Kyle's cabin, a nice, snug two-bedroom, was another quarter of a mile away.

David rose at dawn and built up the fire exactly as Jesse did, as his grandfather had taught David when he was a little boy. As soon as the blaze was high, he put a saucepan of water on. When it began to bubble, he poured it into a chipped blue enamel basin. There was no shaving cream, so he took a bar of Lifebuoy and worked up a lather of sorts. He'd always disliked the carbolic smell of Lifebuoy, but it was all that was available. The blades from his safety razor were all used up, and the only remaining one was dull. Peering into a small mirror fastened to the wall, he pulled the blade down through his whiskers. It made a raspy sound and pulled at his skin until tears came to his eyes.

"What are you prettying yourself up for, Mitchell?"

David turned to see Riley, who had swung his feet over and was sitting on his cot. As always, when Riley woke up, it was instantaneous. There was no blinking or yawning or grogginess. One moment he was asleep, and the next moment, just like a cat, he was fully awake. Riley seemed impervious to cold, wearing only an undershirt and a pair of shorts. His arms were strong, and there were two humps of muscle where his neck joined his shoulders. He was a muscular man, and his hands were hard and rough and work worn. David idly wondered at how little he knew of Riley Case.

"Some Cy-star might drop by," David replied, grinning boyishly. He drew the razor down the other cheek and then under his throat, grimacing, as Riley dressed. He had just finished rinsing his face when Riley said abruptly, "Someone's coming."

Both men grabbed their guns and stepped outside, alert and ready. "It's Grandma," David said with relief.

It was nearly a mile to the Mitchells' cabin, and as she slowly climbed the two steps up to the front porch, David asked, "Anything wrong, Grandma?"

"Nothing except I'm cold and grumpy," Noe replied.

"You're never grumpy, Grandma," David said. "Good thing, too, or Grandpa might trade you in for a giggling young girl."

"Yes, I worry about that all the time," she said. Her cheeks were pink, and her brown eyes sparkled like a clever little bird's.

"Come on inside, Mrs. Mitchell," Riley said, taking her arm. It felt like a child's, small and delicate. It made Riley feel like a great bumbling bear.

Noe entered the cabin and looked around, assessing. "Men just can't fix up for themselves. Looks like a prison barracks."

"Allegra's already been over here, giving us orders and poking around," David said with amusement. "She's going to fix this place up whether we like it or not."

"Good for her," Noe said with satisfaction.

"Uh—won't you sit down, ma'am?" Riley asked politely. "We'll make some coffee. Have you had breakfast?"

"I had a little. I could drink some coffee, though."

David knew his grandmother well enough to understand that something was wrong, but he also understood that she was not a talkative woman. She would talk to them in her own way, in her own good time. As Riley made the coffee, David talked about the things Allegra had wanted to do with their cabin, curtains and rugs and things.

But David was thinking of how Noe and his grandfather had raised him. His father, Noe and Jesse's son, had been an irresponsible, selfish man all his life, and he'd married a woman who was just as bad. David had always wondered why they'd had him. It was easy not to have children, with abortions so readily available. But they had, and they dumped him on Jesse and Noe, then left to go to California. David's mother, who had a kind of tawdry sultriness, was sure she was going to be a Cy-star. The last David had heard from her, she'd been acting in a pornographic play in San Francisco, and his father had been her "manager." That had been when David was sixteen years old. He'd tried repeatedly to get back in touch with his parents, but he'd never been able to find them. It was his greatest sorrow, and he couldn't imagine how it made his grandfather and grandmother feel. Every time he mentioned his father, Noe cried pitifully, so David no longer brought him up.

Jesse and Noe raised David with so much love that he never felt that he lacked anything. They had little in the way of money, but they poured themselves into him so that there was no one on the face of planet earth who mattered to David Mitchell as did the two older people.

He saw how age had marked Noe, and a tiny fear pulled at him, for he knew that both she and Jesse were coming to the end. It was not that he feared for them so much as for himself. He couldn't imagine a world without them, and he fought back a panicky feeling.

He read part of a poem once that he did not understand, but one line of it had grabbed at him and the words had burned themselves into his memory:

And those I love push off from my life
Like boats from the shore—

The words came to him now, and he breathed a quick prayer, *Lord, keep Grandma and Grandpa safe and well—for a while at least.*

When the coffee was ready, the three drank with enjoyment, savoring the warmth and rich scent. "You make a good cup of coffee, Mr. Case," Noe said. "Not many people can, especially when you have to boil it."

"Thank you, ma'am," Riley said sheepishly.

Evidently Noe considered the social niceties over, for she turned to David and stated, "I'm worried about your grandfather."

"Is he sick?" David blurted out, mindful of his previous worries.

Noe gave him a sharp look. "No, David. At least, not yet. But he's troubled in his spirit."

"Grandpa? He's always so—solid. So certain." David frowned and fell silent, studying his coffee as if he could read something in the depths of the steaming liquid.

Riley studied the small woman. He had formed a strong attachment—unusual for him—to the Mitchells. "What are you afraid of, Mrs. Mitchell?"

Noe turned her gaze on the muscular man with the steady eyes. "I'm afraid he'll get out in the woods and step in a hole and break his leg. I'm afraid he'll walk off a cliff and break his neck. I'm afraid he could get lost. When he gets to praying, he just walks like a blind man! Why, one time when he was a young man, he prayed and walked so long that when he finally finished, he was in a different county! He laughed and said when he looked up to get his bearings, everything was different, strange. Sometimes he doesn't pay any attention to what he's doing."

"We'll keep an eye on him, Grandma," David said quickly.

Riley nodded slowly. "Ma'am, if you'd like me to, I'll go out and walk with him."

"I'd like that, Mr. Case." Noe finished the last swallow of her coffee, then stood up. "I feel better knowing that you two will be looking out for him."

As always, Riley jumped to his feet when she stood. Now Noe turned to him and took both of his hands.

"I think God sent you to take care of my husband," she said simply. She looked deep into his eyes, and Riley had the impression that her gaze passed his eyes and searched deep into his brain and even down deeper than that. He felt uncomfortably exposed, though how this woman, so frail and advanced in age, could possibly make him feel vulnerable was a mystery to him.

David said, "I'll walk you back, Grandma."

"No, you won't," she said spiritedly. "I know I didn't sound like it, but I did enjoy the solitude and the walk. Told you I was grumpy. You come up for dinner, David. I'll see you then." She left, a tiny figure in a black coat that reached almost to her ankles.

Riley stood silently, gazing after her. David studied him a moment, but as usual, he couldn't read Riley's face. It was a closed face, guarded, sometimes forbidding. David was uncomfortable intruding on a man's private thoughts, so he said nothing. He was surprised when Riley said quietly, "Your grandparents are really something. What she said—that's so strange. I wouldn't have put up with it if it hadn't been your grandmother or Mr. Mitchell."

"I've noticed you don't like to talk about God much," David said casually.

Riley raised one thick black brow. "Yeah. You started in on me once, and I cut you off so short, you must have thought you'd fallen through a trapdoor."

"I remember." David nodded, smiling faintly. "No trespassing. That's what you were telling me. But I wasn't 'starting in on you,' Riley. I'm just curious. I'd like to know about you and God."

"I'd like to know myself," Riley answered.

The simple honesty of the words impressed David, but he decided not to press Riley. "Well, you'll find Him. Or if you don't, He'll find you."

"Maybe," Riley said noncommittally.

Riley pulled on his long stained Ty-canvas overcoat and worn broad-brimmed gray hat, then picked up his Marlin .30-30. He opened the door, turned, and looked at David with a peculiar expression. "I'm going to look for your grandfather. I don't think that it's the assignment God's given me for the day. I don't even think He's sent me here or brought me here, much less for some noble undertaking. But I want you to know, David, that I consider it a real honor to watch over Jesse Mitchell."

The door closed firmly behind him.

David went back to the table and prayed for Riley Case for a long time.

From overhead the sharp cry of a hawk sounded, and Jesse, who had been sitting with his back against a monumental chestnut tree, looked up. He had time to see the hawk as he fell from heaven, disappearing behind some bushes. There was a thumping sound, a brief thrashing, and then silence.

Jesse got up and brushed the snow off the seat of his pants. He was weary to the point of exhaustion; his feet and fingers felt like dead lumps. He was vaguely surprised to see that dusk had already begun to gather. With dragging steps that marked the snow, he turned to climb up toward home.

He had wandered the woods all day, sometimes pausing to kneel. Once he had even fallen on his face and prayed, for how long he didn't know. During such times, he rarely knew what was happening around him, and now as he turned his mind toward home and Noe, he became aware of the world of pine and snow-covered rock and living things.

Still, in the back of his active mind, he was communing with God. He'd had a difficult time on this long day. It was one of those times when God chose to remain silent. Jesse Mitchell was never discouraged by the silence, however. He kept talking to God.

He'd often taught, *Your best prayers are not those when you feel good. When the heavens are brass and when you're half convinced that nothing will ever come of such foolishness, but you keep praying, why, that's a prayer of faith. And faith can overcome all things . . .*

Suddenly Jesse stopped and called out, "You might as well come out and walk with me."

Riley emerged from a clump of cedar trees. "I wasn't trying to hide from you, sir. I didn't want to bother you. And, uh, by the way, how'd you know I was behind you?" Riley asked with a hint of exasperation. "I'm usually a little bit hard to trace when I don't want to be noticed."

Ignoring the question, Jesse said, "Why don't we go on to the house? I'm ready for some biscuits and gravy."

"You're the boss, Preacher."

They made their way through the falling darkness. A bleak chill lay in the still air, and their breath made little puffs of visible moisture as they trudged along.

For Riley the day had been unsettling. He hadn't had any trouble tracking Jesse, though by the time Riley caught up with him, Jesse had wandered quite far from the cabins. The man, as Noe had said, trudged on blindly, and sometimes he talked loudly.

At first, Riley had decided to walk up and speak to him, tell Jesse that he'd be going along with him on his strange wanderings. But then Riley realized that he was praying earnestly, and truth to tell, it had embarrassed Riley a little. He decided not to intrude. But he still felt odd, stalking along, keeping out of sight. He felt that he was eavesdropping. Riley finally settled on a sort of distance tracking. He kept Jesse in sight, but stayed far enough away from him that he couldn't hear the words Jesse said.

Nevertheless, it had been a troubling experience for Riley. All day he felt the cold touch of a timeless question. During the long day, his reflections went down a long spiral, wistful and hopeless. Riley had never known such passion, such longing and love, as he heard in the old man's prayers. He heard joy, too, true and unguarded, and Riley knew that was a thing so rare that most people never knew it existed.

Certainly there had been no real joy in his life. He had a few pleasurable memories of a friend or two; the brief flash of a woman's shining eyes came to him. His life had been a series of stray pictures that faded slowly, and he allowed them to, for clinging to such things was not his way. Yet he sensed that there was more, that there was a true beauty he couldn't quite grasp, like a piece of a melody, like a fragment of a song he couldn't place.

He glimpsed this unseen, unknown world occasionally. He saw it in Noemi Mitchell's lovely old face, heard it in Jesse Mitchell's prayers. It frightened him a little to think that he missed it. The thought was jarring to Riley Case. He couldn't ever remember being frightened of anything.

Finally they reached the cabin, and Jesse said, "Come in and have some dinner with me, Mr. Case."

"I guess I'll head on back," Riley said uncertainly.

"Oh, I hate to eat by myself. Come on in. You can tell me what you and David are doing. Where you got the cows, for example."

Riley really did want to talk more with Jesse Mitchell, so he accepted the invitation. Twenty minutes later the two were sitting down, eating biscuits and gravy, and Riley was explaining how he and David had found two abandoned cows, both with calves. "They were wandering around out in an old pasture about three miles from here, down in the valley, Mr. Mitchell. There was an old ramshackle barn at the corner, and I guess they had plenty of grass to eat and probably slept in that barn. David and I are turning that old shack behind Mr. and Mrs. Stanton's cabin into a kind of stable for them."

Jesse grinned. "The Lord is good. That's for sure and certain. Hear that, Noe? Better break out that iron skillet, 'cause I'm hungry as a plowhand for some of your good corn bread."

"Butter, too," Noe said dreamily. "If we can figure out how to make a churn, maybe. And if I can talk you two big strong men into churning."

Riley sighed extravagantly. "I don't know what churning is, ma'am, and I'm not sure I want to know. I've already had a shock, trying to milk that cow. She didn't like it, and she let me know she didn't like it. Think I'm going to leave that little chore up to David."

"Then you can churn," Noe said with satisfaction. "But I warn you, you might be sorry you chose it."

Jesse said, his blue eyes sparkling, "Watch out, Mr. Case. When that woman puts you to work, you know you've been working."

"Yes, sir, I've already seen that," Riley said heavily, thinking of the exhausting day. He eyed Brother Mitchell; the older man, for all his high spirits, was pale, and he seemed drawn and chilled. "Well, ma'am, the meal was really good, as your cooking always is. Thank you." He rose and put on his coat, but hesitated as he was going out the door. Turning, he asked Jesse, "Sir, if you don't mind, could I come with you tomorrow?"

Jesse grinned. "You mean, I don't have to pretend I don't notice you tomorrow?"

"Uh . . . something like that," Riley grunted. "I just think someone ought to—to—walk with you. But I don't—want to—intrude or anything. I won't bother you."

"No, you won't bother me, Mr. Case. I'll probably forget you're there." He eyed Riley shrewdly. "I'll be praying, you know. 'Fraid you'll have to listen to that."

Riley fidgeted with his hat for a moment, then nodded. "Maybe it'll be good for me, Preacher. You never know."

Jesse laughed. "Oh, but you're wrong, Mr. Case. God knows. God always knows. I'll see you bright and early in the morning, son. We'll go looking for God together."

TWENTY-ONE

ALLEGRA STRAIGHTENED up, placing her hands in the small of her back, arching until her stomach muscles pulled. She was wearing a pair of faded Ty-jeans that were too big for her, a heavy blue Ty-wool shirt, and a man's shapeless Ty-cord jacket that had seen better days. Twisting from side to side to work the strain out of her back, she glanced over and watched Riley and David bucksaw a log. A brisk breeze lifted the fine sawdust and carried the fresh green-wood scent to her nostrils. The steady cadence of the saw biting into the log was a pleasant sound.

She looked overhead and watched a flotilla of geese in a perfect V and wondered whimsically, *How do they decide who gets to lead? Do they have an election? A committee meeting? Do they draw straws?*

From far away she heard the cry of a coyote, and as always, it was a thin, melancholy sound. She listened to it fade out, wondering if it was a male calling out for his mate. Once again she stretched; her back felt as if it were on fire. *It's so hard to live out here like this. No wonder people—especially women—had such short life spans . . . But David and Riley seem to thrive on it . . . men like them would . . . like Neville, he would love living out here . . .*

The thought of Neville brought a pang to her, and she had to fight back the sadness and the loneliness that crept over her. She had written in her journal the previous night:

I miss him so much, and every day I hope somehow that soon we'll be together. But that hope appears as a sailor who comes to an island and sits on it for a day or two, resting, and then sails off again, disappears, leaving nothing behind . . .

She remembered now, standing in the pale light of the winter sun, how she had considered canceling that line, striking it out, for it seemed pathetic. Allegra was not, and would never be, the type of woman to wallow in self-pity. She had sternly reminded herself that the others were no better off than she. She had thought of David's father, Jesse and Noe's only son. What measure of grief, of sorrow, must there be, to lose your father, your son? Allegra was blessed, she had wonderful parents, and Kyle was her deepest joy.

But still, she and her parents grieved, for Allegra was the eldest of five. She had one sister in Atlanta, one in St. Louis, and a brother and a sister in California. They had heard nothing from any of them since the blackout. She knew her parents worried about them, though Merrill and Genevieve, like Jesse and Noe Mitchell, seemed to have such peace, such consolation, in their relationship with the Lord. Allegra wished she was that strong, but she wasn't. She was lonely and found it hard to find any comfort within herself or anyone else.

She glanced back at Riley and wondered about him, as they all did. His blue-black hair caught the sun, and he had taken off his shirt, so he was wearing only a khaki army undershirt. The muscles in his back rippled as he pulled easily on the saw. Despite the cold, a fine sheet of perspiration coated his dark skin. *And what about him? Does he have someone . . . anyone . . . that he longs for, grieves for?* Even as she formed the thought, Allegra knew that Riley did not, that he was alone. She had some intuition, some depth of perception, about Riley. She'd had it since the first time they met, back in the wilderness. *He has no one to worry about, think about . . . and maybe that's the saddest story of all . . .*

Wearily she turned back to her job, which was washing clothes. It was a task that had to be done, but it was tremendously hard work, especially in cold weather. Allegra stubbornly insisted that she would do everyone's washing, for the men definitely had other, harder work to do, and Noemi Mitchell and her mother were too frail to do it.

Jesse Mitchell made what he called a battling bench. He said he'd never seen one used, of course, but years ago, when he was a child, he saw them in old junk shops—usually someone's barn—and he thought he could tell Riley how to make one. He could remember his mother telling him how, many years ago, women had done their unending wash. Allegra had discovered it was aptly named. Doing the wash manually, with any kind of equipment, was a battle. With a longing that was almost like a physical yearning, she remembered her lovely tri-jet washer and microwave dryer.

Finished with the wash, she separated everyone's clothes. It didn't do any good to hang clothes out in the freezing weather, and the climate was so wet that heavy clothing never got dry. The clothes would freeze, but when they thawed, they were wet again with melted ice crystals. Riley had made crude wooden racks so they could hang their clothes by the fireplaces.

Wringing out the clothes as best she could, Allegra ruefully considered her hands. They were red and chafed, the nails torn down to the quick. She was freezing, exhausted, and wet; she'd never learned how to do the washing without getting sopping wet. It was a miserable job, but she never complained. Allegra, being the kind of woman she was, got great satisfaction from doing it, and doing it well. She eyed Riley and David as they finished stacking her firewood on the front porch. *Now there's some hard work, every day, hand-cutting down trees, hauling the logs, bucksawing them, splitting them, taking the wood to all the cabins . . . They certainly never complain. I sure like that in a man . . . I can't stand whiners . . . That's one thing I loved about Neville, he never complained . . . he never let anything get him down . . . he was a fighter—*

With a shock that took her breath away, Allegra realized she was thinking of her husband in the past tense. She stood, frozen, clutching a heavy, cold pair of David Mitchell's BDU breeches. With characteristic determination, she put the disturbing thoughts away.

The men called their good-byes to her, and she recovered, telling them to come back after they finished to get their clean clothes. Then Kyle came around the corner of their cabin, pulling Mannie and Benny the Blue Bear in his wagon.

Allegra couldn't help smiling. Oddly Mannie seemed to like riding in the rickety wagon. Every time Kyle got it out, Mannie ran, with the peculiar half-hopping gait of the Manx, and jumped into the wagon. Now he sat there, his clown's smile intact, as Kyle dragged him along, the wagon bumping over the rough ground.

Allegra was happy that Kyle had a pet. In the old world (it occurred to her that she was thinking of that in the past tense, too) they could never have afforded a companion animal. And they would never have been able to get a license since they were a military family and moved around a lot. They wouldn't have qualified for the strict licensing standards. Absurdly it was harder to adopt a pet than it was to adopt a child.

It's wonderful that Mannie's so good-natured . . . Kyle plays so roughly with him, but Mannie seems to adore him anyway . . .

The cat had become the boy's constant companion. Mannie still slept at Brother Mitchell's, but every morning he was at Allegra's door, meowing insistently for his saucer of milk and crumbled bacon. He stayed with Kyle most days, though sometimes Mannie walked with Brother Mitchell in his wanderings.

Noe trudged up to the cabin, looking like a child playing dress-up in her long military-cut coat and beret. "Sister Mitchell! I would have brought your clothes to you," Allegra declared.

"Nonsense. If you're kind enough to do this awful chore, I can surely come and get the clothes. Thank you so much, Allegra," Noe said, stuffing the wet clothes into a canvas bag.

"But—can you carry that heavy bag, Sister Mitchell?" Allegra asked doubtfully. "Your hands . . ." Noe's arthritis gave her trouble in cold weather.

"I'm fine, and I'm enjoying the walk. Don't you worry about me," Noe insisted. She turned to watch Kyle pulling the cat and the raggedy stuffed bear in his wagon. He was doing a military march—as much as he could with his short fat legs—and singing, "Noel, Noel, Noel, Noel!" They were the only words he knew to the song, and he sang it at the top of his lungs.

"It's so wonderful to have a child around at Christmastime," Noe said warmly. "It makes it so much more fun. You get to be a child again yourself."

Allegra remarked, "Sometimes I worry about Kyle being all alone. He doesn't have any friends to play with, except that cat."

"It won't hurt him a bit, not a bit," Noe assured her. "When we were raising David, he was alone most of the time. He turned out well, I think."

"Yes, he did," Allegra agreed quickly. "He's a fine man. I'm grateful to him. He's good with Kyle and takes so much time with him."

"Yes, and Mr. Case does, too. Kyle dotes on them both, doesn't he? I guess he misses his daddy." Noe noticed the quick pang of grief that swept across Allegra's face, but the younger woman said nothing. Noe turned back to watch Kyle with a mixture of warmth and pain. David was four years old when his parents left him with her and Jesse.

After watching Kyle for a while, Noe returned to the cabin, and Allegra took their wash in to hang it by the fireplace. She was gratified to see that Riley Case had built up her fire with the newly split wood. He often did things like that for her without being asked, and he seemed embarrassed when Allegra thanked him.

Twenty minutes later Allegra heard the humming noise of a diesel vehicle and ran out onto the front porch. It was Xanthe, lumbering up the mountain and through the overgrown fields in her tough Vulcan. "Hello, hello," Allegra called, waving.

Xanthe got out of the Vulcan, and the two women embraced,

though Xanthe, as always, was a little stiff. Since they had become such good friends, however, Allegra insisted on hugging Xanthe and kissing her on the cheek. She thought that Xanthe hadn't had much affection in her life.

"I brought some things," Xanthe said awkwardly, after enduring Allegra's embrace.

"Oh, that's nice, but I'm just glad to see you," Allegra said warmly. "You don't have to bring bribes, you know. We all wish you'd just stay here with us anyway."

Xanthe flushed. "Well—thank you. Anyway, I brought a few groceries, even though I think you all eat better than we do. But I did bring some staples, like sugar and flour. And I've got some presents for Kyle. Where is he?"

"He's hauling that fool cat around in a wagon. What did you bring him?"

"Call him and I'll show you."

"Kyle—Kyle! Xanthe's here!"

Kyle came roaring around the corner of the cabin, still hauling the wagon. Seeing Xanthe, he started running, and the wooden wheels of the wagon bounced off the ground. Benny the Bear fell out, and Mannie gave a yowl of protest and bailed out, too.

"Hi, Aunt Xanthe!" Kyle beamed, leaving the now-deserted wagon to hug Xanthe's knees. "Did you bring me a present?"

"What makes you think I did?"

" 'Cause you always do."

"Yes, I guess I do, and I did this time, too. Have you been a good boy?"

"Oh, yes," Kyle promised, his brown eyes solemn. He looked like a cherub with his fat pink cheeks and button mouth.

"Maybe I ought to ask your mother," Xanthe teased.

"Mama, I've been real good, haven't I?" he pleaded.

"Yes, I must say that Kyle has been exceptionally good," Allegra said, smiling.

"See?" he said to Xanthe.

"All right. I think you're going to like this one, Kyle." Xanthe turned to the Vulcan, and Kyle grabbed her hand. She seemed bemused, but pleased, too, when Kyle lavished affection on her. She opened the rear door and pulled a bulky object out of the storage compartment.

"Mama! It's a car!" Kyle shouted.

Indeed it was a car, scaled down to Kyle's exact size. "Does it run?" he asked.

"It sure does," Xanthe answered. "But you're the motor."

"What you say?" Kyle entreated her earnestly.

"You have to shove the pedals with your feet. That's what makes it go."

Kyle ran around the car, running his stubby hand over it. It was painted bright red and had metal wheels with rubber tracks around them, a steering wheel, and a hood ornament.

"Where in the world did you get it, Xanthe?" Allegra asked, smiling at Kyle as he clambered into the vehicle.

"One of the antique stores in Hot Springs. I've never seen one before, but this store suddenly put it on display in the window. It's probably very valuable—it must be a hundred years old. I got it for eighty deutsche marks."

Uncertainly Allegra asked, "Is that a lot?"

"I don't have a clue," Xanthe said cheerfully.

The two women stared at each other, then burst out laughing. The world was an absurd place these days.

Kyle jerked the steering wheel around, played with the pretend gearshift, and made the blubbering noise that all boy children make when playing Car. Now he cried, "How do you make it go, Aunt Xanthe?"

Xanthe leaned over and pointed. "You see those two pedals down there? Put your feet on them. Now, I'll give you a little push, and you start pushing with your feet, first one and then the other. You ready? Here you go."

Xanthe gave the boy a push, and the car lunged forward. The two women watched with pleasure as the boy laughed and steered it in ragged circles around them. They chuckled when Mannie, not to be left out, ran forward and jumped on the hood. He clung to it, his claws screeching on the metal. Unconcernedly Kyle reached out, grabbed Mannie's head, and yanked him down into the passenger seat.

"I swear that cat thinks he's a little boy just like Kyle," Xanthe declared.

"It's a wonderful gift, Xanthe," Allegra said. "Thank you so much."

Xanthe suddenly sobered and gave Allegra an uncomfortable sidelong look. "You're—you're welcome. I—I have some more things. Why don't we take them inside?"

The two women carried in the two boxes, and Allegra was pleased to see that Xanthe had brought some children's books. "Picture books!" she cried. "I've about gone crazy trying to make up stories for Kyle. He'll love these! He can already read some words."

"I—I thought you should give them to him for Christmas," Xanthe said. Inexplicably she seemed troubled.

Allegra gave her a shrewd glance, then said with a trace of weariness, "I have some coffee on. Would you like some, Xanthe?"

"Yes, thank you."

Allegra fixed two cups of coffee, then sat down across from Xanthe at the crude table that Riley had built for her. Xanthe lifted the cup to her lips but, before tasting it, set it down and shifted restlessly.

Allegra noticed that her friend was unable to meet her eyes—and was struggling to tell her something. Faintly she said, "It's—it's Neville, isn't it?"

Xanthe was looking down at her hands. She nodded wordlessly.

"I knew it . . . ," Allegra whispered.

Xanthe looked up, her strong features twisted with grief.

"There was no Cy-mail from him, so I checked on his unit. It was posted on the 'net that the 7th Marine Expeditionary Brigade had been deployed to Syria in November," she said in a colorless voice. "Then—then—" She swallowed hard, then went on softly, "Two days ago Colonel Neville Saylor was posted . . . Killed in Action."

All of the blood drained from Allegra's face, leaving her looking pinched and cold. She drew a sharp intake of breath, and her eyes darkened to a muddy brown-green. Xanthe was afraid she was going to faint, and she made a helpless little gesture toward her. But Allegra jerkily motioned her away, then laid her head down on her folded arms. Sobs began to shake her thin shoulders, but she made only a sickly choking noise. Xanthe could hardly stand it, but she didn't know what to do, what to say. Xanthe had never been a very comforting person. Helplessly she bowed her head and prayed.

Finally the terrible straining sobs quieted, and Xanthe looked up at Allegra. She was sitting up straight. Her face was deadly white, and her voice was unsteady. "I—I'm not going to tell Kyle, not until after Christmas."

Xanthe nodded. "I—I understand. But, Allegra, you have to tell the others. They—you need them. Especially your parents."

Allegra nodded shakily. "Yes . . . yes, I will. Later . . ."

"Can—can I do anything? Anything at all?" Xanthe pleaded.

"Yes, you can," Allegra said softly, sadly. "I'd really like to be alone for a while. Could you please watch Kyle? Maybe—take him to see David and Riley for a little?"

"Of course," Xanthe said quickly, rising. "But—Allegra, are you sure? I mean, wouldn't you like for me to go get your mother?"

Allegra shook her head. "No . . . I think . . . the only person that I want to be with right now is the Lord." Fresh tears started running down her face, but somehow, Xanthe thought, it was better than the sobs that had seemed torn from Allegra's slender body moments before.

"All right. Please don't worry about Kyle," she said. "I'll take him to David, and you come get him whenever you . . . feel like it."

Allegra nodded, staring into space, the tears flowing unheeded down her pretty face and splashing onto her breast.

Xanthe awkwardly kissed her cheek. It was cold. "Allegra? I—I—don't know what to say, except . . . I'm so, so sorry . . . and I love you."

With that, she turned and almost ran out the door.

Incredibly Allegra felt warmth on her cheek where Xanthe had kissed her, and then it spread down into the bitter cold of her heart.

"Look! Look! Da-vid! Wi-ley!" Kyle yelled, his child's high-pitched, tuneless call carrying in the still, cold air.

David was outside his cabin, still splitting wood, when Kyle came bursting through the tree line, pedaling furiously.

"Hey, boss, what you got there?" David called with delight. "Can I drive it?"

Kyle pulled to an abrupt stop in front of David's feet, staring up at him accusingly. "You're too big," he said succinctly.

"Guess I am, at that. It's just your size, huh?"

Kyle nodded vigorously, then turned and pointed behind him. "Aunt Xanthe gave it to me. Well, bye."

"Uh, bye," David said to empty air, for Kyle, with Mannie still riding shotgun, had pedaled off.

Xanthe came walking up, though instead of her usual mannish stride, she was dragging a little. Before he even greeted her, David said alertly, "What's wrong, Xanthe?"

"Hi," she said listlessly. "Do I look that bad?"

"No, as a matter of fact, you look really good to me," David replied warmly. "But something's wrong, I can tell. Here, come sit down with me." He took her hand and was surprised at how cold it was. He led her to the porch steps and put his arm around her shoulders. She stiffened, as she always did when he touched her, but she let him stay close. Staring at Kyle as he played happily in his new car, she had a look on her face as if she were in pain. "It's—it's Neville, Kyle's father," she began and found that the burning lump in her throat kept her from continuing.

David sat up alertly. He knew Neville Saylor was in the 7th Marine Expeditionary Brigade. "They've been deployed for combat duty?"

"They were sent to Syria back in November," Xanthe replied dully. "Day before yesterday it was posted on Cy-net . . . Colonel Saylor was killed in action."

David bowed his head. "Aw, man . . . poor Allegra . . . poor little boy."

"Yes."

"How's Allegra doing?" David asked.

Xanthe shrugged, a helpless gesture. "She—seemed to know somehow. But I guess you can never really—prepare yourself for it."

"No . . . no, you can't," David said, thinking about Deacon Fong, his friend. Soldiers were trained to mentally prepare themselves to face death and the possibility of the death of their comrades. But it was no guard against the overwhelming grief when it actually happened.

As if she were about to fall, Xanthe suddenly turned and clasped David around the waist with both arms, clinging to him. David was surprised, but held her close. Even in the moment of grief, he was conscious of her firm body, the strength of her embrace. Errantly David recalled when he first met Xanthe, how he'd thought she was not feminine. It wasn't true; she was womanly, feminine, but not soft. She was strong, and she seemed to grow more in confidence, in awareness of herself as an attractive, desirable woman, every time he saw her. She was certainly desirable to him. He longed to caress her, to kiss her, to tell her how deeply he was attracted to her, physically and in a deeper sense, too.

I'm falling in love with her, David realized with shock. *I thought it was just that I was becoming physically attracted to her . . . she's just the kind of woman that I've always wanted, not needy, not clingy, with courage and heart . . . but . . . in love? Now, in these terrible days?*

Seeming to sense his disquiet, she pulled away from him, her face averted. Then she sighed, a deep, shuddering intake of breath. "She doesn't want Kyle to know until after Christmas."

David nodded thoughtfully, watching the innocent little boy playing.

"I know you and Mr. Case will take care of her," Xanthe said sadly. "But, David, it'll be really hard for Mr. Case, you know. I think he'll probably have to stay away from her."

"Huh? What are you talking about?" David demanded. "Why should he stay away from Allegra?"

She turned to him, melancholy amusement lightening her rather heavy features. "Riley Case is madly in love with Allegra, you ninny. Didn't you know that?"

"Huh? What—you gotta be kiddin' me! How—how do you know? I know Riley never told you, My Commissar! He avoids you like the plague, and besides, getting Riley Case to say anything personal is like pulling a wisdom tooth with pliers!"

"He didn't tell me. He wouldn't do that," Xanthe said disdainfully. "But he is. I know he is. And Allegra knows it, too. And no, she hasn't said anything, either. She wouldn't."

"But—but how do you know?" David insisted.

Xanthe gave him a scathing look. "You're such a *man.*"

"Huh? Oh—forget it. Thanks, I guess."

"You're welcome," Xanthe said. They both felt a little lighter now, and David got up the courage to take Xanthe's hand again. Kyle was singing "Noel" again as he drove around, and it was hard not to feel joy at watching him and listening to him.

After a while Xanthe started, then said apologetically, "Oh, I almost forgot . . . I have a message for you, Puppy."

"Yeah?" David's face lit up, and Xanthe, for the hundredth time at least, envied the melting brown eyes and impossibly long lashes.

"Here, I wrote it down . . ." She fidgeted, going through the pockets in her breeches and overcoat. "The drones, they can't handle all the traffic, so we can't get hard copies . . . here."

Eagerly David read: *Glad to hear from you, Puppy. For now, just stay home and keep watch. That's what we're all doing here.*

"Oh, thank the Lord," David breathed, pointing to the sentences for Xanthe to read. "That means my captain isn't reporting back for duty. They must have a really bad feeling about the Global Union Task Forces and that creep, Luca Therion, too. I hate to call him my commander in chief."

"What's the rest of it mean, David?" Xanthe asked curiously.

And, Puppy, you'll be glad to know that me and your two brothers have come home. If we don't meet here, then we'll all see you at our Father's house. Love from all, Mama Noc.

David frowned. "I'm not . . . sure . . . this isn't any code we talked about . . . and—love . . . ?" Suddenly his face lit up like a child's at Christmas. "They—Captain Slaughter! And that old savage, Rio, and Lieutenant Darmstedt! Xanthe! This means they've all been saved! My whole team! Thank God! Thank God!" He jumped up, drawing Xanthe with him. Easily, for he was a strong man, he gathered her up in his arms and whirled her around, laughing. "My captain! My comrades! Zoan did it, that scoundrel!"

Xanthe couldn't help laughing as David whirled her around and around. She threw back her head and then arched backward and threw her arms into the air.

Finally David set her down, but kept her in the circle of his arms. "The Lord is so good, Xanthe," he said in a low voice. "There's a time for mourning, but He always gives us a time of joy, too."

Breathlessly she nodded. "I'm beginning to see that, too."

They stared at each other, but Xanthe was very conscious of Kyle, so she broke what was becoming a tight embrace. "I—I'm so glad for your team, David. We needed some good news. By the way, how's your grandfather?"

They returned to their seats on the porch steps. David answered in a low voice, "He's not doing so well. But he insists on wandering around, praying, almost every day. He's weak, and I think he's getting another cold. Grandma's afraid that he'll get pneumonia again."

"Maybe I should take him into town to a doctor," Xanthe said worriedly. "It should be all right if he just wouldn't start preaching."

"Don't even suggest it!" David exclaimed. "You might give him the idea, and if he set his mind on it, a whole battalion couldn't stop him. Yeah, we've already talked about him needing to see a doctor." He snorted, a dry sound of amusement. "Riley even offered, as cool as winter, to kidnap a doctor and bring him up here. Grandpa politely refused. I don't know what Riley would have done with the doctor anyway. And I was kind of scared to ask."

"Yes, I can understand that," Xanthe said dryly. "He's not the kind of man that you would ask a lot of personal questions."

David stared off into space, deep in thought. "You know, he and I decided to go with my grandfather every day and stay with him, watch over him, while he's out walking and praying. But you know what? Riley won't let me go. I mean, he doesn't forbid me or anything like that. He just jumps up and gets there first. It's funny because I think Riley is really wanting to be with Grandpa, to watch him, be with him, listen to him pray. Riley acts like he couldn't care less about God."

Xanthe said, "Oh? Like your team acted? Like I did?"

David smiled down at her. "You know, you're pretty smart . . . for a girl."

She smiled up at him for a moment, and he noticed the richness of her lips. He had always liked her mouth. It wasn't soft and pouty looking, the way some men liked; it was firm and decisive, just as Xanthe herself was. Aside from her eyes, they were her best feature. He stared at her and struggled within himself, for he wanted so badly to kiss her for a long time.

As she watched him, realization slowly dawned in her eyes. Xanthe knew, in an instant's revelation, that David Mitchell loved her. A wave, a surging tide, of longing and passion swept over her, and she blushed hotly and averted her eyes.

The moment seemed to last a long time, but like a fragile bubble, it popped when Kyle roared up to the porch and announced, "I want to go show Bruvver Mitchell my car. Bye!"

"Whoa, there, hoss!" David said, jumping up. "I think maybe you better let me and Aunt Xanthe come with you."

"Okay," he relented, adding, "but you can't ride. You're too big." Busily he pedaled off. Mannie was no longer riding, but Benny the Bear was sitting patiently, if precariously, in the passenger seat.

David had to carry the car some of the way, and Kyle ran ahead impatiently, yelling loudly long before they reached the Mitchells' cabin. Xanthe visited with the Mitchells for a short while, but soon it was time for her to leave. David walked her back to the Vulcan. She seemed a little nervous and immediately started to get in the vehicle when they reached it.

But David had decided that he would—must—say something to her, something that wasn't a joke, something to let her know how he felt about her. Gently he took her arm and pulled her to him.

She seemed reluctant at first, but then she smiled up at him, and he got his kiss. It was long and sweet.

"Xanthe, please don't go," he said huskily, holding her tightly. "Stay here with us . . . with me . . . I—"

Quickly she put her fingers against his lips. "No, don't—don't say—anything else, David. It's—it would make it too hard."

He nodded, understanding. "It is hard. And, Xanthe, I just think that the time is growing short. I hope, and I'm going to pray, that soon, you'll come be with us. With me."

Xanthe glowed. This—David—was like an impossible dream.

It was the sort of wonderful thing that she could treasure and hold and think of in the days to come.

She merely told him, "Take care of yourself."

"You take care of yourself, too, Xanthe," David said.

As she drove through the darkening woods, she fought her longings, fought hard. She wanted more than anything to stay with David Mitchell. She dared to imagine marrying him, living in bliss in those cabins, surrounded by friends and love and security . . .

But Xanthe St. Dymion knew that the days ahead held no such promise.

TWENTY-TWO

IT WAS THE NIGHT of the full moon, and Merrill Stanton thought he had never looked out upon a world so lovely and so peaceful. Snow had fallen gently all day, blanketing the woods and fields, softening the spiky outlines of the bare hardwood trees, mantling the evergreens with thick white cloaks. Now, in the darkness, the brightness of the snow had faded to a dusky silver-blue sheen. The faint light of the candle Merrill was holding streamed out, and where the light touched the snow were occasional flashes, as if God had carelessly strewn precious jewels on the steps of the humble cabin.

It's hard to believe that evil is out there . . . hiding . . . lurking in the darkest shadows . . . but it is, isn't it, Lord? That's—that's what You've been trying to show me, to tell me, to make me understand, that it's not just a picture book, it's not just a fairy tale, even though I do feel like that's what we're living sometimes . . . the Woodcutter's Cottage, the Forest Deep and Dark . . . and the Big Bad Wolf—

"Oh! What *is* this? Just—just *look* at this!"

His wife's wrathful mutterings interrupted Merrill's thoughts. He could tell by her tone that she was utterly frustrated, and he sighed as he turned and walked into the small kitchen, which was much like the Mitchells'. Somehow he knew that whatever he said was going to be wrong. It was amazing that he could know that, but he couldn't figure out what the right thing to say was. He and Genevieve had been married for almost thirty-five years, and he still didn't know how to handle his wife when she got upset like this. He sighed deeply and plunged in. "It smells really good, Genevieve," he said with false heartiness.

"Smells good! Oh, yes, but just look at it!" she said scathingly. She was holding towels, folded into fat pads. On the towels was some sort of round black pot that she had just taken out of the oven. In the pot was a brown substance.

"Yes, looks delicious," Merrill observed.

Genevieve slammed it down onto the table. "You don't even know what it is."

"Of course I do!" he blustered before he could stop himself.

Genevieve already looked triumphant. "Oh? So, go ahead. What is it, Merrill?"

"It's—uh—is it—no, wait, I know," he said desperately. "It's one of those—uh—Christmas puddings, isn't it? Like—like Tiny Tim had? The—uh—British—things?"

She was staring up at him accusingly, her cheeks reddened with the heat of cooking. She had a smudge of flour on one cheek, and her eyes were sparkling. "No, it's not a Christmas pudding, Merrill," she said ominously. "You wouldn't know a Christmas pudding if you sat on it. And neither would I."

"Oh. Umm—is it—"

"Oh, never mind! It's a German chocolate cake! I mean, it's supposed to be! But I never made one from scratch before. I always had the freeze-dried kit things, and you just popped them in the laser oven and there they were! But this—this—how am I supposed to know how to get the coconut and glaze separated from the cake? It gets all—tumbled up together, and won't—do right!"

"But, Genny, it smells really good, really! Can't we try it? I mean, it might taste just fine."

"No," she said, her shoulders suddenly sagging. Slowly, as if she were very old, she pulled out the armless wooden chair and sat down. "I was trying to make it for Allegra. It was always her favorite, you remember? I wanted to make her a pretty cake with maybe a sprig of holly on top for a garnish . . . but this isn't pretty. It looks like—like—pudding."

Merrill sat down in the only other chair at the table. "Didn't you know," he said quietly, "that that's exactly what they garnished the Christmas pudding with in those olden times? You know I've read Charles Dickens's *A Christmas Carol* at least a hundred times. The puddings, they were ugly old lumps, but they sprinkled them with sugar and then surrounded them with sprigs of holly and put one on top, a little bit of lady holly, with berries on it . . ."

Genevieve began to cry.

Merrill held her. He knew that she wasn't crying over some silly cake. It was because of the death of Neville, their son-in-law. And it wasn't really a deep grief because of him; they hadn't known him very well. His career in the marines had meant that he didn't have much time off, and since he and Allegra had married, they'd been stationed here and there and finally assigned to Twenty-Nine Palms, more than a thousand miles away.

But Allegra was suffering, and so her mother was suffering, too.

Genevieve wept a long time, and Merrill didn't say any more. There wasn't anything to say.

Finally she straightened and wiped her eyes with the corner of her makeshift apron, a square of white sheet tied around her waist. "He's evil, you know," she said in a curiously colorless voice. "That German general. That von Eisenhalt. Neville died because of him. Perry died because of him. Many, many people are going to die because of that one man."

Merrill sat back in his rickety chair, studying her. Genevieve didn't often say such things. She was a very practical, down-to-earth woman. He was the fey one, the one who mooned around, thinking of fairy tales and dreaming of ancient days and reading dusty, forgotten books.

"You know, Genevieve," he said quietly, "I think the Lord told you to say that. Just that. I think I needed to hear it."

She had been staring into space rather vacantly, but now she focused on her husband. "Maybe," she said cautiously. "I've been thinking of it a lot these past few days. Of that man. Of the evil that's been loosed in this world. We've seen it now, Merrill. It's touched us."

He nodded. "Yes, it has. And the Lord has been—showing me some things, telling me some things. I've had a hard time—working it out. But what you just said . . . it kind of confirms it."

She propped one elbow on the table, rested her chin on it, and leaned forward to listen carefully. That was one thing Merrill had always loved and appreciated about his wife. She listened. She paid attention. It made him feel important, that he really mattered. He took a deep breath. "I think," he said slowly, "that God has been telling me why He brought us here."

She nodded, her face taking on a faraway look again. "At first I thought it was just to get us out of Hot Springs. That was purpose enough for me. But that's not it exactly, is it?"

"That may be part of it, but I think there's more." Merrill hesitated and then said, "I think we're here because of Jesse Mitchell."

"What do you mean?"

Merrill shifted uncomfortably. "I know how weird this sounds, but I think God has been telling me that Jesse Mitchell is a key. He's like a—pivotal piece, a lightning rod, maybe."

"I don't understand, Merrill," she said gently.

He explained it to her, groping for words, but talking, talking, and all the while praying, while the nebulous ideas got a firm hold in his mind. Eventually she—and even Merrill—completely understood.

"You have to talk to the others," she said firmly. "Especially Brother Mitchell."

It was before dawn when the knock came on Merrill's door. He and Genevieve were barely up; Merrill was still struggling with getting the fire started in the cookstove. Unlike Jesse, he wasn't skilled at leaving a fire arranged the night before so that he'd have a good bed of coals in the morning. He had to start over again every morning.

Genevieve hurried to the door and cracked it, then opened it wide.

"Good morning, ma'am, sir," Riley Case said, shifting uncomfortably. He was fully dressed and had his ever-present rifle. Without further pleasantries he said, "Brother Mitchell's not going out today. He's sick."

"Oh, no," Genevieve said, turning to her husband. "Merrill, we have to go up there and talk to them right away."

"Well, let's get dressed first," Merrill said mildly, but his kind blue eyes were worried as he came to the door.

"Talk to them?" Riley repeated. "You're a pharmacist, aren't you, Mr. Stanton? Don't you think you could do something besides talk to him?" He was a little sharp, and Merrill was surprised. Riley rarely showed any emotion at all, and the fact that he was so worried about Jesse Mitchell showed that he must care very deeply for the man.

"I've got some medicine, Mr. Case, but I think that my wife and I have some—um—plans that will help Brother Mitchell even more," Merrill said soothingly. "Now, if you would excuse us, we'll get dressed and go right up to the Mitchells'. And, Riley, would you please meet us there? What we have to say concerns you, too."

"Yes, sir," Riley said, though with a trace of impatience. He started to leave, then turned and said gruffly, "I haven't talked to

Mrs. Saylor. Maybe you'd like to let her know. Whatever." He jumped off their porch and hurried away.

Genevieve watched him go, a thoughtful look on her face. But Merrill didn't notice and merely said, "Let's hurry, Genevieve, since we have to go get Allegra and Kyle."

"Mm, yes," she agreed.

In about half an hour they had gathered together in the Mitchells' cabin. Jesse had been in bed, but when the Stantons arrived, he insisted on getting up. He was pale and hoarse, and he had a deep, racking cough. Noe fussed, but she knew he would do whatever he wanted to do anyway, so she made him put on a Ty-wool sweater and tied a rather ludicrous red-and-green muffler around his neck. Then she made him some sassafras tea with honey, and the sweet scent permeated the small room.

Allegra was pale, with shadows under her eyes, and she seemed to have lost some weight. Riley steadily refused to look her way as he brooded by the fireplace, set apart, as he always was. David sat holding Kyle, who was unusually quiet. He kept casting sad glances at his mother, though she tried to smile and act normally. However, as most children will, he could sense something was wrong.

Brother Mitchell smiled wanly at the group sitting at the table. "I hope you came to pray for me, sisters and brothers," he said. "Prayers of the saints heal the sick."

"That's the first time he's admitted he's sick," Noemi muttered.

"Yes, we'll pray for you, and I've got some medicine that will do you good, Brother Mitchell," Merrill said firmly. "I hope you'll take it."

"I sure will," Jesse croaked. "Lord God made medicine, too."

"Good," Merrill said briskly. "But before we pray, Brother Mitchell, there's some things I'd like to—uh—talk about."

Jesse was very tired, and unbelievably he almost flinched when Merrill said that. However, he reached out and drew the Bible toward him. He had no choice. He was a minister to God's people, and a sore throat and aching head didn't stop them from needing to hear the Word. "Of course, brother. What would you like to study today?"

Merrill glanced uncertainly at his wife. She nodded firmly to him, and while he still seemed to be groping for words, she said with faint exasperation, "No, Brother Mitchell, today it's going to be my husband who ministers to you."

Real pleasure lit Jesse's fever-dulled eyes. "Why, that's good news, Brother Stanton. Real good news to me. I could use a good word from the Lord."

"I—I—" Merrill stopped and said helplessly, "I can't help it, Genevieve, it's like—preaching to Moses or something."

His comment made Jesse and even Noe laugh. "Brother, God is no respecter of persons," Jesse said. "He can talk to you just like He does me. Probably does, only I talk so much sometimes, maybe I need to keep quiet for a change."

"Okay, here goes," Merrill said. Everyone leaned forward, extremely curious. Merrill was a rather shy man, not one to put himself forward. When he did, it was always because he had something important to say.

"The Lord has shown me some things, Brother Mitchell. He's shown me many things, and my wife—bless her—has helped me to see them clearly. In fact, she's seen some of it herself."

"That's scriptural, it sure is," Jesse said with enthusiasm. He already seemed stronger. "The Spirit is confirmed between you."

"Well then you just be quiet and let him talk, Jess," Noe said good-naturedly.

"Sorry," Jesse said a little sheepishly. "Say on, brother."

Merrill leaned forward, his eyes and voice intent. "The world is different now. What the Lord is showing me is that—somehow evil has become more—physical, more—temporal. The forces of evil, instead of being simply spirits, are taking on actual, physical shape. Like Count von Eisenhalt. And many others, I think. Even, maybe, some animals . . . Anyway, the Lord is showing me that He, too, is giving us—tools, tasks, weapons, to fight this evil. And I mean actual, physical tasks and things we must do, tasks we must perform. And you, Brother Jesse Mitchell, are a key, a pivotal point. The forces of good, you see, are being—concentrated here, in you, in this place, just as the devil is concentrating his forces in certain people and certain places. That's why you've been feeling compelled to wander in the wilderness, Brother Mitchell. Because the Lord is showing us that it's not just spiritual warfare anymore. It's here. It's now. It's a real, physical fight."

Everyone sat back, stunned. Even Jesse looked astonished. Merrill took a long, deep breath of relief and waited. Genevieve smiled at him, then took his hand and squeezed it.

"Well, for goodness' sake," Jesse murmured. He glanced at Noemi. "Wife, you're a wise woman. What do you think?"

"I think—no, I know—it's the truth," Noemi said thoughtfully. "It is, Jess. All of us—even I—have sort of sat back and let you do all the work, and sort of depended on you to be everything. But I know now that the Lord's been trying to show us that we've got to do more. That's why you finally gave out, Jess. The Lord's giving you notice that you can't do it all alone."

David asked, puzzled, "But we all pray for each other, and I'm pretty sure we all pray for Grandpa a lot. I guess I don't understand what more we can do."

"Well, I've got an answer to that," Merrill said, growing more confident. "I think that the Lord has shown me why we're here. I mean, each of us, in particular."

Riley Case, who almost never spoke up during their meetings, said, "I'd like to know that myself."

Merrill turned to him and said, "Mr. Case, you've already saved our lives. Literally. And now, I think, you're here to save more lives. I don't know whose. I don't know how or when. But I do have a strong feeling that you will again physically save one—or maybe all of us—from death. In the meantime, I think that you were brought here, by God, to watch over Jesse Mitchell."

Riley nodded vigorously. "I can do that. I'll be glad to do that."

Jesse balked a little. "I don't need a bodyguard. The old devil doesn't want us to die, you know. Then we'll be in heaven, beyond his reach. He wants to turn us away from God."

Merrill listened, and once again he seemed distressed, for he had no thought of correcting a man like Jesse Mitchell. But he knew—he was certain—he had to. The Lord was telling him to, right here and now. "Sir, I don't mean to be disrespectful, but I have to tell you that you may not realize or know exactly what the devil's going to try to do to you. You know better than I do, Brother Mitchell, that he's not omniscient; he's even blind in some things. But one thing I do know for sure is that somehow you're very important in these evil days. God has set you in this place, sir, and if the old devil can kill you, well, it just may mean that a lot of sheep may be lost. I know that we here would be very frightened."

Jesse was bemused and considered this for a while. Then, with a trace of his wicked humor, he looked over at Riley. "You're a good shot, are you, Mr. Case?"

Before Riley could answer, David muttered, "Best I ever saw. Wish I was that good."

Jesse nodded. "Should have known that if the Lord God was going to give me a guardian, He'd give me the best."

To everyone's surprise, Riley looked absurdly pleased and even muttered a low, "Thank you, Mr. Mitchell."

David said a little petulantly, "Wait a minute, he's my grandfather. If anyone's going to watch over him, it should be me. Hey, I'm a soldier, remember? I'm—I'm trained to—to—guard people!"

Merrill said in his most kindly manner, "I know, David. And let me tell you now that I'm only telling you what I feel the Lord has shown me. But you all always have a right to make your own choices and to seek the Lord."

"David, you've been a light of my life," Jesse said gently. "Don't you ever think otherwise."

David looked rebellious for only a moment longer. He was so good-natured and had such a kind temperament that he couldn't sustain any negative emotions for long. "I'm just jealous, Grandpa. I wanta be the big, bad bodyguard."

Jesse, who was looking better by the minute, grinned. "You're just a puppy, you are."

"Aw, Grandpa, don't even start that," David rasped. "My team even calls me that. But nobody here is going to—Mr. Case!"

"I didn't say anything," Riley said, staring up at the ceiling. Almost, but not quite, inaudibly he added, "Puppy."

Ignoring him, David said to Merrill, "You don't even have to tell me, Mr. Stanton. I already know. I knew even before I started acting like a spoiled little kid. There's wood to cut, and hunting, and repairs and maintenance on the cabins, and water to haul all day every day. I can do that. And I know that I'll be thanking the Lord for making me strong and healthy enough to take care of my grandparents."

"You're a good boy, David," Noemi said quietly. "You always have been. I thank the Lord for you every day of my life."

David smiled, clearly pleased. He hugged Kyle, who had long fallen sound asleep in his lap, closer.

"But what about the rest of us?" Allegra asked. Even she seemed to have become a little more animated. "What can I do?"

"You're already doing what might be the hardest task of all, Allegra," Merrill said gently. "You're like our servant already. You wash our clothes, clean for us, wait on us, do so much for us all. It's not much glory, but the Lord knows that we all need help, for this is hard living. Especially Mrs. Mitchell, for her task is to take care of her husband as she's always done. Only we all know that your hands really give you a lot of pain, Sister Mitchell. I think that sometimes you really do need help, maybe with cooking or cleaning or making the bed. But you won't ask for it. Well, I'm telling you now that the Lord has sent Allegra to help you."

"Why, I never . . ." Noemi's eyes shone, and she gulped a little. "The Lord is good."

"It would be my great pleasure, Mrs. Mitchell," Allegra said honestly. "I can't think of anything I'd enjoy more than to feel like I'm—helping somehow."

"So that leaves us, wife," Merrill said, his eyes shining with joy. "Last night we read the book of Exodus about the first battle that the Israelites had. Joshua led the fighting men in the battle against the Philistines, and one thing became apparent. As long as Moses held up his hands and prayed, the children of Israel won. But when his arms grew weary and he dropped them, they lost."

"That's the way it was," Genevieve added. "The power was in the prayers of Moses. Isn't that right, Brother Mitchell?"

"That's exactly right, daughter. And it'll always be that way." The faded eyes gleamed, and he was studying the pair carefully.

Merrill took a deep breath and turned to face Jesse squarely. "What He's told me is this: my wife and I have been brought here to hold your hands up, Brother Mitchell. I don't mean literally—well, then again, it may come to that sometime. But what I mean is, when you pray, one of us will be praying. When you walk and seek the Lord, one of us will be seeking Him for you. When you study the Word, we study. All day, every day. One of us will be praying."

Jesse Mitchell's eyes filled with tears, and he wasn't a bit ashamed. "Bless you, my brother, for your faithfulness. It takes courage to stand up in faith on the Word of God. And I know this is the Word of God. I already feel new strength, new hope—new faith from you. From all of you. Now, let's pray, and I want to praise Him for His victory. Though we'll have to fight and fight hard, the victory is already in Jesus!"

Twenty-Three

Riley Case knew that it was almost dawn, though he didn't understand exactly how he knew. Ever since the blackout he had stopped wearing a watch; occasionally he had a disturbing thought that all the watches in the world had stopped, that they were a symbol of men's foolish beliefs that they could control universal forces such as the flow of time by faithfully wearing a piece of jewelry.

In any case, the little sixth sense that had measured time for his ancestors (before a single Cylex had been made) kicked into play. Throwing the blanket back, he lifted his legs and came off the cot. As he slipped into his Ty-jeans, he deliberately stifled the shiver that ran over his body in the freezing cold. One of Riley's defensive measures was not to give in to mild physical discomfort; he forced himself to ignore such things. He regarded this as a fine exercise in self-control. Pulling on his boots and heavy Ty-canvas drover's coat, he grabbed his hat and his rifle, then left the room, closing the door quietly behind him so as not to awaken David, who was still snoring gently.

He made his sure way through the woods, knowing the path to the Mitchells' as well as he knew the inside of the small cabin. As Riley trudged on, he was aware of the rush and the vigor of the land as it changed from night into morning. He watched the day's color sweep across the sky, as if a powerful hand were scouring the dome of heaven. Up here, in the cleanness of these old hills, the land seemed to waken quickly. One moment it was quite dark and all the stars were clear in the sky—then a thin line of violet light made a fissure dividing earth and the land, and long waves of light rolled out of the east, turning the soft silvery snowscape into brilliant whites and crystal blues. The snow was deep. Yesterday, as they had returned to the Mitchells' cabin after a long day of wandering, Jesse remarked that the winter seemed to be more severe than he recalled from when he lived there many years ago.

Riley's thoughts moved ahead of him as he forged toward the Mitchells' cabin. Day after day he stayed with Brother Mitchell, watching over him. Once Jesse almost walked into a twelve-foot-deep ravine, and Riley was barely able to get to him in time to pull him back from the edge. After that, Riley stayed closer to the older man, though he was extremely uncomfortable to be able to hear Jesse's prayers so clearly. As he listened to Jesse for hour after hour, he became more and more . . . was the word . . . *frightened*? Maybe so, Riley admitted to himself, for he was an honest man. He thought that long ago he had lost the ability to feel fear, as he had lost the ability to feel much emotion at all. Such weaknesses he had conscientiously culled out of himself, along with his illusions and dreams. He had many dreams at one time, but they were like children who went out to pick flowers in a field and did not return. Their loss left a void, he knew, but he always convinced himself that instead of the soft stuff of dreams, he filled that hole in his spirit with a hard-eyed knowing of who he was and his place in the world. He was a solid man, a measured man, and he must plan for and strictly control life at all times.

Of course, his life had been thrown off the track. He was bemused at first, but he recovered. He was fully back in control, and he carefully planned for all eventualities, even in this off-kilter world.

As he followed the well-worn path into an evergreen glade, Riley lifted his head and breathed deeply, appreciatively, of the aromatic scent of pines and cedars. Another of his self-disciplinary tools was that he never took anything for granted. He determined never to grow callous to the beauty, the wonder, of this place and time. Living alone in first one heartless co-op city and then another, Riley thought he would never have the chance to live like this, in the woods, with no commissars threatening to arrest him every time he stepped on some flower or drank from a spring.

What amazed him most, however, was how much he relished the company. His mind shied away from such thoughts as loving his companions and friends, and he especially trained himself never to dwell on thoughts of Allegra Saylor for long. Yet he was glad to have these companions in this odd journey of life. Idly he reflected that they all—the Stantons, Allegra and Kyle, David, and especially Mr. and Mrs. Mitchell—were the best companions to have in these days.

He had been right to follow that far-off unknown fire in the hills. At the time, it was a difficult decision for Riley to make; it went against his common sense and his deep instinct for organized action. Then when he realized they were all a bunch of dunkheads, he was disdainful, as he always was of Christians. He had always thought that dunkheads were rather weak and silly people, deluded by fatuous beliefs. But now he knew differently. These people had an inner strength that he'd never seen before.

Riley was presented with a terrible quandary. If the dunkheads were right and true and strong, then suddenly he was faced with hard questions of life—and death. Although he was not an old man, lately he had been feeling the crushing weight of mortality. Almost against his will, he remembered one of the verses of Scripture that Jesse quoted in a Bible study that Riley pretended not to listen to but couldn't help hearing and remembering. One verse drove into his mind, leaving the words as indelible as if they were pressed into damp concrete and allowed to harden. *It is appointed unto men once to die, but after this the judgment.*

The tiny feeling of dread that always accompanied these hard words started somewhere in the back of his skull. Just a tiny prick, almost unnoticeable, but while the words echoed as if in a chamber, the feeling quickly spread, and only by a grim act of will was he able to force them out of his mind.

As if mirroring the thick veil he drew over certain thoughts and feelings, the landscape suddenly grew gray and flat. Riley looked up at bleak gray clouds plodding across the cheery sun and wondered dully if it would snow again. He picked up his pace. It didn't matter if it was a blizzard. Jesse would probably insist on his lonely wanderings. And however ludicrous it might seem, Riley's job was to watch over him. He didn't want Jesse to take one step without him.

By noon Riley was feeling a little differently.

A few feet ahead of him, Jesse had stopped to stare up into the gray sky. His breath came in steamy expulsions, like incense rising from a censer. He was wearing his long coat and thick boots and his funny red toboggan hat. Jesse had been wandering, almost aimlessly, all morning. Usually he sat down somewhere about midmorning, but on this bitterly cold and gray day he walked slowly, his shoulders and head bowed.

With some irritation Riley reflected, *The old man wouldn't even eat if Mrs. Mitchell didn't make him . . . and he's supposed to be the key to saving the world? It's ridiculous! How did I get myself into this—this—farce?*

From a great distance, Riley heard the long, hungry cry of a wolf. It seemed to go on and on, a deep, angry sound, a warning sound. He glanced at Brother Mitchell. Jesse sighed deeply, as if he were in pain, and began trudging again. Riley followed, more closely than he usually did. Though he never sensed any danger—and he was certain that he would if it was present—on this day he felt a certain reluctance, a certain reservation about letting Brother Mitchell get far away from him. He always observed animal tracks in the fresh snow: deer, rabbits, coyotes, raccoons, mice . . . wolves. Though they hadn't caught a single glimpse of one since they'd reached Blue Sky Mountain, they heard them, and Riley had seen their tracks, sometimes perilously close to the cabins.

Finally Jesse seemed to settle on a place to rest for a while. They came upon a small clearing circled by wild holly trees. The green leaves made a vivid contrast to the snow, and overhead a large fir tree had borne the weight of the snow, while underneath the needles were deep and still green, shielded from the snowfall. Without speaking to Riley, Jesse knelt and began to pray.

Riley moved to a discreet distance where he could still see Jesse but was, so to speak, not in his personal space. Brushing the snow off an upended tree, a giant brought down by the mighty hand of a storm, he sat with some gratitude, for treading through deep snow was hard walking. He wondered how in the world Jesse, at his age, could keep on hour after hour, day after day. Riley held the rifle across his knees, ever alert, his eyes relentlessly searching the clearing and the thick woods surrounding them, his ears keen on the small sounds of the wilderness. Suddenly Jesse started praying aloud. It went on and on, and Riley grew restless. *What in the world can he be saying to God all this time? All the words in the dictionary, and I can't think of a single word to say to God! But he prays all day and half the night—then does it again.*

He couldn't help listening, though he tried hard not to. He couldn't make out the words, yet the passion of the man's prayers disturbed him. Jesse Mitchell cried out to God as if He were right there, standing there, responding to him . . . and Riley thought uncomfortably that there certainly was a Presence in the little clearing.

As the time and the prayer went on, Riley became absolutely miserable. He had tried all his life, he thought, to convince himself that religion was a somewhat laughable, somewhat pathetic, self-deception. But Riley had seen, had heard, and now knew that Jesse Mitchell was not laughable, was not pathetic, and was certainly not deceived by himself or anything else. He was real.

And his God was real.

Finally he could stand it no longer. *I've got to—get away—just—get back in—control, figure out—*

He turned to go but had not gone three steps when he heard Brother Mitchell calling his name. He stopped abruptly, riveted to the spot, for Jesse was crying out, "Oh, God, save Riley Case! Don't let him go on in such misery. He's running from You, Lord, for he doesn't know Your love, Your joy, Your sacrifice for him. Draw him unto Yourself, Lord. Save him and fill him with peace . . ."

Riley felt as if a bullet had taken him in the heart, and it drove the breath out of him. He suddenly found himself weeping. He had not wept in years, not since he lost his mother when he was eight years old. The pain he had felt then, so stricken, so lost and alone, washed over him in a great wave and grew until he felt that he was the most desolate being in the world.

Turning, Riley stumbled toward the small figure. He heard himself crying out, but it did not seem to be his voice. He saw Jesse turn; a youthful light appeared in his blue eyes, and his face glowed brightly.

"Come on in, son!" Jesse cried. "All those who ask forgiveness from Jesus Christ are welcome!"

Riley heard the voice, but he could go no farther. He fell to his knees and began sobbing. He felt Jesse's hands, warm and sure, on his shoulders, and then he heard himself crying out to God. Riley saw that his fears were right—he was going to die, and he was going to face judgment.

But now Riley knew that he was not going to perish.

In fact, he might have just started living.

Riley Case had never been so exhausted in his entire life. As the two were walking back toward the Mitchells' cabin, it was all he could do to pick up one foot and put it down in front of the other one. He looked at Jesse and said rather sheepishly, "I'm really dragging, Brother Mitchell. I can't remember ever being so tired."

Jesse, too, was weary. "Let's sit and rest awhile." The two men found a good-sized boulder, brushed the snow off, and sat down on it.

"This is so—strange to me," Riley said awkwardly. "I'm tired physically, but it's kind of a good, clean thing instead of the beat-up, dingy feeling you usually have . . . and . . . inside I'm—rested or something."

"That's the peace of God, son," Jesse said quietly. "You know, it's been many years since I found Jesus, but I felt that day just like you do right now. I had run from Him and fought Him. He had to bring me into the kingdom kicking and screaming! But the minute I gave up, I felt peace in my heart."

"I can't get over it," Riley said in a low voice. "All my life, ever since I was a boy, I've had this—tight, wound-up feeling inside myself. I've prided myself on keeping everything—emotions, feelings, anger, regrets, anything like that—under strict control. Now it seems that somehow all of those things are—are not—gone or disappeared or absent, but that I don't have to work so hard, to strain, to fight."

Jesse nodded. "I expect you'll still have some fights, son. But you'll find that they're all on the outside, that they don't touch the solid, secure, restful spirit of Jesus that's in you now. The peace of God passeth all understanding."

Riley stared into the distance, unseeing. "Peace . . . yes, peace. Funny you know the word, you know the definition of the word . . .

but you don't get a glimpse of what it really is. So this . . . is peace."

Jesse laughed. "Makes a nice change, doesn't it?"

"Yes, sir, sure does." Riley glanced at Brother Mitchell, whose face still glowed with an inner joy. "What about fear? Does peace overcome fear?"

Jesse glanced shrewdly at Riley's face. It was a hard man's face, his jaw set with grim determination, his eyes far-seeing and unflinching. He was a tough man, Riley Case, and for him to broach the subject of fear—to admit to it, to seek guidance for it—was, Jesse knew, probably one of the most difficult things Riley had ever done. Slowly Jesse replied, "Well, Mr. Case, I think that our Blessed Savior and Lord Jesus Christ answered that a lot better than I could: *'Peace I leave with you, my peace I give unto you: not as the world giveth, give I unto you. Let not your heart be troubled, neither let it be afraid'* . . . *'Lo, I am with you alway, even unto the end of the world . . .'"*

Epilogue

COUNT TOR VON EISENHALT walked with triumph in the ancient lands that had once been a garden and in the city that had once been holy. His face, comely in form, was nonetheless shocking in its glee. For what had once been a garden was full of the stink of death and the dust of bones; the old river Jordan ran dirty red with blood; and the hallowed ground where wise King Solomon's majestic temple had stood was a mound of rubble and the carcasses of the dead. Some New Zionists, profoundly uneasy at the desecration of the holy ground, had dared to express doubt about Tor von Eisenhalt's bloodthirsty victories and the harrowing cult worship he had inspired among the children of Israel. These dissenters were soon found out, and then their bodies were added to the charred remains of the traitorous Arabs that reached almost to the sky, a ghastly, putrid sacrificial pyre on what had long been known as Temple Mount. They were, after all, like the betrayers of old who had believed that God had once sent them a Lamb of sacrifice instead of a lion of war. Had those traitors, too, not been rightly crucified?

For Tor von Eisenhalt swept away the enemies of the children of Israel and gave them untold riches. The children of Israel had, once again, demanded a king and gotten one like unto Saul; and they had wished for a golden calf and gotten gold such as the world had never seen. Tor von Eisenhalt was their messiah.

But even as he rejoiced in the barren hills of Lebanon and the parched battlefields of Golan and the blood-soaked plains of Moab and Judah and Edom, Tor von Eisenhalt was uneasy in his mind. He was drawn—torn, even—because of the unsettling feeling that somehow things in the West were not as they should be. It was not a knowledge; it was not an instinct; it was as formless and hard to define as a cool tendril of air on a hot day or a very faint scent that carries a half-forgotten reminder of the past. He could never quite grasp the exact source of his apprehension, whether it was a place or a certain group of people or a single person. Every time he tried to surround it, to encircle it and then descend upon it, all he could bring to his mind were the most fatuous of images: cats. Big spotted cats . . . little kittens . . . a stupid-looking tomcat that had no tail . . . small wildcats . . .

Though Tor von Eisenhalt felt no pain as mere humans know it, this frustration was such a torment to him that it was almost a physical sensation. It made his mouth dry and his throat tight and his chest burn. It enraged him that he could not envision, could not crush, whatever was standing against him.

It was unthinkable; and so he refused to think of it. Even the most powerful evil may be weakened with the most insignificant mistake.

He turned his inhuman eyes to the east, and to the utter north, for there were murmurings, there were secrets, there were betrayals and the beginnings of dark plots. This he could see clearly, and this he relished. The two great giants, China and Russia, would soon be his footstools; and the blood would run high and thick and stinking up to even the bridles of the great warhorses . . .

Tor von Eisenhalt, for all his dark cunning and ancient sorceries, was still blind and deaf. True, ahead of him lay great and terrible battles, and blood-soaked victories. True, even the great colossus of Russia and the oldest earth of China would be his.

But his enemies were behind him, unseen, in the West, and

though they were few, they were mighty, and they were unafraid.

And ahead of him the earth itself rebelled at his ghastly touch.

The rumblings and unrest Tor felt in the hole of his soul did not come from Russia, China, or any place that could be named. Deep beneath his feet, where even rock ran as thin scarlet liquid, was rebellion. It was called the Pacific Ring of Fire, and it encircled the whole world like a flaming band. Soon it would spew forth in fury, and Tor von Eisenhalt would gnash his teeth in a kingdom of darkness and pain.

In the West, and in other little secure pockets of the world, God's people rested that winter, and were refreshed and renewed as they prepared for the Ancient of Days.

In Chaco Canyon, Zoan grew a garden that was as lush and green as if it had been in the cradle of the Tropics. Every Indian in the canyon, through Cody Bent Knife's testimony, had come to Jesus Christ with a deep and quiet joy that at last they had joined with the true Great Spirit. The Bible was one of the few books that the desert wanderers had, and Lystra Palermo taught it first to the children, and then to all the children of God. They made gardens, sang songs, admired the stars, made friends, and prayed. They were hoping for a long siege, but were preparing for a short bloody war. They grew strong.

In the gentle Ozarks, Jesse Mitchell walked and prayed and rejoiced. His people, too, had gardens, and in the spring, the flowers seemed to grow so rapidly and luxuriantly that they might have been in the most pampered greenhouse. Allegra worked and grew tired physically, but her grief lessened and her gaze began to rest without guilt or fear on Riley Case. The Stantons blossomed, their joy complete, their peace whole. David and Xanthe, without ever saying the words, grew into a love that was best measured by its serenity and security.

Riley Case walked and kept watch.

He thought about how, one day, he would save the lives of the others. He thought about how, and why, he knew that he might have to die to do that.

But mostly he marveled, for he knew peace.

For me to live is Christ,
And to die is gain.

About the Authors

Dr. Gilbert Morris is a retired English professor from a Baptist college in Arkansas. His first novel was published in 1984. Since then, he has become one of the most popular fiction writers in Christian publishing. He is the author of more than eighty novels, many of them best-sellers. Some of his most popular series include The House of Winslow, Appomattox Saga, and The Wakefield Dynasty. His daughter Lynn and son Alan have coauthored many books with him.

Lynn Morris has a background in accounting. She worked as a private accountant for twenty years before she began collaborating with her father on the series Cheney Duvall, M.D. This series has sold nearly half a million copies in five years.

After working in the armed forces and the U.S. Postal Services, Alan Morris began coauthoring books with his father. Their historical series, The Katy Steele Adventures, launched Alan's highly successful writing career. He is the author of The Guardians of the North series and is currently collaborating with best-selling author Robert Wise on a new series.